I0681025

DEADLY

INFILTRATION

Book two of
AGENTS IN HIS SERVICE

By W. Richard Lawrence

Deadly Infiltration by
W. Richard Lawrence
http://www.wrichardlawrence.com/

Published by
Boarding House Publishing
Loveland, CO, 80538

ISBN: 978-0-9774432-1-5
Copyright 2016 by W. Richard Lawrence

Cover design by Phil Lawrence:

Available in print from your local bookstore, online, or from the publisher at:
BoardingHousePublishing.com

For more information on this book and the author visit: wrichardlawrence.com
W. Richard Lawrence
Deadly Infiltration / W. Richard Lawrence 1st ed.

Printed in the United States of America

Deadly Infiltration

AGENTS IN HIS SERVICE

Book One
Fatal Transaction
Book two
Deadly Infiltration

This book is dedicated to
Debbie, my loving wife,
Elizabeth Lawrence,
and Josh Franklin.
Whose input on this novel was invaluable.

Jeremiah 29:11 ESV

For I know the plans I have for you, declares the Lord, plans for welfare and not for evil, to give you a future and a hope.

Romans 12:19-21 ESV

Beloved, never avenge yourselves, but leave it to the wrath of God, for it is written, "Vengeance is mine, I will repay, says the Lord." To the contrary, "if your enemy is hungry, feed him; if he is thirsty, give him something to drink; for by so doing you will heap burning coals on his head." Do not be overcome by evil, but overcome evil with good.

Qur'an (9:5)

When the sacred months are over, slay the polytheists whenever you find them, and confine them, and lie in wait for them at every place of ambush. If they repent, and perform the prayer, and pay the religious tax, then let them go their way; God is all-forgiving, All-compassionate.

Qur'an (8:12)

"I am with you, so strengthen those who believed. I will cast terror into the hearts of those who disbelieve. Therefore; strike off their heads and strike off every fingertip of them"

Prelude

2nd Tuesday in August
7:50 AM

"You wait here, dear. I'll just be a minute." Senator Carl Henderson slipped out of the car and up the stairs to his house. His wife had forgotten her heart medicine and driving back from Colorado Springs was not what he had planned to do on their second day of vacation. *As a U.S. senator, you'd think the pharmacist would have cut us some slack and refilled her prescription.*

Abby lowered her car door window. "I'm sure I left it on the bathroom counter."

He loved her as much as any man could love someone. But lately she was forgetting more and more. She blamed it on stress. He hoped the time away would help. "Don't worry, I'll find it." He glanced back. He would be completely lost without her. She was his right arm, beside him through years of campaigning and work to get where he was today. He punched in the code for the front door but the green light did not flash, nor did the lock mechanism make the sounds he expected. He pushed down on the latch and shoved. The door opened.

She forgot to lock the door. Well, I guess it's good we came back after all.

Stepping inside, he checked the alarm system. *Yep, she missed that too. Great. The best alarm money can buy and it's not on.* He would make sure to arm it before he left.

He felt a presence before he heard the noise. He turned around. A man, several feet away, rushed him. Carl's hand went to his side, instinctively reaching for his subcompact Glock. All he felt was belt. The gun was in the car with Abby. He turned to warn her.

The man's fist smashed into his jaw, turning the warning into a cry of pain. Carl's head snapped back, smashing into the doorframe. Darkness engulfed his vision. He slumped in the doorway.

Slowly, his vision cleared to show the man standing over him. Carl struggled, grabbing at air, trying to get back to his feet. The man was about his size, six foot, how could he wheel so much power in one blow?

"Stay down." The smoothness in the man's movements as he pulled a gun, showed experience.

Carl stopped. The pain turned into a throbbing headache as the adrenalin subsided. Rubbing the back of his head, he checked for blood, but found only a very tender bump, growing in size. "What are you doing in my house?"

The man stepped over him and glanced out the door.

Abby! Carl pulled his foot up, preparing to thrust it into the man's knee.

The large man knelt down swiftly and pressed the cold barrel against Carl's forehead. "Don't even think about it."

Carl dropped his knee back down. The man wore nylon coveralls, rubber gloves, a hairnet and booties. *Why?*

Abby screamed, but it was quickly muffled. Carl leaned out the door to see a second man, dressed much like the first, with a hand covering her mouth, pulling her head tight against his shoulder, as he directed Abby up the steps of their home. His other hand held a gun to the side of her head. Before thrusting her inside, he scanned the mountainside that surrounded the Hendersons' home. On coming through the door, Abby tripped over Carl's legs and landed on the floor beside him.

Fear filled her eyes as she stared into his. "Who are these men? What do they want?" She had the same questions he did.

The smaller intruder looked at the larger man. "Get them up and bring them into the office."

Carl couldn't place the man's mild accent, but it did not sound American.

The first man kept his gun trained on Carl as he grabbed Abby and yanked her to her feet. She let out a yelp. He pushed her deeper into the house before grabbing Carl.

Resistance was an exercise in futility. The man's fingers dug deep as he lifted Carl with only a little more effort than he had put into lifting Abby.

Carl stopped short of plowing Abby down. She was not moving. She looked completely lost and afraid. He needed to do something. But what?

"I'm a U.S. senator and breaking into my home and threatening my wife or me is a felony."

The large man shoved him again, this time into Abby. "Shut up and keep moving." They were herded down the hall to Carl's office in the rear of the house.

The smaller man already stood across the room, in front of the desk. "Senator Henderson, please come over here."

The large man released Carl and continued moving Abby toward the file cabinets across the room from the desk.

"I demand to know why you are in my home. This is a federal offense."

"Yes, we know. I have some questions for you." You would think the man was discussing dinner plans. His calm was unnatural. He was a criminal who had just been caught in the act. He should be concerned, but his actions resembled those more akin to a manager in a board meeting.

Carl glanced at his wife. Her face was pale, eyes wide and unblinking. "Let her go and I'll do as you ask."

"Senator Henderson, you will do as I ask now," the man casually leaned against the desk and nodded toward Abby, "or your wife will suffer."

Crossing his arms, Carl put on a front that had worked for him many times in the senate and he hoped it would here. "Until she is free, you will not get anything out of me."

The intruder shook his head slowly before glancing at the man holding Abby. "Show the senator what his defiance will cost him."

The other man brought his gun down, placing it against Abby's leg. Carl tried to rush him, to stop him, but her loud cry of pain filled the room as the explosive gunshot subsided. Her body began to fold.

Carl stopped. The barrel came into focus two inches from his face.

"Back off before I put the next one between your eyes."

Raising his hands, he backed away. No amount of military training could have prepared him for this. "Okay, okay." He backed off, watching Abby writhe in pain.

"Jonas has eight more rounds in his gun, all hollow points. With your background, you know what that type of bullet does as it passes through tissue."

Carl looked down at the bloody mess where Abby's knee had once been.

"Jonas will put each round into a different part of your wife's body until you do as I ask."

Carl glanced at the emotionless man. Couldn't he see what he was doing? "She needs a doctor."

"You are right, and the sooner you comply the sooner she will receive treatment."

Carl saw a chilling, uncaring cold emptiness in the man's eyes. In that instant he realized one important fact. These men would kill them unless he could take them both out first. "What do you want?" Carl moved a few feet closer to the man by the desk.

"I want to know why a CIA agent sent you files."

"What CIA agent? What are you talking about?"

"Shoot her in the other leg."

"No!" Carl raised one hand toward the man holding his wife, the other toward the desk. "No, I'll do whatever you want, just don't hurt her anymore."

A very evil smile formed. "Very good. We know about the files and the man who sent them to you. I need the decryption key. Where is it?"

How much to tell? How much did they already know? "The only encrypted files on my computer are to do with a sub-committee in the senate, not CIA anything." Henderson hoped they would believe his lie. The files had shown up on his system four days ago.

The small man shook his head slightly before looking at Jonas. "Senator Henderson is either very slow to learn or he thinks we are stupid. Which do you believe to be true, Jonas?"

"We need to hurry." Jonas glanced at the large digital clock on the wall. "You are wasting time letting him stall like this."

Setting his pistol out of Abby's reach, Jonas grabbed a pen off the file cabinet. He jabbed it into the bullet hole and yanked up hard. Abby screamed louder than before as the man's hand became covered in her blood.

As Carl yelled for them to stop, the man pushed the pen down. Abby's hands clawed at her assailant before her head lurched forward. She had passed out from the pain. The man stopped and stared into Carl's eyes. "I can make her feel more pain than you can possibly imagine. Now, give us the key."

Abby roused, lifting her head. Her eyes were rolled back. She couldn't take any more.

Carl desperately needed to save his wife. "The key is in my desk. It's in a hidden compartment that requires my finger prints."

The smaller man watched as Carl walked around to the desk chair. Carl could feel every move he made being scrutinized.

"Hurry up."

"Yes. — Just — give me a minute." Carl sat at his desk. An open laptop sat on the work surface of the desk in front of him with a cable running down to his desktop system. It partially blocked their view of his hands.

The smaller man was moving around the desk. Carl didn't have much time. "Hold up, it's right here." Carl dropped his hands below the top of the desk. He pushed back just enough to reach under and slide his hand over the fingerprint reader. A thin embedded case popped open. He pulled out a jump drive and tossed it toward the closest man, making sure it missed his hands. As all the eyes in the room momentarily followed the jump drive, Carl pulled out his handgun, a Walther P99 from the same box. He brought it up into a firing position, but before his finger touched the trigger, a loud sound filled the room and his left shoulder jerked backwards.

The pain brought to mind images of the Middle East. There he had expected this type of danger. It caught him off guard in his own home.

These men weren't going to let him or his wife live and if he survived much longer he would tell them everything they wanted to know. He had to prevent them from learning the other locations of the files.

The burning pain spread through the upper left side of his body. The hollow point had ripped through his muscles and was causing massive blood loss. He had only minutes to live. Dropping down, he concealed himself behind the laptop. He rested his gun arm on the desk to stop it from shaking.

Abby was vertical, held up by the arm around her neck. The large man holding her hid behind her, his gun pointed at the side of her head. The other man's arm and shoulder were just visible in the office doorway. He also held a gun.

"Your foolish actions will not save you." The voice came from the hall.

"Maybe not, but it will stop you from achieving your goals." It was over. Carl and his wife were dead. It was only a matter of time. His only options were how that end would come.

Abby screamed again. The man had his gun pressed deep into her temple, pushing her head to one side. "The next round will rip through her brain, tearing apart everything in its path."

Carl couldn't let that happen. He had to save her from the pain. As he steadied his hands, he aimed the pistol carefully. He looked into the terrified eyes of the only woman he had ever cared for and mouthed the words, "I love you."

He pulled the trigger twice. Both rounds hit the only pure heart in the room.

1

Tuesday

Sara Beckwith sat on the cold, sterile examination table facing the nurse. The antiseptic hospital smells filled the room. "Hasn't the doctor taken enough of my blood? What is he, part vampire?" Her attempt at humor fell flat.

This was the fourth set of vials she had filled in the past two weeks. And the last two times had been five tubes each. Was she really so sick that they couldn't figure it out?

A chill came over her thin body. Why hadn't she let Derry come with her on this visit? Putting up a brave front had its cost.

She gave an involuntary shudder as she watched the male nurse tie a rubber strip around her upper arm. He then reached for the tubes and applied a label to each one. As the nurse brought the needle near her arm, Sara quickly looked away. She gave a short wince as the needle pierced the skin.

He pulled it back and stuck it in her arm again, searching for the vein. Each time she winced a little more. Were her veins that hard to find? She glanced down at her arm as he found his mark. The dark red fluid started to fill the tube.

Gross. She looked away. The door leading out of the room was four steps from where she sat. Only four short steps. She turned her head to peer out the window but remained seated.

"All done." He placed a white pad on Sara's arm and wrapped her elbow with a strip of adhesive. "We should have the results by the beginning of next week. Let me check with the doctor to see if we need to do anything else."

"Sure." *Take your time.*

Looking around, she saw the same images that she saw every time she came, pictures of mothers nursing their babies. One day that would be her. She and Derry both wanted kids. Their only disagreement was how many.

The nurse's tap on the door interrupted her thoughts. "We are all done. You can go now. Just make sure you stop at the front desk to make your next appointment for the doctor to go over the results."

She slid off the table and started for the door, but only made it three steps. The room spun around her.

"You okay? Here, sit down for another minute. Let me get you some water."

Sara took the seat as she tried to focus on something, anything. "I'll be fine in a minute." As he stepped out, she mumbled to herself that she needed to get to work. Standing a second time, more slowly now, she picked up her bag and headed out of the room, passing a full length mirror on the wall. Her reflection gave her reason to pause.

Her weight had dropped ten pounds over the last two years. She looked more like a skeleton every day, and every drop of blood they took, she wanted back.

———

Jonas released the woman's body, letting it fall to the floor. She was needed no more. He glared at Dace as he reentered the office.

"That was a mistake." Dace was unreasonably calm.

"He left me no choice. He was shooting at me. What'd you want me to do? Get killed?"

"You were cowering behind a woman, you were safe. Now we have two dead bodies and nothing to show for it." Dace holstered his pistol as he walked over to Jonas. Reaching down, he pulled on Abby's arm to turn her over and expose her back. "His caliber was small. The bullets would never have made it through her overweight body."

Jonas glanced at her back. There were no exit wounds. "That's not important now." He started to move around the dead body, but Dace stopped him.

"You assured me the senator would be gone today. Now, because of your incompetence our plans could be in peril." He looked into Jonas' eyes.

A chill went down Jonas' back. He stepped around Abby's body and around Dace as he moved toward the desk. "He shouldn't have been here. I checked his schedule. He was supposed to be on vacation touring the state. He's just another politician you can't trust."

"This is not something to make light of and your poor attempt at humor does not change the fact that you made a mistake."

The senator's body lay behind the desk in Jonas' way. "If you're done chewing me out, come over here and give me a hand."

Dace stepped toward the desk. "What are you planning to do with him?"

"He's in the way." Jonas grabbed the senator under the arms and lifted. The fifty year old was solidly built. "Get his feet."

The two carried him over next to his wife and laid them out side by side.

Dace, after dropping the victim's feet, looked down at the two. "I did not believe any American had enough dedication to kill his wife to hide a secret."

Jonas, a man trained and experienced in combat of all types, disagreed. "It wasn't dedication to his work, it was love for his wife." The senator was a noble man. Enemy or not, it was a shame he had to die.

Dace shrugged and went to work cleaning up any evidence that could identify them.

Jonas glanced at the clock. "We don't have much time. A security drive by is scheduled in twenty minutes."

"Then remove the hard drive and we will take it with us."

"Too risky. The senator's family background suggests he would have installed precautions against tampering on his computer. I won't risk it again." He instinctively rubbed his tender hand with the other. The CIA system they had worked on earlier had sprayed acid on him. It had burned through his gloves as it destroyed the hard drive he was trying to remove.

"He was just a U.S. senator. Blinder was CIA. I doubt the senator would have the same security measures as the CIA agent." Dace's tone was typically disrespectful.

"This house has state-of-the-art security and the senator is ex-Special Forces. So I am sure the computer has some form of protection on it. We have copies of what we need and I will make sure no one else can retrieve anything from the hard drive."

Dace stopped and turned. "How can you be sure? Your bullet

damaged your laptop."

"Only the display is damaged. The data will be intact. All we need is the encryption key."

Dace walked across the room and picked up the jump drive. "I believe you will find it on here." He tossed it to Jonas.

2

Sam Freymen rubbed his face with both hands. Three flights in twelve hours with as many name changes was taxing. Sitting back on the bench, he reached for the newspaper lying next to him as he scanned the Suvarnabhumi Airport on the outskirts of Bangkok. His average height and build and brown hair let him blend in almost anywhere in the world.

Was his cover blown? That's what the coded message had said, but how? He was extremely careful and extremely good. The Middle East was his home. He had grown up in Israel, with both Jewish and Palestinian friends, something his Jewish mother had been in favor of before his sister was murdered. Unlike others in his field, he knew the culture. He lived the culture every day of his life. Now, he was returning to a house that was home in name only. *Is someone waiting there, hoping to kill me?* Others had tried, without success.

Standing, Sam took a walk toward security, stopping short of exiting the area. Looking out the window into the darkness, he checked the reflection. Not perfect, but clear enough to tell if anyone nearby was watching him. The foot traffic flowed behind him. *Good.* He rubbed the dark-brown beard that covered his face. It would be coming off soon.

He returned to a different seat in a different waiting area to await his next flight and a new alias. Two more hops and identity changes and he would be Sam again, and at his mountain home in the hills of Virginia.

––––––––

Slamming the door to his car, Special Agent Lamar Stover marched his large muscular frame toward the FBI building. It was his day off and his and Mary's one-year wedding anniversary. They had plans today. He had talked Mary into finding someone else to watch the youth home today. That in itself was a feat.

Special Agent Booker better have a good reason for ruining his day.

The receptionist's greeting fell flat on the floor as he flashed his badge and rushed past. He regretted his rudeness. The receptionist wasn't the one that had made him come in.

The ride up in the elevator was quiet as no one seemed inclined to talk once inside. Focusing on a spot on the doors, the large African-American worked to control his emotions. This was something he thought should be easy for a forty-three-year-old, but it wasn't.

Lisa Booker was his boss and the head of the Denver FBI branch. Booker's large office occupied the northwest corner of the fourth floor. The floor to ceiling windows gave her a panoramic view of the Rocky Mountains to the west. The room held her oversized desk, two comfortable brown leather chairs and a conference table that Lamar had never seen used.

Lamar's office, one-third the size, was a few doors down and faced north.

Tapping on her office entrance, he put on his stoic face.

"Come in."

He took three steps inside and stopped.

"Close the door."

Turning slightly, he pushed it shut.

She studied him for a minute before speaking. "I received a confidential report from the Department of Homeland Security this morning." She held a folder with red stripes along one edge. She glanced down at it.

"And?"

"It's to do with an internal leak within one of the federal law enforcement branches."

"We get an update on this, every week. What's in this one to warrant calling me in on my day off?"

Closing the folder, Lisa Booker rubbed her index finger and thumb along the edge. "They are making progress on finding the operatives within our government, namely the ones passing information to terrorist groups in the Middle East."

Her hesitation to come out with it spoke volumes. *Is she holding back something? What?* "Do they have names? A list of suspects?"

"No." Finally her eyes met his. "But they have a list of parameters."

"Of parameters? You called me in to tell me they have a list of parameters?"

She locked eyes with him. "Yes, that is exactly what I called you in for."

Was he on the list, or someone under him? Impossible.

"Sit down." She nodded to her visitors' chairs. "Please."

He moved forward and took a seat, sitting up straight. He started to protest.

"Just listen before you speak." She stood and looked at him with a piercing gaze.

He glared back but only for a moment. Now was not the time for defiance.

In most cases she was a stickler for the rules, disregarding all whom she ran over to enforce them. Recruited by the FBI right out of MIT, Lisa Booker was an attractive five-foot-four, thirty-seven year old blonde that still turned heads when she entered a room. But to think she got this post because of her gender or looks would be a grave mistake. Though she could be as gentle as a Fiji Island breeze, those who worked with her knew she could just as easily be as tough as a North Atlantic winter storm. Today looked stormy.

"The report lists several instances of information being gathered from multiple sources." She moved around to the front of her desk.

"Are you going to get to the point?"

"This would require a person who is a computer expert. Like some of those in your department."

Lamar headed up the Computer Analysis and Response Team or CART. There were twelve members working under Lamar, divided into three groups. His field group had two agents and one parolee, which left him short-handed. The second group had six members, all software jockeys running traces, compiling data, and more. The last three members worked in the computer investigation part of the electronics lab.

He started to stand, but Booker held up her hand, telling him to stay where he was. "Everybody at the bureau has access to a computer," he protested.

"But most do not have the skills we are talking about. The report is looking at those with the abilities, the timing and a motive."

"No one in my department would turn against their country. Everyone on my team is –"

"Above reproach? Not everyone working under you is here by choice."

Now it became clear. "Sara? You're saying Sara is a terrorist?" Clenching the armrest, he kept himself in the seat.

Sara was a self-taught computer genius who had been the engineer behind a clever credit card scam a little over two years ago. Lamar was credited with bringing her to justice even though she had been the one to come to him for help, to save the life of her future boyfriend. A change of heart was a powerful tool. With her cooperation, the authorities had been able to bring down the entire organization. Because of her help and at Lamar's request, she was given a light sentence which included parole in which she helped the FBI investigate other computer crimes.

Lamar had taken Sara under his wing and the two had become close. He had seen huge changes in her over the past two years. He trusted her as much as any member of his team, maybe more than most. "You've been after her ever since I brought her on."

Booker shook the folder at him. "This is not from me. Sara fits the profile. I am just letting you know about it as a courtesy."

"Why would Sara be sending information to Muslims in the Middle East? She's a Christian after all. She would never help those types of groups."

"What does her claiming to be a Christian have to do with her greed? People say whatever they need to say to get out of trouble. You know that as well as I."

How could Booker understand the effect God has on someone's heart when she had never experienced it? "I know her. She's like a daughter to me and her faith is real. Christians don't help terrorists or Muslims."

"Learn your history. Christians kill people all the time."

She did not understand. He stood and with his arms hanging at his sides, fists rolled into balls, he took one step closer to her desk. At six-foot-four and two-hundred-eighty-five pounds, Lamar could intimidate most people with just his presence, but not Booker.

"Sit back down."

He was pushing her hard. If he didn't want a suspension, he needed to back off a little. He relaxed his hands. "I would rather stand if I, or anyone on my team is on trial."

"This isn't a court of law and no one is on trial at this time. Now back off."

With a huff, he backed off but couldn't sit down. Moving across the office, to the windows, he resolved to use a different approach, one maybe Booker could understand. He softened his tone, "Sara has been a valuable member of my team for two years, helping us solve numerous crimes."

"Which shows us what? How smart she is? Her position is a perfect fit."

Looking over his shoulder at her, he started to interrupt, but Booker cut him off.

"Sara's not the only one being investigated. All of the offices have been ordered to examine anyone who fits the parameters. There are many people across all the agencies being scrutinized."

Placing his hands behind his back, Lamar turned back to the window to think. Sara was not guilty, she couldn't be. He needed to prove this to Booker. "Okay, I would like to see the list of parameters."

"I couldn't show it to you if I wanted to, which I don't. Your clearance isn't high enough and the only reason you have for wanting to see it is to clear her name."

"Absolutely right." He turned, slowly. "She's –"

"…close to you. I know. That's why you aren't in the position to make this determination." She stepped closer to him. "How long have you worked for me?"

"A little over four years." He looked down at her.

"And in that time, have you ever seen my personal feelings about someone color my judgment?"

He had, but saying so now would only damage Sara's hopes of a future outside of prison.

Booker gave him ample time to answer before turning back to her desk. "I told you when you insisted on adding her to your team that it was a risk that could cost you."

"You've already found her guilty."

"No." She regarded Lamar for a few seconds before dropping her stare. "I will have the investigation conducted quietly, and if we find anything I will inform you before we move."

"And who will you assign to conduct this unbiased investigation?"

"I have not decided yet and when I do, the name will remain under wraps. I am not about to have you trying to influence the outcome."

"I would never do that."

Her eyes flared. "Oh, stow it. I know how you work when it comes to one of your own. You believe your team can do no wrong, but you were wrong once and you could be wrong again."

Booker was right. Tony, one of Lamar's field agents, had covered up his brother's embezzlement. Tony hid evidence important to the case. When the truth came out, Booker had come to Tony's rescue and given him a second chance, letting him keep his job and avoid jail time. Lamar doubted she would do so for Sara. "Have there been any complaints about Sara's work or behavior? Has she broken her parole in any way?"

"As I said, this is not a trial and I will not stand here and debate the merits of someone becoming a Christian."

"It changes a person."

"It can change a person, I know." Booker paused, then in a purposefully measured tone, went on. "But her conversion happened at a very convenient time. It's all a little hard to swallow."

"She could have run."

"To where? And her running would have given her up."

This was nothing but a replay of an ongoing discussion. One he had not made any headway in for years. Lamar knew Christ changed people. Booker refused to believe it or see it. "So where does that put us?"

"What do you mean?"

"With Sara, are you suspending her?"

Booker hesitated, motionless for a few seconds. "The thought has crossed my mind, but no, not at this time. If I did, she would go back to jail. For now she will remain in her present position."

Enough was enough. He regretted answering the phone this morning. He turned to leave.

"I'm not done."

Great. "Yes?"

"This information is not to leave this room. If she is guilty, I don't want her running."

"And when you find her innocent?"

"If that happens, you will have my apology."

"I'll keep my mouth shut." He walked out of Booker's office as her phone rang.

3

Stopping just outside Booker's door, Lamar questioned why Sara couldn't get a break. The corridor was empty and no answer came. He started to leave in order to salvage what was left of this day. It was early and he and Mary could still make it to Breckenridge for a late lunch at his favorite hole-in-the-wall Italian restaurant. At least it would be easy to get a seat after two o'clock.

"Stover!"

Now what? The thought of not answering flashed through his mind. But Booker would just have security stop him before he left the building. He turned around and reentered Booker's office.

The mood in her office had changed. It was back to normal. She was on the phone using her business tone.

Since she had called him back, the conversation must have something to do with him. He tried listening in, but could only hear her side. He moved over to the large windows with his back toward Booker. The glass worked to amplify her voice.

He heard Senator Henderson's name. The media was all over his murder this morning. Lamar stared out at the Rockies as he waited. Clouds were forming in the high country, but Denver was clear and headed for another hot August day.

Booker gave some assurance and hung up. Lamar turned to face her.

"That was Agent Faircloth. He's at Senator Henderson's home."

"What does this have to do with me?" Faircloth had more years with the bureau than anyone in Denver and was close to retirement age. When he retired the agency would lose a good man.

"He needs someone from CART up there right away."

"Standard operating procedure is to pack up any electronics and bring it to the lab where we have the right equipment to work on it."

"And in most cases that would work. But someone hacked into the senator's home security system. It can't be moved here and it can't wait. I want Agent Jenkins on this."

"Todd's at Quantico, giving a class on the art of computer infiltration."

"Where's Tony?"

"Undercover in the Springs. We can send Sara."

"She's not an agent and with all that is going on I'm not sure we want her involved. If she's found guilty of terrorist activities, every case she has worked on will be subject to review. What about someone from one of your other teams?"

"They're not trained in this area and could slip up. If it's that important, Sara's your best bet. Besides, as you said, she's only one of hundreds of possible people under investigation. Are they pulling everyone under suspicion from their work?"

Booker eyed him. "You don't have anyone else that can do this? Or is this your way of getting even with my conclusion?"

"Everyone who has worked with her, including Tony and Todd, will testify she is one of the best programmers in the bureau. She has a natural ability to see things the rest of us miss. If she is found innocent and not used in this case it could come back on you."

Booker stood and glared at Lamar before looking down at the folder on her desk. Opening it, she flipped through the top few pages.

He was winning.

She closed the folder. Crossing her arms, she moved to within three feet of him and looked up into his face. "You are playing a dangerous game with me, and if you are wrong, I'll have your badge before I go down for it."

He shrugged. "Sara will do the job and do it right. I guarantee it."

Their eyes locked in an invisible tug-of-war.

Seconds passed before she broke the silence. "You better be right about her."

"I am." He turned toward the door.

"And Stover,"

"Yes?" He turned back toward her.

The anger was gone, along with her icy tone. "It is very important this is done right. The media will be all over it along with every nosy blogger, upstart reporter, and want-a-be politician in the state. Any mistakes will reflect on the whole Denver office."

She was worried about her job.

"I'll make sure it is done right."

"Everything must be done by the book. I've heard Sara likes taking shortcuts, but not this time."

Sara's shortcuts were one of the things that made her so good. "I'll let her know." Lamar headed out the door before she changed her mind and added more stipulations. He should have stayed home, but then Sara would be without an advocate.

Stepping into his office, he shut the door. First things first. He called Mary and told her he wouldn't be back until that night. She said it was fine, she wasn't comfortable leaving the kids at her youth home anyway. He knew she was just making excuses to cover her disappointment. She was too good for him, another reason he loved her so much.

Next, he called Sara. It rang several times before she answered.

"Catch you in the middle of something?"

"I just got in. I had a doctor's appointment this morning."

"You hear about the murdered senator?"

"Who hasn't?"

Lamar reached for the coffee sitting on his desk and took a sip. He quickly spat it back out. It was yesterday's, cold and bitter. He tossed the cup into the trash. "Faircloth needs us up at the scene. Someone got around their military-spec alarm system and he wants to know how. Grab your stuff and let's get moving. Meet me downstairs in five."

4

Why wouldn't the nurse look me in the eye?

Sara could not get the images out of her mind as she stared out the window of the black FBI car.

Maybe Derry's not the right person.

No, he's perfect for me.

Why would he want to marry me?

What if he's not who he says?

This is crazy. I'm just worrying about nothing.

Wedding jitters is all it is.

Could that be what is causing these stupid dizzy spells?

The doctor can't find anything wrong with me.

Or has he?

She looked down at her bony hands.

Why can't I gain weight?

I try, but half the time food upsets my stomach. I should track that. Maybe I've developed some food allergies.

The pine trees and aspens that lined the hillside brought images of the mountain retreat her church had hosted this past year. She wasn't sure how much closer it brought her to God, but it had brought her closer to Derry. She saw a quiet strength in him.

How could anyone be that wholesome?

Will he really stay by my side no matter what?

No one else ever has. What makes him different?

Pushing her hair out of her eyes, she turned toward Lamar. She was bad company today, wallowing in her own self-pity.

"We're almost there," he said without looking at her.

"Sorry I've been such poor company. It's just –" Just what?

Unfounded fears?

"Anything you want to talk about?" With that rich, deep voice of his, he could have been a singer.

"Not really." Looking back out the window, she saw the cars and TV network vans parked along the narrow road.

"How are the wedding plans coming along?" Lamar maneuvered the SUV through the body of media surrounding the entrance to the senator's mountain home.

"Fine, I guess." She turned her attention toward him and away from those trying to see into the car.

A Deputy Sheriff stood in the middle of the drive, blocking all those trying to enter. Lamar pulled up and stopped. He lowered his window as a second deputy walked over. Lamar showed the man his badge, who signaled the other deputy to step aside.

"You don't sound too excited." Lamar turned his head toward Sara as they passed the deputy who had move aside.

"It's not that." How much should I say? Mary was helping with the wedding plans and anything she told Lamar would make it to Mary. "I went to the doctor this morning."

"It's not bad news, is it?"

"I don't know yet. They haven't gotten the results back."

"Is this about what happened the other day when you passed out in the hall?"

"It's not the first time that has happened. I started having dizzy spells occasionally about four years ago, but lately it's been much worse. I've completely passed out twice in the past few weeks."

"Why haven't you said something before?" He pulled the car to a stop alongside another black FBI SUV.

"I hoped it would pass." As she reached for the handle she felt Lamar's large hand on her arm.

"You know Mary and I are praying for you. She thinks you're too skinny. Have you been losing weight because of this?"

"You've noticed, huh?"

His smile was warm and sympathetic.

She returned a smile. "I'm having trouble keeping a lot of foods down. The doc's not sure why."

"If there is anything we can do, let us know." He turned off the engine.

Of all the agents she had met at the Denver office, she felt lucky to work for Lamar. "Sure."

He opened his door. "Grab your bag and let's hit it."

———

Sara entered the living room with Lamar. Faircloth stood toward the center of the room, facing the large picture window that looked out onto the driveway. He glanced over at them. "I asked for Agent Jenkins. Where is he?"

Faircloth stood a couple inches shorter than Lamar, but was just as heavy. He had more salt than pepper in his hair, making him look well past retirement age. He was half American Indian, the other half no one knew, not even him. The Diet Coke he held clearly was not helping him lose any weight in his midsection. He took another sip as he waited for a response.

"He's in Quantico. Sara can handle this." Lamar barely slowed as he entered the room. "Where do you need us?"

Faircloth turned to the much shorter, redheaded, female Deputy Sheriff. "I'll be just a minute." Faircloth then took a couple steps toward Lamar as he pointed toward the dining room. "The security system's in a small room off the kitchen and is supposed to be *unbreakable*, but obviously *it's not*. Someone hacked in. I want to know how and I want to know today. Can you do that?" His rough tone fit the rumors about him. The word around the office was he had four failed marriages, with five kids in all. None of whom, ever came to see him.

"That depends on how—" Sara began.

"If you can't do it, tell me now before you go screwing things up back there."

She glanced at Lamar, who did nothing. She turned back to Faircloth. "If the information is in the system, absolutely. If not, I will have to track it down and that may take resources we don't have here." It came out sharper than she meant.

Faircloth glared at her. "Don't get smart with me, young lady."

Lamar stepped in. "She wasn't. You asked her a question and she answered." He nodded for her to go.

After one short glance at Faircloth, Sara headed to the rear of the house. The security panel was easy to locate in a large walk-in pantry off the far end of the massive kitchen. Moving one box to the floor gave her room for her computer. She slipped her bag off her shoulder, and retrieved her computer and a small tool kit. Setting them on the open area she had just made, she opened her laptop. Turning to the security control panel, she examined the cover closely before opening it. There were no signs of forced opening. The brand was common enough, but this model was top of the line, used primarily by the military, not private citizens.

Wonder what he was hiding to need this?

After unscrewing the cover, she located its USB ports. She grabbed a cable out of her bag and connected her computer to the control panel. Bringing up the port access, it asked for a verification code.

"You don't miss a trick, do you?"

"You always talk to the equipment?" It was Lamar.

"Only when it gives me trouble," she answered without looking up.

"What'cha got?" Lamar hovered just outside the doorway.

"Nothing, I just got started. I need to call in and— oh, wait a second." She found the numbers on a tag next to the system. "I got it. Just give me a minute." After entering the code, she brought up the menu. It displayed the status of several dozen motion sensors. At the bottom of the list were the window and door sensors. "This is crazy."

"What's crazy?" Lamar took a step closer.

She didn't realize her comment was audible until Lamar had asked his question. She stepped back and leaned against the wall as she gave him a rundown of the sensors. "This place has better security than most banks."

"Any idea how the intruders got past it?"

"I have some ideas."

"I'm listening."

She stepped up to the control box and pointed out the parts of the system as she talked. "As with many security systems today, what gives them the ability to do what you want also adds weaknesses. This one has three different forms of communication— phone, internet, and its own two-way radio. Having all three makes it nearly impossible to block an alarm going out. If you tamper with any one of them, an alert will be immediately sent to the security company via the other two communication routes."

"And how does that work against them?"

"It also gives you three ways to tap in."

"Is that what they did?" Lamar stepped over to where he could see her screen.

"Maybe, I don't know yet." She stopped working for a second and turned to Lamar. "Why did the Hendersons need this much security? I mean, even for a senator this is overkill."

"Apparently not."

"Did he have any enemies that we know of?"

"Maybe. His father was pretty high up in the CIA and his wife's family has lots of money. Oil people from Texas."

"Well, Faircloth was half right. This system is close to unbeatable. Whoever killed the senator was a computer expert."

"Okay. So tell me how they did it." Lamar's phone began to sing. He stepped out and pulled his phone out of his pocket.

Sara needed more information on this unit. She contacted the security company.

The operator on the other end of the line had been expecting a call from the FBI. Bad news travels fast and they were more than willing to help. Something like this pointed to a hole in their system and they wanted to know what it was.

They gave her a temporary login and password to the senator's directory within their network. They also told her about a hidden directory within each system that was not in any documentation. It was there mainly for maintenance and catastrophic failures.

"Anything yet?" Lamar was back.

"Shouldn't you be off somewhere else, bugging somebody else?"

"I wish I could, but that was the director. She wants everything computer related double checked, two agents verifying each part."

"You think you can keep up with me?" Sara gave him a smile.

"Not for a second, and I'm not going to slow you down by having you explain everything. But in case anyone asks, I was right here with you all the time."

"You're not really needed, you know." She smiled down at her keyboard.

"Yeah, maybe, but we haven't had a U.S. senator murdered since

Robert Kennedy."

"Who?"

"Robert Kennedy, the senator –"

She continued to work. She knew who he was, but it had happened way before she was born so she thought she would tease Lamar.

"Anyway, this is big news and every base needs to be covered."

Lamar turned and caught the attention of the Deputy Sheriff who was cutting through the kitchen. He went to talk with her, giving Sara time to work.

He returned with new information. "The senator and his wife were not supposed to be here. The killers may have known that."

"I'll put my money on it. The security company was notified that the Hendersons would be gone for a week starting yesterday." Sara read the data off her screen.

"Does it also say how the system was bypassed?"

"It wasn't. Someone entered the master passcode. It gave them complete access to the whole system except for the hidden file."

"Hidden file? Good. What does that show?"

"Don't know yet. There is only one of me."

"And all my questions are slowing you down."

She knew he was only trying to help. "I will be going through the hidden file next, but it could take a while. It's a record of the status of the system, including any changes. To keep it a manageable size it's coded and compressed."

"Can you decompress it here?"

Sara made a face as she twisted a little to see him better. "Maybe. I need to see how big it is."

"Let's do it back at the office. Do you need anything else while we are here?"

"Yes, the documentation says each control panel has its own backup files. There is one by each door. I need to download the files from each one."

"I'll let Faircloth's team know."

"Know what?" Faircloth stepped into the kitchen. Lamar filled him in.

"We knew they must have had the code to the system. That's not new information." His comments weren't directed to Lamar but Sara.

"They tried to erase everything, but the system has a hidden compressed backup."

"What does it tell you?"

Lamar stepped between Sara and Faircloth. "My team will go over it in Denver. We will let you know as soon as we have something."

Lamar stood with his back to her, blocking her view of Faircloth. The room was quiet and she could only imagine the face-off between them.

Faircloth blinked first. "Have her check the computer while you're here. It was warm when we arrived."

————

Entering the murder scene, the smell of blood mixed with an array of forensic chemicals hit Sara. Her pulse raced as the world spun for a few seconds. Oblivious, Lamar pushed past her. Once everything came back into focus, she scanned the room for a clear path to the desk. Both bodies were laid out side by side next to the filing cabinets.

The coroner knelt next to one of the corpses. He looked to be in his own little world as agents and forensic experts stepped over and around him. He shifted and the bloody bodies came into view.

Sara looked away.

Agent Elle Bosh was directing the activities of the room like a shop foreman. She was about Lamar's age, forty-ish, and looked part Asian. She was short and stocky.

Kent, one of Faircloth's men, sprayed something on the filing cabinets while Chris stood holding a light next to them. It showed something splattered across the front. Blood most likely. She had seen the two around the office a lot and even though Chris was of average height and size for a male, he looked short and heavy when walking next to Kent's skinny six foot four body.

Everywhere she looked, they were finding evidence of what had happened here. Sara stared at the desk as she moved forward.

"Hold up." It was Elle.

"I'm here to work on the computer." Sara avoided turning to see the bodies again. The smell was stronger the farther she went into the room.

"I know who you are." They'd worked on the same cases, but never really talked with each other. The other members of Lamar's team were the ones who usually interfaced with others in the bureau. "We are done with this area." The agent used both hands to mark out a space in which Sara could work. Try to stay in these bounds."

Elle turned back toward the bodies. "I hope you find something. We're sure not finding much." Stopping, she looked back and addressed Sara. "If you need a chair, you'll have to get one from another room. The desk chair's been bagged and tagged. I think the senator was shot in it."

Sara did not want to think about that. She glanced at the area behind the desk. The wall was covered with dark red spots. "I can stand."

"That would be better." Elle grabbed Kent by the arm, giving him more instructions.

Sara checked the surface of the desk for missed evidence, like blood. Finding the area clean, she pulled out her laptop and set it down. Connecting the two computers with a LAN cable, she slipped a jump drive into a USB port in the senator's system.

Turning on the senator's computer, she brought up the bios and had it load from the jump drive. The senator's computer was now a slave to hers, giving her complete access to all the files on his hard drive and bypassing most security.

Sara dug through the directories and files, checking access dates and times. A lot of activity had taken place that morning, too much for a normal work day. Someone was definitely hiding something. She ran a program looking for partial files, or file fragments. Several files and one directory had been erased that morning. The activities spanned a ninety-two minute window.

She looked for Lamar. He was kneeling next to the coroner, talking. She called to him and he walked over. "Got something?"

"Does the coroner have the time of death?"

"He's placing their deaths at the same time, around 8:10, give or take."

She glanced at the two bodies on the floor. Someone was finally putting them into bags. "The file system shows activities starting at 7:04 this morning and lasting 'til 8:36."

"What were they after?"

"I can't say. They erased and copied over much of the hard drive. It's going to take more time and equipment than I brought with me to figure this all out."

Faircloth stepped into the room, tossed his empty can into an FBI trash bag and looked at Sara. "What do you have for me?"

This man seems to know when to show up for a repeat, every single time. "Not much." She gave him the same details she had given Lamar.

"So, nothing here either." Disappointment was evident. "Pack it up and take it back to Denver." He looked at Lamar. "When will Todd get back?"

"He's coming in late tonight."

"Good. Have him take this over."

5

'Core dump' again.

Derry Conway could not figure out what he was doing wrong. The program was due tomorrow and it had worked until he added the last function. Removing it fixed the core dump problem, but the function was needed to complete the assignment. His instructor had told the class this task was tricky. No kidding.

Leaning back in his chair, Derry stretched his 5'8" body, as he asked himself why he let Sara talk him into this summer class. She had far more confidence in his abilities than he did.

Well, his 4.0 GPA would soon become a thing of the past.

His phone sang the old TV show 'Dragnet' theme song. It was Lamar. He answered, "What expert advice does the FBI need today?"

"Very funny. Are you going to be around tonight?"

"Yeah, I've got a killer program due tomorrow and I'll be working on it most of the night. Why?"

"I just wanted to make sure you would be around for Sara. She's going to need you tonight. It's been a rough day."

"Is she involved with that murdered senator?" The senator's murder had been all across the web today. It was big news. The media was mixed on whether it had been a home break-in or a murder-suicide.

"You know about that, huh? She went to the scene today and it really shook her up. Just be there for her."

"Absolutely. Thanks for the heads up."

"Good man." Lamar ended the call.

Here he was, worried about a computer program while Sara was working on the biggest murder case in recent Colorado history. Derry had been trained in martial arts from the time he was small. He was only a hundred and forty-five pounds, but his training had taught him how to use every ounce in a fight. He would do anything and everything to keep Sara safe. He would even lay down his life or her. But when it came to helping Sara with her emotions he often felt lost. He whispered a quick prayer for wisdom and determined to listen more than he talked tonight.

He glanced at the time. If Lamar didn't keep her late, Sara should be home anytime. A couple of years ago Derry had rented his converted garage to Sara. But now that she was on probation she was living next door with their mutual friends Kevin and Natalie Knight. The two rooms they rented to her were small so she spent most evenings at Derry's house. Tonight would be no exception as he was sure she would need his company. Picking up his phone again, he put in a call to a local pizza place for a delivery, and tried to go back to work. Every sound had him looking toward the front door.

Standing, he moved toward the living room as he heard the familiar creak of his front screen door. Sara was here.

Heading for the door, he glanced at his laptop on the dining table. He closed it as he walked by. The last thing she needed tonight was him bugging her for help with his homework.

She pushed on the stuck front door. The 1920's home, with its off plumb walls and doorways, along with the uneven floors, gave the home character, he was told. If that meant more work for him, then yes, this home had tons of character.

He grabbed the handle and yanked the door open. She fell through but caught herself.

"Sorry." He reached out for her.

"You could have warned me." She pushed past him and dropped her bag on the floor next to the couch. Sinking into one corner, her arms reached out to engulf one of the throw pillows. She sat silently.

Moving in behind her, he gently rubbed her bony shoulders. "You okay?"

"That feels good, but," Sara twisted her shoulders out of his hands, "I just don't want to be touched right now."

He moved around to the front of the couch and sat close to her. "You sure you're okay?" He studied her with his grayish-blue eyes, a color she said she found interesting, but which he felt was dull and boring.

Her gaze was on the floor. "After a terrible start this morning, I spent the rest of the day around dead bodies and blood." She gave a shiver and hugged the pillow tighter.

"Anything you want to talk about?"

She peered over at him. "You know I can't say anything about an open case."

"Okay, but I thought you didn't go to— ah."

"Murder scenes?" She cut him off quickly.

"Yeah."

"I don't or shouldn't, but everyone else that could do it is out of town. That left me."

"I heard they think the senator killed his wife."

Sara gave him a sharp look. "Can we change the subject?"

"Sure. Sorry. How'd the doctor's visit go? I know I should have gone with you, but we had a big meeting at work." Derry was an account manager for a local accounting firm. Since meeting Sara his interest in computers had grown. When his boss saw how good he was with computers he encouraged Derry to go back to school to get a computer science degree. So he was busy juggling his job and school and still trying to find time to spend with Sara. He felt bad about missing the appointment. He would make up for it by totally focusing on her tonight.

Her gaze flickered toward him, then back to some invisible spot on the floor in front of her. "He just wanted more blood and a hair sample." She reached up, took a few strands of her dark-brown locks, and peeked at them. "Maybe I should give them some for your hair next time." She peeked at him.

"Hair sample? Really? But you can't use mine, it's too light of brown to pass for yours." Derry placed his hand on the side of her neck as he ran it along her straight hair.

"Yeah, and yours is too wavy." She released her strands, tossing them back in place. "And they wouldn't say why they wanted my hair."

"I'm sure it's nothing serious." He dropped his hand off her shoulder.

Her eyes shifted away, toward the floor. "You sound just like Lamar."

"Is that a good thing or a bad thing?" Derry smiled at her as he stood to answer a knock at the door.

"Whoever it is, tell them to go away." Her voice was muffled by the pillow in which she hid her face.

"Can't. I called them. It's dinner."

"I'm not hungry, but you can eat."

He returned with a pizza along with two plates and a can of Coke for himself and one of Pepsi for her. He placed them on the coffee table.

She took a whiff. "Okay, maybe one slice." She grabbed a plate and opened the box to retrieve a piece. "I have a follow-up appointment next week." Sliding back into her corner, she bit into the warm pizza.

"More tests?" *She's eating, that's a good sign.* Sara loved pizza and he knew it. It was her comfort food.

She shrugged. "I sure hope not." She wiped her mouth with a napkin. "I just hope they can find whatever's wrong before our wedding. I'd hate to disappoint you on our honeymoon." She gave an impish smile.

"Just don't think about putting off the wedding."

She reached over and patted Derry's cheek. "I wouldn't do that to you." Her face held a dramatized sad look.

"Better not."

The smile disappeared. "I just hope I can get my mother to come."

"Have you told her yet?"

"I thought you said you wanted to be there when I told her so she could meet you. You're not backing out are you?" She took another bite.

"Of course not. After what you told me, I'm looking forward to meeting her." He gave a huge grin.

"Liar." Sara shifted her gaze out the back window, as she set her half-eaten slice of pizza down. "You may get out of it yet." Her words were soft.

"Still no luck getting ahold of her?"

"I've gone by her apartment three times in the last two weeks. Nothing, no sign of her." She took another sip before she rose and walked to the rear sliding glass door. "That place she lives in is a real rat trap. It stinks of booze and who knows what." She nodded toward the converted garage in the backyard. "You find a new renter?"

"I think so. He said he'd move in this weekend."

"If he doesn't work out," she turned and gave a soft smile, "could I rent the place?"

"You miss the place that much?" He smiled at his own humor. She was the reason he had fixed the place up to begin with. Sara had come into his life when she was on the run. She had betrayed her corrupt boss and he had tried to have her killed. God intervened and allowed Derry to rescue Sara. While she was recovering from her injuries he had fixed up the garage then rented it to her.

"No, you know I can't move back in. I was thinking for my mom."

He should have thought of this before. "Of course."

"I really want her out of that slum." Sara's gaze fell as the slight smile faded. "That lifestyle is killing her. I need to get her someplace where I can take care of her. Get her off—" she didn't finish her thought.

This was not the cold woman he had met more than two years ago. God had worked a miracle in Sara's heart and Derry wanted to help any way he could. "I'll call the guy and tell him something has come up and I can't rent it to him." He took a bite before setting his plate down and joining her at the rear door. He slipped both arms around her. "Family comes first."

She snuggled into his well-defined arms. "'Family', I like that." Pulling back, she looked up into his eyes. "Thank you."

He stared over her, at the garage, her old home. "It looks a lot better with the new siding and roof."

She spun around in his arms and faced the glass door. "And it only took you two years." Breaking free of his arms, she moved back to the couch and took a piece of pepperoni off his plate. She stuck it in her mouth and licked her fingers. "The last time I visited my mom, she didn't even know who I was. She told me to get out." Sara regained her seat. "Her mind is going."

Sara had been twelve when the courts took her, her two brothers, and two sisters away from their mother. After a few years alone, her mother had started drinking and slowly spiraled into alcoholism. Six months ago Sara had reconnected with her mother after using the FBI database to locate her. Her mom lived in a rundown apartment off East Colfax, in one of the least desirable locations in the Denver area.

"I'm sure it is temporary. Good food and getting off the booze will help." Derry took one last look out the back. *How would it be to have an alcoholic living there? She was going to be his mother-in-law but would that make it any easier? Would he have to spend his days and nights keeping an eye on her?* He turned toward his love. For Sara he would do whatever it took to give her mother a good life. "Tell your mom about this place and how it's next door to your home." Derry moved back to the couch and took a drink of his Coke.

"If she's there."

"This weekend we'll both go to her apartment. If she won't listen to you, maybe I can convince her."

Sara hesitated, "You think she'll listen to a perfect stranger before she listens to me, her daughter?"

"Well, I wouldn't go as far as to say I'm perfect, but if you believe that—"

"You know what I mean." She gently kicked him with her toes.

He shrugged and smiled. He knew it had been a rough day for her and it was nice to see her smile.

She snatched another slice of his pepperoni.

"Hey, give that back." He reached for her hand.

She shoved the pepperoni into her mouth. "You weren't eating it."

"I was going to, you little thief."

Sara smiled. "That's why you're marrying me isn't it?"

Derry moved his plate out of her reach. "Nope, I'm marrying you for your body."

"You are one desperate man. You sure it's not for my brains, my genius IQ?"

She was the smartest person he'd ever known and she had never set one foot inside a college classroom. "If only you would use your powers for good instead of evil."

"Now where's the fun in that?"

———

Picking up the sheet of paper, Nasir scarcely glanced at it. It didn't matter what was on it. It gave his hands something to do as he waited. He tossed it back. The paper floated off the back of the makeshift desk. He let it fall to the floor of the small room.

He stood and walked five paces to the window. Looking out onto one of the many dirt alleys of Puerto Palomas, Mexico, he longed for this task to come to an end. In the dim light, he could see the dirt that covered every building and car in sight. The view reminded him of home, but the taste in the air was different.

He glanced at his watch.

11:57 PM

The shipment the truck was carrying needed to get across the border soon, before some over-zealous Mexican Federal Policeman started to wonder about a truck sitting on the side of the road within sight of the U.S. checkpoint.

He glanced at the young man sitting across the room. "Anything?"

Mekka listened to the radio transmission, holding the headphones up to one ear. They were monitoring the U.S. Border Patrol's communications. He shifted his gaze toward Nasir and shook his head. "Nothing so far."

Where was Ortiz?

Had he been caught? Backed out? He'd better not. Nasir was paying him good money for his simple part in this operation.

He walked back to his desk and checked the time again.

12:00 AM

They had maybe a half hour at the most. A cancellation tonight would cost him only money. The chemicals in the back of the truck, could be purchased on the open market but not in the quantities they needed without a licensed manufacturer being involved.

Mekka suddenly sat up.

"Are we ready?"

Mekka laid the headset on the table. "Agent Ortiz has rotated into position."

"It took him long enough. He better not be having second thoughts or his wife and daughter will pay with their lives."

"He gave the code word," Mekka confirmed.

"Call Rukanah and send him across. I want to know the minute he clears customs. Also, remind him to change his plates once he is ten miles across the border. Have him call me once he is back on the road. I will give him the rendezvous location at that time."

Mekka pulled out a burn-phone and relayed the message.

Nasir took a five gallon can of diesel fuel and poured it around the inside edges of the tiny room. The fire would most likely spread to the surrounding buildings. He said a short prayer for the children who would die tonight as he tossed the match and walked out.

6

Wednesday

Fighting the sleep that strove to overtake him, Rukanah took another sip of the strong coffee. It was not as hot as he liked. The sun intensifying over the distant hills blasted his eyes. After sitting and waiting the first half of the night, then driving the second half, he looked forward to finding a hotel and catching some much needed sleep. He had no clear instructions for after the delivery, and sleep would be good.

He turned off the main road into the parking lot of an abandoned warehouse at the edge of Silver City, New Mexico. Getting out, he looked toward the town and wondered if this place even had a hotel. If not, the truck's cab would do.

Within minutes, five vans from around the country, all of different makes and colors, pulled up. They backed up to the rear of Rukanah's truck. Each of the vans had a single occupant. These men got out and joined him.

He turned toward the rising sun and offered to lead in Fajr, their morning prayers.

The driver of the red van laid his hand on Rukanah's shoulder and turned him back. "While we are in the land of the Kafir, we are not to draw attention to who we are. Our prayers to Allah are best done in secret for now."

"I am not afraid." Lack of sleep or maybe too much caffeine was making him say things he normally wouldn't. He didn't want to be looked at as only a delivery boy to these men. He wanted to show these men he was as brave as they were.

"But those are our orders and we are to obey. This country may say they accept us, but they do not trust us."

He wanted to disagree, to tell the world he belonged to Allah and he wasn't scared of anyone. "But the Qur'an tells us to pray five times every day."

"It also tells us if we are in a position of weakness, not to tell the idolaters we are followers of Allah."

"Maybe you are right." Rukanah longed to be home with his family, to hear the call to worship echoing off the buildings.

"Soon, very soon, Sharia law will rule in this land and the infidels will be the ones who will have to pray in secret. But now we should get to work, I have a long drive ahead of me."

Rukanah opened the rear of the truck. Grabbing a pair of rubber gloves, he offered a set to each of the others. "I am told that in its present state it will not hurt you. So it is up to you if you want to wear the gloves or not."

The men looked at each other, then each quickly grabbed their gloves and put them on. Each man transferred three two-gallon, yellow, unmarked plastic canisters into his van. They all worked carefully as no one wanted to take a chance of the contents spilling on their clothes. Within fifteen minutes the group dispersed, each van heading toward a different destination.

————

Walking down the hall toward the conference room, Sara reviewed her notes. The report wasn't complete, but it was all she had. As she neared the door she took a sip of her coffee.

"Hey, watch where you're going."

Todd was standing just inside the door. She barely avoided spilling coffee on him and herself. "Sorry. Welcome back."

He gave a stiff smile. "Yeah, thanks." But he didn't move. He looked like he hadn't gone to bed since returning to Colorado.

"Why are you just standing in the doorway, in everybody's way?" She stepped in beside him.

"I'm making sure no one took my seat." Todd rubbed his face and gave a big yawn before he progressed into the room and took the same seat he always did, in the farthest back corner. If he could attend these meeting via Skype, he would. Sara took a seat next to him at the large oak table that filled the center of the room.

He flipped open his laptop and started typing.

"Not ready for this meeting?" Sara leaned in to see his work.

He turned the display away slightly. "My being here is a waste of my time. I've been gone for a week and have a lot to catch up on."

"When did you get back?"

"Last evening, then I came here for a few hours."

Sara opened her laptop and pulled up her presentation. Her status as a parolee kept her out of most of these meetings. Normally, either Todd or Tony reported any work she did for them. But someone wanted her here today and Lamar had told her not to be late.

Lamar and Faircloth walked in together, Lamar with a cup of coffee, Faircloth with his Diet Coke. They took their seats on opposite sides of the room.

Yuck! Diet pop first thing in the morning. That stuff will kill you.

She took a sip of her coffee to get the imagined sugary taste out of her mouth.

Within the next thirty seconds Elle, Chris and Kent filed in one at a time. They took seats along Faircloth's side of the table.

The last person to enter the room was Dr. Carpenter, a slim man in his late thirties. He was the best Medical Examiner the Bureau had. "I've got a phone conference in half an hour. Can we get started?" He dropped into the chair closest to the door.

"We were just waiting for you." Faircloth stepped to the front of the room as Lamar took a seat next to the doctor. "We'll have you go first, Doctor." Faircloth took a seat at the front corner of the conference table, opposite the door and Lamar.

"Thanks." Clutching his tablet but leaving his yellow notepad behind, Dr. Carpenter jumped up. He tapped the tablet's screen and pictures of the bodies popped up on the large LCD monitor in the front of the room. The doctor reported the results of the autopsies he had conducted along with the information from the coroner. Most people in the room already knew everything he said. Sara leaned over to Todd. "Make any progress on the hard drive?"

"Not yet. I spent some time on it last night. I left my program working on it when I went home," he whispered.

The doctor glanced at his report. "I sent the bullet fragments along with skin samples to Elle for analysis. Any questions?" His report was short and to the point.

Elle asked, "What about those large dark areas, bruises if I were to guess, around the wife's neck and on her arms?"

"You would be right. They likely occurred shortly before her death. They were from a large and very strong person who held or restrained her. I checked and the senator's hands do not match the pattern. His hands are a little too small." He glanced at his watch. "I need to run. If you have any more questions, call me or stop by." He grabbed his notepad and rushed out the door. Everyone sat silent for a few seconds at his abrupt exit.

Faircloth looked across the room. "Lamar, what have you got?"

Remaining in his seat, Lamar gave his report. "I have a team monitoring the suspected terrorist chat rooms, internet sites, phone activities and texting. They are looking for an increase in activity and for key words. We did a twelve hour backtrack from the time of the murders. Several sites showed an increase in activity after the story hit the news, but no change was noted within twelve hours prior to the murders." Lamar leaned back.

"Ok. Elle, you're up."

Elle hit a key on her computer, sending images to the main screen as she moved to the front. "Dr. Carpenter's data coincides with my scenario. The blood splatters we found on the floor and file cabinets indicate that one shot was fired by a pistol pressed against Mrs. Henderson's leg." Elle used her cursor to show the location on the picture. "I have not had time to reconstruct the bullets, but by their weight and shape, I can confirm the leg shot and the three rounds found in the senator's body are 9mm hollow points. The two shots that killed Mrs. Henderson were 380 light load hollow points, or commonly referred to as home defense rounds. This is the same type as those in the pistol found next to the senator's body. I will have them reconstructed by the end of the day and if all looks good, have a striation pattern to run ballistics."

Elle brought up the next slide, showing the senator's desk. "The senator was sitting at his desk when he received all three rounds, one to the shoulder, one to the chest, and one to the head. The round to the chest must have passed through something close to the senator prior to making contact with him as the bullet had spread some before making contact, but did not have time to start tumbling."

Faircloth asked, "What sort of something?"

"It was fairly hard, not flesh unless it included a bone. And I'd say not more than a half inch thick. However, I could not find any holes that were unaccounted for. I did find a few small fragments of plastic embedded in the bullet. I hope to have identification by the end of the day."

Sara raised a hand and Elle nodded to her. "Could the plastic pieces be from a laptop display open on the desk?"

Elle glanced at the senator's office layout she had put up on the screen. "Maybe. Except no laptops were found with a hole in them."

Faircloth cut in. "What makes you think it might be from a laptop?"

"The intruders were using something to bypass the desktop's security. A laptop is the most likely tool to use."

Elle glanced back at the slide. "That would make sense."

Faircloth's hands were resting on his oversized belly. "Do you have enough fragments to test for that?"

"Maybe, I will have to check."

"Run the test and let us know. Also, if you have enough, see if you can tell the manufacturer of computer."

Elle looked a little lost. "I'm not sure—"

He dropped his hands off his round belly and sat up a little. "Do what you can. Now, please move on."

A new slide appeared. "Dr. Carpenter's report gave the angle for the entry wounds that killed Mrs. Henderson. Whoever shot her was at a sitting level." She looked around the room. Then, moving toward her chair, she added, "We did not find any other forensic evidence within the office. It was swept clean. We are still processing the rest of the house."

Faircloth turned to Chris. "You're up." Christian Carter was the newest member to Faircloth's team. He was young and athletic and walked quickly to the front.

The only new information Chris added was that the senator's car had been driven that morning far enough to bring the engine up to operating temperature for at least forty-five minutes. No one in the area had seen, heard or noticed anything. Chris' long legs took him quickly back to his seat.

Next, Kent Richardson, the senior agent under Faircloth, went through his report. "There were no fingerprints in the house other than the Hendersons'. Most of the surfaces in the senator's office, along with other parts of the house, were wiped clean. The intruders even raked something over the rug to remove any shoe prints. However, we did find several hair and skin samples outside of the office. We are testing them to see if they belong to the Hendersons as well."

Faircloth nodded then turned his attention to the back of the room. "Todd, I know you haven't had much time on this but let us know what you have."

Todd slowly rose, his bloodshot eyes fixed on his computer. He kept his eyes down as he moved to the front of the room. He looked as if he'd never been in public before as he stood with his arms crossed and his hands flat against his ribcage.

"I came in last night for a while and then returned at five this morning to work on the senator's hard drive." His speech was fast, a nervous habit from his childhood that he never shook. "It was a wise choice to wait until I arrived before handling the hardware since the senator's computer had an acid tamperproof device on the hard drive. Not something sold at your local computer store." He smiled and looked around. No one else understood his humor. "Away, you should be glad I was the one who removed it from its case. One wrong move and acid would have sprayed the inside of the drive, destroying the disk along with any skin it touched."

"Thank you for coming back to help. Now, did you make any progress?" Faircloth asked.

"I learned that several files were erased and the portion of the disk that contained those files had been overwritten, maybe several times. This makes it next to impossible to render a complete image of the files."

This was the same thing Sara had told Lamar yesterday. She started to interrupt but Faircloth beat her to the punch. "But you have something?"

"Um, yes. It appears the overwrites took place between 8:30 and 9:00 AM yesterday, after the senator and his wife were killed."

Absolutely nothing new. Sara looked at Lamar. Maybe he would point out the obvious. He glanced at her with a look of understanding, but said nothing.

Todd looked down at the floor before going on. "I was only able to retrieve fragments of the deleted files. Nothing usable, but my best guess is the files were programs, images or encrypted data, not regular word documents."

"Encrypted files? Not surprising these days." Faircloth half mumbled.

"What about the senator's backup files?" Lamar asked.

"I followed up on that this morning. Not everything on his computer was included in the backup. I will run a pattern matching program to see if the deleted files were included in the secured backup."

Todd slid his hands into his pockets. "I'm sending the hard drive over to the lab. They may be able to retrieve something more." Once done, Todd stood in the front looking around awkwardly.

"Anything else?"

"No, not at this time." Todd retreated to the back of the room.

"Sara."

As she passed Todd, she whispered. "You should use my program."

"It's not ready or released."

"What have you got on the home security system?" Faircloth looked annoyed.

She hastened to the front and brought up her first slide. "At 5:37 PM, the night before the murders, the security company's database was hacked into. The hackers downloaded the senator's security access codes at that time. The break-in at the company was done using government access codes from a bogus IP address."

She changed slides. "At 6:24 AM, the senator's security system received these access codes via the Internet, disabling the security system, but not shutting it down."

"If it wasn't shut down, why wasn't there a log?" Faircloth asked as he jotted something on his notepad.

"The system recorded the entry actions in a backup log as well as in the system itself, but the system's regular files were erased. This backup log was hidden from normal view. As you can see," she pointed at the top of the slide, "the front door was opened at 7:17 and again at 7:52. The second time the door stayed open for six minutes. The front door was opened again for less than a minute at 9:09. During this two hour period the motion detectors recorded movement in all of the rooms on the main floor, but no movement upstairs. We know the senator and his wife did not return home until about 7:50 that morning so they could not have opened the door the first time. And they were dead during the last noted activity."

Faircloth looked up. "How did you determine they could not have opened the door the first time?" His tone was lifeless.

Does he really care about my report? Sara pulled up a different slide. "I took the liberty of doing a back trace on the location of the Hendersons' phones. At 7:00 AM both phones were on I-25 north of Denver. Using the log from the cell towers, they arrived home about 7:50. My guess is they came in and caught the intruders by surprise."

"Maybe, but unsubstantiated."

Sara felt every eye in the room judging her. "It is a reasonable assumption if they were not expected to be home yesterday."

"Do you have any more facts?" The irritation came through loud and clear.

Right. Report the facts and nothing but the facts. "The next activity was at 9:40 when the deputy arrived."

"Fine. I need to know who broke into the security company database and entered the code to the senator's home. Make it your top priority."

"I already tried. Both IP addresses are dead ends."

"Tried? In only a few hours you have tried all possibilities?"

The room was deathly quiet. "Yes, I tried and every route I took was a dead end. These guys are good."

"Explain to me how a couple of murderers are better than one of our top computer geeks."

Was this an insult or a challenge? She glanced around the room. No help there. "The location from which the hack originated appeared to come from a government system. I traced it. It led out of the country to an unknown exchange with a service that would be illegal if it operated within our borders. These types of services pride themselves in being untraceable. This service routes numbers through dozens of servers, each one branching off to more servers, creating a web of connections, with no end point."

"That's it? There has to be a place where it started."

"Sure, but there is no way to determine which node it is without running a full verification on each point. I am working on this, but so far they all look like the real thing."

"So instead of no starting point, you now have dozens?"

"Exactly. The IP address used to access the alarm company's database and the one used to call into the home both go through the same company so both are essentially dead ends."

"I want you to hack into this offshore company and find out who bought these services."

"But that's —"

"Is it a U.S. company?"

"No."

"Are their systems inside the U.S.?"

"No, it doesn't appear they are."

"Then do as I ask."

Her cheeks burned. *Just because a company is out of country doesn't give us the right to break international law or U.S. law.* Sara dropped her head and shuffled back to her chair.

Faircloth stood and returned to the front of the room. "Before I go over my findings, I just want to mention how important this case is. It's clear these murderers are professionals. The media is having a field day with it and Agent Booker has received calls from D.C. on this. This needs to be resolved ASAP.

"I talked with Mr. Chauncey, the senator's aid. The senator had planned this vacation over six months ago. Mr. Chauncey said Senator Henderson had made it clear nothing would get in the way of this time with his wife other than a direct attack on the U.S. Capitol. He gave me a copy of their itinerary. The Hendersons were staying at the Broadmoor Hotel in Colorado Springs. We now have a good indication when they returned home, but we don't know why."

Elle interrupted. "A phone call maybe? Or a text?"

Sara responded, "I'll check their phones and emails."

"Fine, but don't let it detract from your other assignments. If you need help, ask Todd."

"I'm sure I can —"

"This case is too important for any screw ups." Faircloth looked around the room. "That goes for all of you. If you have any questions, if you are not one hundred percent sure of your work, have it checked."

Glancing back at Sara he added, "That goes double for our less experienced and untrained team members. Okay, now get to work."

7

Walking down the hall toward Dace's office, Jonas rubbed the stubble on his chin. He was approaching thirty-six hours without sleep. The door was open. He stepped in.

"Close the door." Dace stood by his office window, staring out.

After he obeyed, Jonas walked closer to the window. The view was not to his liking. There was nothing out the window but glass, steel and cement, the signature of the Denver Tech Center. It was all too new, too clean, and without personality. He focused on Dace. "What is so important?"

"Have you deciphered the files?"

If he had, he would have notified Dace. "The decryption key is not on the jump drive."

The man slowly turned. "What do you mean?" Each word was clearly pronounced and emphasized.

"The drive contains Henderson's personal banking information, their wills and his retirement information, along with a few other logins and passwords, but nothing useful for finding out what's in the encrypted files."

"Have you tried those passwords or account numbers?"

"Yes, of course, and in every conceivable variation. They appear to be what they say they are." *He does not think I know my job.*

"If the drive did not contain the key, what was on it that the senator was willing to die for?" Dace glared at him.

He went home last night. He got sleep and now he stands there and questions me? Jonas stepped a few feet farther in and placed his hands on the back of one of the chairs for support. The answer was so obvious. "That's not why—" *Never mind, Dace could never understand a noble act like the senator's.* "I checked each number against the banks listed and all of them panned out."

Dace's gaze dropped to the floor for half a second. When it came back up, there was laughter around the edges. "So, you are admitting you are not the computer expert that you have claimed to be."

"No. I'm saying I have wasted a full day on misinformation. I am saying I still don't have the decryption key." *It's that look again. He's studying me, the little frog.*

Dace took a seat behind his large chrome and smoked-glass desk. Picking up a two-inch silver coin, he rolled it across his knuckles, back and forth.

Jonas looked away. It was only a game, but Dace played it masterfully. Jonas rubbed his shoulder to hide the chills that ran down his body. "Decryption is not that easy. It is a very specialized field." Turning back, he studied his cohort. The man sat unblinking and expressionless.

He'd kill me if it furthered this mission.

Dace stopped the coin. Then, holding it between his thumb and index finger, he slowly spun it, studying it. "Is this something you are unable to complete? Should I bring in someone *trained* in this area?"

"Without the key I am unable to decrypt the files. I have run all of our tools on it without success." It was not an answer, but Dace was not really asking. Jonas moved to the front of the chair and dropped, sliding into a slump. Rubbing his eyes, he wondered why, after more than three years, he was still here, working with this mad man.

Laying down the coin, Dace stood and walked around to the front of his desk. "You did not answer my question. If you are unable to complete the task then we must find someone who is."

"I could send the files overseas. We have a team in Cairo that can handle this."

Dace's stare bore into Jonas. "The people in Cairo do not need to know what those files contain. It is vital that we keep this information local."

Jonas was not a young recruit but he still could not lock stares with Dace. Especially not in his sleep deprived state. He looked down at the floor. This was not a discussion or a brainstorming activity. This was Dace telling him what to do. Wearily Jonas looked up. "And what do you propose?"

Dace's smile sent another chill down Jonas' back. He then returned to his seat and continued, "We need someone outside of the group that is expendable. Someone who can decrypt the files, but won't be missed."

Jonas stared at Dace. "Any other conditions you want to add to make this completely impossible?"

"Yes. We must be able to control this person. We must have someone watching them at all times."

"And I suppose you want them here in the next ten minutes?"

"Do you see any humor on my face? We are talking about the success of our mission. I feel confident that in our vast array of Homeland employees you should be able to find said person."

Jonas sat up a little in his chair. "There is someone in New York that might work."

"I am glad to hear my trust in you did not fail us this time. Who do you have in mind?"

"Her name is Kai Luana. She is a decryption expert. And she does not have any family or close friends to ask questions. Plus she has worked with Gabriele before. They were friends in New York. We can use Gabriele to keep an eye on her. But if you want Kai here fast, you will have to sign a priority one request and that could raise some eyebrows."

Dace followed through without any hesitation. "Have the request on my desk within the hour. The request cannot mention file decryption. Is that clear?"

"I'll get right on it." Jonas rose to leave.

"I want Gabriele to keep an eye on Ms. Luana outside of work as well."

"That can be arranged."

"Once the files are decrypted I want Gabriele to kill the woman and dump her body somewhere not to be found."

"That won't be a problem." Jonas again moved toward the door.

"This meeting is not over. We have another problem."

Now what?

Jonas moved back to the chair and plopped back down.

After a short pause Dace began, "It appears you missed

something yesterday."

Games, always games when he wants to tear you down. "What are you referring to?"

"The FBI found a backup file on the senator's security system." Dace opened a folder on his desk.

"That shows what?" What had he missed? Was there a hidden camera in the house?

Dace scanned the folder on his desk. "A file lists each time we entered or left the home yesterday. It also has information on how you disabled the security system."

This was nothing. "That's it? They confirmed someone was in the house when the senator was killed. That became a moot point the minute the senator came home." *I've got real work to do.* He started to get up again.

"That is not all. They are also working to retrieve data off the hard drive. Your attempt to remove the files was a failure."

Jonas stood, shaking his head. "Look, you may have time to play these games, but I don't. There was nothing left on that hard drive of any use to anyone." He moved toward the door. "Now I have a request to write up." He headed toward the door.

"This is not a game. How can you be sure your removal was complete when you put a bullet through your own computer?"

Jonas halted and turned. If he did not listen to what Dace had to say, every failure from this point on would be put on him. "What exactly have they found?"

"They have found part of a data file and they are working on it."

"Part of an encrypted file is trash. It cannot be read or decrypted."

Dace peered at him. "You are certain?"

"Yes."

"And if they are able to retrieve a whole file, are you certain they will not be able to decrypt it?"

Jonas stepped forward and leaned against the back of the chair. "You seem to be monitoring their work. If you see a problem –"

Dace was on his feet. "If I see a problem it will be too late. We need to know what they know before it shows up in some government report." He took a breath and moved the folder on his desk. "I want you there, as part of their team."

"That would be a huge waste of my time."

Dace moved around his desk to within one foot of Jonas. "None of your daily activities are more important than this mission. We are very close and we cannot take the risk of being uninformed. You will go to the daily meetings and you will do as I say."

"Yes, sir." Jonas knew he was beaten.

Dace walked back toward his desk. "I just hope that all our efforts are not in vain." Suddenly he stopped and turned. "The man who put the encrypted files together was CIA. Are you sure none of his work has shown up at any other agency?"

"It's impossible to be one hundred percent sure, but I have been monitoring the CIA reports. There has been no mention of the files and so far we are the only ones that know where Blinder's body is. I feel confident we have taken care of all copies of the files."

8

Thursday

Sara checked the time. The meeting should have started ten minutes ago, but Faircloth was busy talking in hushed tones to two male visitors in the front of the conference room. She tucked her hair behind her ear and tilted her head toward them. The words were garbled, but the tones were clear. Faircloth was not a happy camper.

"What are you doing?" Todd glanced at her, then at the trio.

"Hush, I'm trying to find out what's going on."

"That's rude, you know."

"Whatever. It's holding up the meeting. I want to know why."

He mumbled, "It's none of your business," as he went back to typing on his laptop.

She glanced over. He was pulling up data from the computer lab. "Any luck?"

Todd answered without looking up. "Luck has nothing to do with it." A hint of his lopsided smile formed and was gone just as quickly.

Faircloth moved to the center of the room. "Sorry for the delay. But *Homeland* feels they need to be part of *my* investigation."

The larger of the newcomers moved to the back and took a seat two chairs over from Sara. Everyone in the room caught Faircloth's tone as several pairs of eyes shifted between the men. The other visitor stood in the front with a smug, self-satisfied look.

Faircloth nodded toward the smaller man. "This is Agent Patrick Landry." Then pointing toward the back, "and this is Agent Curtis Hewitt. They are from the Department of Homeland Security. Someone higher up feels it would be wise to have Homeland involved in our investigation. Agent Hewitt will be joining us in our meetings. You are to copy him on all official reports."

The little man spoke up. "We are to be copied on all reports related to this case, official and non-official."

Faircloth stared at him. Landry did not blink.

"Fine, on *all* reports."

Faircloth was missing something. It took Sara a minute to realize what it was. He did not have a Diet Coke in his hand. This case must be getting to him.

Landry moved to the center of the room, next to Faircloth. "I would like to say a few words to your team." It was not a request, and he did not wait for an answer. Faircloth took a seat across from Lamar. Again, the three members of Faircloth's team were sitting on the same side as him.

Landry spoke as if he were in charge. "We are not planning to take over your investigation or direct you in your day to day activities. We are simply here to offer Homeland's services...."

Great, I get to spend the afternoon listening to a nothing speech. She looked around the room at the others working the case. They all occupied themselves with their various iPads, notepads or whatever they had bought to the meeting. The little man in the front did not seem to notice.

Sara glanced at Todd's display. He was typing numbers into his slides. "Still don't have enough data?" she whispered.

He glanced at her. "We made progress."

"Do you have a complete file? Do you know how many files were deleted?"

Todd shrunk a little. "As I said, we are making progress." He turned away from her slightly.

The message was clear enough. She watched him work. It was more interesting than the political speech droning on in the front of the room.

"Okay, let's get this show on the road." Faircloth stepped to the front as Landry took a seat near Hewitt. "Stover, is anyone claiming responsibility? What's the chatter saying out there?"

"Whoever is behind this is staying off the Net. This is not standard for a terrorist group. Usually they want the world to know what they've done."

"At this point we do not know, nor can we assume it was

terrorism. Don't rule out politically driven actions, espionage, or even a failed robbery."

"We haven't. I've contacted my counterparts at the CIA and the local police departments. They all have their ears to the ground and will keep me informed if anything shows up."

"Anything else?" Faircloth pulled a can of pop out of his coat pocket.

Sara covered the tiny smile that started to form. It was good to see Faircloth hadn't given up his trademark drink.

"There is a lot of talk on the streets. Everyone is speculating, but none of our sources have anything we can follow up on."

"What kind of speculation are we talking about?" Faircloth opened his Diet Coke and downed half the can.

Lamar glanced at his iPad. "Everything from, it never really happened, to the hit was ordered by the President to remove political opponents. But nothing credible or useful. We will continue to monitor the Web. We've set up a new list of watch words that will trigger the system. We also ran a back trace for cell phones and GPS signals in the area at the time of the murders. There were some that didn't belong, but when we checked them out, everyone had an alibi. Whoever is behind this did not have active cell phones with them at the time of the murders."

"We didn't happen to have a satellite overhead at that time or cameras in the area?"

Lamar shook his head. "I tried that, too. Nothing."

"Keep looking. Elle, you're up. Do you have anything for us?"

"A little."

Faircloth took a seat as Elle took her position in the front of the room and brought up her presentation. "We were able to reconstruct the 9mm rounds and can confirm that they came from two different pistols. However, we were only able to get a usable striation pattern off two of the rounds. I'll run ballistics on them and feed them into our national database, but I am not counting on any hits."

"Were the patterns unclear?" Hewitt asked.

"The patterns are fine. But it is clear these guys were pros. I am sure the guns they used are throwaways and untraceable."

Hewitt nodded.

Sara noticed a very slight upturn on the corners of Landry's mouth. *Does he admire these people? Murderers that can outsmart the cops?*

"So you didn't find any usable evidence that can help us track these killers?" Hewitt said it more like a statement.

Elle focused on Hewitt. "We found some DNA that did not belong to the senator or his wife, six samples to be exact. How many belonged to the intruders, if any, is unknown at this time. I am running some tests to determine that."

Hewitt seemed to be running the show with his questions. "If you do not have suspects to match them against, how will this help? It would take months to compare against everything on file. And it may not even belong to the intruders."

"You're right. But there is some new software that will speed things up, and can give us a physical profile for the people that the DNA came from."

Faircloth turned to Lamar. "Can you give me a rundown on this new software?

"Sara and Todd are the experts on it."

"Okay, Todd can you explain it in a way that we all can understand?"

"Ah, sure. It's based on the principle of population distribution and grouping of the polymorphisms within specific phenotypes —"

Faircloth cut Todd off. "Sara, how about you?"

Sara knew everyone in the room could see her smile, but she didn't care. When Todd was caught off guard he always spoke over most people's heads. Was it intentional? Maybe. "It's a program that groups DNA markers based on gender, ethnicities, hair and eye color, approximate age and general build. Then it compares the DNA sample in question against these groupings to narrow the search and give us a possible physical characterization profile."

"Physical characterization profile?" Landry asked.

"Yes, in general, an ethnic group will have most facial and physical features in common. Such as build, height, weight, eye color, shape of nose and ears and even skin tone. The ability for this to work is dependent on the purity of the person's heritage. Someone from a small village in China would be much purer in this case than your average Californian for example. So if I were to run the Chinese person's DNA through this program, I could get a very close likeness. The results from the Californian will be broader but still helpful."

Now Landry was controlling the flow of the meeting. "So if your DNA were run through this test would it come back describing you? Maybe identify you as extremely slim and that your whole family has this slight build?"

It wasn't some tag in her DNA that told her to throw up half her food. "I— maybe, but in some cases other factors do come into play." *And you don't need to know about my family.*

"Thank you." Faircloth turned back to the front of the room. "Elle, continue."

Landry interrupted again. "Where were the DNA samples found?"

Elle glanced at her slide. "Three in the entryway, two in the kitchen and one near the door to the study, most of them are hair samples."

"None of them are from the room where the murders took place?"

"That room was clean. But we know the perpetrators used the main entrance. One or more of the samples found in that area may belong to them. One of the samples is a piece of skin. It may have come off in a struggle."

Landry nodded. "So at this point we have little information on the intruders?"

"We have *some* information. As I stated, we know that at least two men carrying 9mm guns entered the Hendersons' home while the senator and his wife were en route. We know at least one of the men was strong."

"Justify your hypotheses." Faircloth had been at this business a long time and took nothing without some sort of proof.

"Looking at what we know about the crime scene I can deduce that it would take a minimum of two men to move the senator's two-hundred and thirty-five pound body. He was lifted from the desk chair and carried to where his wife's body was. His body was not dragged. If two men carried him, one or both had to be fairly strong. He could have been moved by three men of average abilities, but with the other evidence, at this point, I can only justify two intruders."

"You said men, is that because of the strength needed?" asked Faircloth.

"Mostly. It also has to do with the way they were killed. With the wife being held and shot in the leg at the same time, would suggest not only a strong but also a large person, because of the reach that was required. Demographics puts that into the male side of probabilities."

Faircloth nodded. "While you're making your educated guesses, what else do you have?"

Elle brought up a slide containing a simple layout of the study. It showed four figures in different locations and several red lines. "As per Dr. Carpenter's report, we know the senator was shot three times: shoulder, chest and head, all 9mm." She placed her cursor on the figure at the desk. "Only a few other marks were found on his body. His wife's body on the other hand, was abused. Bruises were found on her neck, shoulders, abdomen, and legs. She was shot three times. The first time, in the leg with the barrel pressed against the flesh. A small round object was pushed into this hole and used to torture her as shown by the damage done in and around the bullet hole. She was also choked and hit multiple times."

"All this looks very reasonable. Little guesswork involved. Do you agree they were trying to get information from the senator?" Faircloth asked.

"Absolutely. It's my working scenario and the only one that fits." Elle glanced around the room. Others nodded. "The senator was at his desk. His wife was about here, next to the file cabinets." Elle showed each place with her cursor. "We are sure she had been shot, knocked around, and almost strangled. The senator reached under his desk to a hidden safe. He retrieved his pistol—"

"Wait. Are you saying he shot his own wife?" Faircloth asked. Two red lines went from the senator's location on the map to his wife.

"Yes. Only two rounds were fired from his pistol. We matched the rounds that killed Mrs. Henderson to the ones in the senator's pistol. We matched the type of powder found on Senator Henderson's skin to the bullets found in his gun. And finally, we matched the trajectory of the rounds to the height and direction of the surface of the desk, where the senator sat."

"So, he got ahold of a gun and he used it to kill his wife. Why?"

Elle stood still as an uneasy silence enveloped the room.

Lamar's soft voice broke the silence. "To stop the pain. To save her from any more torture."

9

The room was silent except for the whispers. While it was not unheard of, each trained person in the room wondered if they themselves possessed the bravery to sacrifice a loved one in order to save them from the intense pain being inflicted by mad men who would surely kill them once they had what they came for.

Sara studied the faces in the room, looking for someone to challenge Lamar's words, but no one did. Her scan landed on Todd, who was the last to come to grips with it. His face went through confusion, shock, disbelief, understanding, and landed on anger.

Faircloth glared at the table as his head swiveled back and forth. "The men who did this don't deserve to breathe my air." After a few murmurs of agreement, the meeting moved on. "Kent, you're up."

Sitting up a little straighter, Kent gave his short report without getting up or looking at his notes. "I walked the neighborhood, checking for home security systems that might give us an image of the perpetrators or their vehicle. It was a bust."

"Chris?"

He had questioned the neighbors that were not available the first day. Nothing.

The meeting slowly moved past shock to determination as each report gave little or no new information. "Todd, you're up."

Todd hesitated before making the decision to stand and walk to the front of the room. He never once looked up or at any of the room's occupants.

"The lab was able to retrieve a few more data fragments from the hard drive, large enough pieces to determine with a seventy percent confidence that the file or files were encrypted."

He brought up a slide showing several lines of what appeared to be random numbers and letters, with a different tag next to each line.

Sara found a little humor in his presentation of hexadecimal code. No one in the room could possibly understand the code or the tags. And even she would need to spend a fair amount of time studying the code fragments to see what he was talking about.

"As can be seen here—"

"Todd, can you just give us a summary and not a computer science lesson?"

"Ah, yeah, I guess." He skipped to the next slide. "The patterns were compared to several known patterns, documents, images, and so on. The structure is different. It could be complied code or some other unreadable data.

"Why do you think it may be something other than parts of a program?" The question came from Agent Hewitt.

"I ran the bits of code against all programs Senator Henderson had backed up. They don't match and the senator has no programming abilities that we know of, so that rules out him writing his own code."

Lamar jumped in, "Statistically, on any senator's computer, you won't find much of interest other than low level classified government secrets. It's against the law to store anything above 'confidential' on a home system."

Hewitt nodded.

Todd continued. "With such small fragments, we have not made any progress in determining what the data is or how many files were deleted. But if we rule out computer code, my next guess is, they were encrypted files. But then again, if they were encrypted government files, they should have been backed up. And the deleted files were not in the backup."

"Any idea what type of encryption was used?"

Todd's hands slid back into his pockets. "Again, the fragments are too small."

"So, you're at a loss, too." Faircloth exhaled the statement.

"We are still hoping to gather more data off the hard drive. If I can get a complete file, I feel confident I can decrypt it."

"And when do you think that might be?"

"That is indeterminate at this point in time."

"You don't know?"

"Correct, that is what I said."

Only twice did Todd's eyes meet Faircloth's and even then it was for only a fraction of a second each time.

"We might be able to help. We have a state of the art computer lab in New York. They have some very advanced techniques for retrieving data." Hewitt offered.

Lamar shifted in his chair, leaning forward. "Our lab is just fine and Todd and Sara are excellent at what they do."

"I'm sure they are. Their records are well known. However, we also have some highly trained people and another set of eyes won't hurt."

"I'm—"

"Agent Hewitt," Faircloth cut Lamar off. "we will copy you on our progress and keep you informed." He looked back at Todd. "Anything else?"

Todd looked surprised at the question. "No, as I stated before –"

"Sara, you're up."

She passed Todd on her way to the front of the room. Stopping, she hesitated as she looked at Lamar until he gave her a nod. "First, I understand how important this case is, and— I believe what I was asked—"

Faircloth cut her off. "We all know you have reservations about what I told you to do. Now please move on. We don't have all day to hear you spill your conscience."

She stopped and straightened up her shoulders. "I was able to hack into the offshore company that provided the routing for the phone and internet access to the security company and the senator's home. I found the account number linked to these transactions. I'm going through the company records now to see if I can find a name, business, location, or country attached to that account."

"So you were able to make progress on this. Good." Faircloth actually sounded pleased for the first time this meeting.

"I also ran through both the senator's and his wife's calls and emails for the thirty-six hours leading up to the murder. The only things of note were several calls to pharmacies in the Springs."

"And how might that relate to the case?"

"If one of them was sick, that may have been the reason they returned home."

"Did they call a doctor?"

"No."

"Do you know if they went to see a doctor?"

"Nothing indicates they did."

Faircloth glanced down at the table as Sara waited. "Still, you have a point. — Kent, follow up on this. If one of them was sick or had a medical condition and forgot their medication, they may have returned for that reason." He looked at Sara. "Anything else?"

Sara headed for her seat. "No, that's it."

Todd spoke up as he typed on his laptop. "Mrs. Henderson had a heart condition that required medication."

"That answers part of the question. Elle, see if she had run out of her prescription or if it was left behind. It may or may not have been picked up in the house inventory."

She nodded.

Using the table for support, Faircloth rose from his seat. Leaning on the table he addressed the room. "The senator and his wife have been dead for over forty-eight hours and we don't have any solid leads as to who or why. I need results. — Elle, stay on top of ballistics data and DNA evidence. If the intruders weren't expecting the senator to be home they may have slipped up on the guns. — Todd, everything points to the missing data. We need to know what it was. See if there are any encrypted files on the computers at the senator's office in D.C. — Sara, go after that offshore company and stay on it. Also go through the senator's emails, phone records, text messages and any other electronic form of communication for the last nine months. Find out what he was working on. — Kent, that encrypted file had to come from somewhere. Find out who the senator worked with both inside and outside the government. — Chris, interview his staff. Find out if the senator said anything unusual recently that might help here. If he felt threatened, he may have told one of them. Also run a background check on every staff member."

Taking one quick glance around the room, Faircloth added, "Okay, you all are dismissed. Let's get to work. Chris, make sure the homeland agents make it out of the building." He headed for the door.

10

Friday

Jonas reached for the noisy phone on his desk and placed the receiver to his ear. It was Dace. He decided against a greeting. It did not matter, as the man on the other end left no room for one.

"Report to my office immediately."

"What's this about?" The line went dead without an answer. Jonas slowly put the handset back instead of slamming it. These interruptions were having an impact on his work. After locking his computer, he rose and took a deep breath to relax his mind. He didn't want to walk into Dace's office with his head filled with distractions.

Forty paces and thirty seconds later he stepped in without knocking. "What is so important?"

Dace sat at his desk, flipping that stupid coin of his. The urgency was gone from his tone. "This agent Jenkins sounded very confident that he will be able to recover more data from the hard drive."

"He was blowing smoke, nothing more."

"An American expression. Are you willing to stake your life on it?" His eyes pierced deep. The question carried more significance than Jonas' statement.

"I only bet on sure things. I'm monitoring his work to make sure neither of our lives are at stake."

Dace tossed the coin aside and stood, placing his fists on top of his desk. The previous calmness was gone. "And if he does recover enough data, then what?"

"First, if he does extract more data I will personally see to it that the situation is contained. And second, we have the full files and we can't decrypt them. I don't believe this Todd Jenkins would be able to do it either. Even if he does believe he's the top programmer at the Bureau."

"I hope for your life and mine you are right."

Jonas faced the window, preventing Dace from seeing his contempt. "I'll take care of my end, you worry about yours. Is your chemist on track?"

Jonas didn't notice Dace moving toward him until Dace crowded into his peripheral vision. "You will do as I dictate. I am your leader and superior. If you are unable to function under me, I will remedy that problem. Do I make myself clear?"

If he could change one thing about Islam, it was the way leaders were picked. One's understanding about the Qur'an did not always translate into a superior understanding about life or espionage. "Yes, you are very clear."

"Good." Dace's gaze burned into Jonas.

One quick twist and that little weasel's neck would snap. Jonas turned back toward the window.

Dace moved away. "Now, when will Ms. Luana arrive?" He took his seat at the desk.

Turning around, Jonas looked down at Dace. "She'll be in tonight. I have Gabriele meeting her at the airport."

"Satisfactory. Make sure all the safeguards are in place. If she learns what we are doing or who we are, I want her life ended immediately."

———

Booker stared at Faircloth. The reports on the senator's murder were not good. At this point, they had nothing.

"I want your opinion on this case. Not what you have put in the reports, but how you feel about the team and their work."

Faircloth, slouching in one of her guest chairs, looked up at her with his bloodshot eyes, something he had twenty-four-seven. "What are you looking for, exactly?" Distrust came through in his tone.

After working under me for three years, you would think he would learn to trust me. Booker sat at her desk. Folding her hands together, she raised them and rested her chin on the fingers. "Relax Agent Faircloth. I'm not trying to hang you out to dry. If I didn't believe you were up to this task I would have pulled you before you set foot in that mountain home. I'm here to help, but I have everyone up the chain of command, including the President, breathing down my neck. They want to know why we don't have any suspects."

Faircloth reached up with both hands and rubbed his oversized face. His age showed more and more with each passing day. This could be his last investigation, one last chance to make a name for himself. "We have nothing because there is nothing. Whoever killed the senator were experts and they have gone through great pains to keep their identity hidden."

"Are you confident no one on the team is sabotaging your efforts?"

"Are you asking if someone at the Bureau is behind these murders? Someone on my team?"

"You have said in your own reports that whoever killed the senator knew FBI procedures. If that is true, we could have someone on the inside helping them."

He nodded in agreement. "Or someone who left the Bureau or someone who works in a different agency. Just because they know our procedures doesn't mean they are on my team."

"So you trust the team? Everyone you are working with?" She studied his face. The man must spend his weekends playing poker, for his face gave nothing away.

"I would not have anyone on my team that I did not trust."

"You asked for Todd and did not sound too happy about using Sara."

He stood and paced toward the window as he spoke. "That has nothing to do with trust. She's not field material. I thought she was one of those programmers that likes to sit in the dark and talk with her computer."

"And now?"

"And now, she's doing better than I would have expected. She's a lot sharper than I had given her credit for."

Booker waited for him to stop and face her. "Keep me informed about her work. You are right about her not being field trained."

Booker hesitated but decided against giving the warning that flashed through her mind, be careful Faircloth, *Sara knows enough about our procedures and is sharp enough to be the one sabotaging our efforts.*

———

"What's that over there?" Linda pointed down the hillside a little ways off the trail. Their weekend getaway to the back country in Rocky Mountain National Park was cut very short when she had slipped down a 30-foot incline.

With Robert supporting her, they were heading back to his car. He wanted to take her to the emergency room. She strongly disagreed, saying it was only a twisted ankle and some ice was all it needed.

He glanced down the hill. "It's a body. That's what happens to hikers who refuse to go to the doctor when they need to." His sarcastic comment trailed off, as something down the slope drew his attention.

"No, that's what happens to men who won't listen to their girlfriends." Linda jabbed his side.

He only half heard what she said as he studied the tangled mess. Something made of cloth was intertwined in a bush between two large gray boulders. It appeared to be a coat covered in something. Blood, maybe?

She started to hobble on.

"Hang on a minute." He moved her to the uphill side of the path, and sat her down on a fallen tree trunk. "You wait here."

She scooted back on the log a little as she stretched out her sore ankle. "Where are you going?"

"I'll be back in just a minute." He didn't want to worry her if it was nothing, and if it was what he thought it might be, he didn't want her to see it.

Cutting between the rocks, pine trees, and bushes, he worked his way carefully down the incline.

A coat covered with dirt and large dark red spots lay tangled in the bushes. The flies and odor told him more than he wanted to know. He stepped closer and carefully lifted a branch.

The animals had clearly worked on the remains. A body had been pulled most of the way out of a shallow grave. Disturbing the canopy that covered the corpse released an overpowering smell. He dropped the leaves, covered his mouth and stepped back.

He wanted to look away, but couldn't take his eyes off the form as he yelled up to Linda, "Call 911."

———

"Kai, over here." Kai heard a friendly voice over the noise of the Denver airport.

She saw her former co-worker Alex waving in the crowd of fifty or so people, all waiting for someone at the exit of the monorail at Denver International Airport. Some of the tension from this rushed transfer left her stomach at the sight of her friend, a woman who had helped her so much when she was new to New York. Kai cut across the moving mass of those trying to get out of the airport. "Hey, what are you doing here?"

Alex stepped around a woman pulling a suitcase and gave Kai a hug. The two were as different in appearance as two young women could be. Kai was tall and slim, with long, straight, black hair from her Chinese mother and the darker skin from her Hawaiian father. Alexandra was shorter, stockier, with short blond hair and a light complexion.

"I couldn't let you spend your first night here alone in some hotel. I've got an extra room in my apartment. You can stay there tonight." Alex grabbed Kai's shoulder bag. "Let me help you with that." She turned and started walking.

Kai scrambled to keep up. "We need to stop by baggage claim."

"That's where I'm headed, or don't you remember DIA's layout?"

Kai pulled her carry-on. "I remember it mostly, but it has been a couple of years. You sure I won't be an inconvenience?"

"Not at all. As I said, I have an extra room. Hey, if you like you can rent the room. Homeland is paying you for temporary housing, right?"

Everything on the trip was happening quickly, not that Kai minded. New York was getting a little stale. "That's what I was told. They said to rent an apartment on a week-by-week basis. They gave me a list of places that the government accepts."

"I'm sure bunking with your supervisor is also acceptable. I'll set it up." Alex gave a devilishly sweet smile.

"Temporary housing is normally expensive. What exactly are you planning?"

"As you said, temporary housing is expensive."

If you're planning on cheating the government I get half." Kai liked the games Alex played.

"Seventy-thirty, it's my apartment and I am your boss. If this comes out I would get blamed."

"But I'm the one giving you this opportunity. Sixty-forty."

"You could stay in a hotel while you're here. I know how much you like them. Sixty-five-thirty-five." Alex smiled up at Kai.

"Fine you win. Sixty-five-thirty-five."

"After utilities of course."

"You are a real turkey, you know."

"And normal rent for the room."

"I think a hotel is sounding better all the time."

"Fine, sixty-five-thirty-five but you still pay half of the utilities."

The friendship picked up right where it had left off in New York. Kai glanced at Alex while they waited for her bag. She was the truest of friends.

11

Saturday

Sara was walking across the lawn as Derry pulled up into his driveway. Shutting off the car, he stepped out and started walking toward her.

"Forget we're planning to see my mother today?"

He raised the white bag he carried. "Nope. Just went to get some doughnuts and coffee." He gave her a peck on the cheek.

A small giggle escaped her mouth. "You are one sad case. You use any excuse you can."

"What's a road trip without some little sugar bombs and caffeine?" He followed her around the car.

"A twenty minute drive is not a road trip."

He reached for her door and held it open. "You know, with Denver's traffic, it could take a lot longer. Maybe as much as thirty minutes." He gave her his kid smile. It worked as always, but she wasn't about to let him know that.

She patted his rock hard belly. "Once we're married, I'm cutting you back on the sweets. I can't have you becoming one of those overweight, bald headed, good for nothing husbands." She took the bag and started to get into his car.

"Once we're married, I'll have *all* the sugar I need." Derry slid into the driver's seat.

She hit him. "That was bad."

He shrugged. Before closing the car door, he added, "Don't worry, I won't talk this way around your mom."

She took her coffee out of the bag and set the bag by her feet, away from Derry.

Backing out, he quietly said, "You think I can't reach them?"

"You have to drive. I'll take care of the food." His comment about her mother brought despair with it and she wasn't sure why. It was her mom they were going to see, the mother she has missed for over ten years. The mother that showed what ten years of destruction and loss can do to someone. Was she afraid of what Derry would think of her after meeting her mom? She started to say a silent prayer.

He glanced over. "What's wrong?"

How could she tell him she had reservations now that she had forced him to come? "Nothing, why?" She pushed her hair back and reached into the bag, grabbing a chocolate doughnut. Slipping off her shoes, she placed her feet on the dash and slouched down. She took a nibble. It was so sweet. She followed it with a sip of hot black coffee, the way she had learned to drink it at the Bureau.

At a stop sign, Derry studied the map on his phone.

"I told you how to get there. Don't you trust me?"

"I just wanted to get the route in my head." Derry turned at the corner and headed out of their neck of the woods. He then cleared his throat and glanced at her sugar bomb.

"You think you get one?" She gave him a deadpan expression.

"I bought them."

"So?"

He quickly reached over and grabbed the one in her hand before she could move it away. She tried to get it back.

"Hey, don't mess with the driver."

"You want my coffee too?"

"If you don't give me mine, sure."

The game didn't feel right today. She reached into the bag and got his coffee out, handing it to him. She then retrieved another doughnut for herself.

"You never give in this easily and you rarely eat anything with this much sugar." He held up the doughnut. "So what's wrong? Is it work or something else?"

She'd have to answer sooner or later, but she procrastinated by taking a bite of the new doughnut.

She knew it was wrong to lie to him, but she just could not tell him what was really on her mind. She decided to tell a half-truth. She wiped her mouth with her hand. "It's work."

"The case isn't going well?" Derry glanced at her as they headed south. His blue eyes pierced deeply into her soul.

She hoped their kids would get his eyes but knew the chances were slim. "You know I can't say anything."

"You don't have to; I see it all over your face. If your team is having trouble finding who did it, you might try reading the newspapers. Every news service out there has its own opinion as to who did it and why."

"I'll make the suggestion."

They worked on their doughnuts and coffee in silence for the next several minutes.

The sugar bothered Sara's stomach. The last thing she needed was to barf just before seeing her mom. She stopped after eating about a third of the sugary ring. "You want this?"

"You've barely touched it."

She tossed it back in the bag and sipped more coffee. It helped. She studied him as he drove, asking herself the same questions she had asked herself a hundred times before. *How can someone like him love me? He can have any girl he wanted. Why me, a skinny sickly twig with a bad past?*

He made loving him so easy. He listened when she needed to be heard and smiled when her spirits were down. He knew her deepest, darkest secrets, understood them, and still loved her. "What I'm about to share is completely confidential."

"Of course." He gave his kid smile again. She hoped he never lost it.

She worked on the phrasing of the question, not wanting to give too much away. "Are people and companies outside of our country given the same rights as those inside?"

"Not an easy answer. It all depends on the judge hearing the case, but foreign countries shouldn't be covered by our constitution. The rights they have depend on the treaties we have with the host country in most cases."

Sometimes his random understanding of things surprised her. "So can we, the FBI or CIA, do things to them that would be illegal to do to U.S. based companies?"

"Yes, sometimes. And in the case of a murdered senator and his wife, things change. Much of what is overlooked, or prosecuted, is based on public opinion instead of the law. It's not right but it's the way things are today."

He glanced over. "Does that help?"

His answer helped on one level, but it didn't make her feel any better. "Yes." She looked out the window and wondered what would happen to her if the media found out about her hacking into companies based in other countries. Would they understand or would she be just another FBI scapegoat?

––––––––

Kai had spent the last several hours reviewing what Alex's team had done with the standard decryption tools. They had not made any progress in decrypting the files, but their failures would tell her where to go next. Her back ached and she rotated her shoulders to gain some relief. She hated the tiny closet of a room they worked in. Her face was to the wall with Alex lined up behind her. She turned around to see her friend's forehead over the top of her monitor. "Who set this place up?"

Alex stuck her head just above her display. "Agent Hewitt, why?"

"Because it *stinks*. I'm here with my only view a cinder block wall while you're there, staring at the back of my head."

"Which has a tiny streak of gray." She smiled.

Kai reached back and touched the spot. "That's where I fell out of a tree and hit my head on a rock. I was six years old. And you don't have to remind me."

"It's nothing, sweetheart." Alex's southern accent was turned up.

"Why can't I rotate my desk around and butt it up against yours?" A little bead of sweat rolled down Kai's temple. It was okay, in a minute the air conditioner would kick on and drop the temperature to where a sweater would be needed.

"Hewitt set it up this way and told me not to change it." Her smile was gone but she sounded like she cared. "Sorry."

"But he didn't tell me." Kai gave a mischievous smile.

"He said we must have a double vision protocol in place on this project."

"So you're here to spy on me?"

"Your clearance isn't high enough to work on this project alone.

But I'm not spying on your every move, I just need to make sure all the right protocols are followed."

It doesn't matter what you call it, it's still spying. "And getting wanded this morning on the way in, what was that all about?"

"Again, it has to do with our different levels of clearance. This project is very sensitive and above your clearance. But you have the skills we need. So I have to make sure you are not compromising the data in any way. Speaking of that, how is it going?" Alex asked sweetly.

"Haven't you been peeking over my shoulder?"

Alex pushed back from her desk and hit the wall next to the door. "You're too tall for me to watch over your shoulder. I have to look around you."

Kai glanced back at her screen as she twisted her upper body and stretched out her stiff muscles. "I am about finished reviewing what has been done."

"So, what have the tests shown you so far?"

"That whoever encrypted these files was good. But I have determined a few things that should help me get started."

"Such as?"

"Such as there is no backdoor, at least none that are in our database."

"That's why we sent for you, honey."

"You know, Homeland has a whole team of highly trained people in New York that would love a chance to work on this. And using them would make it go much faster."

Alex shook her head and gave a disappointed look. "And I thought you were the best."

"Maybe I am— but as they say, ten heads are better than one."

"Ten, huh? Are you admitting defeat already? Oh, and after all I did to build you up to Landry and Hewitt."

"Not all encryptions can be cracked without the key." The air conditioning was on again. Kai rubbed her hands on her upper arms hoping the friction would generate some heat. "If we have to work in this sardine can, can't they at least fix the air conditioning? I'm not a piece of test equipment that needs to go through temperature cycling."

"I'll see what I can do about the swings in temperature. As for getting help from New York, sorry, that's a no."

Standing, Kai moved away from the vent that blew cold air toward her.

"You can always redirect that."

Kai reached over to the vent cover and pointed the air at Alex. "There, maybe this will help remind you to get it fixed."

Alex raised her face toward the air and smiled.

"You like that?"

"It doesn't bother me. So what do you need to finish this project?"

"Caffeine. Do you think we could get our own coffee station in here?"

"And what part of your desk are you willing to give up?"

"Not mine, yours. It needs to be centrally located."

"Not going to happen." Alex glanced at her watch. "It's a good time to take a break. We might want to grab some snacks, too."

Kai started for the door. "Unlike some in this room, I don't have a sweet tooth."

"Lock your computer."

Kai turned, reached back and hit the key to lock her system. "Before we step out, I want to know why we have all the high security on this project. I mean, we can't send it to New York, no one else is allowed in here, I can't have internet access or a cell phone while I'm in here, and I can't step three paces down the hall without locking everything up."

Alex's hand rested on the door handle. She lost all emotion in her face. "I probably shouldn't be telling you this, you don't really have the clearance, but when you crack these files you might find out some of this anyway." Alex lowered her voice as if someone could hear anything coming through that steel door. "It's believed these files list hundreds of terrorists around the country, their activities, associates, Middle East contacts and funding. Many of whom work inside our own government."

"All the more reason to have the lab in New York decrypt them. The sooner we know who they are, the faster we can round them up."

"We are sure some of these terrorists work in Homeland and are in managerial positions. We cannot take any chances of the wrong people seeing the contents of these files."

"Where'd these files come from? I mean, how did we get ahold of them?"

Alex showed a little pride in her smile. "I only know part of the story. It has to do with some undercover work and a whole lot of luck. It was passed on to Hewitt by the field agent who found it. At this point you are one of only five people that know of its existence and we want to keep it that way until we have time to sort through the data."

"You're right, my clearance is not high enough for something like this. Why am I working on this?"

Alex stepped in a little closer. "It has nothing to do with clearance. It has everything to do with trust. As I said, we believe some fairly high up people are on this list. If clearances were one hundred percent reliable then we wouldn't have people in a position of power on the list."

Kai had heard rumors about a leak. This all made sense. "Why me? I have not been around long enough to build that kind of trust."

"You also have not been around long enough to be on the list. We needed the best encryption-decryption expert from that lab of yours and we had to have someone we knew would not be involved."

"How do you know I am not one of the terrorists?"

"I suppose no one really knows for sure about someone else, but when Hewitt and Landry came to me, you were the one I felt I could trust. So I threw your name in the hat for this job. Hewitt checked your background and after he and Landry reviewed it, they made the decision to bring you in."

"What convinced them that I could be trusted?" She would never betray her country, but how could they know that?

Alex leaned in. "We know about your father being in the CIA and how he was killed. It tore you up pretty badly. Hewitt figured after that you would never turn against your homeland."

The pain of that memory destroyed Kai's mood. She hadn't put anything about her father on the paperwork for this job, other than the fact he had died five years ago. "I never said anything about that to anyone." Kai pulled back as she watched Alex. It bothered her that Alex knew this part of her past, but what did she expect? Her dad was part of the government. His death would show up in a background check. They never caught the man who had killed her dad. It was suspected he worked for the North Koreans, Chinese or some other Asian country. They said they tried to find the person, but never did. She wondered if they really cared. And she had left out that information for good reason. She didn't want anyone to know.

"Even though you did not include it in the information you gave to Homeland, a background check on you revealed your father's connection with the CIA. Hewitt reviewed your father's file before agreeing to bring you in on this project."

Kai did not like the turn this conversation had taken. "Okay, then how about trusting me on one more thing."

"Tell me what it is and I will see."

"If I am going to decrypt these files I need some tools from New York that I don't have access to here. Your system talks to the outside world. I need you to download them."

"Give me the list and I'll see what I can do."

12

The ride to Sara's mother's apartment was not what Derry had expected. Sara's talk was soft and shallow, never allowing the conversation to venture too deep. She was worried or hurt about something, but today she would not let him in. His heart ached when she hid like this, but he'd learned over the last two years that he had to wait her out. When she was ready she would let him in.

"That's it." Sara nodded at the old rundown two-story apartment building, built in the shape of a wide U with outside walkways and wrought iron rails.

He pulled the car to a stop in front. The structure had been built in the sixties and lacked any form of maintenance for the last few decades.

"It's not half as bad of a dump as you made it out to be. I'll bet only part of the roof leaks and I'm guessing it has cold and cold running water, and flow through ventilation in every apartment."

Sara slowly turned her head and looked at him. "Is that your poor attempt at humor?"

"Best I can do on short notice."

With a blank expression, she turned away. "I'm going to see my mom. You coming?" She opened the door and stepped out without waiting for a response.

Following, he felt the gap between them widen, the same gap he'd felt the first time she returned from a visit with her mom. Was it painful memories from her childhood or guilt for the poverty her mom lived in? He hurried to catch up.

The walkways were filled with broken toys and items destined for a bonfire. Some of the apartments had cardboard or wood where glass should have been. There was loud music coming from somewhere that echoed against the walls. The area where a lawn should have been, was covered with long dead grass and dirt overlaid with cigarette butts and other forms of trash.

Derry grabbed Sara's hand. She tried to pull away, but he held on. This area made the part of town he grew up in look safe and upper class. He didn't think Denver had places like this anymore, but every large city has its deep dark secrets, places they don't want anyone to know about.

Scanning the walkways and building, he decided Sara should never have come here alone. Working for the FBI was no protection against a bullet or men with knives.

Two half-naked, dirty faced, young children sitting on the bottom step glanced up at Derry and Sara and studied them just long enough to determine if they were a threat. Wide eyed, they saw they were not and went back to their nothing world and looked away. What a way to live.

Sara pulled her hand loose as they stepped around the kids and headed for the second floor.

"What's your mom's apartment number?"

She turned left at the top of the stairs. "It's this way." He followed as they weaved through the chairs, boxes, and other obstacles left in their path.

Most of the doors were missing their numbers or had them hand written in marker or carved into the wood.

Sara slowed to a stop. The window next to the door was covered with a heavily stained and tattered curtain. She took a deep breath before knocking lightly. This was followed by more knocks separated by only a few seconds. Each knock was louder until she was pounding.

He reached for her hand to stop her. "Hey, are you trying to wake the whole building?"

Her face was hard and cold. "She's drunk, I know it. I'm just trying to wake *her*."

"Maybe she's not home."

The next door down opened. "Ain't no one there no more." The gruff voice belonged to a wrinkled old woman with gray scraggly hair that stuck out in all directions. Her grimy face was wedged between the door and the frame. She stared with bloodshot eyes. "So stop all your pounding or I'll call the cops."

Sara took a step toward her. "It's my mother's apartment. What do you mean no one lives there?" Sara's voice was weak but challenging.

"It ain't hers no more. Now stop all that racket and go away." She started to close the door as she kept talking. "Can't get any sleep with all that noise."

"Wait." Derry stepped closer. A horrific smell of marijuana, stale cigarettes and body odor assaulted his senses. "We're trying to find her mother. Do you know where the woman who lived here moved to?"

"If'n she were a good daughter, her mum would have told her." The old woman glared at Sara, answering her dare. "It's your own fault you can't find her." The door started to close again.

"She is a good daughter. She's come several times trying to find her mother." He started to reach out, but the horrified look on the woman's face stopped him. "Any information will help."

The woman opened the door a little as her eyes went from Derry to Sara and back. "What's in it for me?"

"What?" Sara gasped.

"I said what's in it for me? You hard of hearing, too?" The door opened a few more inches, allowing more of the stench to pour out. The woman stood full in the doorway as she scrutinized Derry. "You look like you got lots of money. You ain't gonna miss a few bucks."

Sara stepped forward. "Why you little druggy! We're not going to give you money so you can just get high. It's a simple question. Do you know where my mother went?"

"I don't do none of them illegal drugs. I ain't one of them meth junkies. I just need some stuff to help my pains." The woman rubbed her left shoulder. "My government check ain't come yet and I need some medication."

"You're a li—"

"Will twenty work?" Derry stepped forward, reaching for his wallet. *Chastising the woman won't change her.*

The woman challenged Derry, "Twenty? Can't hardly buy anything with that. — I know you got more. A couple of rich kids too busy spending their money to come around and see their own mum." She continued to massage her shoulder.

Derry pulled out the bill then opened his wallet and showed the woman the inside. "That's all I have. You want it or not?"

The woman reached for the bill as he pulled it away.

"Hey."

"After you tell us what we want to know." He held the twenty up just out of her reach.

The woman didn't blink as she gawked at the twenty. "Your mum moved out about a month ago. Now give me the money."

"She doesn't know anything and you'd better not give her anything." Sara stood defiant, arms crossed, staring at Derry.

Derry stared down at the old lady. "Did she say where she was going?"

Not once since the bill appeared did the old woman's eye leave it. "Yeah, said she was going to live with her kid or something like that."

"I'm her kid. You're too stupid, or too stewed to know anything." Sara's glare shifted between the two of them. "She'll say anything to get more drugs." Sara grabbed the twenty out of Derry's hand.

"Hey, if'n you don't give me my money, I'll call the cops on you."

"Go ahead. I work for the FBI." Sara stared the woman down.

"FBI? I don't want nothing to do with'n the FBI. Get away from my door." She disappeared as the opportunity slammed shut.

"Told you she didn't know anything." Sara held the twenty where Derry could grab it as she headed down the walkway.

He moved in behind her. "Let's go talk with the manager. He should know something."

"It's a waste of time, but if it makes you feel better, sure."

The manager's apartment was on the first floor in the right front corner of the 'U'. A middle-aged, obese, woman answered the door. She surveyed the two of them. "Are you two looking for an apartment? I have several openings and it's a great place for a young couple to start out, real low rent."

"We're looking for Catherine Ramos in apartment two-thirty-four. She's her mother." Derry pointed at Sara.

The woman gave Sara the once over again. "Your mother? You got some I.D?"

Sara reached into her bag. "My last name is Beckwith. My

mother went back to her maiden name after my father died."

The woman glanced at Sara's driver's license. "Different last names. You got something to show she's your mom? A picture or something?"

Sara peered down in her bag. "Ah — no. Not with me."

"No picture? Nothing?" The manager glanced at Sara's bag.

"No, I was taken away from my mom shortly after my dad was killed. I just reconnected with her a couple of months ago."

Doubt covered the woman's face. "I'm sorry, it must have been rough on you, but without something to prove you're related, there's not much I can do."

Sara turned toward Derry with tears forming.

Derry, seeing Sara was having trouble at the thought of losing her mom again, explained to the manager why they were looking. "We're getting married soon and I wanted to meet her mom. It's important, please."

The manager stood unmoving, studying them both. "Maybe I can get a message to her, if she left a forwarding address."

Sara cheered up. "That would be great."

"Come on inside. It's too hot to be standing out in the sun." The woman turned and left them at the door. "I'll be perfectly honest with you. I was glad when that young man told me she'd be moving out. She never paid her rent on time and the place stunk. I'm not sure if I'm ever going to get that smell out of her place."

Sara perked up. "What young man? Did he have a name?"

"Most likely. We all seem to have one. It should be in my records." The woman lumbered around a small desk that was surprisingly neat. Plopping down in a large chair, she took a few seconds to catch her breath. "You know your mom wasn't all there. I was happy to see her go."

"Yes, you said that."

"Well, I just want you to know how I felt." The woman reached over and opened a file drawer. "I don't mean to sound uncaring, but your momma's got some real problems upstairs." The woman pointed at her own head.

"She's had a rough life." Sara moved around the side of the desk. Derry stepped in closer.

The woman flipped through the file drawer before pulling out a slip of paper. "Here is the record for that apartment." She read it over. "She left owing me two month's rent."

"And you expect us to pay?" Derry had seen this game before.

"She's her kid, right?"

"You can't hold us responsible for her bills." Sara tried to see the paper, but the woman tipped it back where Sara couldn't read it.

The woman stared at Sara before answering. "No, I guess not. Like I said, I was happy to see her go."

"Do you have her new address?"

The manager put the paper back in the drawer.

"Nope. I asked, but I never got one." She turned toward Sara. "Sorry."

13

Monday

What's wrong?

The message popped up on Sara's display. She glimpsed over her shoulder at its sender.

Everything.
Sorry to hear. You need someone to talk to?

Swiveling around in her chair, she faced Todd. "We could actually talk face to face you know."

He kept typing. She read the message on her display.

Yeah, but this way I can work at the same time.

Todd, Sara, and Tony shared an office that held four desks, but the fourth desk sat empty, and Tony was gone for a few weeks on an undercover assignment. Not being management, they did not have the luxury of a window or overstuffed chairs for visitors. Lamar told them anything as nice as an overstuffed chair would only serve as a bed for Todd and he would never go home. Todd thought a chair to sleep in was a good idea. Most of the other programmers were out on the floor, stuck in cubicles.

Sara stuck her leg out and pushed Todd's chair, spinning it around.

"Hey." He tried to turn back but she continued pushing against the chair. "Fine." He scowled at her. "But it's wasting time this way. I don't need to see your face to talk with you."

"And you wonder why you don't have a girlfriend."

"I don't wonder at all." He put his hands on his knees. "So, talk."

He meant well, he just didn't have any social graces.

"Derry and I tried to go see my mother this weekend."

"Is something wrong with her? I mean besides what you told me the other day?"

"She moved out and didn't leave a forwarding address." Sara was pushing his chair back and forth. He scooted back a few inches, out of the reach of her legs.

"Well, that explains why she hasn't answered her door." He gave his dorky smile. "Did you ask the management?"

"Yeah, but we got nothing. I don't think the manager cared."

In his best "I know everything" voice, Todd added, "You know, tenants are supposed to leave a forwarding address, but it wouldn't matter. Most apartment managers would never give that kind of information out. Did you tell her you worked for the FBI?"

Sara tilted her head. "I should have, but I don't think it would have helped.

"You could have told her it was an investigation."

"You told me that was illegal." She tried unsuccessfully to push his chair.

"And you don't want to end up in the slammer again." His short nasal laugh had really bothered her when she first met him, but now it was just Todd.

His sense of humor was the worst she'd ever encountered. "My life is good now. I'm happy, or maybe I should say content. I don't want to lose that."

"Content? After all the work you did to find your mother and now she is gone, how can you be *content*?"

She looked up in his eyes. How could she be content? She was sick and she had just lost her mother again, but yet— "It's more than that. I'm content with—oh never mind, you know what I mean."

"Well, I wouldn't give up so easily."

"I'm not. I have some ideas." She told him everything that happened at the apartment building. "If it was someone from the Department of Human Services that moved her, it should be in their records. Or maybe they filed a change of address at the post office. If I could log into the DHS system, I might be able to find out where she is."

"What happened to not bending the rules?"

"It could take weeks to go through the official channels and I really need to find her before the wedding. It's not really hurting anything to take a peek at their records on my mom."

"You can't get into that system without my help." He leaned back and crossed his arms.

"Yeah, but you'll help me. Won't you?" She gave him a sweet smile.

"You think you can get your way by flirting with me?"

Changing to a slightly pouty expression she played the next card. "No, I would never do that."

He shook his head slightly as he looked away. "Fine, but you need to be careful. If you're caught, I'm not covering for you."

"No one will find out. So, can I use your login ID?"

"You'll owe me for this one."

"I know and I'll be careful."

"If you get caught I could lose my clearance and maybe my job."

"I'd end up in jail, and you're worried about losing your clearance? You're all heart."

He gave a barely noticeable shrug. "Do you remember the rules? Only log on while I'm here and only in the same room. Also—"

He had at least fifteen of them. "Yes, I know. Don't go to any unauthorized sites or any place that could bring the attention of upper management. Make sure no one sees me using your log in. Keep a record of everything I do, and forward it to you and if I am caught, I stole your password and you will hang me out to dry."

"That's not all of them."

"It's a summary of most of them."

"Fine, I guess that is close enough." A slight smile formed. "And any risk must have a reward."

"Reward? And what would that be?"

"You go to the meetings for me for the next three weeks."

"You know I can't do that."

"Okay." He looked around the office. "You bring me some homemade cookies."

"If you had a wife, she could make you all the cookies you want."

"Women are too needy. They want you to pay attention to them and do things with them. My life is just the way I like it."

"You are the biggest nerd I've ever seen."

"Whatever. Is it a deal?"

"Fine, what kind of cookies?"

"Oatmeal raisin. And one more thing."

He always asked for oatmeal raisin, not her favorite. "What?"

"I heard they were tightening security around here. Be careful."

"Of course. I always am."

14

Sam's pocket vibrated. Setting the folder down, he welcomed the distraction. The leak that brought him home could be anywhere or anyone. Looking through his personal records of his missions in hopes of finding something helpful was like searching the North Pole for a particular snowflake. He slid his phone out and glanced at the caller ID. It was his boss.

"Freymen."

"Hi Sam. It's Nick. Sorry about your business trip."

Nothing they said was what it sounded like. No phone was ever truly secure, even an encrypted one. "Yeah, it took two years to set it up and for what?" He looked out from his covered porch. A row of rolling dark clouds was pushing its way up the valley. Rain would be here soon.

He closed the folder to keep the papers in place in case the wind picked up. He inhaled deeply. The moist air filling his lungs removed some of the tension. There was nothing in this world like the smell of the Appalachians.

"We had no choice. The deal fell through. We could not afford to waste any more assets on it." Meaning others had died because of the leak and they didn't want to lose him, too.

"I think I could have persuaded the deal to go through. I am sure I could have negotiated a contract in the next few weeks." Something was coming down and he was close to finding out what.

"We know, but it wasn't your call."

All this was in his report, nothing new.

"We have a possibility of finding the resources we need someplace else." Another source.

Sam stood to pace. Nick was a good boss. He was upfront and

honest. Not what the public pictured for a department head at the CIA.

"A new business arrangement always takes time, something I don't believe we have before they go through with the deal." Whatever was about to happen, would happen too soon for a new asset to infiltrate a new group.

"Perhaps, but I believe you were lucky in those negotiations. It could have cost you all you had. If it weren't for your friends in the Israeli company, we'd have nothing more than another broken deal and your name showing up on some forgotten wall." *Meaning if not for the Mossad, I'd be dead and they would put a star on the wall at CIA headquarters.*

"If this deal goes through with some other country, it will hurt U.S. interests at home." Sam spun around and headed the other direction. He could see the rain down the gorge about a mile off. "Isn't the risk of one person's assets worth the assets of hundreds of Americans?"

"If I believed you could have pulled it off, then yes, but that's not the case."

Sam tightly gripped the phone. Did Nick understand what was at stake? Of course he did, he had to. "My assets are extremely secure. I want to go back and finish the deal."

"There will be other opportunities, but you've been working hard. As soon as we get your notes and other documents I want you to relax for a while. Are you at home?"

"Yes. Why?"

Sam had three locations he called home. One was this cabin in Virginia, one in Israel and the third known only to him up near the Canadian border.

This small cabin sat near the top of a hill in the western mountains of Virginia. The cabin had three rooms and a large back porch. It had been built in the early forties by a man fearing a Nazi invasion. The walls were thick and the bedroom had a trapdoor that led to a bomb shelter. Sam had added a tunnel that ran a few yards past the tree line. He didn't think he needed it, but it made the paranoia of the cabin complete. From his back porch he had a good view of any car coming up the road, which, given the terrain around his home, was about the only way to get there.

"You are about to have a visitor."

"I see the car. What's this about?"

"Joelle can answer any questions you have" Joelle was Nick's niece and just a few years younger than Sam. But she'd been in the company three years longer than he had.

Sam glanced at the clock on the microwave. "She's just in time for dinner."

"As long as you sit at the other end of the table." A bad running joke between the two men, one Joelle either was unaware of or didn't care about.

"After all these years of working for you and you still don't trust me?"

"It's because of all those years that I don't trust you."

A vehicle pulled up in front of the cabin. A second later, a car door slammed followed by footsteps crossing the porch and a knock on the door. "She's here." Sam cut through the living area of the main room.

"Perfect timing, she'll take care of everything." The line went dead as Sam gave his greetings to Joelle.

"Welcome back." She stepped past him and into the great room of his small cabin. She went to the only large, flat, unoccupied surface in the room, the table that served as workspace and eating space. Putting her briefcase on it, she took a quick look around the living area. "So this is where the great spy lives."

"You expected something different?" His cabin was very simple and little was visible to give any information about Sam's likes, dislikes, or interests.

"Yeah. I'm not sure what, but this isn't it. Anyway, I don't have much time, and we have a lot to cover. Take a seat."

"Maybe later."

She opened her briefcase and withdrew a folder. "Suit yourself. You talked with the old man, right?"

"Your uncle, yes. Does he know you call him that?"

She went on without an answer. "We need you in Denver tonight."

"What happened to my time off?"

"Who said you get time off? We have a situation out there that needs your touch."

He started to pace. U.S. missions were always risky. The CIA was

Deadly Infiltration

not supposed to operate inside the borders, but they did. "What's so important in Denver?"

"Agent Blinder was murdered. We need to know why." She glanced up at him as he crossed the small room. Using the pen she held, she pointed at him. "Please stop, I can't concentrate while you're walking back and forth."

"Sorry." He stopped next to the table. "I heard Ryan left the company a few months ago to start his own business."

"A cover that apparently didn't work."

"What was he working on?" Sam dropped into a chair and reached for the folder.

She picked it up before he touched it. "The leak. The same one that brought you home early. As nearly as we can tell, he was getting close and the men who killed him gained access to our computers and learned about it. He was found dead in Rocky Mountain National Park. His body had been dropped into a shallow grave." She laid the file down where he could see a couple of the pictures. "Some animals found him, and pulled him up, and did a number on him. He was ID'd by a card found in his pants pocket. Once his body is back here we will run other tests."

Sam looked at the open folder. Reaching over, he picked up a couple of the photos from the crime scene. Ryan's body was unrecognizable.

"Did you know him?"

"We came in contact on a few missions."

After a short pause she retrieved the pictures. "The last report we got from him was a little over two weeks ago. At that time, everything sounded normal. When he didn't file his report last week we started a very low priority search. We couldn't risk sending in assets or calling anyone to learn what had happened."

"If it wasn't for the grave, his death might have passed for a mountain lion attack," Sam observed.

"That and the fact he was tortured."

"He was? Do you believe they got anything out of him?"

She leaned back in her chair. "Seen any news since you've gotten back?"

He glanced around his cabin, "Only what I see on the internet."

There was no TV.

"Hear about Senator Henderson?"

"Of course. Impossible not to."

"Because of the leak, we have not and may never tell the FBI, but we are convinced that his death was a direct result of information gathered by Ryan Blinder."

"How are these two connected?" Sam focused on her.

"Through us."

He waited for more. *Had Senator Henderson been involved in the CIA?*

She laid down everything in her hands. It was clear this was a subject she knew well. "The senator's father was one of our agents. In the years before he died he trained young field agents. Blinder was one of his last students, and from what I understand they were close. It makes sense that Blinder would reach out to one of Agent Henderson's two sons if he was in trouble."

Sam understood this. He had grown very close to his own mentor and his family. When his mentor was murdered because of a botched case, Sam almost quit the CIA. It tore the family apart. "Reached out? How?"

Joelle shifted her weight, uneasily. "We do not have any information on anything that Blinder was working on for the last two weeks. This is the part we are completely guessing about. We believe that whatever Ryan discovered was dumped somewhere he considered safe. And the senator's home makes sense."

"In an attempt to keep it away from his killers?"

"Yes, but we think it didn't work. Somehow they found out." She picked up the pen and ran it back and forth through her fingertips as she stared at it.

Sam leaned in. Joelle waited for him to speak. "If he was worried about a leak within one of the agencies, why not upload the files to the dark net or some secure offshore backup?"

She tapped the pen against the table edge and looked up at Sam. "My guess, he didn't think it would be safe even there." She handed him a bullet list of security breaches.

He gave it a quick read. Blinder had identified twenty-seven separate leaks in just the last year, occurring in every branch of law enforcement. "Who could have access to all of this information? No one agency could be doing this."

"That's what we thought, but all of our systems are interconnected on one level or another. The internal firewalls are not as stringent as the external ones. Once a good hacker has gained access to one federal agency, they can gain access to the others."

"If that's true, they would know about me."

She tossed the pen aside and looked over at him with her hazel eyes. "We are sure they do. That is why we brought you home. So everything we do is a risk right now. Uncle Nick feels that you are the best choice for this mission."

"Best for success, or most expendable?" He smiled at his own question, but worried about the truth of the selection.

She held his gaze. "I worked on the profiles of all the available agents." Her stare broke off. "You have a sixty percent chance of returning. The next closest was forty-seven percent." She spoke more softly, "I may have too much faith in your abilities, but I tried to be honest on my assessment."

Did she really care about him? Most people in the office considered her to be more machine than female. "How am I going in?"

The caring face vanished quicker than it had appeared. "I worked up a profile. We are not going to hide the fact that the terrorists most likely already know who you are. You've been on assignment for two plus years. You deserve and need time off after learning your mission was a bust."

He shrugged in agreement.

"You like hiking, the mountains, and all that outdoor stuff. You will be on vacation. It's only natural."

"So you want me go on vacation?"

"Yes, that is the plan."

"It didn't work for Ryan."

"This time it's different. Deep in our database Mr. Blinder was still listed as working for us and on active duty. You will be listed as on vacation with no mention of this mission anywhere, in any system."

Sam stood. It didn't sound right. "And if I need to break a law here and there? I'll end up in jail?"

Joelle pulled a paper out of the folder. It was from the White

House. "We will get you out."

He took the paper and read it over. It gave him complete immunity for any white-collar crimes and misdemeanors committed in this case, and if need be, full powers to pull in and control any and all parts of the investigation. "How did you get the President to sign this?"

"We gave him the information that Mr. Blinder and our other sources have gathered and showed him the strong link between them and the internal leak or leaks within our agencies."

"And that did it?"

She smiled. "No, we also pointed out that the Secret Service's computers were also interconnected in the same manner and that they could be hacked anytime. This would nullify almost all of his security."

"You put the fear of God in him?"

She shrugged. "We do what we must to save this country."

They became quiet as rain began to beat hard on the steel roof. "I know you need to get going, but that dirt road will be impassable for a while after this storm passes."

She peeked out the front windows. Everything outside disappeared in the white-gray of the heavy downpour. "I brought my jeep." She showed no concern.

"Okay. If you're sure you can handle the roads. I have a couple more questions, then I'll let you go."

She gazed up at him. "Well?"

"If all of the agencies' systems are suspect, I won't be communicating through them. Do you have a secure plan for communications?"

"Of course. You can use the dark net."

In most cases that would be the perfect answer. "That requires unique software. I need a way that can be done from any system. Something that, if my computer is found by the wrong people, won't give me up. I'm going to use a unique, non-standard IP address." He reached over and took her pen. "I will be filing all my reports at this location and Nick can post information for me there as well." He wrote out the address. It did not follow the IPv4 or IPv6 protocol.

She picked it up and looked at it. "You sure this will work?"

"I've used this method before in the Middle East. This is a different address, but it will work. Give it only to Nick, and tell him not to use it at work or at home but to hit a cyber-café or someplace like that."

"Everyone knows those are not secure. I don't think Nick will go for it."

"You are right. Everyone knows they are not secure and would never be used, including the people we are after."

"Good point."

"The first password is the name of his favorite niece."

"I should be able to remember that."

"Making an assumption there, are you?"

"I'm the only one in his family that will talk to him, so no. No assumption made."

"His wife still talks to him. The second password is the name of his dog, Cobalt."

"Got that too. Anything else you need before I leave?"

"No. I think that about covers it. Be careful. The roads will be nasty for a while."

"Will do. And good luck." She left without a backward glance.

15

The nurse led Sara and Derry past the examination rooms to a doorway at the end of the hall. He tapped on the open entrance. Large windows with drawn shades covered the far wall. The office was only big enough for intimate meetings between two or three people. "Sara Beckwith is here." The nurse turned and left without another word.

Sara turned and looked up into Derry's eyes.

"Come in, have a seat." Doctor Rosales was a very slim man, with a full head of gray hair. He was in his mid-forties, or so Sara thought. He sat behind his cluttered wooden desk, with medical folders stacked a foot high on the corner closest to the door.

Derry slipped his warm hand into hers.

The doctor looked around the stack that blocked his view. "Is this your husband? Your records list you as single."

"This is Derry, my fiancé. You called and said you had my test results and you needed to talk with me about them. If it's okay, I'd like him here too." She tightly gripped Derry's hand.

"Yes, please, have a seat before we get started. If you're to be married this concerns you as well."

Not a good sign.

Letting go of each other's hands, they filled the two chairs facing the doctor's desk. Sara sat on the edge of her seat, hoping to hide her fears. "Do you know what's wrong?" She folded her hands together on her knees.

"Yes, I believe so." Dr. Rosales paused. "We ran the blood workup twice to make sure." He continued as he read through the file on his desk. "The test results show you have small amounts of Cesium, Boron, Cadmium, and even a tiny amount of Polonium plus elevated levels of several other heavy elements. Many of these should not be in your body at all."

Sara slid back in the chair as Derry's hand come over to hers. "What do you mean by elevated levels and how could the ones that aren't supposed to be there get into me?" Her voice was weak as the furrows grew between her eyebrows.

The doctor removed his glasses and set them on his desk. "Individually these levels are higher than we like to see, but in themselves will not cause the types of problems you are having." He paused for no apparent reason. "However, the combination of the elements that have shown up are rare, almost unheard of in this country, and there isn't a lot of data on their effects."

"What aren't you telling me?" Her shoulders drooped as she looked him in the eyes.

The doctor reached for his eyeglasses but instead of putting them on, he folded them and held them in his tightly closed fist. "We feel that the combination of all these toxins together is having a long term effect on your health, one your body is no longer able to fight against—without help that is." He studied the open folder again. "What type of work do you do again?"

"I'm a computer programmer."

Derry leaned in. "She doesn't work around chemicals, only electronics." He shifted in his seat before sliding back to where he started.

Using one hand, Dr. Rosales pushed back from his desk. "How long have you been working at your present job?"

"About two and a half years."

"Many of these heavy elements stay in the system for as many as thirty years unless you do something to remove them. Where did you work before this job?"

"Thirty years? — I was a programmer for a Denver tech company." She pulled her hand away from Derry's.

"Did that company use chemicals? Or have you ever worked or lived next to a chemical company?"

Sara thought back. "No. I've worked in an office most of the last four years and I'm sure none of the companies around me were chemical companies. Occasionally I work in our computer lab at the FBI. They have solvents, but all of their solder is lead free."

"None of that would cause this."

"I don't know of any place where I would have been exposed to chemicals."

"Have you traveled to third world countries, eaten their food or drunk their water?"

Derry cut in, "She has never even left Colorado. Could she have been exposed to these chemicals by living in an old house?"

The doctor answered without looking at Derry. "If it were just lead that we were concerned about I would say that was possible. But there are too many chemicals that aren't very common in our part of the world. Here's a copy of the report." He handed Sara a couple pieces of paper.

She read through them while Dr. Rosales went on. "I ran the results past a colleague who specializes in this area. We feel that the combination of all these elements have thrown your body out of balance. It's like a very slow poison. There are treatments to lower these levels and I suggest you start them as soon as possible. But I want to warn you they take time, months, maybe a year or two. I advise caution in your activities until we get your system back in balance. But the bright side is we don't believe there will be too much permanent damage."

"What kind of permanent damage are you thinking?"

"These chemicals have damaged your health. That will take a long time to recover from and there may be side effects to all this."

"Like what?"

The doctor read some of his notes. "Dr. Brewer said with these chemicals it's possible to have permanent damage to your reproductive system. In later years, as you mature, other problems may arise including cancer, arthritis, liver or kidney problems. But let us not get ahead of ourselves. Just take it easy for now and we will get you into treatment as soon as possible."

Why does everything have to happen at once? "What do you mean by take it easy? You want me to sit around and do nothing?"

"No, not exactly." Dr. Rosales stood and walked around to the front of his desk, pausing in front of her. He peered down. "You just need to cut back on your physical activities. These treatments can be hard on a person and you are already very underweight, to an unhealthy level. You can't afford to lose any more weight or you may end up in the hospital. Dr. Brewer will have a dietary plan for you to start after she meets with you. You will need to follow it. Am I clear? It will be part of your treatment program and hopefully bring your weight back up." He handed her a card. "Give this office a call and set up an appointment with Dr. Brewer as soon as you can."

Sara barely glimpsed at it before slipping it into her pocket. "Thank you." She looked away to wipe the tears. Derry's arm reached around her shoulder.

"What about my wedding? Will this treatment interfere with that?" she asked without looking up.

"Meet with Dr. Brewer. She can answer those questions for you." Dr. Rosales reached behind him and picked up Sara's folder. He scanned it while Sara composed herself. "She also wants to run her own tests."

Derry moved to stand. "Thank you for your time."

"And remember, until we get this taken care of, do not try to start a family." The doctor's warning hit her hard. No family, no babies.

But I want children, I love Natalie's kids and I want some of my own. "How bad would it be if we did?"

"We have two problems. First, your body is not strong enough to support a pregnancy. It could kill you as well as the baby. The other concern is that these chemicals could cause physical or mental deformities in the baby." He closed the folder and walked back to his chair. "If you have any more questions, please take them up with Dr. Brewer."

Derry reached down for her hand. She let him pull her up. They turned for the door as the doctor made one last comment.

"Maybe you were exposed to these chemicals as a child. How long ago it happened doesn't really matter, so long as we get it taken care of."

Sara squeezed Derry's hand as the answer hit her. She needed air. She needed out of the building.

16

Luca Clayton stretched for the fourth time in twenty minutes. Her shoulders ached. Ten hour workdays were not any fun, but she didn't see any alternative if she wanted to get promoted. Almost all of her coworkers at Homeland Security were gone. Many had left early, like they did every day. They hoped to miss the New York rush hour. Luca, on the other hand, stayed late nearly every day, hoping to make a good impression on her boss.

She read the most recent report one more time. A U.S. border guard named Ortiz and his wife had been killed in their home near the U.S./Mexico border. Rare, but not unheard of. Their teenage daughter was at a friend's house when it happened. She discovered the bodies on her return.

If this was meant as a message to other border guards why kill the wife? And why in their home? Was it to show that the drug cartels can reach into the U.S.?

Were they getting that brave? Were they now bringing the drug wars across the border? That would be a risky move. If the U.S. sent troops in, it could shut down their pipelines into the U.S.

And why him? He worked the border crossing, not along the fence where you'd expect problems. Did he double cross one of the cartels?

She brought up Ortiz's bank account records. It showed twenty thousand dollars deposited five days before his murder. That must be it.

If I find where the money came from we could inflict some real damage on the cartel and my boss would get off my back.

She started a program that would back trace the money. While her computer did the work, she stood to stretch again. Luca looked out the windows across the large room filled with cubicles. Her gaze swept across the nearby waterway to the New York Yacht Club. How she would love to be on one of those boats. That is, if she didn't get seasick so easily. She was surprised when a small window popped up on her computer so quickly. Most of these searches took much longer. Whoever is behind this did not try very hard to cover their tracks. But the results were not what she'd expected. The money had gone through four banks but originated in Egypt.

Well, it's not drug money. Not unless the Mexicans were now working with terrorists.

Why would terrorists kill a checkpoint guard? What was the money for? It had to be for turning a blind eye to something coming across the border. But what?

Everything at each checkpoint is recorded. She brought up Ortiz's schedule. He had only worked three shifts between the time he was paid and the time he was killed. She pulled up the video of his crossing station for those shifts. It did not take long to find something out of the ordinary. Shortly after he took over inspections, a white panel truck flagged for inspection passed through his station without the rear being opened. She read his comments. He documented the rear being opened and the truck containing women's dresses. She watched on. All other vehicles were searched during his shift. Only the truck escaped inspection.

What could be in the truck that was worth his life? It would not be people. They sneak across the border every single day. And it could not be something radioactive. That would have set off alarms. What else could it be? And where did the truck go after coming across?

It was a long shot, but, crossing her fingers, Luca ran a search through the tens of thousands of police reports from that part of the country, looking for a white panel truck. She set the priority to locations closest to the border.

After grabbing another cup of coffee and daydreaming out the harbor window, she returned to see several reports flagged. The one that caught her attention was from a small town in New Mexico.

The local police had received a phone call early the morning after the truck entered the U.S. Someone had seen several men moving canisters out of the back of a white moving truck into several panel vans.

The report stated that the men were at an old, unused warehouse and wore green chemical gloves. The local police responded to the call, but had found nothing when they arrived.

Chemicals?

Luca took a sip of her coffee, hoping to gain the energy to think this through. What kind of chemicals would terrorists want to bring into the U.S.? Chemical weapons of some sort. If it were chemical weapons, where did they go? How many vans did they have?

It was getting very late, but she had something worth following up.

Returning to her desk, she wrote up a report on what she had found and sent it to her supervisor. Almost as an afterthought, she also sent an email through her private email account to her friend who worked for the CIA.

———

The ride home was stone cold silent despite Derry's best efforts. He was hurting for Sara, but right now she needed his strength. She waited in the car, eyes straight ahead, as he walked around the car to open her door.

Slowly and without looking at him, she stepped out.

"Can we talk about this?"

He walked beside Sara as they approached the Knights' front door.

"What do you expect from me? You heard what the doctor said." Sara turned away and reached for the door.

He slid his arms around her. "He said there are treatments, things we can do. We will get past this."

"*We* will get past this? It's me that's sick, not you."

He gently turned her face toward his. "You are to be my wife. The two shall become one." He stopped. She was going through something impossible to imagine unless you have been through it yourself. What could he say to help? How could he make her understand that she wasn't alone? "I love you with every fiber in my body and I promise I will never leave you as long as I am on this planet. We will make it through this together. Trust me. And if you can't trust me, trust God. I don't believe He saved you just to have you die now."

She froze. "I do trust you. But—"

"But what?"

"I don't know. I trust God, too. That's not it." She pulled her face free from his gentle fingers.

"God loves you and will only do what is best."

"And what if, in His mind, the best thing for me is to die?" She quickly pulled away from Derry. "And don't say that's impossible. Thousands of believers die every year. How can you say God will keep me alive when my whole world is being destroyed, when everything I've ever wanted is being yanked out of my hands?"

She had a point—on one level. "God loves you more than I ever could. He laid down his life for you. I believe with all my heart that He has a plan for us in all of this and that plan does not end this year or next."

"If He has a plan I can't possibly see what it is."

"Neither can I, but I trust God, nevertheless." He tipped her face upward. "This is something I never told you because I was kind of ashamed."

She gazed into his eyes, waiting.

"Remember that day when Levy tried to kill you? I rushed back in to save you."

"And you did."

He looked down. "Not really."

"What do you mean, not really? I would have died if you hadn't been there."

"I thought that I could save you on my own. I trusted in my own skills as a fighter. But I nearly died. That goon Vance was about to stab me."

She peered deep into his gray-blue eyes waiting silently. His muscular frame always gave her a level of security and comfort.

"He beat me and I knew it. I gave up. I had nothing left in me to fight with."

"You never gave up. You fought to the end. I was there. I saw you."

"You were there, in that basement. But you weren't in here." He pointed to his heart. "And here." He pointed to his head. "I gave up, completely. I knew that not only could I not save you, but I learned it wasn't up to me to save you. That's when I knew it was God's decision.

I had to accept His will either way, live or die."

Was she going to lose faith in him as a man? This made him sound wimpy, but it was the truth. "That's when God brought Lamar into the basement. Lamar shot Vance, saving me and ultimately saving you. But all of that was in God's timing and plan. None of what happened was by our own wills."

Her head tilted slightly, "What does all that have to do with my situation now? It's completely different. I am not trying to do any of this in my own strength. I am just trying to live a normal life. That's all."

"It has to do with trusting God completely, no matter the outcome."

Her glare became hard. She no longer looked deep into his soul, but blocked him from seeing into hers. "You're saying I should sit back and do nothing and God will step in and fix everything?" She pulled back and crossed her arms.

"No, I'm saying you should trust Him."

"I DO." Tears lined her eyes. "But this has nothing to do with my trusting Him and everything to do with my past, with my life before I met you."

He reached for her hands but she would not let him hold them. "God forgave you for everything you did before, even before you asked Him to. This is not a punishment for something you did in your past."

Before he could say more, she stepped back. Staring into his face, she challenged him. "We all must pay somehow. It's no different than if a murderer comes to God; his victims don't rise up out of the ground alive and well. Someone who broke the law has to do time. Coming to God may give you forgiveness, but it does not erase the things you did or that were done to you. They are still there and still very real. I am just being punished for what someone else did to me." She turned away and walked into the yard.

Following, he stayed near her as she circled in her own fumes, arms crossed tightly across her chest.

When she began to slow down and relax a little he asked, "Who?"

She stopped and looked him in the face. "The Motovas."

"The man who *raped* you?"

She nodded. "It was his sons who did that, but he knew they did it and he didn't care." Her eyes and nose were red and wet. "But he and his wife did *this* to me."

"The chemicals? How?"

She looked out into the street. "I don't want to talk about it here." She kept walking in ever widening loops. When her feet crossed into his yard, she changed course toward his back porch.

He caught up with her as she took a seat in one of his lawn chairs. Looking up she asked, "Can I have something to drink? And not one of your Cokes."

"Sure. You know I keep Pepsi around for those without taste." His humor fell flat.

When he returned he took a seat beside her.

He waited as she took several sips. An eternity passed before she spoke. "He was always bringing chemicals to the house. He had a small lab in the basement. I didn't know what they were and I didn't care. Whenever I caused trouble, he would lock me down there. After I found cameras hidden around the house, I promised myself I would never let them record me again. I stole a kitchen knife and hid it under my pillow. I knew if I used it I would have to pay, but I couldn't take the thought of—"

He waited, he had never asked her about her past. She had opened up once so he knew the bare facts. He knew her foster family had abused her. He loved her and none of what had happened was her fault. He figured she would talk to him about it if she needed to. He wanted her to heal, not to be reminded of her past.

"Anyway, one night the oldest boy forced his way into my room, again. When he grabbed me, I grabbed the knife and went for his face. He thought he was so handsome. I got two deep slices in before he punched me, hard. When I came to, he was standing over me, holding the knife. The gashes were wide, blood dripping from his face. It felt good to know I had hurt him."

She paused. "As punishment I was thrown in their soundproof basement for the rest of the night. I'd been there before and knew there was no way out. But cutting him showed me that I could fight back. I found a screwdriver in the father's lab and pried open the cabinet containing the chemicals. It was filled with glass containers. I started throwing them as hard as I could against the wall. I hoped they were worth lots of money."

She looked out into the yard. "With each crash my hate grew. When I ran out of jars I overturned the cabinet and started breaking things in the lab. I yelled and screamed as I went. In the end, I sank to the floor and cried myself to sleep. In the morning, after Motova had gone to work, his fat wife made me clean up the mess with my bare hands. I ended up with several cuts on my hands and feet. The chemicals must have gotten in that way. I ran away two weeks later. I felt a little sick at the time, but attributed it to fear."

Sara stared into Derry's eyes as more tears flowed. "I had no idea I was killing myself that night. But it wouldn't have mattered, I wanted to die so badly then I would have done it anyway."

Leaning into his arms, she cried the soft words, "And now I want to live. I want a life with you."

17

Tuesday

The sip of coffee burned her lips, but her mind barely noticed. She was dying anyway. And now, after a miserable night, she had to spend the morning in another stupid meeting. Sara stepped into the room as the meeting was about to start and headed to her customary spot.

"Man, you look terrible. What happened?" Todd wrinkled his nose and raised one corner of his lip, forming a sneer.

Todd was acting like the jerk that he was and she did not want to put up with it. She turned around without an answer and headed toward the front. She slumped into the empty chair next to Lamar.

His face held a mixture of mild surprise and concern. "You okay?"

"I'm fine." Opening her laptop, she brought up her work. Lamar did not need to know her life story, even though he already knew more than most.

"If you need some time off, let me know. Once this case is solved I will see what I can do."

"I'll be okay." *My parole doesn't come with a vacation package.*

She could feel his eyes on her. She focused on her monitor. He lightly laid his hand on her arm. "I mean it. If you need time off for health reasons I can get it arranged."

"Thanks." *But no thanks.*

"Let's get started and I better hear some progress." Faircloth stepped through the door with his Diet Coke and laptop. Taking a seat toward the front he added, "Elle you're up first." He finished off the Coke and tossed it into the trashcan as Elle got up and walked to the front.

"The bullets pulled from the senator have been reconstructed and their patterns were used to search the national database for a match. With no match in the national database, the search has been expanded to the international databases. However, without one central repository for all ballistics, the new search will take much longer. As for the DNA profiling, we have learned one of the men was of Germanic ancestry. His DNA indicates he is a large man, blonde hair, blue eyes and our best guess is that he is around thirty-five years old. Now that I have a profile to narrow it down, I'm running the information through our DNA database as well as through the European database for a match. It could take up to a couple of weeks to complete the search."

"Sounds like you're doing all you can. Anything on the other intruder?" Faircloth reached into his coat pocket and pulled out another Diet Coke.

"Not at this time. We were able to match the remaining DNA samples to family or friends who admitted to being in the senator's home sometime in the week leading up to the murders." After a short pause for questions, Elle moved back to her seat.

"Well, we have a start. Kent?"

He remained in his seat. "Mrs. Henderson had a heart condition. The Hendersons had contacted three locations in Colorado Springs, trying to refill her prescription. But according to the medical records, she had two weeks left on her last refill and they would not give her more medication. I checked the inventory we made of the home and her heart meds were found in their upstairs bathroom, sitting on the counter. If I were to bet, I'd say that's what cost them their lives."

"So they returned home for her medicine?" Faircloth jotted something on a notepad.

Kent nodded.

"Anything else?"

"Nothing worth taking up time in this meeting."

"Chris."

Chris also remained in his seat. "I talked with Senator Henderson's Colorado staff and followed up with their whereabouts. Nothing has popped up."

"Keep looking. Todd?"

"The lab is still running static scan on the hard drive. I made a few changes to increase our chances of retrieving data but it is slow going."

"How long before you get enough to work with?"

"That's hard to say. With each pass we are getting closer. If a small file is among the data that was deleted and we get that file in its entirety I can get started on decrypting it."

"Let me ask it this way. What are the odds of finding this small file?"

Todd, slouching in his seat, kept his eyes on his laptop. "I can only say at this time we believe there is a good possibility that a small file was included. But having never seen the data before, I really do—"

"Lamar, is there any hope of getting anything usable off the hard drive or out of Agent Jenkins?"

Lamar gave a short chuckle. "I don't think there's much hope for Todd. As for the hard drive, the possibility becomes slimmer with each pass and with each pass we are taking a risk of doing more damage than good."

"What percentage has been recovered?"

Todd looked at his laptop. "Not knowing what was deleted—"

"Give me a number, a guess."

Todd shrugged, "Somewhere between eighteen and twenty-three percent."

"And in the last pass, how much new information was added?"

Todd studied his computer. "Approximately one point three-seven percent but the pass just before added maybe four percent."

"*Great*. Thank you." Faircloth changed his attention to Sara. "Do you have anything?"

"I traced the hacker's account information through the host company and I was able to correlate the usage with an account out of Egypt."

"Good. Who owns the account?"

"I've narrowed it down to two groups, both using the same bank. I should have an answer sometime today."

"Good work."

"And, sir?" This could cost her Todd's friendship, but right now she did not care.

"You have more?"

"Well, sort of."

"Let's have it."

She resisted the urge to look back at Todd. He would say it wasn't ready, and maybe he was right. "I might have a way to read the hard drive."

Faircloth's eyes shifted between Sara and Lamar a few times before resting on Lamar. "Does she really have something, and if so why aren't we using it?"

Lamar sat up straight and folded his hands together. Twisting in his chair he asked Sara, "Are you talking about your Multi-Frequency Full Signal Analysis program?"

"You can't use that! It's still in development." It was the most energetic Todd had been in a long time. He was halfway out of his seat.

And the battle begins. "It's close to a usable state. With just a few more hours of work it could be ready." Sara remained calm.

"Your project is not even at the alpha stage. It is extremely premature for you to make this commitment, and the Bureau can't risk the loss of data."

What a jerk. "I've run over a dozen successful tests."

"And even more failures."

She took a deep breath. "Yes, early on I did have several failures. But I have made significant progress in the last three weeks."

Faircloth focused on Sara. "Why are you bringing this up now?"

"It's still in development, but since the static scan is not able to give us the data we need, this is worth a shot. With a few more hours of work it will be ready."

Faircloth shifted to Lamar. "Tell me about it."

"Sure." Lamar leaned back in his chair before going on. "Sara came up with this idea a few months back and ran it past a group of developers. After some tweaks, it was felt the project had real possibilities. Todd was assigned to oversee her work."

"Too much detail. Will it work or not?" Standing, Faircloth looked at Todd.

"I have not seen any data leading me to believe it can. However, in previous tests, the data was destroyed around fifty percent of the time."

He is so stinking antagonistic. "I sent you a report two weeks ago with much better results." Sara turned to squarely face Todd.

Todd gave a forced smile that was really no smile at all. "Sorry, I was busy preparing my lessons for the class I taught at Quantico. But I can look over your report as soon as this case is solved."

Oh, what a dirty little trick. Push it out so it will never see the light of day.

"Can you tell us how it works?" The question came from Agent Hewitt.

"Sara?" Lamar nodded toward her.

Finally, someone is interested. "Multi-Frequency Full Signal Analysis has been in development for several months. It's designed to read corrupted or badly damaged disk drives by physically exciting the surface of the disk with a wide uniform beam, or wide frequency spectrum, at an extremely low energy level. This will excite the molecular structures of each section of the drive, looking for ghost patterns. Then it will read and store each pattern and determine the one with the highest validity. It then uses the patterns obtained by the static scan to test the new patterns."

"Pattern validity?" Faircloth looked around the room.

Todd cut her off before she could explain. "*Her theory* is that the pattern validity can be found by comparing it to similar patterns. But that's not the issue. The problem is hitting the surface of the disk with energy. If the energy level is even a little too high, it can destroy whatever data is there."

"That's why I need a few more hours to set everything up." Sara picked up a pen that lay in front of her and rolled it back and forth between her hands.

"You believe she can make this happen? Reading the senator's disk?" Faircloth addressed Lamar.

Sara answered. "If I can zero in on the energy needed for this manufacturer, yes. The problem is, each manufacturer and family uses a different alloy ratio. The test must be finely tuned to each family of disks."

"How long will that take?"

"At least half a day, maybe more. And that's if I work full time on it." She saw Todd, in the back of the room, staring at her. His face was turning red and his lips were pressed tightly together. She ignored him and finished her thoughts. "I need time in the lab to work on it."

Faircloth turned to Todd. "Your method has until tomorrow morning. If you have not made significant progress by then, you will hand the drive over to Sara."

"Sir?" Sara turned back toward Faircloth. "What about the bank accounts in Egypt? If I spend the day setting up the disk test I won't have time to follow up on the accounts."

He looked back at Todd. "I want you to pick up her work on the bank accounts."

"*Fine.*" Todd slammed the lid on his laptop, stood, and walked out of the room.

18

Sam looked out of the 'cabin' window in Breckenridge at the bare mountain peaks. This so called cabin came with four bedrooms, two full bathrooms, a hot tub, large kitchen, dining room, and two living rooms, each of which had a sixty-inch TV mounted on the wall and hundred gig secured Internet. The men and women that vacationed in this town did not want to be without their luxuries.

Denver was over an hour away, but this was where the company had put him for his *R&R*. His idea of a vacation was at a place without TVs or even running water. Turning back to his laptop, Sam took his browser to private mode and entered the IP address that he had given Joelle. There he found the coroner's report with pictures from Ryan Blinder's autopsy as well as files on the murders of Senator Henderson and his wife. Sam viewed them without downloading them. If someone gained access to his system, he wanted it to be clean.

Ryan's body had been badly damaged by animals, that much was clear. The cause of death however was loss of blood from numerous wounds from a serrated blade. A sketch also showed several bones had been broken in the rib cage, hands, arms, feet and legs. A notation stated probable cause of the breaks was a blunt object such as a hammer. It was reminiscent of bodies that had been recovered in the Middle East after questioning by Hezbollah or ISIS.

What were the killers looking for, and did they find it?

Maybe. Something led them to the senator. Most people would cave under the pain.

He read through the FBI reports on the senator. What the murderers had done to Mrs. Henderson showed they were still looking for something that they had not found. *They had obviously taken files off of the senator's computer. Perhaps they were looking for the encryption key.*

Sam had been on the web site longer than he should have. If someone was tracking him, they could be mirroring his display right now. He shut down the browser, removed all temp files and rebooted his system.

He needed to get out of the cabin to think. His whole home could fit in the living area of this place. He needed more privacy. Walking out the door, he headed to the closest trail head, less than a quarter mile away. Coloradans loved their mountains. The trail he was on was fairly crowded. After spending ten minutes with the day-hikers, Sam cut off the beaten path and into uncharted areas to be alone and think.

What do we know or think we know?

Ryan was on the trail of and may have found the inside leak.

He had a file or files that are now missing, but we don't really know what was in those files.

We believe the files were dumped or sent to the senator.

The senator was forcefully questioned before he was murdered.

The murderers removed files from the senator's hard drive that we can assume were the files in question.

The FBI believes the files were encrypted, but only have tiny fragments of them.

The branch over his head started to sway. It took several seconds for the rustle of the limbs to work its way down to the base of the trees. He peered up between the tree boughs. Clouds with off-white edges that turned to gray-black in the center were moving across his porthole to the heavens. *Rain, maybe.*

He continued wandering up the hillside between the underbrush and gray rocks. The landscape held its own peacefulness and strength. It had its influence on the stress that had built within him over the last two years.

A bright flash of light brought a crashing boom overhead. The deep bass roar rolled down the mountainside followed by many repeat performances. Rain was definitely coming. He continued on.

Something had brought Ryan out to Colorado. Was the leak here?

He heard it minutes before he felt it. Rain worked its way through the pine needles to the forest floor as the temperature took a nosedive. Neither the rain nor the lightning strikes alone could drive him from this solitude, but teaming up together they had that negative consequence. Sam headed back down the hillside.

The answers Ryan had been looking for were in Denver, not in a high end resort hidden away from the worries of everyday life. Sam would remedy that situation tomorrow morning. The risk was worth it.

Entering his room, Sam felt uncomfortable dripping water across the patterned hickory wood floor. After changing into something dry and cleaning up his wet trail, he opened his computer to look at maps of Denver.

An email from Luca was sitting in his mailbox. She was an attractive young woman he had met while working with Homeland a while back. She believed him to be an analyst like her. Her overpowering desire to succeed had the outcome of leading her down false trails, but also gave her the ability to find correlations that others missed.

She wanted his opinion about a possible link between a border guard who had been killed and the possibility of chemicals being used by terrorists. She attached several files and summarized the facts as she saw them.

It was known throughout the agencies that one terrorist group or another was always trying to get something past the borders, but rarely did they kill a border guard. That would make it too high profile.

Sam sat back and added this information to his case. Could the upcoming attack be chemical or biological?

Luca was good at what she did and her insight could prove very valuable to this case. A link was possible, but more work was needed. He asked her to keep him informed of anything else she discovered.

19

Tapping his fingers on the steering wheel, Jonas' mind whirled as he waited for a green light.

Can Sara's program read the hard drive? She sounded so confident. Jenkins has his doubts, but he seems to be the type of person that doubts everything he didn't invent himself.

He glanced at the driver of the car next to him, a young punk singing to his music. Jonas tuned back to the long red light.

If she is able to develop a way to read the hard drive then she may be smart enough to decrypt the data, something that my people have not been able to do. I could use someone like her, and with her past, blackmail is possible, but that will take time.

The turn lane next to him started to move. The young punk punched it and his tires squealed slightly. Jonas smiled at the car's lack of power.

She seems to be very close to her boss. Approaching her would be very risky.

I could kill her, but Stover would only put someone else on the project, maybe Jenkins. So, if I can't kill her and can't turn her, what does that leave?

His light went from red to green as a plan formed. He was ten minutes from his office, but this needed to get started immediately. Sara was most likely in the lab right now, working on the hard drive. The window of opportunity was narrowing. He reached for his phone and made a call.

"It's Jonas. Has Kai made any progress on the files?" The answer would determine his course.

Alex's fake sweet southern accent quickly changed as Gabriele's slight German accent surfaced. "She spent the weekend reviewing all of our work and has an idea of how to proceed. She made a list of software programs she needed from her lab in New York. I downloaded them to her computer and she has been working with them. She believes she'll be able to decrypt the files."

"Do you think she can do it?"

"I think she can, but it will take time. She said because the tools are experimental they will take more interaction, more tweaking. It may be a week or so before we have something."

"That's too long. The FBI is working on it now and we need to stop them. I have a new assignment for you."

20

Sara watched as Todd grabbed his laptop and walked out. He was not happy. But he needed to understand that he was not the only one on site that had a brain. She grabbed her laptop and walked out a few yards behind him. Halfway back to the office she turned toward the elevators and headed down to the first floor.

Cutting out the back of the main building, she took the enclosed corridor to the electronics lab. The room was filled end-to-end with racks of equipment and workbenches. She headed toward her work area in the right rear of the lab. It was close to the station that was static scanning the senator's hard drive.

"Sara, you slumming it again?" James peered around a rack of computers. It had taken her months before she was willing to call him by his nickname, Smiley.

"No, not really. I've been ordered to get the Multi-Frequency Full Signal Analysis up and running tonight."

He gave her his most charming smile. He was a joker and fun at times.

"What a name. Rolls right off the tongue, doesn't it? You need to come up with something shorter or at least an acronym."

"If it works I'll name it." She moved past him.

"You talk about it like it's a pet or your kid."

After the news from the doctor his comment hurt. "Whatever." It was not his fault that she was in a bad mood. "Maybe you can call it something different. What can you do with M-F-F-S-A?"

"Miff-sa, no. It sounds like a mafia hit-squad."

"It might be. I am Italian you know."

"Why don't we call it DDR, the Dead Disk Reader?" He was

proud of his wit.

"Too easily confused with Duel Data Rate. Sorry, already taken." She joked enough to keep him happy, but it was not helping her mood. *Why did he have to call it my kid?*

He was typing on a keyboard that stuck out from the rack of equipment running the static scan. He looked at the monitor above the keyboard. "This isn't giving us anything. You want it now?"

"Not yet. I still have a little more work to do before I can try out my program." She peered into the plexiglass cabinet housing the senator's hard drive.

He stepped back. "What are you looking for?"

"I just need the model number." Most of the drive was hidden from view.

"It's right here." He pointed to his screen."

She jotted it down on a sticky note.

"Hey Smiley, you coming?" It was Vincent, another one of the techs. He was heading down the aisle in their direction.

"Oh, I almost forgot." The smile was a permanent fixture on his face.

"What's going on?"

Smiley logged out and headed toward the door. "It's just another Bureau time sink, mandatory safety training. Like something in this lab is dangerous." He glanced back at Sara. "If you were a nice person you'd go in my place."

"Well, we know that's not going to happen."

"Some friend you are." He joined up with Vincent and Cindy, the third technician. "Don't get lonely while we're at this two-hour meeting." As they passed through the door, James offered to buy Cindy a beer if she went in his place.

"And who'd go for me?" The voices disappeared as the doors slid shut.

The fans on the equipment added to the eerie feeling of the empty lab. Sara glanced around the room, she was truly alone.

She walked back to her workstation and grabbed a disk drive in the same family as the one from the senator's home computer and plugged it into her test setup.

Using the Mil-spec disk erase program, she removed all the data from several sectors of the drive. This would take a few minutes.

She brought up another window and logged in as Todd. She should send him an email, letting him know she was about to use his ID to do a search, but he might say no now. Besides, he didn't need to know she was searching for someone besides her mother.

The FBI had access to all public records. She narrowed her search to Colorado, with an emphasis on the Denver area.

```
Last known name: John Motova
Aliases:
Approximate Age: 45-55
Sex: Male
Ethnicity: White
Nationality:
```

He was Russian or of Russian descent but she was not sure of his citizenship status. Best to leave it blank for now.

There were several other optional questions, but she hoped this would be enough.

While the computer searched, she pulled the drive out, disassembled it and placed the first platter into her MFFSA tester. Setting up low energy levels, she started the test.

Bringing the other window back up, she found that the search had failed. No one with that name, in that age group, lived in Colorado. She really wasn't surprised. His whole family was nothing but a bunch of scum. They probably had to change their names or move out of state.

Going back into the records from the time she was forced to live with him, she retrieved his driver's license number, Social Security number, birthdate, and bank account number. She ran a trace on each one. The license number and Social Security number came up dry. The bank account information showed the date he closed the account. To trace any money he had, she needed to log a case ID which she didn't have, making that route a dead end as well.

There are always other ways to find someone. She had learned a lot while tracking down her mother. Pulling Motova's driver's license picture she started a facial recognition search against all driver licenses issued in Colorado around the time he dropped off the radar.

Hearing a human voice, Sara peeked around her rack of

equipment. There was a woman standing near the lab door, looking around.

"May I help you?"

"I'm looking for Sara Beckwith?"

"I'm Sara."

The blonde woman headed down the main aisle, then turned toward Sara.

Sara iconified several windows as the stranger approached.

"Hi. I'm Alex Taylor from Homeland Security. Agent Hewitt asked me to see if you need a hand." She had a definite southern accent.

"No, I don't think so. It's a one-person job." *Great. More interference from Homeland.*

As she approached, the woman extended her hand. "You sure I can't help?" She had a firm handshake.

"There's not really anything you can do." Sara peeked at the iconified window running the search.

The woman moved in beside Sara. "I'd really hate to go back empty handed. Would you mind so terribly much explaining to me how your setup works? You know, in case Agent Hewitt asks me."

Sara had a few minutes. "Sure." She launched into a lengthy explanation.

The woman was no dummy. She asked several good questions and even had a few suggestions. All Alex's attention to detail made Sara temporarily forget about the search. Sara talked as she reassembled the drive.

"And you came up with this on your own? I am very impressed. The Bureau is lucky to have you." Alex smiled sweetly.

Sara was a little surprised at the comment. "Thank you." She then started the disk scan on the test section.

"Well, thank you for filling me in. You're a real sweetheart for showing me all this." Southerners could sound so nice.

"No problem."

Alex turned and left just as the results of Sara's test popped up on the screen, eighty percent recovered. Good but not good enough. For encrypted files she needed close to a hundred percent. She tweaked the parameters and reran the program.

Taking a quick glance around the lab to ensure she was still alone, she brought up her search window. She had a hit, Brian S. Halter. *You can change your name, but if you don't change your face, you still get caught.*

She gathered all the information the government had on Brian Halter and downloaded it to a jump drive. Still alone, she went further. She Googled his home and workplace.

Life had not been good to Brian Halter. *Good, let's see if I can make it a little worse.*

She hacked his company computer to plant incriminating evidence, but stopped when she realized he was the only employee.

He owns his own company, but lives in a rundown trailer? Must be a small company. Maybe I can make him lose all his customers.

She went to his email inbox. One email caught her attention. The email had gone back and forth several times and included two attachments. He was having a long conversation with someone and she wanted to know who and why.

He was explaining to someone, identified only by a number, about saving money and time, as 2-Methylpropyl was classified as harmless and could be ordered premixed. The savings on equipment to the five sites would be approximately forty-two thousand dollars.

Five sites? If he's dealing in this type of money and has five locations, why is he living in a 1970's trailer?

The lab-rats were back. She'd have to work on this later.

———

Returning from a meeting, Agent Lisa Booker noticed the small red-letter window on her computer monitor.

```
Warning: Agent Todd Jenkins login in conflict.
Room 231 -office
Computer lab
```

With the latest security measures adopted by the FBI, she was seeing this window a couple times a week from different staff members who forgot to logout in one location before logging in at another, but never before for Agent Jenkins. He was a real stickler on computer protocol.

She logged the locations and times before reaching for her phone. She needed to call Agent Jenkins and check on this.

———

Deadly Infiltration

"Jonas, it's all set up." Gabriele made the call from the FBI parking lot.

"Did you have any problems?"

She opened the car door as she took a quick glimpse around. Some training never leaves you. "No, Sara was so busy telling me about her project, she never saw me stick the jump drive into her system or remove it. The program is downloaded and I'll be able to access her project from my office." Taking a seat, she started the car.

"Tonight I want you to sabotage her program."

"I could do that, but she might see it before she starts tomorrow. She's very good. I have something in mind she won't see coming."

21

Wednesday

She couldn't lie in bed any longer and pacing was sure to wake Alex, who was the last person Kai wanted to face right now. That girl explained things away far too easily.

Seeing the faint morning light creep past her shades, Kai slipped out of bed, into her running clothes, and silently crept out of the apartment.

She loved the feel of the brisk air in the morning, something rare in New York in August. Heading toward the park, she glanced at the beautiful reddish-orange sunrise as the first rays peeked over the flat eastern landscape.

Why me? I'm not the smartest or best or most experienced decryptionist. Gordon, along with half a dozen others, can run circles around me, and his background is impeccable.

Kai almost hit another runner stopping to tie his shoes. Wearing dark clothes at this time of day was a good way to get rammed.

If they really checked my past, how could they not know about my time on the streets or working for Levy? The real surprise was that Homeland hired me in the first place.

Either Hewitt is the dumbest manager working there, or he's up to something.

But what?

Someone was smart enough to only grant me a confidential clearance, and that much was most likely because of Dad. But his involvement in the CIA ended more than four years ago.

Her mind filled with memories of her father, their times playing and talking. Something he often said came back to her. 'Once in the family, always in the family.'

Could those words be true? Is that why I am the one they brought out here to decrypt the files?

She cut into the grass to miss an elderly woman with a small yappy dog. The woman acted like controlling her pet was more work than she could handle. It was not the type of dog Kai would choose. She liked dogs in the seventy pounds and up range. One day she'd be able to buy a house and get herself a couple of real dogs.

If this is because of Dad, Sam would know. And if not, why did they pick me? And that whole line about what was in those files. If it were true, there would be a hundred geeks working on them not just me, an expendable hacker.

She shook slightly at the sound of her phone alarm. She had just enough time to get back, shower and eat.

———

Kai babbled about nothing while the blonde woman drove the car. One question remained unanswered. *Is Alex really my friend?* Kai took a quick peek across the tiny console that separated them. Was she talking too much?

Her father told her any change in your actions or attitude was enough to give you away. If Alex was hiding something from her, which of course she was, she would see a change if Kai did not shut up.

Is Alex a spy?

For whom and why?

Spies are never your friend. Her dad made that comment after almost every mission. But what about Sam? He's a spy and he and Dad were best of friends. Sam was a good friend, one that could be trusted. I wonder what he's doing these days.

"I heard you leave before sunrise this morning. Did you seriously go running?"

"It was great. Seeing the sun come up as you're out in the morning air gives life meaning."

Alex gave a short snort. "You're not serious. Life meaning?"

"How can you not want to get out of bed on a morning like this?" Harassment is always a good way to hide suspicion.

"I have no problem pulling the shades to keep the world out."

Alex was acting differently this morning. *Does she suspect something? Or am I just being paranoid?* Kai studied every movement Alex made. *What will Alex do if she learns I don't trust her or Hewitt? Maybe she doesn't care.*

"Ready to show me some results today?" Alex pulled the car into a parking place facing the building.

"I sure hope so." *Alex will tell Hewitt if she suspects something.*

Exiting the car, Kai rubbed her hand over the small bump made by the jump drive under the waistband of her pants.

The two headed in, past the receptionist, to the small locker room at the back of the break area. Kai grabbed an orange and Alex took a Danish as they passed the snack table.

"How can you eat so much sugar and not get diabetes?" Kai set the orange just inside her open locker as she proceeded to empty her pockets, placing their contents inside, past the orange. As Alex took a bite of her Danish, Kai pulled the jump drive from her waistband and laid it just behind the orange, out of view.

"Ready." Kai lifted her arms.

Alex wiped her mouth with her hand and brushed her hand off against her pants. Reaching into her locker, she pulled out a wand, the type TSA used, and ran it over Kai's body.

"What. No complaints today?"

"Sorry, kind of tired. I didn't get much sleep."

"Yeah, that's what you get for making those early morning runs." With no beeps, Alex put the wand back into her locker.

"It was a short one." Kai reached for the orange and let her fingertips pull the jump drive along with it.

"Where did you go?" Did she really care or was Alex checking up on her? Alex seemed more attentive now than when they lived in New York. Now she always wanted to know where Kai was going, what she was doing. She acted as if it was just idle chitchat, but it wasn't. Alex picked up the remainder of her pastry and motioned for Kai to lead the way out of locker room.

"I made it about halfway to the park. Not even two miles round trip." Kai acted like she was wiping water from the orange on to her jeans as she slipped the drive into her pocket. As they passed through the break room, she grabbed a few napkins.

Alex reached over and flipped through them. "Just making sure no one hid anything in there," she said with a laugh.

What have I gotten myself into?

———

Stepping into the electronics lab, Sara surveyed the room before heading to her work area. The world looked a little better today. Natalie had told her last night that a good night's sleep always helped. And she was right. Natalie and Kevin Knight were the family Sara had never had but had always wanted. Living in their home was a blessing.

Turning down the aisle, Sara just caught sight of Todd talking with James. They stood at the static scan setup. He did not look up until she was a few feet away, and when he did he just looked through her.

Is he still mad?

It didn't matter. Last night's results were good. Ninety-eight percent good. That was the amount of data she was able to recover. Now she was ready for the senator's disk.

She stopped next to James. "Good morning." It was meant for both of them, but James was the only one to respond. She looked at Todd. "You mad at me? Can't say good morning or anything?"

With a perplexed look on his face he peered at Sara. "Oh sorry, I was thinking. Good morning."

"Thinking about what?" She took a tiny step closer. Todd was a good friend even if he had the social graces of a hermit crab.

"I want to try a few more things with the hard drive."

She raised an eyebrow. "Have you talked with Faircloth about this?"

He answered without looking at her. "I'm the lead on this. It should be okay. I just need it for another day or so." His speech was faster than normal. This was a habit that showed up whenever he felt uncomfortable or personally challenged.

"And who will take the blame when Faircloth finds out?"

His look was close to priceless. He'd lost but could not admit it. "I suppose you want it now?"

Sara tried to suppress her smile, but failed. "In a few minutes. I need to set a few things up first." She heard Smiley give a short quiet chuckle as she moved past.

Dejected, Todd told her he would have it to her in a couple of minutes. She went to her setup and tapped the spacebar. Everything had been left on, giving the equipment its greatest stability and her best chance at success. Todd showed up before she had everything done.

"Thank you for bringing it to me." She placed it on her workbench to disassemble. He did not leave right away. She looked up at him. "You okay?"

"I don't mean to be acting like a jerk, but this is supposed to be my job, you know?" He stared at her, not her screen.

"And you don't think I know what I'm doing?"

He ran the palm his hand up the back of his neck, across the top on his head, landing on his mouth as he spoke. "No, it's not that."

"You think I'm dumb?" It was a game to her.

"No, I think you're pretty smart." He let his hand drop away.

"Just nothing close to as smart as you?"

"No, that's not what I'm saying. I—" He wouldn't look her in the eye.

She waited. She was not going to let him off the hook. He was at a loss.

"You are very smart. The work you've done without any college training is totally amazing."

"But with your MIT training you can do better?"

He grabbed one of the tall chairs, pulled it over and dropped in. "It's like this. I spent seven years studying computer science at MIT. I came out top of my class. I've taken over a dozen post graduate classes, and you come in with no real training and can do everything I can, some of it better."

That was a compliment, a real one. Todd never gave those. Nothing could stop the smile from spreading across her face. "So you want me to act dumb to make you feel better?"

"No, that's not what I mean and you—" He looked at her and stopped. "Are you enjoying this?"

"Absolutely. Aren't you?" She covered her mouth as the giggle sneaked out.

"Fine, just stop making me look bad and getting me in trouble."

"If this works I'm sure you won't be in trouble."

"Not that. It's using my login while you're down here. I had to cover for you yesterday."

"You said I could, and after the meeting I didn't want to bug you. I just—"

"Agent Booker called me. She found out that I was logged in down here. I told you that new security measures have been put in place. I can't be logged in at two different places at the same time."

"I'm sorry. I didn't mean to get you in trouble."

"I told her I was helping you with this project and I forgot to log out. You'd better be glad I like you. If she found out what you were really doing you'd lose your parole status."

Jail. He didn't have to say the rest, she knew. She reached over to give him a hug. "Thank you."

He stiffened and pulled away. "Don't."

"Sorry." She gave a catlike smile. "You don't like hugs?"

"I do, from the right people. Did you find her?"

"My mom? Ah, not yet."

"It shouldn't be that hard. You know where she was living. Don't tell me you need my help." He gave her a sheepish grin.

If it made him feel better she could put up with his help. "Maybe." Otherwise he may tell her she couldn't use his login again.

"Next time do it in the office, not down here. In fact, it might be best if we just did it together on my system."

"Okay." *Next time it will look like it came from your system and Booker will not be the wiser.*

"Well, since I told her I was helping you, tell me what's going on—just in case I get cornered in the hall or something." Todd glanced at her equipment as she began a quick rundown of what she had done last night.

22

It was ten minutes after eight when Alex logged in. Running the numbers in her head, Alex hoped she wasn't too late. It all depended on how much of an early bird Sara was.

She took a sip of her coffee. It was getting cold. Rather than letting it go bad, she downed the cup. *Caffeine.*

She wanted another cup or maybe three, but it was too much work to make Kai logout, leave with her and lock up the room just to feed her addiction. Tomorrow morning, she would bring her own cup, three times the size of the cups in the break room. She didn't have time to leave right now anyway.

"Did you have a hot date last night? You didn't get home until after midnight," Kai asked while she logged onto her computer.

"No, nothing like that. I just had some work to catch up on. I don't mean to be rude, but I am still behind. I need to concentrate. Besides you have work to do also."

"So you really do have a job besides watching me work?"

Alex ignored the jab as she started typing. Kia shrugged her shoulders and turned back to her computer. *Good. Hopefully that will keep her busy.*

It only took a few minutes for Alex to establish the pipeline between the Homeland network and the Denver FBI building. This made it look as if she were on site in the FBI building. Little did the other agencies know that Homeland not only could do this, but had been given the okay as part of their charter. The only drawback was that the connection was logged at her end, but in a few days that would not matter.

Once in, she located and mimicked the FBI's IT department,

allowing her to bypass many of the safety nets that had been set up to stop someone from snooping around in or controlling a system.

After routing to the lab, she searched through the different systems for her program. It was loaded on Sara's workstation.

"What?" The cry came from Kai.

Alex looked up. "What's wrong?"

"Oh, this software. It locked up my computer." Kai pounded on her keyboard.

Alex gave a very slight laugh at the stress relief. "Well, you'd better fix it." *And please don't do that again.*

Kai was pushing her chair back. "Whatever you say, Boss." She reached under her desk. "I've got to do a hard shutdown and hope my computer comes back up."

"Okay, but can you keep it down?"

Kai leaned down to press the power button on the computer that was sitting on the floor beside her. "Sorry."

Alex turned her focus back to her work. Once on Sara's system, she set up her program to run in the background. Other than taking up some CPU cycles and a little memory, it was invisible to Sara.

Next, she brought up two windows. One was a mirror image of Sara's user interface. The other tapped into the ports connected to Sara's test system and displayed the firmware commands Sara's program was feeding them.

Alex studied each command. The twenty-four minutes of sitting, watching and waiting finally paid off. At 9:07 Sara typed in the power levels and frequencies to be applied to the disk drive's platters.

Quickly Alex retyped the firmware commands to supply forty times more power and ten times the frequency range than Sara requested. The tester repeated back the commands, which Alex intercepted and changed to the original numbers before sending them on to Sara's display.

The lag time would be longer than normal. Alex watched to see if Sara did anything about it.

After a short wait, Sara entered the command to start the test. Alex could now relax.

Kai started complaining again. *Now what?*

———

Kai slipped the jump drive from her pocket as she leaned down. She turned off the computer and slipped the jump drive in the back before turning it back on.

Sitting back up, she copied the encrypted files plus everything that Alex had downloaded from the New York office onto the jump drive. Giving a sideways look back, she saw that Alex was very intently watching her own monitor. Good. She would not notice what Kai was doing.

Kai restarted one of her programs and ran it on one of the encrypted files. She gave it impossible parameters to ensure it would fail. It quickly did.

Complaining that the computer had locked up again, Kai repeated the process to retrieve the drive.

As Kai sat up, Alex stood and moved around next to her. "Maybe this new software wasn't a good idea after all."

"I told you it could still take a while. I just need to find the right program."

Sam walked the streets around the home Ryan Blinder had rented. The houses in the area had average sized lots with six-foot wood fences, a few in need of repair. It was a typical mid-level 80's housing area. Most of the homes were well cared for, but some weren't. A few had yards of brown grass filled with dandelions and Canadian thistles.

Ryan's house did not stand out. The grass needed to be cut, but the yard and house were average looking, a dwelling few would notice or care about.

Sam took a casual glance around before hopping up the steps. He was surprised to find the front door unlocked.

Opening the door, he stepped in. After closing it he stood quietly listening. Nothing. Someone other than the police had been here. The place had been tossed by professionals and he doubted the investigating officers would even have noticed. Drawers were not closed all the way. From the dust and imprints on the carpet, several items and a few pieces of furniture had been moved. It looked typical for many homes, but not for a CIA operative.

Were the men who killed Ryan really pros? If so, they should know he would never hide anything where amateurs could find it.

Heading to the basement, Sam knew the killers had found something. The smell of acid and melted plastic lingered in the closed in space. A deformed laptop lay on the floor in a corner near the water heater. He covered his nose with his shirt as he approached the destroyed computer.

Using a piece of steel lying next to the water heater he lifted the lid. The acid booby trap had done its job and hopefully had done a number on the killers as well. Any information that might have been on the computer was completely destroyed. There was only one thing left to do with the useless pieces of plastic, metal and silicon. If left behind and found by the local police, it would raise questions as to why an everyday sort of guy had this type of security on his computer.

Sam headed back upstairs. Grabbing a few tee shirts out of Ryan's closet and some plastic bags from the kitchen he returned downstairs. With one tee shirt covering his mouth and nose to keep the odor out, he wrapped the other shirts around the computer and slipped it into the plastic bags. Taking it out to his car, he tossed it into his trunk. He would find a dumpster and drop it off in another part of town.

23

Derry paced in front of the Mexican restaurant waiting for Lamar. As different as the two were in appearance, the big man was the closest thing Derry had to a father.

Coming around the corner, Lamar skipped the typical greetings. "So, what's so important that you needed to call me away from the office?" Lamar sounded tough at times, but the man would give his last breath of air to anyone he cared about.

"I might be blowing this out of proportions but— it's Sara."

Lamar studied the ground, as if looking for the right thing to say. Raising his gaze back to Derry's face, he asked, "What about her?"

This was not the response Derry expected. "Can we talk inside?" *Something else has to be going on and this is not the place to talk about it.*

"Sure, but I don't have much time. I'm sure you know about the case we're working on."

"Yeah, it sounds like a tough one." Derry reached for the door.

Lamar's arm stretched out and stopped him. "How much has she told you?" It was a cold question.

Derry hesitated. "It's all over the news." The agent wasn't satisfied with the answer so Derry continued, "Sara hasn't said much of anything about it other than she is part of the team."

Lamar took a half second to process the answer. He lowered his arm. "I'm sorry, but I had to ask. Everything on this case is on a need to know basis and—"

Derry pulled the door open. "I've heard— on the web, — that the Bureau is stumped on this one."

Lamar followed him into the restaurant. "I guess that's no secret."

Derry stepped up to the hostess. "Can we get a booth please?"

She turned and scanned the colorful room filled with bright tables and chairs, before taking a look at the room layout page in front of her. "Yes, would a corner booth work for you?"

"That would be great."

She led the two men to the back of the restaurant and gave them their menus. Another worker dropped of a basket of chips and two dishes of salsa.

"Now what do you need to tell me about Sara?" Lamar opened his menu, but stared at Derry.

Derry talked about the doctor's visit and the chemical poisoning from her time in the foster home. Moving his menu aside, he moved closer and lowered his voice. Lamar sat silently as Derry went on. The only interruption was to give their orders. Derry finished his monologue with the events that took place at her mother's apartment building.

"That's a hard pill for her to swallow. What are you doing to help her?"

The waiter warned them about the hot dishes as he set their plates down before heading back to the kitchen.

"What can I do?" Derry stared down at the food. "I've told her no matter what it takes, I am there for her, but—"

"But what?" Lamar asked between bites.

"She's hurt and mad, and I'm afraid she's going to do something that will get her in trouble."

"You mean like use the Bureau's resources to find her mom or the man she blames for poisoning her?"

"Yeah, something like that." Derry lifted his head and stared into Lamar's eyes. "What would happen if she was caught?"

Lamar leaned back in his seat. "Last time, when she was looking for her mother, I turned my head and didn't do anything. That won't be the case this time. And if she goes after her foster parents in any way, she'll land back in jail."

"That's why I wanted to talk with you. I've tried to talk sense into her, but I know it went nowhere. She has a lot of respect for you. And you being her boss and close friend, I was hoping you could make her see the light, so to speak."

Lamar pushed what was left of his lunch around on the plate

before speaking. "Any other time I would be more than willing to help her or you, but—" He set his fork down and crossed his arms with his elbows on the table. "I could get fired for what I'm about to tell you, and don't breathe one word of this to anyone." He dropped his head forward as Derry waited. He spoke softly. "Things at the Bureau are crazy right now and it's not just the murder case. Everyone is being watched closely, everything we do is being recorded. Now is not the time for Sara to go off and break the rules, hacking into systems she has no business in. If she does, I won't be able to protect her. And if I try, I could end up in a cell of my own."

———

"Hungry?" One thought had occupied Kai's mind for the last hour, and it wasn't food. She had to get out of the tiny room. The jump drive was nicely tucked away and out of sight. But all she could think about was finding some place to hide it before she got caught. But how could she get away from Alex's prying eyes?

"Sure, why not? It's a little early, but I could use a good meal and some more coffee." Alex stood as Kai locked her system.

"How about we go get some sushi?" Kai knew that Alex hated sushi.

Alex stopped at the door. "Raw fish? Are you sick or something?"

Kai worked the angle. She needed time alone outside of the building. "What's wrong with sushi?"

"It's gross. Fire was invented for a reason."

"It wasn't invented, nor that hard to discover. A little lightning strike and poof, fire." Kai made the motions with her hands.

"Yes, it happened when a dinosaur got hit. The cavemen found it made the dinosaur easier to catch and cooked food tasted a lot better. You can go get all the uncooked meat you want tonight. What's wrong with the cafeteria for lunch?" Alex stepped out as Kai followed. Once the door was secured, they headed toward the locker room.

"The cafeteria? Talk about food making you sick. Come on, let's go get some fish wrapped in seaweed. The lunch menu at this sushi place is about half the price of dinner."

"So, you get food poisoning for half price. The answer is still no, unless they serve something else that has seen a flame."

"It's called All Sushi All The Time. I heard they have some of the spiciest sushi around. But they only serve sushi as far as I know." Kai licked her lips.

"Oh, spicy raw fish, that's *so* much better. And who thought of that name? Are you sure it's real?" Alex's face contorted.

"Raw is better for you as long as they prepare it right. I remember when my cousin got ahold of some bad sushi once. He was up all night. We ended up rushing him to the hospital. Good thing we did, he almost died." A complete lie, but it had the desired effect.

Alex's small smile faded.

"But this place should be okay. I haven't heard of anyone dying after eating there."

Alex went to her locker, pulled out her phone, and Googled the restaurant. "You have to be kidding, this place has one point eight stars. One comment said fish found on the side of the road would be better."

"So, a lot of people don't know good sushi when they eat it. You can't always trust those ratings." Kai knew the place was a dive. She wasn't sure how it stayed open. When she had lived here before, her friend Mike tried taking her there once, hoping to impress her. He was such a cheapskate. But after smelling the place, they had walked out without trying the food.

Alex read her screen as she talked. "This place sounds like a dump. How'd you hear about it?"

"Oh, when I went running this morning I took a break to catch my breath and ended up talking with this cute guy. He said he just started working there, and said I should stop by for lunch."

Alex shook her head. "You need help. Do you know that?"

"So you don't want to go? Come on, it could be fun. He might have a friend." Everything a girl doesn't want to hear.

"Absolutely not. And if I were any kind of friend, I wouldn't let you go either."

"You are such a prude. If you're not coming, can I use your car? I kind of told him I'd be there." Kai gave a dorky smile as she moved toward the door.

Alex's face relaxed a small amount. "What if this guy turns out to be a stalker?"

"I doubt it. I told him I worked for Homeland. He thought that sounded cool."

"You are one desperate girl. Here are the keys. Just don't be gone too long."

"That all depends on him."

24

What kind of an airhead does she think I am? I can't believe she fell for that.

Kai started the car and headed toward the Sushi bar, which happened to sit a half block from a Walmart. If Alex was monitoring her, she would probably be tracking her cell phone.

Pulling into the almost empty lot of the restaurant, Kai parked the car. She hid the jump drive under the passenger seat. A feeling of relief washed over her. Kai left her phone in the car and walked to Walmart where she bought two burn phones and a salad for lunch. While there, she used one of their demo computers to retrieve the phone number for a computer store owned by an old acquaintance. Kai knew Ted from her time working for Levy two years ago. Like Sara, Kai had been involved in Levy's illegal credit card scam. Kai had left Ted holding the bag when she had run away after Levy was exposed. Hopefully Ted had a poor memory or was very forgiving.

Walking back to the parked car, the odor of the eating establishment stung her nostrils. It was bad, and no love for sushi could bring her to eat there. She sat down in a small grassy area upwind to eat and make a few calls.

"Ted? It's Kai."

Silence.

"Ted, are you there?"

"What do you want?" It was not the greeting she had hoped for, but at least he had not hung up on her.

"I see you still own that high-end computer store."

"Yes, I still own the store. I didn't run like you did."

"I'm really sorry about that. You didn't get in much trouble over all that, did you?"

"No, not at all. Everything was fine after I turned state's evidence and told them everything I knew about Levy and his operation. It was the only way to keep the place and stay out of jail." Slowly his tone was changing.

"I never said anything about you to anyone." Kai swallowed a bite of food.

"It didn't matter. They found me when they investigated Levy's finances. He had given me the loan to open the store."

Silence.

"I really didn't want you to get in trouble, but when I saw the report on TV about Levy's arrest I panicked."

"I didn't have that luxury."

"Did you tell anyone about me, — you know, working for him?"

"Sara asked me to keep your name out of it, not that I would have said anything to the cops about you anyway."

"Thank you. I owe you, both of you."

"You most certainly do."

"Is there anything I can do to make it up to you?"

"Not calling me again would be a good start."

"I said I was sorry."

"Look, I've changed. I'm not into that sort of stuff anymore. I couldn't be even if I wanted to. I'm on their list."

"Whose list?"

"The cops. They stop by every once in a while to keep me straight."

Maybe this was a bad idea.

"You shouldn't be calling me. They might be listening," Ted continued.

"I'm not on the run. I work for—I'm working for a security firm. We do a lot of stuff for the Feds."

"Really? With your background?"

"I'm clean and I intend to stay that way."

"Good, I hope you do." She could tell he was thinking. "You hear anything from Sara?"

So he still has a crush on her. "I heard she's working for the FBI as part of her parole."

"Yeah, I heard that, too. I also heard she was engaged to the guy that saved her from Levy."

"Engaged? Really? He must be quite a guy to win out over you?"

"Nice try."

"Hey, anyway, I should be going. I need to get back to work."

"Glad to hear all is going well for you. If you're ever in the area you should stop by and say hi."

"I will. And I'm happy to hear everything has worked out for you."

After he hung up, Kai regretted the call. If he was being watched, her call might have been recorded. It might make its way back to Alex or Hewitt.

She turned that phone off and started to toss it, but changed her mind for now. Grabbing the second phone, she made what she thought would be the harder call. She sat for a minute as her mind replayed the numbers that were beaten into her head so many years ago and wondered if they would still work today.

She took a sip of water and one more bite of her salad before she hit the sequence of numbers. They routed the call through the CIA and out again. She would leave a message and hope he would call her back.

"Hello?"

———

Rushing down the hall, Sara glanced at a wall clock. She was ten minutes late for the update meeting. Something had gone wrong with her setup in the lab and Faircloth would not be happy. She stepped through the door.

Elle must have just finished giving her results. She walked past Sara as she headed back to her seat.

Faircloth picked up his pop can. "Glad you could join us, Miss Beckwith. You're just in time to give your report."

"Ah, can you give me a minute?" Sara held her laptop in front of her and made a gesture with it. "I just got the results from the hard drive."

"Something positive, I hope?"

Sara stepped in and set her stuff on the table. "Not really." Faircloth's glare bore down on her.

"Your test failed?"

"Sort of." She couldn't meet his eyes. She looked toward Lamar, not much better.

"I'm waiting. The whole room is waiting. We don't need a formal report. Just tell us what happened."

Sara needed help, anything would do. She peeked at Todd. His expression was blank. No help there. *Is he enjoying my failure?*

She opened her laptop but gave the results that were burned into her mind. "I've been in the lab for the last hour trying to figure out what happened. The disks are shot."

Faircloth's eyes bore deeper somehow. "What are you talking about? You were only supposed to read them. You said your test was fixed and there was no risk of damage." His face was turning red with each word.

Sara let her shoulders droop, making herself appear shorter. "Something went wrong."

"Something or someone? Did you make a mistake? Is it your fault we just lost our only evidence? Our only lead?" He seemed to grow along with his statements.

"No, I don't think so." She could not shrink anymore.

He flung his empty pop can at the trashcan and missed. His voice took on an icy tone. "Your test destroyed the hard drive?"

"I think so."

"You THINK so? Aren't you sure of what you did?"

"I need time to look into it. None of my settings were high enough to damage a hard drive. I plan—"

"Take your seat."

The room remained silent. Dropping her head as low as she could, she headed to the back of the room. Todd gave her a poisonous look. She slipped into a chair a couple of places away from Todd and kept her head down, trying to hide behind her computer screen.

It took several long seconds for Faircloth to speak. "Lamar, I want this investigated ASAP. Find out what went wrong and who's at fault."

"It will have to wait until this case is solved. I don't have the manpower right now."

"Don't forget." Standing erect, he scanned the room as he ranted. "Can't anyone in here do anything right? It has been over a week and we have no leads whatsoever." His scowl was aimed at everyone, but spent a lot of it's time pointed at the back of the room. "Are you telling me that a couple of killers are smarter than the FBI? Not one of you has found one piece of evidence that we can use." He looked back at Agent Hewitt. "Maybe we should hand this off to Homeland. You want it?"

Hewitt gave a condescending smile. "I'm sure your team is doing the best they can."

Everyone's attention shifted between Hewitt and Faircloth. Anyplace was better than looking into Faircloth's black eyes.

Faircloth walked over to the wall. Picking up his pop can, he crushed it and dropped it in the trashcan. He then planted his hands on his hips as everyone in the room waited for him to turn back around.

Finally, Faircloth turned to Todd. "Do you have anything, or was this whole meeting a waste of time?"

"While Sara's program was running this morning, she helped me track down a few leads."

Sara glanced at Todd. *Honesty.*

"And did they pan out?" His attention was on Todd only.

"She found something out of place."

Was he setting her up for another fall or was he actually helping her?

"What do you mean out of place?"

"Sara, you know the details better than me."

Faircloth shifted back to Sara. "Well?" His black eyes looked deeper than before, a bottomless pit to fall into.

"Ah, when we were looking through Senator Henderson's credit card expenses I came across a USPS shipment to a PO Box in Texas. The shipment occurred the same day that the files showed up on the senator's computer."

"So he shipped a package to Texas. So what?"

Todd interjected. "The shipment went to his half-brother Frank."

"You have more than that, I hope."

Sara was happy to let Todd do most of the talking. "Yes. Frank used to work for a military subcontractor in the Middle East. While he was guarding one of the oil wells it was attacked. He was the only survivor. Afterwards, he went off the deep end. Two days after his rescue, in the middle of his debriefing, he got up and walked out. He just disappeared. Six months later, he was found back in the States, and no one knows how or when he came back, or where he was in the meantime."

"That would make an interesting storyline for a movie, but what in the world does that have to do with this case?"

Get to the point, Todd.

"Because of the senator's position and the questions surrounding Frank, the two have not communicated in over four years. There have been no phone calls, no emails, no visits between them until this shipment."

"And suddenly the senator sent him a package. Did this brother Frank receive a call or email about the package? Anything?"

"No, sir. Just a package mailed to his home."

"Call Frank and find out what it was."

"We tried. He doesn't have a phone. After his time overseas something in him snapped. He's a real loner now. He owns a hundred acres southwest of Fort Worth, in the middle of nowhere. The closest town is Granbury."

"Does he have a job? Can you call his employer?"

"He doesn't have regular work. He picks up day jobs here and there."

"Well at least it's something." Faircloth changed focus from Todd to the room. "We need a team down there tomorrow to find Frank and this package." Faircloth surveyed his team. "Chris, you and Kent head down there in the morning and find this guy. But be careful. If he has gone off the deep end there's no telling how he will respond to a couple of FBI agents showing up at his door. Todd, I want you to go with them. If Henderson sent him the files we're looking for, I want you there to look at them."

"Sara's the one who found this lead."

Todd was a field agent who never liked the field much.

"That may be true, but I can't send a parolee out of state."

"I would like to go along." It was Hewitt.

"Sure, why not. As long as you don't get in our way."

"No problem. I'll meet up with your team at the DFW Airport."

25

On the Canadian side of Rainy Lake near the Minnesota border, Nasir paced at the home of a fellow believer. *If the West only understood what the one true god required of us, they would not be so eager to accept us.*

The location of this crossing had been chosen because of the thousands of waterways linking the two countries. It made it nearly impossible to follow every fishing boat that moved freely in these waters, and most of the U.S. registered boats were only given cursory observation.

He stopped pacing and glimpsed out the window, toward Windy Point. It would have been a beautiful view if the rain ever stopped, but the rain was his friend today. The heavier the better for concealing his men and their actions.

"Where is the boat? I tire of waiting." It was the smelly Russian.

Nasir turned away from the window to face him. "It will be here soon. What does it matter to you? Are you in a hurry to be out on this lake in the middle of a storm?"

"I grew up in a fishing boat. This is nothing. In Mezen Bay, the water can go from smooth as glass to ten meter waves in a matter of minutes. Crossing this little pond is child's play."

Nasir wondered if Russians were as tough as they claimed, or if bragging was just part of their culture. He turned back to the window. "Good. You will have a chance to show your skills. The boat is here." A thirty footer came into view as the rain eased up a little. It headed for the long pier twenty meters downhill from the house.

"They are here," one of Nasir's men said as he entered from another room. He carried a walkie-talkie in one hand. Cell coverage was spotty in this area, and monitored. All phones had to be off until they were safely across the border.

"Head on down and get the cargo loaded. Take Rostislav with you." Nasir wanted the Russian out of his sight. He was needed, but not in here.

"Yes, sir." He headed toward the front door. Rostislav slowly stood and followed, scratching himself as he went. The man was a tool, an expert in operating the equipment they were bringing into America, but not a believer. Tools had their uses, and once that use was over they could be discarded.

Nasir went to locate the owner of the home. "Jeffery, we are leaving. I want to thank you for the use of your home."

Jeffery was sitting at his computer. He rose and progressed toward Nasir. "It is an honor to be of service to an Imam such as yourself."

The two men embraced and gave the non-contact kiss on the cheeks. "Your reward will be awaiting you in paradise."

Nasir grabbed his coat and headed down the outside steps toward the dock. The boat floated at the far end. As he approached, he watched Rostislav grab the last crate and hoist it to his shoulder. He handed the large box to a man on deck who stacked it with the others. The size of the crate was due mostly to Russian packing material. What they lacked in quality they made up for in quantity.

This equipment had cost Nasir dearly, but it was the most important piece to his mission. Everything else, if necessary, could be reacquired, but not these. It had taken two years of work to locate and another six months to steal from a Russian military storage unit. They were parts to a chemical weapon the Russians denied ever existed.

The light rain changed suddenly to a downpour as the wind picked up speed. Nasir climbed aboard just ahead of the Russian. "How long before we can get underway?"

"In this weather, the equipment must be tied down below deck. I will let you know when we are ready." Rostislav passed Nasir and moved on ahead with the rest of the men. He really did know his way around a fishing boat.

"I am the captain. Sorry we are late. The weather, you see." Nasir turned to see a bearded weathered face. The captain's eyes were young, but his face showed many years at sea.

Nasir stuck out his hand and shook the captain's. "Your timing is fine. May Allah bless you and your crew."

The seaman gave a slight nod as his eyes shifted toward the front of the fishing trawler. "This way." He turned and headed forward with Nasir in tow. Entering the bridge, the captain closed the door behind Nasir.

"Much better." The captain turned to the man at the wheel. "Go help John and Nat get those boxes below and make sure they're secured."

"Yes, Captain."

The captain's attention followed the man until he was off the bridge and the door was closed. Once the two were alone, his shoulders dropped a little as he turned toward Nasir. "Not all of my men share in our belief. You must be careful what is said around them. Some are loyal followers, but others are typical American Christians. What faith they have is weak and only comes out when they fear for their lives."

"That will be their downfall."

The captain nodded and gave a grunt of agreement. "They serve on this boat for money and that is all. I pay well and they keep quiet about what they see. But we do not want to take chances at this point."

The pilot reentered the bridge. "Captain, we can get underway. The last crate is tied down and Nat is casting us off." He stepped around Nasir to the boat's helm. Grabbing the wheel and controls, he applied a small amount of power as he looked over his shoulder toward the dock.

"Excellent." The captain studied the onboard radar. "And we've timed it just right to lead the next squall south. That will help keep us hidden."

Nasir turned to see what the pilot was looking at, a man on the dock throwing a rope on deck as he quickly followed. No sooner had he made it onboard, when the power from the engines increased and the floor rumbled as they moved away from shore. With every minute, the wind grew until they hit the channel. The driving rain made it impossible to see much past the bow. The pilot watched his instruments more than he looked out the window.

"Heading, sir?" The pilot waited for the captain's response.

"Take us into Black Bay." The captain joined Nasir. "I know where we can safely unload. I have two vans waiting close by. I will call them when we are ten minutes from our destination."

"That will be perfect." The rain blew against the window, completely blocking any view. The son of the dry lands of the Middle East was not as comfortable on the stormy sea as these sailors. Nasir said a silent prayer to Allah.

26

Returning from his weekly trip to town, Frank parked his car behind his 1980's doublewide trailer. This made it impossible for anyone driving down the road at the end of his quarter mile long driveway to know when he was home.

Beside him on the car seat was a package from his half-brother, Carl Henderson, *the Senator*, a man who refused to talk to him or help him. Carl said Frank was a nutcase and told him to stay away.

Frank stared at the package. He had almost tossed it in the trash in town, but his curiosity had gotten the better of him.

Why contact me now?

The package contained a note with two short sentences. 'Remember Dad and keep this safe. Our lives depend on it.'

What about Dad?

Carl's dead.

Is this going to kill me?

The brothers had only two things in common, their father and his secrets.

When he was young, Frank idolized their father and his work in the CIA. Their dad had been a spy and helped to keep this country free. Frank had wanted to be just like his dad.

Now, after he'd experienced what it took to ensure that freedom, the lies told to the American people, Frank hated what his father had done. The American government spent more resources keeping itself in power than it did protecting its citizens. And they were always sneaking around spying on everybody. No one was safe. Now it looked like Carl had learned that the hard way.

Frank glanced down at the brownish-yellow package.

What have you gotten yourself into, Carl? What have you gotten me into?

'Our lives depend on it.' What can be so important?
Is it some of your government secrets that killed you?
And now you've sent them my way.
Why?

He stared out the window. No one lived within two miles of him, and that's just what he wanted, solitude. Maybe he should have bought land in Alaska, but it was too cold there.

Picking up the package, he let the jump drive slide out the open end, into his hand.

This could have a tracking device in it. It needs to be shielded. Its signal must be blocked.

Frank hated technology. *Any computer anywhere can be tapped into. How could everyone not see that? Computers make it so easy for the government to see what you're up to.*

His training in Iraq had shown him that. He had learned a lot of things there.

Palming the device, Frank stepped out of the car and walked to the edge of the trailer. The driveway was clear all the way to the road. Out on the state highway only three cars were in view, normal traffic for this time of day.

He examined the device again.

'Our lives depend on keeping this safe.' Who wants this? Who was willing to kill for it?

It has to be the government. The people Carl worked for. I told him they could not be trusted. He said I was nuts.

I've got to keep this safe, away from them.

He walked over to a lone tree that stood a few hundred yards from his home. Dropping to his knees on the far side, he slid a large flat stone to the side. He brushed the dirt away from the lid of an old military small missile case that was buried lid up in the ground. He opened it and peered inside. The heavy metal case and water tight seal kept the contents safe from water and government scanning.

The cylinder held his passport, birth certificate, deed, car title, four hundred ounces of silver and ten ounces of gold. The gold was his "bribe" for serving his country.

Serving? More like killing to protect big businesses.

He dropped the jump drive in.

After replacing the lid and tossing the rock back in place, he brushed away knee and foot prints from the area. The sun was going down and he was hungry. After one more quick look around, he headed in for a bite of food.

Carl and Abby were dead because Carl trusted the government. Abby was a good woman, too good for Carl. Wish I could go to the service, but that would be a sure giveaway. They would find me and kill me, too.

Grabbing a box of cereal, Frank sat down at his table to eat dinner. He emptied it into a bowl. Not much there. Standing, he checked the back room for more. He was out.

Man, I'll have to look for some work tomorrow. Now is not a good time, but I need food.

A car pulled up to a stop just outside his trailer. Rushing out of the back room he glanced out the window. Two men in suits stepped out of a car.

They found me!

His fist pounded against the wall and he rushed into his bedroom. Grabbing his rifle, he yanked the trap door open in the floor. Dropping through, he quickly and quietly lowered the lid back in place. It was a routine he practiced two times a week, minimum. He crawled under the flooring toward the rear of his home.

Footsteps sounded above him. He waited a few seconds for the men to move back toward the living area. He pushed a panel aside to see the last dim glow of the sun.

Perfect.

His car sat fifteen feet away. A short sprint. He could make it.

He slid his gun out and started crawling through the opening when cool steel pressed against his neck.

"I got him."

Frank's rifle was flat on the ground. A man's foot held it down. The fifteen feet to his car turned to miles. Unless—

He reached over with his other hand and grabbed the leg of his assailant. If he could throw the man off balance—

The explosion burned the side of his neck. Pain stung deep as a voice said something about being stupid. Was the voice talking to him?

His hand went to cover the blood.

Arms grabbed him, pulled him up, and dragged him around to his front door. They threw him inside. He rolled across the old stained carpet and stopped next to a kitchen chair.

"I ain't telling you guys nothin'."

The larger man put Frank in a seat while the smaller one did the talking. "Mr. Henderson, my partner did not mean to hurt you. We only came here to ask for your help. Once you answer our questions we will give you a ride into town to get that wound taken care of."

Frank held one hand against his neck. The man handed him a kitchen towel to press against it. "You're liars. You killed my brother and now you've come to kill me."

The small man gave a smile. "No, you misunderstand. We had nothing to do with your brother's death. We were sent here to track down the ones responsible for his murder." The man pulled out a badge. "I am Agent Landry and this is Agent Hewitt, we're from the Department of Homeland Security."

"I know most of the murders in this country are committed by the government. You think I'm dumb or something?" *The only way you could have found me is through the tracking device Carl sent me. I should have thrown it in the trash.*

The speaker looked at the other man. "I see I am wasting my time here."

"Absolutely, so why don't you two leave. I can take care of myself," Frank chimed in.

The small man looked into Frank's eyes. "You are right. Your brother suffered greatly before he died, and if you do not want to experience the same, you will tell us where the package he sent you is."

The world was starting to blur just a little. Frank had experienced this before, the last time he was shot. "What makes you think he'd send me anything? You should know he hasn't talked to me in years."

Landry stepped back and paced around the trailer as he talked. "We are part of the government, and we know he sent you a package."

"Then you should also know I only go to town once every two weeks."

"Are you telling me you have not retrieved this package?"

"I have not been to town in over a week. I don't know anything about a package. What's in it anyway that's so important?"

"If you don't know anything about the package, why did you run when we came up your drive?"

"Maybe that's because no one knows about this place, not even my dead brother. If you found it, it can only mean you want to hurt me. So, yeah, I tried to hide until you left."

"With your rifle?"

"I have to be able to protect myself."

"Yes, I am sure you believe that. Where is the package?"

"Even if I had this package, I would not give it to you. You killed Carl."

Landry stepped in a little closer, and nodded to the other man.

Hewitt's large hand reached around the back of Frank's neck, pushing Frank's hand aside. As he squeezed the wound, pain shot through Frank's body. "Stop, please. I don't know anything."

The man stopped, but the pain barely lessened.

"Where is the package?"

Frank gingerly held his neck. He couldn't take any more pain. Everything he had run from was coming home to haunt him. "If he sent me something it's still in town, at the post office."

Landry sat back and crossed his arms. "What is your PO Box number?"

"Don't have one. I use general delivery. I don't get much mail." He leaned forward as his head started to spin.

"In Granbury?" Landry glanced up at Hewitt.

"Yes." Frank barely got the words out before he passed out.

Landry looked at Hewitt. "We are not getting anywhere. And we do not have time to play his paranoid games. We can find the package ourselves. If it is not here, I will check out the post office tomorrow while you and the FBI are investigating his death." He turned back to Frank and put a bullet in his head.

27

Thursday

Sara closed the door to her office. Todd was in Texas and Tony was on assignment, so she had the office to herself today. Her work on the senator's murder was on hold until Todd returned, so today was the day she would destroy John Motova's life.

She logged in as herself. No alerts would pop up in IT or anywhere else to tell Booker she was doing anything wrong. She did not need Todd's login for what she was about to do. Then she set up a program that allowed her to hack into Motova's/Halter's company computer system without being traced.

Now he would suffer. Not the same way she had, but suffer he would.

What would get the police's attention? Drugs. He was a chemist, he could be into making meth.

She created a purchase order for six cases of Ammonia Hydroxide, enough to make several kilos of meth. That should get someone's attention. But he could say he was using it for other purposes. So she created another purchase order for red phosphorus and iodine. Each PO was posted as having been filled in the last couple of weeks.

With this evidence on his computer, no one would believe him when he denied involvement. And with the inventory missing he would look as guilty as Ted Bundy.

He would fight the allegations, of course. He would have to hire a lawyer to prove his innocence. But lawyers cost money and good lawyers cost lots of money. If he was broke, he couldn't fight. He would go to jail.

She pulled up the company's bank accounts. The records showed over five hundred thousand dollars spread across three different accounts. Sara was shocked. Where did he get all this money? He certainly was not spending any of the money that his company had made. Well, that did not matter now. He was going to lose it all.

Sara brought up another window and set up several offshore accounts at banks that didn't play well with the U.S. government. She had learned how to set up hidden accounts outside the U.S. before coming to the Bureau, but working for the FBI had taught her which banks would be safe for her to use.

She then started the transfers. Each account was drained down to five dollars. The money was transferred in several dozen moves so as to not raise any red flags.

It took the whole morning, but what else did she have to do? To hide her tracks, the money went offshore through the new accounts and was routed through half a dozen banks. With each transfer, the amounts were changed as well as the currencies. Finally, the money landed in her new numbered account. A nice nest egg for when her parole was up.

One more thing and I'll be done and so will Motova.

She logged out of his system and accessed the DEA database. She added Brian Halter's name and address to the watch-list of suspected drug manufacturers.

She jumped as the door behind her opened.

"You got a minute?" Lamar's tone was friendly, not businesslike.

Sara killed the window before swiveling around to face him. "Sure, I was just finishing up a search on the senator's case."

He stepped into the office and dropped his large frame into Todd's chair. "I heard about your visit to the doctor's office."

Sara had a startled look. Lamar started to reach out his hand but pulled it back. They were at work and there were rules he had to follow. "I had lunch with Derry yesterday. He asked me to keep an eye on you."

"I'm fine." She didn't really want to talk about it. She was taking care of the problem.

He leaned in and this time let his hand touch hers. "I know you think your foster father has destroyed your life."

"Only because he did."

Lamar nodded as he went on. "But have you ever wondered where you would be if things were different, if you had been placed with a different family?"

"Yes, I wouldn't be sick right now. I wouldn't have had all those terrible things happen to me."

"That's probably true. But you wouldn't know Derry, and it's possible you wouldn't even know God."

———

A red letter window popped up on Booker's screen.

```
Warning: Possible unsanctioned activities under
Sara Beckwith's account.
```

She had her. Booker reached for her phone and called Tony.
He didn't answer so she left a message for him.

———

Landry and Hewitt had been unable to find the package at Henderson's house, even though they had turned the place inside out. They even stripped Henderson's car, but came up empty. So Landry had decided to try to find the package at the Post Office. Landry entered the second post office in Granbury. The first one did not have any mail under general delivery for Frank Henderson or a PO Box under his name. He walked up to the counter, bypassing the line of customers and flipped out his ID. "I'm Agent Landry from the Department of Homeland Security. May I speak with the Postmaster for this location?"

The old man behind the counter reached for Landry's ID and pulled it closer. He examined it, comparing the picture to Landry. "You can never be too careful these days. Hold on, I'll get him."

The postal worker left and returned three minutes later with a younger man in tow. "Yes, what is this about?"

"Can we speak in private?"

The Postmaster opened a door in the counter. "This way."

Landry stepped through and informed the man he was working with the FBI, investigating the murder of a senator. He then asked about any mail for a Frank Henderson.

"I'll check, but if you want it you will need to get a warrant. You know that, right?"

"Yes, of course. At this point we are trying to establish which post office Mr. Henderson uses."

"A warrant could be set up to work at all of them."

"Yes. You are correct. However, that would take much more

time. The package we are looking for might be under general delivery."

"General delivery you said? That will take a little longer. Wait here."

The Postmaster returned ten minutes later. "It appears Mr. Henderson did not use this post office. We don't have any record of mail coming through here for him for at least the last six months. That's all the further back our active records go. You might try the other post office in the area."

Landry turned and left without a word. He had been lied to. How could he have not seen that? Hewitt was with the FBI team. The package had to be at Henderson's house. Landry would have to contact Hewitt and let him know to keep looking at the house.

28

"The guy's a loner and a wacko. We don't know what to expect out here, so be extremely careful." Kent, the team leader, didn't have as much time at the Bureau as Todd, but he had a lot more time in the field. Also, he had taken several courses in profiling. He understood Henderson's thinking.

Hewitt finished his phone call as the car headed up the long drive toward the old doublewide trailer.

Todd, in the backseat with Hewitt, was busy looking at a satellite image of the area. "There is nothing out here."

"The front door's open." Chris was the driver and sat next to Kent. He slowed the car and tilted his head forward, attempting to see through the doorway. "Not a good sign."

"This doesn't look right." Kent added.

"He might be in there ready to shoot the first person through the door." Hewitt said.

"You Homeland people really don't trust anyone, do you?" Kent asked. "Maybe he just wanted some fresh air."

"I haven't always been at Homeland, and I've had too many people try to kill me not to recognize a bad situation. Remember the old Russian proverb, 'even paranoid people have enemies'."

"It's 'even a paranoid has some real enemies', and it's believed that Golda Meir said that to Henry Kissinger during the Sinai talks in seventy-three," Todd quietly remarked.

Chris chuckled as he glanced over his shoulder at Todd. "You really are a nerd. Or maybe you're just making that up."

"I know it because I read. You should try it sometime."

"Who has time to read?" Chris slowed even more as the car

neared the trailer.

"Well, admitting you are paranoid is the first step to recovery," Kent replied as he pulled his Glock out of its holster.

Chris pulled to a stop near one corner of the trailer. Anyone inside would have to step out to get a clear round off.

"Hewitt, you're with me. Chris and Todd, take the back." The four disembarked.

Kent and Hewitt went around to the front door as Todd followed Chris around back.

As Kent entered the trailer, he immediately knew something was wrong. The place had been tossed. He and Hewitt carefully passed through the living room into the kitchen where they found a body lying in a pool of partially dried blood. Kent tightened his grip on his gun and moved it to a firing position before clearing the rest of the rooms.

Finding the back door locked, Chris and Todd completed their circuit of the trailer and entered the front door. They followed the voices to the kitchen where they, too, saw the body. Chris holstered his Glock and pulled out his phone. Blood and other material covered the north side of the kitchen. He took several pictures of the crime scene, bumping into Todd. "Mind moving out of the way?"

It took Todd several seconds to respond. He finally stepped aside.

Chris went back to work. "It's different when it's real," he said to Todd as he worked.

"Yes, I just thought he would be alive. That's all." Todd talked, but stood rigidly in place. He could not tear his eyes from the horrific scene in front of him.

Chris stepped next to him. "Mind doing me a favor? Could you run out to the car and get the fingerprint scanner?"

"Uh, yeah, sure."

As Todd stepped out, Kent nodded to Chris. "Thanks. I think he'll be okay in a minute. Finding the body in this condition is a little unexpected for us all."

It took Todd longer than it should have, but he returned with the scanner and a better attitude. He placed the dead man's right index finger on the screen. The results were quick. It was Frank Henderson.

Chris placed his hand on Frank's back, the body was at room

temperature. "The blood on the floor looks mostly dry. I would say he died last night. The coroner can get a better reading when he gets here."

Kent reached for his phone and placed a call. He filled Faircloth in on the situation. Kent's next call was to the local police, followed by a call to the Dallas FBI office.

Chris and Todd continued to examine the crime scene, taking more photos. Obviously Frank had died from a gunshot wound, but they could only speculate as to why. Was Frank simply in the wrong place at the wrong time? Or were the murderers looking for the same thing they were, the package from Senator Henderson. If so, had they found what they were looking for?

Kent joined them. "People like Henderson are very paranoid. They rarely hide things they deem important in 'normal places'. Chances are, he has a hiding place in an unlikely location." He looked down the narrow hall that ran the length of the trailer. "It's most likely outside of his home."

Kent paused, staring at the floor for several seconds. "I may be wrong, but I suspect whatever Senator Henderson sent to his brother is still here, and we will find it in a secret hiding place either under the trailer or somewhere on the property. Todd, you and Hewitt look for a trap door. See if you can find a hiding place below the trailer. Chris and I will look outside."

Kent and Chris surveyed the landscape around the trailer. There were a few trees and bushes, but mostly dry grass. "If there is a secret hiding place, it should be near the shrubbery. Let's fan out and see what's out there."

"Someone's been out here recently." Chris pointed at shoe prints between the clumps of grass that dotted the landscape.

Kent stopped Chris from proceeding any further. "Get some pictures before we step all over any evidence that might be here."

The two men walked on either side of the prints as the trail led them to the base of a tree.

"What have we here?" Chris took a few more pictures before dropping down and moving a rock aside to reveal a metal lid.

"Hold up." It was Kent. "Check for wires or pressure switches. It might be booby trapped."

"Ah, good point. Can't be too paranoid." Chris smiled as he

carefully checked the lid. "Can't see anything."

Kent stepped back as Chris slowly turned the lid to unscrew it. Lifting it off, Chris peered down the deep, dark tube. Kent looked over Chris's shoulder. "See anything?"

Chris adjusted the camera in order for the flash to reach the bottom and took several pictures. Bringing them up on the camera's display, he zoomed in looking for traps or wires. "It looks safe. I think we found his treasure. Clever hiding place. I need to get me one of these things." He switched his phone from camera to flashlight mode. Reaching in, he pulled out a small white tube with a green lid. He slowly opened it. "Silver dollars."

Just then, Todd and Hewitt approached. "We found a tunnel under the trailer, but no hiding place," Hewitt reported.

"Those tubes are from the U.S. Mint." Todd remarked.

Chris looked over his shoulder at Todd. "Is there anything you don't know?"

"If there was, I would study it," he said with a deadpan expression.

Kent stepped closer. "What else is in there?"

Hewitt crowded in as Chris pulled a third handful of white tubes out. "What's all this?"

"Henderson's buried treasure." Kent grinned at Hewitt.

"So, he buried it." Hewitt commented quietly.

"Wouldn't you, if you lived in a tornado magnet?" Chris said as he bent forward and reached his arm in deeper. "I think I found something else." He came back up with a jump drive between his thumb and index finger. He handed it to Todd. "See what you can find out."

"I need my laptop." Todd headed toward the car. Hewitt followed as Kent and Chris finished going through the items from the hidden stash.

"Do you suppose that's what was in the package?" Hewitt walked next to Todd.

Todd glanced over, giving Hewitt a strange look. "It's what we came for. Why else would Henderson bury it?"

Pulling his laptop out of a bag, Todd set it on the back seat, out of the sun. He plugged the jump drive in and opened its main directory. There were five encrypted files and one text file, titled "Frank." He opened Frank's file.

```
"Frank,
Be careful and do not share or store the files on
this drive on any publicly accessible system. Muslim
terrorists have infiltrated one of our federal law
enforcement agencies. Their identities, along with
information on their plans are stored in one of the
encrypted files. To keep the information out of the
enemy's hands, Dad's field encryption method was used
on these files. If something happens to me, you know
how to open these. Make sure the information gets to
the right people.
Carl
PS. Please forgive me for the way I've treated you
over the last few years. I put politics ahead of
family. I was wrong."
```

Todd shut down his laptop and pulled the drive. "Got it." He shoved it into his pocket.

Hewitt reached out his hand. "I can make sure that makes it back to Denver tonight. I'll hand carry it, and you can stay around and help Kent and Chris."

Todd gave Hewitt a horrified look. "I'm not a murder scene investigator. I got what I came for and I'm out of here as soon as I can arrange a ride to the airport. You can stay around and process the crime scene with those two."

Hewitt stepped closer to Todd, boxing him in. "This murder is FBI business, not Homeland. There's no reason for me to stay. I'll take the drive and get it back to Denver."

Todd pushed past him, "Do you mind? I don't like people that close."

Two sheriffs' cars pulled up next to their rental car. Todd stepped toward the new arrivals as Hewitt moved back. Speaking to the first office to get out, Todd said, "I need one of you to give me a ride to the airport immediately."

29

"So why the short day? Not that I mind." Kai reached for the car handle.

"Agent Hewitt needs me to make a run up to Cheyenne tonight. And since two people are required to be in that room at all times, you get a break." Alex had stopped the car in the roadway in front of their apartment building.

"Thanks. Maybe I'll get an evening run in."

"You could call that sushi guy. I'm sure the smell of fish washes off."

"No thanks. That was some of the worst sushi I've ever had. You were smart not to come." Kai made a face.

"Any raw fish is bad."

Kai slipped out of the car, but turned back before closing the door. "What time do you think you'll be back?"

"That all depends on Denver traffic. Speaking of which, I need to get going before I-25 backs up."

"Later." Kai shut the door and headed into the building.

Alex pulled away and found a secluded spot about a half mile from their home. She shook off her "Alex" persona and once again became Gabriele. She pulled up the message from Jonas, a priority one assignment. She had someone to kill and data to recover. Her target was scheduled to land at DIA at 5:40. Given the layout at DIA, it was impossible to make it out of the airport in less than twenty minutes, and it could take as much a forty-five. She had at least two hours before the target would be available.

What do we know about this man? She opened the attached file. It was Homeland's file on FBI Agent Todd Jenkins.

He had grown up just outside Fort Meade, Maryland with middle class parents. He was the third child of four. He earned his Doctorate in Computer Science from MIT and was top of his class. The FBI had recruited him before he even completed his studies. He worked part time for the Bureau until graduation. After receiving additional training at Quantico, he asked to be assigned to Denver.

Enough of the facts. Alex scrolled down several pages, past his list of projects and accomplishments. She went to his psychological profile, something that was monitored throughout an agent's career. Todd was a recluse, rarely went out after work with his team or anyone else. He had never married or had any live-in girlfriends. Over the last five years he had had seven online relationships, none lasting more than three months.

What a loser. I wonder if he could handle a real woman.

Most of his extra income went to high-end computers, software tools, and doctorate level classes. He was often a guest speaker at the academy, giving training sessions or lectures on computer threats. He spent most evenings at home in on-line chat rooms or in small discussion groups covering a wide range of topics. He was considered a borderline genius.

Retrieving his address from the file, she pulled up information on his apartment complex. It had assigned parking, six digit coded building entry, and cameras throughout the parking area, as well as at the end of each hallway inside. Some people certainly liked their privacy.

She spent most of an hour studying the files.

After a short trip to a storage vault to retrieve two black bags, Gabriele headed over to Todd's home. She checked the time as she pulled into the parking area across the street from the apartment building. She had maybe thirty minutes if Todd's flight was on time.

Slipping on a dark blue hoodie, she headed across the street. Approaching the entryway camera from the back, she slipped a device out of her pocket and pointed it at the camera. After holding the button for two seconds, she headed to the next camera, and the next, hitting each one with a relatively mild EM pulse. It was not powerful enough to kill the cameras permanently, but they would be offline until the power was reset or the magnetic charge had time to bleed off, about two hours.

Returning to her car, she opened the trunk. She placed the

hoodie and EM device in one bag and retrieved a small vile of liquid and a small sewing needle. She carefully applied some of the liquid to the end of the needle. Lastly, she grabbed a dark brown wig.

Moving to the driver's seat, she set the needle carefully in the tray beside her and slipped the wig on. She checked herself for loose hairs one last time. She was ready.

She moved her car across the street into Todd's assigned parking place.

Popping her hood, she disabled her car by loosening the plug leading to the car's computer and waited for her victim.

————

Special Agent Tony Castor met Special Agent Lisa Booker at Skyline Park just off the 16th Street Mall in Denver. "I hope this is important. This meeting could blow my cover, and I am close to having all the evidence we need to shut that company down for good."

Booker sat on a park bench in the shade of one of the tall buildings that surrounded the mall. "I read over your latest report. We have enough information to get the warrants, and if the evidence is there, we'll find it. Right now I need your skills for a much more important and immediate case." Booker's attention was on a homeless man pushing a cart filled with his worldly goods.

Tony took a seat next to Booker. "That company is sending valuable technology to the Chinese. With it, the Chinese will be able to monitor our military's communications and nullify any military action we may need to take against them in the future." Tony spoke in a whisper. Even here, surrounded by homeless street people and mall shoppers, the wrong person could hear what he was saying.

Booker turned her head toward Tony. "This company is only one of a dozen that are a threat. You think they're the only ones putting money ahead of security?" she challenged him.

He fell back against his seat. "So we shouldn't go after every one of them?"

"We should and we will. But with our limited resources we have to hit the highest threats first."

"National security isn't the highest threat?"

"It is, but any threat from the Chinese is several months or years away. We have a bigger problem in our backyard right now. And you have the skills I need to solve it."

He studied the ground. "If I'm off this case, why meet here? Why not at the office?

Surveying the area, Booker made sure no one was close enough to hear her before proceeding. "You've been undercover for a while."

"Five months."

"Have you heard about a leak in one of the agencies that is feeding intel to the Middle East?"

"Yes, it's not that unusual. We've had leaks before."

"This one's very good, and I believe it's out of the Denver office."

"Do you have a suspect, or are you just convinced it's out of your branch?"

"I have evidence of who it might be." Booker reached into her briefcase. Pulling out a file, she handed it to Tony. "Everything is in here."

She watched people passing by while he read.

"Sara?" He lowered the folder and stared at Booker. "You think Sara's the traitor?"

"Not necessarily a traitor as much as an opportunist."

"Changing the name doesn't change what you think. Sara would never betray her country. I've worked with her for over two years and I know her too well to believe she would send intel to Islamists."

"Read on and it may change your mind." Booker crossed her arms as she nodded at the open folder.

Tony read more. Looking up he stated, "I don't believe this. You can't really believe that Sara ruined the hard drive on purpose. And this unexplained computer access has not been investigated. It proves nothing. There is likely a reasonable explanation."

"Are you saying you are willing to let your personal bias get in the way of doing your job?"

"No, but because I am close to her, I should not be the one investigating her. Upper management would never allow it."

"They don't know at this point." Booker turned her body slightly toward him to drive her point home. "You and Todd are the best computer people on site, and Todd is busy working the senator's murder with Sara. I have this evidence, enough to send her back to jail, and the last thing I want to do is show my hand. If someone else is the leak, that would allow them time to run. If I send it up the chain of command and I am wrong, it could cost me a lot."

"I've worked with her for more than two years. In the same room with her and Todd and you want me to run checks on her? Why not use someone else in Lamar's group? Someone who is not as close to Sara as I am?"

"Can't." Her face betrayed her. "Lamar doesn't know, and I want to keep it that way."

Tony sat back. "What's going to happen to me when Lamar finds out?"

"If I'm right, nothing."

"And when I prove you wrong?"

"If I'm wrong and you spent your time proving that, Lamar will be thankful that I put you on it and not some *yes* man."

"Did I even have a choice on this?"

"No. You owe me too much."

Tony knew he was trapped. He owed Booker for her protection in his brother's case.

"I need a way to monitor Sara's activities and not be seen. We have a very tight system to keep people from doing exactly what you want me to do. How am I going to get around that?"

Booker pulled out a second folder and handed it to him. "As far as anyone at the office is concerned you're still undercover. I don't want your face seen around the office."

He took the folder and opened it. "Nineteenth and Stout? You want me to work at the old FBI building? I thought it was shut down years ago."

"It was, but we still own one floor there. It has power and a direct trunk line to the new building."

"What about a computer? Anything left there would be at least two generations old."

She nodded at the folder. "There is a privately held credit card in there, not tied to anyone or anything at the Bureau. Buy what you need, computers, food, hotel room. Don't go home. I want you to stay off the radar. Also, there are keys in there to the second floor of the old building and all the access codes to come in through the backdoor of our systems. The codes are good for one month."

Leaning forward, Tony closed the folder and tapped it against his hand. "If I can't prove to you that you've got the wrong person by then, I might as well find a new place to work."

30

Entering the apartment, Kai walked to the window and watched Alex's car go around the corner at the end of the parking lot. Even with the car out of sight, Kai stood unmoved. Somewhere in the back of her brain a fight was going on. How had her friend become a suspect, someone she didn't trust? Her mother told her from the time she was little that she had a discerning spirit, whatever that meant. She blinked and brought the conflict from the back of her mind to the front.

What is that girl up to? Using some made up reason for me to stop work on a high priority project that's not complete doesn't make any sense.

Kai turned away from the window and glanced around the living room of their two-bedroom apartment. Everything was neat and clean. She turned back toward the window.

This whole setup reeks of a cover up. And keeping me completely isolated from the rest of the building, more cover up.

Kai moved to the center of the window and glanced both directions, checking both entrances to the parking lot.

A trip to Cheyenne for Hewitt? I don't think so. If only I had a car I would be right behind her, finding out what she's hiding.

The only cars entering or leaving the parking area were ones she'd noticed before, just ones belonging to other residents.

Heading down the hall, Kai stopped at Alex's bedroom door. Taking a deep breath, she questioned her own sanity one last time. *What if Alex is hiding something? Then what?*

Using her shirt sleeve, Kai turned the handle and slowly opened the door. She looked in before taking a step across the threshold, nothing out of the ordinary.

Where would I hide something?

The room had clothes on the floor and a stack of papers in the corner, next to the bed. Invading her opponent's domain, she crossed over to the bed to examine the pile. She knelt and carefully flipped through with one hand as she held the stack in place with the other. They were Homeland documents about her, giving flight information and outlining her project.

Nothing of use here.

Going through the closet and dresser also proved to be useless. Standing in the middle of the floor, she scanned everywhere for anything that might help her solve this mystery. The room was without a personality. There were no personal items at all.

A little unusual but not unheard of.

Kai turned to leave. Stopping, she bent down to examine the heater air return vent behind the door. It didn't look right. The paint around the edge of the cover had been neatly cut. There was some wall paint on the cover, but a very thin straight line separated it from the wall. Someone had taken the cover off after the room was painted.

Dropping to one knee and using her phone, she shone a light through the slits. They all pointed up, nothing to see.

Heading to the kitchen, she retrieved a butter knife. Carefully she turned the screws. They went a quarter turn, stopped and popped out. Not what she expected. That was not standard. Why make a permanent cover with quick release screws?

She carefully pulled the cover away and looked inside.

She discovered a black leather bag. She lifted it out. Opening the bag, she found two large bundles of money. One bundle was hundred dollar bills. The other was hundred Euros. She counted each stack, nine thousand dollars and seven thousand Euros. She set it aside and reached back in the bag and pulled out two envelopes. One had a U.S. diplomatic passport with Alex's picture but the name printed on the passport was Julie Bowman. Tucked inside was an open international flight ticket, good for one year. There were two other documents verifying her identity.

The other envelope had a German passport for Gabriele Dieter. The picture was that of a younger Alex. Flipping through, it was clear this passport had been well used. There was also a birth certificate and a paper listing four banks along with account numbers. Kai pulled her phone out and took pictures of everything before putting it all back.

Alex is a German spy.

A chill ran the length of her body as her eyes went to the doorway. *If she's a spy, would she know I was in her room? How?* Kai looked at the carpet around her, Alex's footprints were everywhere. *Good.* She put everything back and examined the area. With a few steps of her own, the carpet took on that uniform un-vacuumed look. Lastly, Kai examined the door. Had Alex put something where the door met the frame? Nothing Kai could see. She backed out as she pulled the door shut the same way she had opened it.

————

Todd was tired but excited. He had the jump drive, and after playing around with it on the plane he felt sure he could decrypt the files. Home was only a few minutes out of the way. After a quick bite to eat, it was off to the Bureau for an all-nighter. If he could have the files decrypted by morning, he could get another citation to add to his collection. Hitting the brakes, he stopped short of ramming the car that was in his parking spot.

Of all the days for people to be breaking the rules.

He backed up and headed toward the visitor's parking. He'd get their license number and call management.

Great. Visitor parking was full. He didn't have time for this. Not today. He headed across the street. There he found open parking. He'd only be there for an hour or less so he tried not to let the inconvenience bother him. On his way to his apartment he slipped his phone out to take a quick image of the car's rear license plate.

As he took the first picture the driver's door opened.

He shoved the phone in his pocket as an attractive woman about his age stepped out.

"Are you taking a picture of my car?"

"You are in my parking place."

"Oh, I'm terribly sorry." She had a sweet smile and soft voice. "I didn't know they were assigned."

"They are." He pointed to one of the signs a few spaces down. "You need to move your car."

She looked behind him. "It's not in anyone's way."

"It's in mine. You should move it."

"In your way? Where's your car?"

"Why does that matter?"

Her smile grew. "I mean, if you don't have a car, it doesn't really matter if I'm in your spot for a little while."

"I had to park across the street. And if anything happens to my Honda, you'll have to pay for taking *my* assigned parking spot." He was coming across much harsher than he intended.

"I'm really sorry, but I can't move my car." She looked worried and hurt.

He looked around the lot, then back at her. "You parked it there. You should be able to move it." It was only logical.

She shrugged her shoulders. "I was headed home and my car started acting funny. I pulled in here and it died. I had to coast the last few feet." She turned and glanced at her car, making a disgruntled face. She was kind of cute.

"If it won't start, you should call a tow truck or a friend. You need to find a way to move your car. I'm in a hurry."

"Okay, I'll try to get it started." Slipping back into the driver's seat, she reached for the keys and cranked the engine a few times. It turned over, but didn't fire up.

He moved next to her open door to get a better view.

She looked up at him. "I am so sorry, — I just moved here from Maryland and I don't know anyone in town. I don't even know who to call for help." She had just the faintest hint of an eastern accent. She sounded a lot like his favorite cousin.

"Maryland?" He should stop being such a jerk and help a fellow Marylander.

"Yes. And everything is so peculiar out here."

"What brought you out here?"

"I needed to make a new start. Hopefully find new friends. But I feel so out of place. Maybe I should have stayed back east."

"Well, Colorado is really a great place to live. It's just a little different is all. You'll get used to it in no time." What was he saying? The seafood was only mediocre and it just didn't rain enough here.

"Yeah, that's what everyone keeps saying. But people here just can't understand. The pace of life is different, no one ever dresses up to go out, there aren't any good shows. It's nothing like home."

"I understand. I'm from Maryland, too." Todd leaned back against the car behind him and slid his hands into his pockets. He felt the jump drive. He'd get back to it in a minute.

Her face brightened. "Really?"

He liked being able to brighten up her day. "Yeah, really. What part of Maryland are you from?"

She pushed the door open a little more, almost hitting the car he was leaning on. He reached over to stop it and kept a hand on it.

Her eyes went to his hand, as she smiled. "Thanks." Looking back at his face she continued, "I grew up in a little area just outside of Laurel, about halfway between D.C. and Baltimore." She swung one leg out as she turned in her seat toward him, propping her other foot up on the doorframe edge. She wore a black pantsuit with a purple blouse, obviously a business woman. "A place called Maryland City. Ever hear of it?" Her smile was warm, inviting.

"Really? That's not more than a couple of minutes from my old house, where I grew up."

"Wow, how awesome is that?" Her blue eyes went wide. It was very attractive. Why had he started off like a self-righteous idiot? He shoved one hand deeper into his pocket, wrapping it around the drive. What chance did he have with someone like her? "I didn't mean to act like a jerk. Maybe I can help."

She reached up and touched his hand. "Oh, that would be great." Her fingers were soft and warm. "You think you can fix my car?"

"I can at least look." Work would be there in an hour, but she wouldn't be.

"If you do fix it, I'll buy you dinner, if you're not busy tonight." Her smile and glistening eyes were inviting.

"Dinner? Tonight?"

"Sure, it's the least I could do for a knight in shining armor." She looked almost embarrassed to say it.

"I can't –"

Her hand was on his again. "Come on. It will be fun. We could talk about home."

"No, it's not that. I really –"

"Oh, I'm sorry." She pulled her hand away. "You've got a girlfriend. I should have known."

"No, I don't. I mean not right now." *She's coming on to me and I'm saying no. What's wrong with me?*

She tilted her head a little with the slightest of smiles. "You do like girls, don't you?"

"Yes, of course. I just ah – It can't be tonight. I have to go to work."

"Oh. I'm sorry. What kind of work do you do?"

She was so charming.

"I'm an FBI agent." It sounded like he was bragging, not what he meant.

Her eyes got big. "For real? Maybe you could tell me all about it on our date, I mean during dinner." Her cheeks turned a little red.

How long would it really take to decrypt those files? As long as they are ready by morning. "Pop your hood."

She turned and leaned into the car. "Sure."

He heard the hood release and moved around to the front of the car. Sliding the secondary latch over, he opened the hood.

She came up beside him. She had a fresh scent about her. He breathed it in as he spotted a loose plug.

"There's your problem. A connector came loose." He reached for it and pushed it back in. "Ouch!"

"Did you hurt yourself?"

"No." He pulled back and looked down at the front grille. "Something just poked me, that's all." His hand went over to his right side, closest to the woman.

"Oh, I'm sorry. Is the car fixed now?" She was moving around to the driver's door.

"Should be, go ahead and try it."

The car started up.

He walked around to her window.

"You sure you don't want that dinner tonight? I could meet you at a restaurant. When do you get off work?"

Oh, it hurt to turn her down. "Can we make it tomorrow night, please? I really would like to talk with someone from home."

She looked very disappointed. "You sure you can't put off going in for a little while?"

"No, I wish I could but I have to get to work. I've already stayed too long."

She didn't say anything, but she stared into his eyes for several seconds. "Sure, tomorrow night it is. We can meet at the Olive Garden around seven, the one just up the road."

"Seven it is."

As she drove off, he rubbed his side where something had poked him. It was very tender. Pulling up his shirt revealed a red spot about the size of a quarter. Maybe it was a spider bite.

31

Keeping an eye on the exit of Todd's building, Gabriele checked her dash clock for the fifth time in thirty minutes. It had been long enough for the poison to disable the target. Reaching over, she grabbed her phone and logged into a private node on Homeland's computer system. She needed the security code for Todd's building. She committed it to memory before stepping out of her car.

Her life would have been so much easier if he had come with her. Then she could have hidden his body where it would never be found. Well, that did not matter much now; within a few days the world would be busy with bigger problems.

Grabbing the EMP generator out of the trunk, she headed up the four steps to the apartment building, hitting each camera with an EMP as she went.

Before entering, she peeked through the long, narrow window beside the door. A camera was mounted in the upper left corner of the small lobby, farther away than desirable for the EMP pulse to be effective. She pointed her generator at it and held down the button for a count of twenty and hoped it was long enough.

On entering the lobby, she kept her head down as she slid into the elevator. The cameras inside were situated in such a way as to make walking in from a blind spot impossible. Tomorrow she would tap into the building's security system and erase her image.

She found Todd's apartment. Reaching into her pocket, she pulled out a pair of thin rubber gloves and put them on before tapping on the door. It took three more attempts before she heard movement inside.

As the door opened Todd's pale grayish face showed surprise.

"What are you doing here?" Todd used one hand on the door handle to hold himself steady, while his other hand was pressed against his side.

"I just stopped by to thank you again." She slipped past him and into his apartment, as Todd put out a hand in a weak attempt to stop her.

"How'd you get in the building?" His speech was starting to slur. "How'd you find my apartment?"

"Oh, a nice man let me in and you told me where you lived. Don't you remember?"

He shook his head as his eyes dropped. He was looking at the floor. "No, I would never…" He looked confused.

"Are you feeling okay? You don't look very good." She glanced around his messy living area. A half-eaten sandwich sat on the kitchen table.

"I'm fine, but you need to leave. I've got to get to work." His shoulder dropped against the door edge for support.

Taking a step back toward him, she gave him her sweetest smile. "Here let me help you before you fall into the hall." He swayed, trying to avoid her, but she reached around him and pushed the door closed. "You don't need to go to work tonight. We can stay in and I can take care of you. It will be fun."

"What do you mean? Get out of my home." He tried to reach for the door handle. Before he could, she grabbed his hand and pulled it away. He almost fell, but managed to remain standing.

"Leave? I just got here." She was turning on the charm, but wondered if it was even necessary.

"No, you need to get out, please. You shouldn't be here." He pulled his hand away and tried once more for the door.

He was more determined than she'd expected. "Why do you need to go to work tonight? What is so important to make you want to miss an evening with me?" She moved her face to within a few inches of his.

He pulled back, hitting his head on the wall.

"My work is none of your business. I've got the evidence to solve a murder case." His left hand went down and lightly tapped his pants pocket. Slipping away, he went around her and toward his couch. He weaved as he moved across the floor. The couch was less than ten feet away, but each step he took was slower and farther off course. "I'm call— building secur—"

He faltered. The effort he had put into trying to kick her out was speeding up the process.

"Go ahead." Standing by the door she watched as the poor man stumbled and clutched the window drapes. She rushed toward him and grabbed him around the waist. "Can't have you ruining my day by falling out the window."

"Wha...?" His eyes were glassy, his head wobbled as he worked to free himself from her grip.

She directed him toward the brown couch that was covered with papers and books. She let go of him as he fell into a half sitting, half lying position. He mumbled something that didn't matter to her. She reached into his pocket. The drive was right where he said it was. After slipping it into her own pocket, she started frisking him for his phone. It was not on him.

Standing and moving away from him, she glanced around the room. Hearing a noise behind her, she turned to see Todd sitting upright, looking at her.

"Are you okay?" She moved toward him and dropped to her knees beside the couch. "You passed out, and I was so worried about you."

"What are you still doing here? I told you to leave."

The man had more resilience than she gave him credit for. "I know, and I was about to leave when you passed out. I couldn't just leave you on the floor. You need a doctor. Where's your phone? I'll call one for you."

He somehow made it to a standing position. "Leave. I'm calling—" He stopped and looked around. "Phone, where is my phone?"

"I don't know. I was hoping—"

He half pushed her aside while using her as a prop. "Move." He started for the dining table.

She turned to see the phone beside his half eaten sandwich. Sticking one leg in front of his, she pushed him forward. He tumbled, crashing into a chair, then let out a moan as his body hit the floor. He tried once more to get up before his body relaxed.

Stepping over him, Gabriele picked up the phone, opened the

back and removed the battery. She placed both the phone and the battery in her pocket. The picture of her car did not need to end up in some FBI database. She pulled a small packet from her other pocket and sprinkled the tiniest amount of its contents on the meat he had been eating.

Stepping back, she dropped next to him and checked his pulse. It was still there but weak and slow. His eyes were open and blank. His skin was a pasty white. Sweat collected in small droplets on his forehead. She carefully picked up his head and turned his face toward the kitchen. She did not want to see his dying eyes. Reaching into his pockets again she grabbed his car keys.

The first time she had killed a man she wondered what kind of life she was taking. Was she robbing the world of a great person? Since then, she'd learned that life goes on and people were rarely missed for long.

After moving Todd's car into the parking space he had wanted so dearly, she went back to the apartment and returned the keys to the lifeless body before leaving.

32

Friday

The coffee was not fulfilling its promise to Sara. She mindlessly entered her office as she glanced at Todd's empty seat. She could use him today. She needed someone to talk to. Her muscles were sore. She had not slept well. She plopped into her desk chair.

Turning on the monitor, she leaned her elbows against the table, her head in her hands. She rubbed her eyes as the nightmares from the night before ran through her mind. Destroying the life of the man who had hurt her should have made her feel great. But she wasn't feeling great. She was feeling guilty.

All the commitments she had made to God seemed so hollow now. She had failed her first real test. *What's wrong with me?* She knew it was God's job to decide when and who He punished, not man's, and most definitely not hers.

So now she had one job to do, to set things right. She needed to undo the damage she had done yesterday and leave things up to God. If God wanted to hurt John Motova He would. And she really hoped He would.

She logged in and brought up a window. As she started to type in the command to hide her work, she wondered if even this was wrong. But if she did it in the open it would show up in the Bureau's database, and what purpose would that serve but to land her back in jail?

"Where's Todd?"

Her hands shook as her heart froze. Was she caught?

She peeked over her shoulder to see Faircloth standing in the door of her office. How long had he been there?

Closing the window, she swiveled her chair around to face him. "What was that?"

"I asked you where Todd is. Have you seen him this morning?"

His seat was still empty, but she thought it should be. "Isn't he in Texas with your team?"

Faircloth leaned into the office a little, emphasizing each word. "If he were, I wouldn't be here looking for him." He glanced at Todd's desk, and his demeanor became harder. It was clear his mind was fighting with itself. "He hasn't been in today?"

"Not that I know of. I haven't seen him." Her mind kept going back to the work she had started before the interruption.

"Can you tell if he's been in at all in the last twelve hours?"

She looked at Todd's desk again. "That's the way his desk was when he left for Texas. But I can check his log file if you need to know absolutely."

Faircloth hit the side of his fist against the doorframe. "Of course I need to know absolutely! Why else would I be asking?"

Her body twitched at Faircloth's show of frustration. Her muscles tensed and her jaw clenched. She turned back toward her computer, hoping he didn't see her reaction, and in a few seconds brought up the log. She informed Faircloth that the last entry for Todd was from yesterday morning.

"We need to find him ASAP. He has a jump drive that we think has the same files as those removed from the senator's computer." He glared at Sara. "Do you have his home number?"

"I have his cell number."

"Call him. Find out where he's at. I need him in here pronto."

Anything to get this jerk out of here. Sara grabbed her phone and hit Todd's number. It went straight to voicemail. She left a message.

"Locate his phone."

"I don't have the authority—"

Faircloth stepped closer, red faced and nostrils flared. Sara pushed further into her chair. "You're telling me that after two years in this office you can't run a trace on a phone?" His breath reeked.

There is plenty of room in here, he doesn't need to crowd me. "I don't have clearance–"

"I don't give a hoot about some clearance. Can you do this one simple task or not?"

She stared hard at Faircloth. He was telling her to break the rules again. "Yes, just give me a minute." Sara turned to her computer and brought up a new window. Every muscle in her back grew tense as she reminded herself again and again that Faircloth was one of the good guys. Logging in as Todd, she ran a search on his phone. The room grew hot during the fifteen seconds it took for her system to declare it was unable to locate his phone within the Denver area.

"Are you sure he made it back last night?" *That came out wrong, but Faircloth has no right to talk down to me.*

"Of course I'm sure." His voice filled the small room.

"His phone must be off," Sara volunteered.

"There's a way to turn it on and find it, even if it's off. Do it."

"But–"

"Do it and stop giving me reasons why you can't perform your job." With each word his voice rose and he took a half step closer to Sara.

She would do it, but not because Faircloth was giving her orders. She would do it for Todd. He was her friend. She entered the commands to turn on his phone and ping it for confirmation. The signal did not bounce back. "It's either out of reach or the battery's dead." She spun back around to see Faircloth hit the doorframe again and say a few choice words about never trusting something so important to someone like Todd as he left the room.

Todd has issues, but he is very trustworthy.

Sara stared at the door for several seconds before standing to stretch her back muscles. She began to walk slowly in a small circle. Faircloth had been way over the top and it had brought back old emotions, ones she never wanted to feel again. She placed her hands on her hips as she circled. *Does he think I have some magical way to know where Todd is?* She dropped her hands and made several fists, relaxing her hands in between each one. Does he imagine coming down on me like that will make Todd suddenly appear? Shaking the last bits of anxiety out of her hands and arms, she dropped back into her seat and started her own search for Todd.

———

"Wait in the break room, I'll only be a minute." Alex had said that twenty minutes ago.

Really?

Kai couldn't believe a thing Alex said. Or was it *Julie or Gabriele*?

The lady she had thought of as a friend was anything but. Pacing around the room wasn't helping, but Kai couldn't sit still. *What was Alex up to?*

Seven steps to the door and seven steps back to the coffeemaker.

Study how you act when things are going well, and use that to hide what you know. More of her father's wisdom. A little late now.

Alex had said she would be in with Hewitt and Landry, discussing classified material. *Yeah, right. Maybe they are talking about how to get rid of me since I have not been able to decrypt those files. Or maybe she knows I was in her room.*

That would mean Landry was part of whatever Alex is involved in. That's crazy. How could someone that high up in Homeland be—be what? A terrorist? Impossible.

The answers were not in this room. And finding them could cost her her life.

I may be dead already.

Kai headed out of the snack area and turned deeper into the building, slowing as she approached her objective. The door was closed. She took a quiet peek back before stopping just outside Landry's door. A female voice could be heard on the other side.

"There is no trace of my having been in his apartment. It will look as if he died of food poisoning, rancid meat to be exact." The voice lacked its southern charm.

"That is not the real problem you have forced us to face. Your operation was poorly executed and therefore dangerous to the success of our objective." *Landry*, but with a slight French accent.

None of them are who they say they are.

"If we had found the drive in Texas before the FBI got there, we wouldn't have needed Gabriele's help." It was Hewitt.

"I left you down there to find it and you failed."

Landry's voice stayed even, as Hewitt's increased with the insult.

"And what did you expect me to do? Kill the rest of the team by myself? That would have surely tipped our hand."

Kai moved in a little closer as she waited for a response.

"I see I should have stayed behind with you. Then we would not be in this situation."

"We don't have a situation." Alex spat out the words. "We have a dead FBI agent and I have the drive you want."

"It will not take them long to figure out that he was murdered. As soon as they realize the jump drive is missing, they will know it was murder regardless of how you tried to cover it up. I want you to plant evidence leading them to someone else."

The room on the other side of the door was quiet for several seconds before Hewitt disrupted the silence. "Who are we talking about?"

"One person on the FBI team is much smarter than management gives her credit for." Landry's voice took on an oily sound. Kai felt slimy just listening as the conversation continued.

"I'm listening. Who would you like me to sic the FBI on?" Alex purred.

"With Jenkins out of the way, the FBI has only one resource left who can create problems for our teams. Sara Beckwith has the computer skills to track us down. Fortunately, you have already laid the groundwork for us. Since Sara's test destroyed the evidence from the senator's computer, she is already suspect."

Hewitt interrupted. "She can't be that smart. Alex had no problem fooling her."

"She may not have great people skills, however her computer skills are extraordinary, and that is where I believe we are the most vulnerable. Computers leave trails that the right person can follow." Landry spoke evenly.

"I have made sure everything we have done is untraceable," Hewitt objected.

"And yet, Ryan Blinder followed the trail that you supposedly hid. How is that possible?"

Silence.

"With the right evidence, they will believe Sara is Jenkins' murderer as well as their leak," Landry continued.

Sara? My Sara?

The silence lasted several seconds before Alex answered. "I can do that, but it will cost you extra."

"It always does with you." Landry was irritated.

"What kind of evidence do you believe is needed, dear sir?" The clipped German accent had been replaced with the familiar southern accent.

This woman thinks this is all a game. Kai glanced around the hall again before moving her ear back against the door.

"The FBI needs to find confidential files in her possession, files covering their Middle Eastern operations. Jonas will send them to you."

"I can plant the files on her system. — As for framing her for Jenkins' murder, I'll put a picture or two of Sara on the security cameras from Jenkin's apartment. Then I will find an eyewitness who saw her at his apartment last night." Alex sounded proud of herself.

"That will do. And I want her to know about the evidence before she is arrested."

"Why? That will give her a chance to run."

"I am counting on her to evade capture. The longer the pursuit, the more resources the FBI will put on the chase and the less chance they will discover what we are up to. The timing of her escape must be handled correctly."

"For this to work the way you want, I will need to monitor Sara's whereabouts at all times. And I will need to know the right time to feed the information to the FBI and to Sara."

Alex is a snake.

"Use whatever resources you need. Our time is growing short. We cannot afford any mistakes at this late date," Landry instructed.

"Rest assured, I will make it happen. The cost is twenty grand in Euros, plus the money for killing Jenkins. American money will lose its value very soon."

What? Why?

"You will be paid for your work. However; if you fail me I will have Jonas end your life. Do you understand the conditions?"

"I was not hired to fail, and I won't."

"You are awfully arrogant."

"I have retrieved the jump drive. I have destroyed the hard drive from the senator's computer. I have Kai close to decrypting our copies of the files. When I fail you can question my attitude, but until then it's not arrogance. It's fact."

Kai pressed her ear harder against the door.

"And where is this jump drive?" Landry was becoming impatient.

"When I see the money transfer, you will see the drive."

"Twenty thousand will be deposited in your account tonight."

"Deposit the full fifty."

"Quoi? Votre prix est trop cher." Landry spat.

Hewitt translated. "He said your price is too high."

"Ich weiß. Don't you think I can understand his barbaric language?"

"French is not a barbaric language. We do not speak with the sounds of the gutter."

So Landry does have emotions.

"No, you speak with your noses—"

"Enough." Landry stopped the degrading conversation. "I will not pay the full amount until the job is complete."

"I killed an FBI agent with less than three hours' notice. I will plant evidence to point to Sara and make her run. This will also be done without the proper time to prepare. If you feel my price is too high, you may bid the latter work out and only pay me thirty for Jenkins' death, and I will leave this doomed nation. But if you want the rest of the work done, it is another twenty, making the total fifty."

The room was silent as Kai waited for an answer.

"I have already agreed to the fifty, however; you will not receive your final payment, until this mission is complete."

"When those devices of yours go off, every bank in the world will freeze all major transactions."

"I am impressed that you are so understanding of international economics, but it is an insult to suggest I do not honor my commitments. Thirty thousand Euros will be deposited in your account tonight. In the morning, I expect to see the drive on my desk. As for the rest of your payment, I will personally ensure it will be in your account before you leave that morning. But I will not pay you for work you have not yet done."

What morning? What are they planning that would shut down the banks?

"Fine. I will get right on it," Alex grudgingly agreed.

Kai heard movement. The meeting was over and she needed to get out of there fast.

As quietly as she could, she rushed down the hall. As she was rounding the corner, a door opened behind her.

Tony ran traces on Sara's computer activities for the last week. He also looked for any of Todd's activities that had timing overlap problems. When he was done, he couldn't figure out what Sara was up to. Things weren't adding up the way they should. On two separate occasions, a computer she was logged into had a window with Todd's login. That in itself was not a problem. Many times, when two software writers were working on the same project, this happened. The problem was twofold. First, there were no active team projects while the senator's murder investigation was underway. Second, Todd was logged in at a system in a different part of the building from where Sara was logged in and both windows showed activities at the same time. That should not happen.

It was obvious Sara was using Todd's login to look up information she wouldn't normally have access to. She had tracked down information on a Brian Halter, and had added his name to the DEA watch list for possible drug manufacturers.

Why would she do that?

Running a background check on Mr. Halter, Tony found his history only went back six years.

Who was he before he became Brian Halter?

It did not take long to find out who he really was. The new identity setup was sloppy. Before he became Halter, he was John Motova, a Russian.

If Sara was working with terrorists, why bring attention to Motova?

If he was a terrorist, then doing nothing would benefit him the most. Her actions could only serve to hurt him. This made no sense whatsoever.

To find the answer, more digging was needed. After three more hours, he felt he was finally getting somewhere. Sara had set up a very secure tunneling system to hide her work. During that time, she poked around in Halter's/Motova's company quite a bit and looked into his bank accounts.

Was someone paying her to find out about Motova and his company? Did she have a hunch about him?

After a very long morning, Tony could only prove that Sara had broken a few laws by wrongfully using government resources. That would put her back in jail, but these were not terrorist activities. There had to be more.

―――――

Swinging by the locker room, Kai grabbed her pack. This place was not Homeland Security. It was a nest of terrorists. A place for them to hide out until they could wreak destruction on America. It was time to save her own skin and get out of there. She was twenty feet from freedom when she heard the voice. "Where are you headed?"

Kia turned but kept walking backwards. "Ah, just out front to stretch my legs."

Alex eyed her shoulder. "With your bag?"

Kai stopped. She was caught if she did not come up with a believable lie. The door was just behind her, only a few feet away. The sunlight was coming in and hitting the floor, inviting her to run. Could she make it? *And go where?* "You were in a meeting and I didn't know how long it would last. It's past lunch time and I'm hungry. I thought I'd head out for some food."

Alex stared into Kai's eyes.

She doesn't believe me.

Did she see me in the hall?

Come on, say something, anything.

Alex gave a slight smile. "Were you going to walk?"

"Yeah, the fast food places aren't too far away."

"I'm sorry, but we have a long day ahead of us. We may be here late, and taking time for a long lunch is not possible. It'd be better if we just ate in the cafeteria."

This was the sweet Alex talking, the Dr. Jekyll. In the meeting she had been Mr. Hyde.

"Work late on a Friday night?"

"You need to get those files decrypted. I thought it would be a piece of cake for you once you got the right software."

"Me too, but I'm still having problems." *And I will never decrypt them for you or any of your co-terrorist buddies.*

"Staying late tonight might help you then."

33

Todd, where are you? First, let's make sure you actually made it back to Colorado. I can get the flight information from his email.

Using his login, Sara checked Todd's inbox. An unread message contained his flight number. It indicated a landing time in DIA of 5:40 P.M.

She tapped into the airline's system. The flight had touched down five minutes early, but had to wait for a gate. The plane pulled up to the gate a few minutes later. The airline manifest confirmed Todd had checked in at the gate at DFW.

So he got on.

Someone else could have used his ticket.

I doubt it, but crazier things have happened.

As with every commercial airport in America, cameras at DIA were prolific. The TSA database had images for the jetway on Gate C47, Todd's point of debarkation. His gate was about as far away from the terminal as a person could get. The footage showed he had gotten off the plane ahead of most of the pack. Using the multitude of cameras, Sara followed Todd's path through the airport, onto the underground train and out to his car. Everything looked normal. It did not appear anyone was following him.

The last image she inspected was him paying the parking fee. Unless someone was lying flat on the floor, he was alone.

Did he head for home or try to come here?

She checked the FBI's database for those entering and leaving the site after hours. Agent Jenkins' name did not appear on the list.

Home it is.

She hacked into his apartment building security. This was illegal without cause, but Faircloth had already given her permission, sort of.

———

Jonas was true to his word. The files showed up on Alex's system within minutes.

So, what kind of evidence did they give me?

Alex trusted Jonas to a point. He would be up front with her as long as it didn't cost him much. But that Frenchman, she didn't trust him at all.

The first file contained pictures and dossiers of eight CIA agents who were or had been working in the Middle East. The second file had information on Muslim informants in the same area. File number three listed logins, passwords and IP addresses for Israeli Military defense systems.

How in the world did Jonas get these?

This was more than enough to put Sara or anyone else away for an eternity for treason. But Alex had to make Sara run so she would not have a chance to defend herself. And to make sure she ran, there had to be proof that Sara killed Todd.

Alex tapped into Todd's apartment building security system to replace her picture with Sara's. But when she went into the directory to find the footage from the day before, she saw that the file was already open. Someone else was viewing it.

A trace led to the FBI. Someone at the bureau was on top of it. Was she busted?

Probably not. They are just looking for Todd since he did not show up for work.

Alex waited for the file to close. Once closed, she edited the file, putting Sara's face in place of her own. After closing it, she modified the timestamp to the day before.

Alex moved on to motive. Why would sweet little Sara kill her friend? Let's make it look like he found out that she had purposely destroyed the senator's hard drive and threatened to expose her. If she was the leak, she couldn't let him get away with that.

Going to Sara's computer in the FBI's computer lab, Alex changed the log file and timestamp, to show that Sara had entered values that she knew would destroy the senator's hard drive. This proved it was done intentionally. Going over to Todd's computer, she placed a copy of the incriminating log file there as well. She then created an email from Todd to Agents Stover and Booker with the log file as an attachment. Finally, she moved the email to the trash bin, making it look like Sara had hacked into Todd's computer and deleted the file before he could send it. Motive established.

Now, how to best use the files that Jonas had sent her. First, she encrypted the files. No one would believe that Sara had sensitive information like this without it being encrypted. She then pulled out a jump drive and loaded the evidence on it. As she envisioned how this would all play out, she thought about how much trouble they were having decrypting the files they had taken from the senator. She decided to make sure the FBI did not waste too much time decrypting the files she had just loaded. She created a file of her own, one she knew would get everyone's attention. Then she encrypted it with the simplest encryption program she had and added it to the other files on the drive. She would place the jump drive in Sara's apartment later.

Alex sat back, satisfied with her work. She noticed Kai was quiet. Not silently working, but completely quiet, no clicking from fingers bouncing around the keyboard, nothing.

Is she upset about having to work late?

"Having trouble with the new software?"

Silence.

"Kai." Alex leaned forward and tapped the young woman's shoulder.

"What?" She answered, but did not turn her head.

"I asked if you were having any problems. What's wrong with you?"

Kai turned. "Sorry, I was reading something. I just discovered that there is a way to run batch jobs with this program. In fact, it says that a batch program is the best way to use a program like this. It's supposed to be self-learning. It takes the results of the last run and uses that for input parameters for the next try. It can make several passes without oversight."

"Did you come up with this so you can get out of working late?"

"That's one benefit. But the program will keep working after we leave. That way, it can run all night, even while we are sleeping. I can swing by here in the morning to see if it was successful. If not, I can start

it again with different parameters. It can work all day tomorrow, too."
Kai gave a big smile.

"What a con. And you just now found this?"

"Yep."

"Big plans for the weekend huh?"

"Not so much. Since I am out here in Colorado I thought I could start training for a marathon. I'd like to get some long runs in tomorrow."

"What is it with runners?"

"It's an addiction."

"Okay, if I can get a few more things done, we can call it a night and take the weekend off."

Alex thought of one more thing to put the last nail in Sara's coffin. She brought up Sara's Homeland file and started going through the images. It only took a few minutes to find the one she needed. It looked as if it could have been taken outside Todd's apartment building. Alex loaded it onto a spare phone that could not be traced to her.

———

"How concerned should I be that Todd has not shown up today?" Faircloth stood in the doorway of Lamar's office and gave him a rundown of the morning.

Lamar quickly stood. "What? Todd is missing?"

"Yes. He returned to Colorado last night, but never showed up for work."

"Todd's a very reliable agent. Him not showing up to work last night is reason enough to start looking for him. Have you sent someone by his apartment yet? Has anyone checked accident reports? Todd always comes to work, even if he's sick."

"I sent a team over to Jenkins's apartment a few minutes ago. They'll call if they find something," Faircloth explained.

"Someone should have told me about this first thing this morning." Lamar pulled out his phone.

"Who are you calling?" Faircloth wanted to know.

"I want to see if Sara knows anything about Todd's whereabouts." Lamar listened to the phone ringing on the other end.

Faircloth's phone buzzed as the same time. After he answered he covered the mouthpiece and said to Lamar, "My team is going in now.

It will be just a minute."

Lamar nodded as he spoke to Sara. She told him that she had verified that Todd arrived in Denver and went straight to his apartment last night. She did not see any indication that he had left the apartment.

"We have a team over there right now. I'll let you know what they find." He ended the call and asked Faircloth to put his phone on speaker. Faircloth held it where both of them could listen in.

"Agent Faircloth, we found a body in the apartment. It's Agent Jenkins."

———

"Tony, this is Lisa."

Using her first name could only mean bad news was coming. "*Yes*, Lisa."

"We just received word that your friend and co-worker, Todd, died last night."

"What? How?" *Todd? Dead? No way.*

Her voice was easygoing. "At this point, we do not know. The police at the scene said there was no sign of a struggle or forced entry."

"You're telling me he just got sick and died?" *I don't believe it.*

"I'm not telling you anything like that. Someone may want us to believe that, but his death is too convenient. I'm having it treated as a murder."

"I'm coming in. I can help."

Her response was quick and decisive. "No, you stay right where I put you. Until proven otherwise, I'm considering his death to be connected to the senator's murder."

"Why?"

"He returned from Texas last night with a jump drive that he believed contained the files that we have been working to recover from the senator's computer. This was our first real break in the case, and I can't believe that he just happened to die at this time."

"I am the best person to look over those files. I need to be there."

"No, the longer we work on this case, the more I believe all of this is tied strongly to a leak within the Bureau."

"Exactly. And with Todd gone, and with Sara's low clearance, you need me there."

"I need you right where you are. You can do far more if no one knows you are looking into their activities."

"But –"

"I will copy you on everything we find out. Stay put for now."

34

The first two agents Faircloth had sent to Todd's apartment were busily taking pictures of the scene as Kent and Chris walked in the door. They had left Texas early in the morning, and upon arrival at the airport were instructed to head straight to Todd's apartment. They had to step around several Denver police officers and the county coroner to reach Faircloth. Kent complained about too many cooks in the kitchen.

"We need to find that jump drive, ASAP!" Faircloth's voice was a half notch below a yell as he impatiently paced around the tiny room.

Faircloth stopped long enough to look down at the coroner who was taking pictures of the body as he spoke. "As soon as he gives permission to move the body, go through Todd's pockets."

Chris nodded his head. "Do we have any idea how Todd died?"

"I cannot see any blood or obvious damage done to his body. But the coroner will not speculate on the cause of death. We will have to wait until Dr. Carpenter has a chance to examine the body and Elle has a chance to do all of the bloodwork."

Chris looked down at Todd. He experienced a sharp pang at seeing a team member and friend dead on the floor. It looked like the coroner was ready to move the body. Chris knelt down to see if he could check Todd's pockets.

The man was reluctant to let anyone touch the body, but agreed to go through the pockets in search of the jump drive himself. It only took a few moments for the coroner to confirm that there wasn't a jump drive in his pockets or anywhere else on the dead agent.

Faircloth was clearly frustrated. "I want you to search every nook and cranny, every possible place in Todd's apartment, car, and in the path leading from his car to his home, any place that Todd may have dropped the jump drive. Until I see proof to the contrary, I'm treating this as a murder and a theft."

After an hour they came up empty. Faircloth slammed his hand against the wall. He took a deep breath to calm himself and decided to take a different approach. Turning back toward Kent and Chris he said, "Ok. There is not much more we can do here. I want you two to get back to the office ASAP and find out how the murderer could have learned that Todd had the jump drive. We have a big leak somewhere. Someone must be monitoring our reports. So whatever you find, I do not want you to send it to me via the computer system. You call me, or you come talk to me in person. Until we close this hole, we need to make sure all classified information on this case is kept out of our electronic networks."

"Wouldn't Sara be better at that? I mean, if someone is in our systems, she would be the one to find them," Kent responded.

"You can work with her, but I want someone I can fully trust overseeing this, and that means someone in my department."

———

Feeling his phone vibrate, Tony slipped it out of his pocket. He didn't need to check the caller ID, as only one person would be calling him at this number. "Yes, Agent Booker."

"I've got more data for you on Todd's murder."

"Are we sure it's murder, or is that still an assumption?" Agents often got killed in the line of duty, but not agents like Todd.

"I am operating under the assumption that it is murder. His death is just too convenient for the terrorists." Booker relayed the information she'd received from Faircloth.

"Assuming that this was murder, how could the killer have known that Todd had the jump drive in the first place?"

"They are obviously monitoring our computer systems. And Sara is the perfect candidate to be able to tap into anybody's computer anywhere onsite. Give me an update on what you've found out about her."

"I found some questionable activities on Sara's part. I just sent you a report."

"No, don't send anything electronically for now. I will have to delete it immediately."

Tony heard the clicking of her keyboard while he waited for her to come back. "It's been removed. Now tell me what it said."

He informed her about Sara's actions and what she had done to Brian Halter/John Motova.

"And she did this right under our noses, without raising any red flags on our systems?"

"Yes, she's good at hiding her work."

"Whether she's behind Todd's death or not, she will have to answer for this."

———

After learning about Todd's death, Sara said she was not feeling well, so Lamar had sent her home to get some rest. Then he called Derry to let him know what was going on. Now Derry pondered what he'd say to Sara as he waited for her on the front stoop of his home.

Seeing her car coming up the road, Derry moved to meet her at the curb. "I heard about Todd. I'm so sorry." He reached out to her but she pushed past him.

"Yeah, I'm sure it's all over the news." She moved toward the front door of the Knights' home, her head down and her tone a mix of anger and determination.

"Lamar called. He asked me to check on you." Derry hurried to stay up with her.

She didn't slow down or look back. "I'm fine and I hope you boys had a nice chat about me. I'm just here to grab a quick bite and a change of clothes." Reaching the front door, she turned to him. "I don't think I can join you and the Knights for movie night tonight."

Of course not. He reached out to her again. "I know. I just wanted to make sure you're okay. You know I'm here if you want to talk, or even if you don't."

She looked past Derry, into the nothingness of green grass that spanned the distance between the house and the road. "I don't know who's behind this, but I'm going to find them. They can't get away with killing Todd. He never hurt anyone." A tear made its way down her cheek and hung on her chin before she wiped it away.

Derry tenderly held her face and wiped more tears away with his thumb.

Other than Lamar, Todd was the closest thing to a friend she had at the Bureau. Sara often told Derry how much she enjoyed working with Todd. He never brought up her criminal past or the reasons she worked at the FBI. To him, she was a colleague, someone to compete with, to talk with, someone who understood him when he went on and on about computers. She bushed Derry's hand away and reached for the door handle.

"Honey, please don't shut me out. I'm here to listen, to give you a shoulder to cry on."

She released the handle. Slowly, she looked up at him as the dam broke. Her arms went around him and she buried her face in his chest. He pulled her in tight.

"Why would anyone want to hurt him?"

He held her as she cried herself out. Finally, he asked, "I know you can't tell me who, but do they have any leads that you know of?"

Keeping her head against his chest, she murmured, "Not really. I need to get back and help them look for the murderer."

"You're helping?"

"I'm just doing some of the computer stuff."

Sliding his hands down her arms, he took hold of her fingers. He kissed the top of her head. "I'll be praying for you."

"Thank you. We really need God's help on this." She pulled away. "*I* need His help."

"You know I will always be there for you, no matter what. I love you more than you can imagine."

She glanced at his shirt. "I got you all wet." She wiped her eyes with the heels of her hands before brushing her fingers across the wet area of his shirt. "I look terrible right now. I need to get cleaned up and get back to work."

———

After a change of clothes and a light snack, Sara headed back to the office. She had not seen the crime photos from Todd's apartment, but her mind continued to flash imagined images of his dead body. The thought of him lying dead on his apartment floor made the acid in her stomach churn with promises of regret for the little snack she had eaten. Twice she pulled to the side of the road to wait for the fight inside her to settle down. Each time, her resolve to find Todd's killer increased. No matter what the cost or how many rules she had to break, this person would be found.

The FBI building was in sight when her phone sang Lamar's song. She pulled through the stoplight and to the side of the road before answering. "I'm on my way back in. I'll be there in a few minutes." Her strength was gone. She had trouble doing the simple task of holding the phone steady next to her ear.

"Where are you right now?"

"Just down the road, close to Sam's Club. I just went home to clean up a little. Why? Did something come up?" She switched hands. That was better.

"You need to come straight to my office when you get here." His voice was cold and hard. Losing one of his men was difficult, the poor man. Tears formed in her eyes.

"I'll be there in three minutes. What's going on?" She brushed the wet away.

"I need to talk to you before Faircloth gets ahold of you. It's about—just come straight to my office. Better yet, I will meet you at the entrance."

She shifted the car to park. "Lamar, what is this about? Does this have anything to do with the work I did this morning to look for Todd?" His tone wasn't right.

"We are looking into anything out of the ordinary."

Just great. With everything else going on, someone's raising a stink about me doing an illegal search for Todd's phone? "I had Faircloth's permission, no, his orders, to use Todd's account this morning. If he's trying to burn me over that—"

"I will see you in the lobby in three minutes. I will apprise you of the full extent of the allegations then."

Did Faircloth or someone else find out about the money? I should have moved it back, or better yet never taken it to begin with. I am so stupid. She hit the steering wheel with her fist. "Look, once we find Todd's killer, I'll—" *Don't say too much.* "—answer any questions you or Agent Faircloth have." *But if they know about the money I took, no way would they let me work on Todd's murder.* She pushed her hair back off her forehead as she slouched down in her seat. *How much could they know? I covered my tracks. Did I miss something?* The inside of the car was getting hot. She turned the air up.

"Just get in here right now."

She had heard this tone before, but never towards her.

"Look,—"

"Get in here immediately."

"Why?"

"Sara, I am in your corner, as always, but I have to let the system work. You asking questions and not coming in, is only going against you." He paused for a second, "See you downstairs in three."

A large truck blasted its horn as it went around her into the Sam's Club parking area. "But—." She pulled the phone away and looked at the screen. He had ended the call.

She tossed the phone on the passenger's seat. Tears were flowing now, making it hard to see. These idiots at the Bureau are so worried about the dumbest things. Jerks.

It has to be about the money. So now they want to question me about moving someone's money when Todd is lying on some cold steel table. It's so wrong. I'll give the money back. I was going to anyway.

She reached for the wheel as the muscles in her right hand shook. She needed something more to sustain her than the small snack she had eaten at home. She reached in her glovebox and pulled out a nut filled energy bar. Lamar would have to wait two minutes. She opened it and took a few bites. Soon she was feeling better. As she munched, she watched the evening shoppers at Sam's, wondering if any of them had lost a good friend to murder.

Ignorance is bliss.

Finishing the last bite, she shoved the wrapper down between the seat and the console. She'd clean it out later, she told herself. She put the car into drive as her phone chimed. Keeping her foot on the brake, she read her text.

`The FBI knows you killed Agent Todd Jenkins.`

What? She stared at the crazy message. What kind of sick joke is this? She checked to see who sent it. It came from a five-five-five number, a fake.

She put the car back in park and sent a response.

This is a sick deranged joke, and I don't think it is very funny.

This is not a joke. Evidence has been found to prove it.

Who are you? What are you talking about?

The response came immediately but didn't answer her question.

Someone saw you at Todd's apartment last night. They know you killed him.

I couldn't kill Todd. This idiot is making— Lamar's voice echoed in her head. *Get in here immediately.* It wasn't about the money she took. The screen blurred as tears ran again. *How could anyone think I would hurt Todd? He's my friend.* She typed in a response.

I was home last night, and I have a witness. No one would believe I could ever hurt Todd.

Your boyfriend is not a credible witness. They have a picture of you outside Todd's apartment.

This person had an answer for everything.

How? That's impossible. I wasn't there.

It had to be a guess about Derry. She stopped typing. She knew how easily pictures could be changed and how much the police believed in them.

They have a witness that says you were fighting with Todd. They have a picture of you there.

This is crazy, the whole world is going crazy. Sara stopped to think. Who would do this to me? And why?

Who are you? Why are you saying this?

It does not matter who I am. Here is the proof that was sent to your boss in the last hour.

Two images came onto the screen. The first was an image of her and Todd talking outside of his building. It was a picture that someone had taken, but she didn't know when, certainly not last night. A second image was a police report. Zooming in, she read a detailed account from a neighbor who claimed she and Todd were outside his building arguing. The person heard them yelling and was worried about the girl's safety and took the picture just in case.

Who is this? And how did you get my number?

She did not get a response. Whoever this was, had made a mistake. She would show all of this to Lamar. He would see it was a set up. She went to save the pictures but could not find them. All of the text messages were gone.

This person's good.

Her phone sung Lamar's tune again. She answered. "Sorry, I had to stop and eat something."

"You promised me you would be here in three minutes. That was ten minutes ago. Where are you?" His tone was stern.

"I got sick and had to eat something. I'll be right there."

"You had better be."

"Is this about Todd's murder? Is someone saying I killed him?"

"You need to come in right now. Faircloth has some questions about your whereabouts last night."

This can't be happening. "Look, I was with Derry last night. You can ask him."

"I'm not part of this investigation right now, but you need to get in here right away. Faircloth has a few questions to ask you and the longer you take to get here the worse it will look."

The streets, buildings, and cars around her started to move on their own. Her mind fought to keep the world stationary. "I'll be there in five minutes."

"You said three, make it three." The line went dead.

She knew she was being framed. But how could she prove it? She went back to the text message screen and searched. Nothing. No proof anyone contacted her. *Why are they after me? And who is this person who can send messages and have them disappear that fast? Who wants me in jail?*

It did not matter. She knew this type of game and she could prove her innocence, given the time and resources. Only one problem. She doubted the FBI would give her the time and resources she would need when they believed she had killed an FBI agent.

No. Someone had tied this case up into a nice, neat, little, package.

She felt sick. She looked so guilty.

Would jail be so bad?

That's if she was lucky enough to get jail. *This is Colorado and they have the death penalty.*

Her nice clean little life was over. Everything she had ever wanted was right there, just out of reach. Why did she even think she deserved a good future? Tears flowed, as her chin quivered. *Good bye.* She was leaving it all behind, friends, Derry, a good job, and God.

Would God go with me into hiding? He went with the Israelites when they went into exile.

Putting the car in drive, she immediately started regretting what she was about to do. With one quick glance over her shoulder, she pulled out into traffic. Coming to the entrance to the Sam's parking lot she pulled in, turned around and headed away from the FBI building. Another failed test.

35

John Motova entered the abandoned and mostly empty grocery store on the edge of Detroit, a dying city with too many unused buildings to monitor. The police had their hands full. Increased criminal activity and high unemployment rates went hand in hand, and there was little hope of improvement.

He looked around. Men were working at different tasks, all toward the same final goal. His dream was becoming reality, and soon the world would know.

His wife's cousin, Omar Rostislav, sat and watched. Rostislav was the trainer for much of the work. John approached him. "Where is Nasir?" The news John possessed could jeopardize this operation.

"He is over there, in the middle of a meeting. He does not want to be bothered right now. But you are forgetting something. Where is my greeting?"

John had spent too many years in America, and his mind was on the mission, not family. "Omar, I am so sorry." John gave him the traditional Russian greeting, a hug with a light kiss near each cheek.

"It is good to see a face I know. These men you have joined with are not like us. They are cold, heartless."

"They are doing the will of Allah. That is not heartless." To the casual observer these men may have seemed cold, but John knew them to be true believers. And one could not have the type of dedication this work required without a burning love for Allah and his one true prophet, Mohammed.

"If you say so. Your wife told me to tell you, hello."

"You talked with her?" John had sent his wife back to her childhood home in southern Russia, close to the Ukrainian border. After this project was over, he planned to join her there. "Is she okay?"

"I stopped by for a short visit on my way out of the country. She told me your sons refused to leave America."

John glanced at Nasir once again. The meeting was filled with hushed voices. He turned back to Rostislav. "They wanted to stay and profit from the chaos that will be coming. They have become capitalists of the lowest kind. They feed off of others' troubles. They are lost to me and to Allah." He spat on the ground, a sign saying his two boys were dead to him.

"I am sorry to hear this. How do they plan on making this money?"

John noticed the twinkle in his cousin's eye. He stared up at the large, godless Russian. "Are you hoping to profit from our work, too?" Rostislav was a pig of a man, but he was family.

"Why not? Is it wrong to take money from those about to die?"

John shook his head. "Allah does not want us to punish this godless nation for personal gain, but to bring them to the one true belief." He needed to talk with Nasir and this interruption was taking up too much of his time. "And do not let Nasir hear you talk like this, or you will die with the others." John looked down at the floor covered with trash and muddy footprints. "If that happens, my wife would never forgive me." Looking back up, he forced a smile.

"When did you become such a zealot? You were not always like this." Rostislav was becoming uncomfortable.

He was right. Up until a few years ago, all John cared about was the moment. He had no thoughts of the future or what would happen if he died. His boys had learned that lesson all too well. Live for the day.

"Is it so hard to believe I have found the true path?"

Rostislav shook his head as he stepped back. "You are just like *them*." It sounded dirty coming out of his mouth.

"Maybe you should learn from *them*. Your life would finally have meaning."

"It has meaning. I am being well paid to teach your friends how to destroy this great country. Money is all the meaning I need."

John could not believe that his own blood would kill millions for a few thousand dollars. To kill for Allah was divine, to kill for revenge was acceptable, but to kill for money was horrifying, a sin that required death. He needed to get away from this worm before he regretted bringing him in on this project. "You need to get back to your training, and I need to talk with Nasir."

Rostislav shrugged and headed toward a large table where one man was working. John walked toward Nasir.

"Excuse me, sir, but may I have a word with you?"

"I am in an important meeting. Can it not wait?"

"The matter may affect the outcome of our mission."

Nasir stepped closer. "What is it?" Clearly he did not like the interruption.

"It is a private matter."

Nasir looked him full in the face. He stared for so long, John began to wonder if he had made a mistake. "This way." Nasir nodded his head.

The two left the group and walked to a corner of the large room. "It is almost evening prayer time. Is there a problem with your formula, this great nerve agent that cannot be detected?"

Nasir always talked down to John, as if Arab believers were better than other followers of the Prophet. "The formula will work as it was delivered to you; however, someone may know of our plans."

Now he had Nasir's attention, "Who? How do you know this?"

"The money is missing. It was transferred out of my accounts." John watched his eyes closely. In Russia, this news was enough to get John killed.

Nasir stared at John for several seconds before answering. "How do I know you did not take it?"

"I have no reason to. I am the one who came to you with the idea of this attack. I put up much of the money we're using. I took out loans against my company and house, to help finance this project. If it were not for me, you wouldn't have a plan. You would still be sitting—"

"Enough. For now, I will believe you. You say someone took the money. How?"

"They hacked into my computer and found the bank account information."

"Why was this information on your computer? Even I know computers are easily attacked."

"To keep my real identity out of this, I used an alias to set up a company. All transactions had to be done over the Internet and I did not want a trail leading to me."

Nasir shook his head. "Why are you so afraid of the Americans knowing who you are? Do you plan to stay here after the attack? That would not be wise."

John hung his head low. "It was to protect my boys."

"You Russians. Things are always about your family, a family that does not believe as you and yet you protect them. Who do you believe took the money?"

"I have a program on my computer to reverse track anyone who taps in."

"But not one to stop them? What did this program show you?"

"The break-in came from the FBI."

"What? Are you sure?" This was the first reaction John had seen from this normally calm man.

"Yes, I think so. They were good, but the program says it came from the FBI Denver office."

"Who inside the FBI could know about you?"

"I don't know. My program could not get past their firewalls."

Nasir looked down, arms crossed, as he paced a few feet away. Looking back at John, he gave an answer. "I have a contact in Denver. I will find out who did this. I will get our money back. And if needed they will die sooner than the others."

36

Why would someone murder Todd? Derry wandered aimlessly in his backyard. *Who would be dumb enough to kill an FBI agent?*

A gust of wind rustled the leaves over his head and shook loose a few small branches from his cottonwood. Picking one up, he tapped it against his leg as he patrolled the grass for answers that weren't there.

Poor Sara. God help her. She has to be falling apart. She's been through enough, Lord. Please, help her through this.

Was God listening? Yes, of course, but would He help?

He knew God was there, at least he knew that in his head. But today he felt alone. His girl was hurting and there was nothing he could do.

The sound of a car pulling up out front made him stop and listen. Was it Sara?

The laughter of a man and woman dashed his hopes.

She shouldn't be working tonight. She is not well enough to take this kind of stress.

Maybe he could stop by her office. Maybe he could convince her to come home and rest.

No. The place will be crazy tonight, and I'd only be in the way. I doubt they would even let me in the building right now.

The theme song to Dragnet piped out of his pocket. He reached for his phone. It was Lamar. His fears for Sara grew.

"Hey big guy, is Sara okay?"

"Where is she?" Lamar sounded rushed.

"At work. She left here about thirty minutes ago. She should be there by now."

"Well she never made it. Did she say—"

Deadly Infiltration

"She was very shaken up. I told her not to go back in. Did you try calling her? Maybe she's hurt or changed her mind about going back to work. She really shouldn't be there right now." Derry headed into his house to grab his keys.

"When did you see her last?"

Derry thought back. "Thirty, maybe forty minutes ago. She was petty torn up."

"What'd she say to you when you saw her?"

Something was not right. Lamar was acting strangely. "Not much, only a little about Todd's murder and how she wanted to find out who did it. Like I said, she's hurting."

"Did she say anything else?"

"No. It was hard to get much out of her. You know how she is when something is really bothering her. Todd was her friend."

There was a pause before Lamar went on. "Was she antsy? In a hurry to get out of there? Acting different?"

"No,— yes. I mean she wanted to get back to work, but that was all. And I've never seen her so shaken up."

"Did she tell you why she went home?"

"To get cleaned up and grab a bite of food. You know how that stuff at the caf—"

"When she left, what did she have with her?"

This has gone far enough, even for Lamar. What's wrong with him? "I don't know. I wasn't paying attention. Her bag, maybe. What does she normally take with her places?"

"That's it? Nothing else?"

"Listen, I said I don't know. I had no reason to take an inventory." Derry, realizing he was giving his phone the death grip, relaxed his hand a little. "Look, if she hasn't made it to work yet, then I need to go look for her. She might be hurt or something."

"You stay home. Is that clear?" It wasn't a request, but a command.

"She's my future wife, my responsibility. If she's hurt, I need to help her."

"Trust me on this, I am very sure, she is not physically hurt. You need to stay home and stay out of this."

"What aren't you telling me? What's this all about?"

"If you hear from her, you call me immediately." Lamar left no room for debate.

"But—"

The line went dead. Derry threw the stick that he still carried across the room.

I don't care what Lamar says. Sara's in trouble. She needs my help.

He grabbed his keys and turned toward the front door. Sara's car was fourteen years old, with over two hundred thousand miles. Maybe it broke down along the way. *Then why hasn't she called for help?*

Hearing Sara's song, he stopped two feet from the front door as relief washed over him. "Are you okay? Do you need help? Lamar called and was asking—"

"I can't talk long. I just called to tell you I'm fine. I need –" She didn't sound right, something must have happened to her.

"Are you at the hospital? Were you in an accident?"

"I need to leave for a while." It sounded distant, so much like a goodbye.

"Leave? What do you mean 'leave'? Like I was saying, Lamar called. He wants to know where you are and so do I."

"I'm sure he does. Look, I can't tell you much but— someone framed me."

"Framed you for what? What do they think you did? Where are you? Whatever it is, let me help."

Her sniffles caused him to pause a few seconds. She was scared and he wasn't letting her talk. He closed his mouth. Less than a second went by but it seemed like an eternity.

"Someone planted evidence indicating I killed Todd. And I need to—to hide for a while, be on my own. It's the only way to—"

"You can't be on your own right now. That's crazy. Look, I will help you. I'll do whatever it takes. Tell me where you are."

"No, I can't pull you in. You stay out of this. I— I need to find out who set me up, and I need to do it on my own."

"No one will believe you killed him. Just tell me—."

"You're making this hard— Maybe I should just say goodbye. I love you."

"Sara, dear," He slowed down and took a breath. "How did they set you up? We – I will talk to Lamar."

"That won't help. They have pictures and witnesses — it doesn't matter. I need to go."

He moved to his front window, looking out at nothing. "Tell me where you are, please. I'll come help." *Please God, don't let her disappear.*

The line was quiet for several seconds. "I'm sorry. I have to go. I will always love you."

———

Her world blurred again as Sara sat in her car, holding her phone. It was over, everything was ruined. The world she so desperately wanted to be a part of, had suddenly been yanked away. To survive, she had to think like her old self. It was the only way she would make it.

May God forgive me.

She wasn't sure He would. Not when she knew in her heart what she would have to do to clear her name. The ends might justify the means, but justify and forgive were two different things.

A conversation grew louder. It was a large group of travelers passing by her car. She turned away, and wiped her eyes.

Enough.

Why did I call him?

It was a mistake. One she would not make again.

As the group loaded their bags into the back of an oversized SUV she reached for her door handle. Witnesses were good. Grabbing her bag, she slipped out and slammed her door. They looked over. "You gotta close it hard, it's old," she said, smiling as she walked away.

Heading into DIA she went near one of the ticket counters that served international travelers. Pulling her phone out, she talked into it as she waited for the right person to come along. It didn't take long. A woman a few years older than Sara was trying to check a bag that was over fifty pounds. The woman opened the suitcase on the floor and started pulling things out. Sara walked over.

"Excuse me, but I couldn't help overhearing that your bag is too heavy."

The woman looked up, frustration written all over her face. "What about it?"

"Well, I'm going to England also, and I might have room in my bag for some of your stuff."

The man behind the counter stepped up. "I'm sorry Miss, but

unless you know this woman, you can't do that. It's completely illegal."

"Doesn't matter." The woman pulled a container of liquid out. "I'll leave this behind. I can get more in London, I hope."

Sara reached down to help the woman close her suitcase. "I was just trying to help."

The woman smiled at her, as the man told her to get back in line.

Sara headed toward the line as she saw the suitcase with her phone in it go onto the scale. She walked to the end of the queue then out of the ticket area. She next went to an ATM and pulled out as much cash as her cards would allow before heading out of DIA to the RTD bus stop.

———

The minute Booker stepped into the office without knocking, Lamar knew the news had made it all the way to the top.

"Your girl ran."

For the last hour, Lamar had been on the phone calling Sara, leaving her messages. This was so unlike her. "I can't believe she's behind this. We don't know the whole story."

Booker marched over and using her index finger, drove her point into the top of his desk. "I'll tell you the whole story. The whole story is she's gone back to her old ways. She's a thief, a spy, and now a murderer."

Lamar was on his feet. "She did not kill Todd. And I don't believe for half a second that she's a spy."

Booker glared into his eyes. "She was seen at Todd's apartment last night. Did you know she was there?"

"I heard."

"And now your little girl has left the country."

"What? How do you know that?"

Booker stepped back and crossed her arms. "She was spotted at the airport. We have information she's on her way out of the country, London we think."

"DIA? I can't believe it. Are there eyewitness accounts?"

"Yes, and we traced her phone. She boarded a flight to London about an hour ago. We just missed getting her before the plane took off." Booker's smile was hard. "I've contacted people in London. They will be there waiting for her."

Lamar stepped around his desk. He needed to get control of this situation before things got any worse. "I'll bet my badge she won't be on that plane, and never was."

Booker's eyes widened at his wager.

He went on, "She's not stupid. We only caught her last time because she came to us. Do you think after working here for two and a half years, she'd be so dumb as to leave that wide of a path for you to follow?"

"I have someone going through the boarding video. If she's not on that flight, we will find out which one she is on. I'm not that dumb either."

"If she left a trail that ended at DIA, my guess is she's still in town."

"If we come up dry, I'll take your advice into consideration. Until then, stay out of the way. Am I clear?"

"I can't sit by and—" He did not finish before she spun around and stormed out.

"You mess this up or get in our way, and I will have your badge." Her parting words trailed behind her.

———

Luca Clayton was the last one at work again. She was preparing to leave when a message popped up on her screen. It was an alert. It should have gone to her boss, but he had left early and forwarded all low level activities to her. He said it was his way of mentoring her into management. She brought up the notice. It was a facial recognition hit. Some software program in Detroit had identified a face as belonging to a suspected terrorist, known only as Nasir.

Now what?

She went to the guidelines that her boss had given her and read through them. Following protocol, Luca forwarded the information to the Detroit office of Homeland Security. She hoped they would be able to find this man.

When she was finished, she logged off and headed out. Glancing at the clock, she saw this little work detour had cost her an hour and a missed date.

Great, another blown Friday night because of work and no one will ever notice.

37

Sara is being framed for Todd's murder? Unbelievable. What will Sara do or, better yet, what would the old Sara do? Run.

Okay, where? Where would she run? Someplace where she would feel safe.

Derry stood halfway between his dining table and the front door, bouncing his keys in his hand. He was coming up with answers, but they were all dumb, useless answers. Walking over to the couch, he dropped onto its edge as he gripped his keys tightly. His mind raced in too many directions to follow.

Why would someone frame her?

She could never kill someone. Never.

Every beat of his heart weighed him down more. The woman he loved was being destroyed by someone. If he could only find out who and pound them into the ground.

This is insane.

I've got to do something that will actually help Sara.

She's smart and she knows Denver.

Okay, I can stay and wait for the cops to set up surveillance on me, or I can go find her.

Derry gripped his keys and moved toward the window. Only the normal collection of cars lined the road. He had a little time.

He needed supplies. Grabbing a backpack, he shoved his laptop and charger in and headed out the back door. Taking one last look around, he got into his car.

Twenty minutes later, he walked into the electronics department at of a nearby Walmart. The store was busy, making it easier to do several separate purchases without notice. With each purchase he used a different credit card and got the maximum cash back that the card would allow.

Before leaving, he hit the food section, grabbing a few of bottles of water, some energy bars and a several bags of Sara's favorite trail mix. His pack was filled with food, of sorts, along with four prepaid smartphones. Would that be enough? He hoped so.

Target was just down the street. He ran the same game there. He picked up two more phones and some more food before one of his credit card companies texted him that his credit card might possibly be stolen. He responded and figured he'd pushed things far enough for tonight.

Sitting in the Target parking lot, he debated about running past his house once more. He could grab some clothes for himself and some for Sara. He decided that was too risky, the house would likely be under surveillance by now.

He needed to go dark, as they say. He pulled the battery out of his phone and shoved it into his pack. Stepping out of his car, he locked it and walked away. Hopefully no one would notice it for a few days.

———

Getting off the bus at 16th and Stout, Sara walked half a block to the 16th Street Mall. Turning the corner, she entered the world of restaurants and high-end stores. The foot traffic of shoppers, diners, and meanderers mixed in well with the hybrid buses that traveled its length. The air was filled with the smells of food, car exhaust, recently resurfaced asphalt, and shoppers after a long day in the hot sun.

Turning northwest she merged in with a large group of young and old. The bottom floors of the tall buildings were filled with inviting businesses. Between the storefronts stood the downtown panhandlers, some begging right next to help wanted signs that seemed to have become permanent fixtures in businesses across Colorado.

The walkways were filled with cops and cameras. The odds of the FBI knowing her whereabouts at this moment were slim. Sara wanted to keep it that way. Facial recognition software was limited, but still a threat to her freedom. Her top priority was to keep her face away from the cameras. She needed to change her looks, to cover as much of her face as possible without being obvious. Maybe a large, floppy hat would help.

Her shorter stature came in handy as she tucked herself in with a group at the other end of the spectrum. This really limited her travel as she had to go where they went.

If she could stay out of sight for a few days, the FBI might believe she had gotten past TSA and was on one of those flights out of DIA. But for now, she was in great danger. Within the hour, every law enforcement department in the country would have pictures of her, America's most wanted. It wouldn't take long for the software she helped enhance, to go through the DIA security videos to learn she never got on that plane.

Head down, she glanced to the side to assess her options. On a little grassy knoll across the roadway, were half a dozen homeless asking for money or food. One of the women sitting back ten feet or so from the others caught her attention. Her outfit was perfect. A black and white bandana completely covered her hair, a scarf went around her neck, and oversized cheap sunglasses made it impossible to see more than a fraction of her face. Not even the best software could identify her. It was hot out, but no one gave the homeless a second thought. Sara made a diagonal line across the road.

"Hey, you got a minute?"

The woman did not look up or make any movements. Sara moved in a little closer and touched her shoulder. "Hey, would you like to make some money?"

"I ain't in the mood." She spoke in angry tones without looking up.

"You don't want to make some money?" *Wow, that must sound bad.* Sara started to rephrase her question, but the woman slowly rotated her head toward Sara, revealing an angry face.

"No, I ain't in the mood for whatever you want me to do. Now leave before I call the cops." She slowly returned to watching the crowds, her expression now lifeless.

"It's not what you think."

"That's what they all say." Complete distrust coupled with hatred. "Now leave me alone." The woman stood and walked toward two men begging at the edge of the small hill. She whispered to one of them before dropping to the ground between them.

The grimy man looked over at Sara. "Hey lady, maybe I can help

Deadly Infiltration

you. What are you looking to buy? Whatever it is, I can get it for you."
He smiled cunningly.

Chills ran up her back and arms, while his gaze traveled the length of her body. "Never mind." Sara moved back toward the main walkway, keeping her head down.

The man called to her as she walked past. "If it's girls you like, I can arrange that too. How much money you got?" The taste of dirt filled her mouth. She wanted to spit it out, but refused to let him know he was affecting her. She moved on. He was the lowest form of sewer rat, a user of people, taking advantage of those weaker or too naïve to know better.

If this were yesterday, she would have put in a call to Lamar. He had friends in the Denver Police Department who would do something about that callous, excuse of a human. But not today.

His words haunted her as she moved back into the crowds, now going southeast. Were all the vagrants so heartless? Was having a soul something that hindered your chances of survival on the streets? As she passed another group of displaced people, she looked into their eyes. Many were empty, without that spark that said, *hey, I'm a person.* She wanted to reach out and say, you are better than this. But even if she wasn't on the run, she wouldn't. How many of them would react the same way as those others had?

Coming to a crosswalk where two police officers stood brought her mind back on track. She tucked herself in behind the group waiting to cross. Drifters walked past the cops and cut across the street without being seen. She needed to become one of the soulless, to become invisible. For that, she needed a homeless outfit. But where does a person buy *rags?*

A thrift store. They don't sell rags, but maybe they might have something that would work.

For homeless shopping, ask the homeless. A lone guy playing a scratched up violin stood near one of the stores. He was fairly good as attested to by the crowd that stood around him, listening. Sara arrived as he was ending a set. He told the group he'd be back in fifteen and asked for support. As his audience paid and moved on, she worked her way in. He was a world apart from her previous encounter. He spoke with the eloquence of an educated man. He told her where he brought his clothes and pointed out that the deals were much better than paying for anything new. She headed for the small secondhand shop in the thirteen hundred block of East Colfax.

It was a short walk. Sara marveled at the difference as the city transformed from its daytime personality to nighttime. Each step felt longer as the sun's rays retreated behind the foothills. The day cooled down quickly as the light disappeared. Sara picked up her pace. The store was filled with used, but still nice clothes. She thought about getting some and taking them out back and rolling in the dirt. Stupid, but it gave her a usable idea. Going around to the side of the shop, she found the donation rejects in a small dumpster that sat next to the loading dock.

After waiting for a couple of cars to pass, she jumped headlong into the discard bin. The aroma that filled her nose staggered her. It wasn't what she'd expected. Something was dead in there, and she did not want to find it. Her always queasy stomach rebelled, adding to the revolting smells. She took a minute to recover, before she turned away from her addition to the confined space to search the opposite side of the box. She carefully moved an old, brown, coat that was pushed up in one corner. The inhabitants below scurried for a new hiding place. Mice, lots of them.

She went to the other corner of the container, grabbed a handful of clothes and flung them over the side. She followed right behind them. Landing near them, she kicked at them with her foot before reaching down to examine her haul. Hopefully, they were now empty of rodents. Using only her thumb and index finger, she picked up each piece and examined it. She had retrieved a stocking cap, a length of old cloth, a shirt, and a pair of pants. She could make them work. The rest went back in the bin to help with the rodent housing.

After shaking them out once more, she rolled them into a bundle, and headed into the store. To complete her transformation, she bought an old Army coat three sizes too big, a pair of oversized sunglasses and a highly used, threadbare backpack.

She asked the clerk if she could use a dressing room to put the clothes on. On stepping out, the clerk gave her an *are you kidding* look.

"I want to play a prank on my boyfriend." With her good clothes in her pack, she left before the woman could ask her any more questions.

The last red rays of the Colorado sunset glowed in the west. It could have been beautiful. She wondered what Derry was doing.

She shook off those thoughts. She needed to find safety for the night. Downtown Denver wasn't LA or New York, but a girl alone was an easy target.

38

Saturday

Alex sat at the kitchen table, working on her computer, completing the evidence to prove Sara's guilt. She had not seen Kai this morning, but heard her making all kinds of noise in her room. She hoped she would either stay in there, or be gone today. Either way, Alex did not have time to make conversation or babysit. This mission was drawing to a close. All the games were coming to an end.

Hearing Kai's bedroom door, Alex started to close her laptop, but before she got it shut, Kai rushed through the living room and was halfway to the front door.

"I'll be back in a few hours."

Great news. "Going for a long run today?" Alex left the lid open enough to keep the laptop from going into standby.

Kai wore her running outfit and carried a large black backpack. It looked heavy resting on her shoulder.

"Last night I searched for upcoming marathons in the area and found out about the Aurora triathlon next month. I am thinking of entering so I need to start a training regimen." She hoisted the pack of gear. "This being the first cool morning we've had in a while, I thought it would be a great time to start. I'm going to head over and look at the course and give it a try. I will also need a new bike, so I'm not sure when I'll get back."

"You're insane. What about checking on your results at work?" Alex's thumb rubbed the edge of the lid, waiting to reopen it.

Kai leaned against the wall. "It might be done by now, but I doubt it. Can we do it after my run? The weather is just perfect for running right now."

"Sure, tell you what. I need to run a few errands this morning anyway. I'll run by work and check on it. What do I need to look for?"

"It should be clear, it will either say complete and list the decrypted files or say run unsuccessful and list a results file."

"That sounds easy enough. I'll call you once I check on it. Just don't go so far you can't make it back if I need you." Alex really did need to run by the office and this gave her a good excuse.

"Thanks, I owe you for this one." Kai pushed off from the wall. "Give me a call, and if you need me I'll catch a taxi."

Alex gave a half-hearted wave as Kai opened the door and stepped through. Once alone, Alex raised the lid and relaxed a little as she reached for her coffee. Taking several long, slow sips, she finished reading through the information from Jonas.

The evidence was good. It would only hold up for a week, maybe two, but that would be long enough.

Logging into Homeland's computer system, she went to a directory filled with everything they had on Sara. She searched through the files for surveillance footage of Sara. All of these files had date and locations in the headers. And most of the footage was close to two years old. Sara's hair was shorter at that time and had been dyed.

Perfect.

Alex picked out four videos of Sara.

She took the clips and inserted them into the video records for various cameras in Denver. This would allow the FBI to find Sara through their facial recognition software.

With a little digging, they would know the footage was faked. But people believe what they want to believe or expect to see. No one would scrutinize this too hard for a while.

Grabbing more coffee, she returned to her seat as her phone buzzed. It was Roux. *Oh, great.*

"Yes, Dace?"

"Don't use that name over a non-secure phone line."

"Yes, of course, *Agent Landry.*" He was so ridiculous sometimes. She should not push it. "What can I do for you?"

"We have a new problem, and your computer skills better be able to solve it."

Or what? "I'm listening."

"I just sent you an email on your private account. Someone at the FBI is investigating one of our *partners*. They confiscated money needed for the completion of the project. I need you to find out what information they have and who all is involved in the investigation."

"That's it? Just find out who took the money?" *Easy enough.*

"No. As I stated, this money is needed for the completion of our work. I would like our money returned. Your payment will come from it."

"And if I can't find it or for some reason I can't move it, then what?"

"Then I would say all your work for us has been, how do the American say it? Pro bono."

"You had better be careful. I'm not a person to be trifled with."

"I would like for you to think of this as a form of motivation. I will send you the location where I want the money to be deposited. Once all of it has been moved to that location, I will ensure your payment."

"How much money are we talking about?

"The FBI took half a million dollars."

"Not even the FBI can take that kind of money without a paper trail a mile wide. This should be easy. I will get right on it."

"One more item."

"Yes."

"I do not believe Kai is needed any longer."

———————

Glancing over her shoulder at the second floor apartment window, Kai looked for a figure peeking out. *No Alex, that's good.*

She repositioned the weight that was cutting into her shoulder.

Can't believe she didn't notice anything. Only a Navy Seal would try running with this much weight. And starting to train one month out for a triathlon, seriously?

She headed toward a bus stop a few blocks away. Maybe she should have left more stuff behind and replaced it when she started a new life. She would need to get a new name and hope Homeland didn't try tracking her down. She knew in her heart that other than living as a hermit in the woods or moving to a different country, they would probably be able to find her if they wanted to. But she couldn't stay around.

After a short bus ride to DIA, she would take a flight to another state. Two other people waited at the stop, both were occupied with their phones. Kai checked the time. The bus should arrive in fifteen minutes. She dropped her pack to the ground, took a seat and looked back toward the apartment complex, a place she never wanted to see again.

A black Toyota Camry pulled to a stop in front of her as the passenger window was coming down. Was someone from Homeland following her? She turned her face and started walking away, leaving her worldly possessions behind. She paused. If she ran now, Homeland would know something wasn't right. She turned back and reached for her pack, keeping her head down.

"Kai, get in."

What? She lowered her head a little to see into the car.

"Kai, get in the car."

"Sam!" She never thought seeing him would bring so much relief.

He reached over and pushed the door open. "We need to hurry."

She moved closer, but whether it was relief at seeing him or a small amount of disbelief that he was actually there, she didn't obey his command. "What are you doing here?"

"You called me, remember?"

"Yeah, but how'd you know I'd be here?"

"We need to talk. Are you going to get in or do I need to come around and toss you in?"

"I'd like to see you try." Opening the back door, she hoisted her pack in before taking a seat up front. Leaning over, she gave him a long, tight hug. "I've missed you." It had been five years, but he looked the same, as handsome as ever.

Accelerating away, he checked his mirrors.

She couldn't take her eyes off him. He was home, safety, and protection all rolled up inside a person. "Ok, how did you know where I was?"

He smiled, but his eyes were serious. "I've been monitoring your apartment all morning. I see you're still into running." He nodded at her outfit.

She leaned back in her seat. "I'm definitely running today, as far away as I can get." With his help she could really get away. "But what are you doing in Colorado?"

"Officially I'm on vacation. But it looks like our paths crossed for a reason. I need to find out more about your work at Homeland. That's why I picked you up today, Sis."

Kai was not his sister, but Sam had worked with Kai's father, and they were very close. "You're after the people I'm working with? That is so weird. Well, I have a lot to tell you."

Sam pulled into the parking lot of a city park and turned off the engine. He looked over at her for several seconds before speaking. "When we talked the other day, you told me you had suspicions about your situation at Homeland, but did not know what was going on. You also said you had copied the files you were working on. What have you learned since we last talked?"

Kai was still flustered. "I'm leaving. I was heading to DIA just now to get as far away from them as possible. I'm working with a bunch of—"

"Murderers?" Sam broke in.

"Yeah, they killed an FBI agent named Todd Jenkins. I overheard them talking about it. And they are planning to pin it all on an old friend of mine named Sara Beckwith." Sara may have been a little bit of a snob when they had worked together, but Kai liked her a lot. She knew Sara was not a killer.

"Who did you hear talking about this?"

"My roommate Alex, her boss, Agent Landry, and another agent named Hewitt. Alex said she had killed Jenkins. I'm afraid they might know I heard them. I think they might try to kill me." Kai began to shake.

Sam squeezed her shoulder for reassurance. "It may be worse than you think. That may not be their only murder." Sam told her about Ryan Blinder's murder. He also told her that he believed Blinder's murder was tied to the senator's murder as well.

"And I was hoping you were here just to save me." Kai knew it was a childish thing to say, but deep down she was hoping to be saved, to be taken away from all this.

"Sorry, Beanpole."

"I haven't been called that in a long time." The nickname warmed her heart.

"I will do my best to protect you. But I need you to help me with this case. There is much more at stake than you realize." Sam's eyes were intense. Kai could not keep looking at him.

"Do you know why they are doing all of this?" Sam's voice was easy, reassuring.

"Doing what? Killing people?" *Oh no. Here it goes. He is going to work it around to make me think I should stay.* It was the same tactic her dad used on her every time he wanted her to do something she did not want to do.

"If they had only wanted to kill a few people, they could put out a hit. Why set your friend up as the killer? I mean of all the people in Denver, why her?"

"Landry said something about her being too smart."

"And is she?"

Kai thought back to her days working with Sara and all she'd learned. Sara was not only the best coder she'd ever worked with, but she could also read people. She knew just how to push their buttons and did so on a regular basis. "Yes. She's smart, maybe too smart for her own good."

"So, she might know something that Landry wants to keep away from the people she works with. Make her run and that problem is solved. Next question. Why infiltrate Homeland Security? That takes years. Why all the secrecy about decrypting a few files? What's in them that is so important that they would kill at least four people? Have you had any luck decrypting the files?"

Kai responded with a weak, "No. This is the strangest encryption I have ever encountered."

"Good. At least they don't have that information yet."

"So you think they are up to something bigger? That's why you're here?" Kai crossed her arms and looked him straight in the face. She did not want to get any more involved in this than she already was.

"They are part of a bigger plan."

"A plan to do what?"

He looked toward the floorboards as he talked. "Sometime within the next couple of weeks a massive attack is planned against American civilians."

"How massive are we talking?"

"The death toll could be in the hundreds of thousands, or even the millions. But we don't know what kind of attack or what the targets are. I really need someone I can trust on the inside to help me get this information before it's too late."

"I already told you who is responsible. It's Alex, Hewitt and Landry."

"Is that the whole group? Who helped them get past the background checks and infiltrate Homeland Security? Who are they sending information to? What are they actually planning? And what's important enough in those files to kill a U.S. senator, his wife, a CIA agent, and an FBI agent and then blame it all on your friend Sara?"

Kai dropped her arms and picked at the seam on the seat. The answer to every one of his questions was, "I do not know." *But I should care.* She was a software jockey, someone who worked with computers and liked it that way. Every time she got involved with human beings it did not turn out so well.

Sam watched the conflicting emotions play across her face. Finally, she looked at him and smiled halfheartedly. "I guess I'm too much like my dad. He never ran from anything in his life."

"So you're in?"

She nodded. "I just hope I don't end up dead like Dad." This was crazy. Why had she said yes? "Did I tell you I found a couple of fake passports for Alex?"

"How?"

"I went through her room while she was gone."

"And they were just lying out or in a drawer?"

"No—, I found them in the furnace air return vent."

"You are quite the little spy already. Do you remember the names on the passports?"

"I can do even better. I took pictures." Kai texted the images to Sam.

"See, you are already involved and on the inside. I need your help. Your country needs your help." Sam reached over and placed his hand on top of hers. He gave it a light squeeze. "I want you to know I would never voluntarily pull you into something like this. But time is running out and you are in the best position to help me. If you run away now, they will send someone after you and I could not protect you. This way, I can cover your back. And if at any time you feel your life is in danger, call me."

She gave a nod as her heart weighed heavy with her decision.

"Since you were planning to run away, I assume you have the copied files with you?"

"Yes, they are the only leverage I have against them."

"I am hoping those files will tell us where to begin."

"That's if anyone can read them. I certainly have not been able to crack them."

"I think I can. But I need someplace to work that has a high end system, somewhere where no one can hack in. And there can't be any cameras around. We can't have anyone seeing us working together."

"I think I know just the spot."

Kent reached for his phone. The call was from one of the pool of software specialists that worked for the Bureau. "Kent here."

"This is Branden. I know the idea is that Sara left the country, but it didn't feel right to me. I mean, I don't know her that well or anything, but she has a boyfriend here and all, and I just—"

"Cut to the chase."

"I have been running a facial recognition program on city cameras around Denver, you know, looking for Sara. It's not perfect—"

Kent cleared his throat.

"Anyway, I got a hit. Well, I think it's her. It's a close match to the Bureau's pictures of her."

"In Denver?"

"Yes. That is what I have been trying to tell you."

Kent sat up. "Where at?"

"Near the downtown area. Actually on the south end of downtown." Branden gave Kent the camera's location.

"How old is this data?"

"Maybe ten, no make that fifteen minutes ago."

Kent killed the call and put one in to Faircloth. Kent had just received a warrant and was on his way to search Sara's apartment. So it was decided to send Chris to look for Sara downtown.

Checking out of the rat-trap motel, Derry made the firm commitment to sleep in the streets next time. Anything was preferable to this place. The whole night he dreamt about little tiny things crawling on him, biting him. In the morning, when he showered in the algae covered stall, he found hundreds of itchy red dots covering his body.

He could not get out of the room fast enough, as he added one more task to his list when this was over. He would call the Health Department about this flea infested hole.

Heading down the street, he stopped to grab a bite at a fast food chain. He stayed longer than he should have, downing one cup of coffee after another. It was weak, but after several cups he was finally waking up.

Now what? How do I find someone who doesn't want to be found?

His last words with her told him the old Sara, the one he had met in that Greek restaurant close to three years ago, was back. He had a few ideas where that Sara would hide.

Holding the hot cup of coffee between his hands that rested on the table, he closed his eyes.

Dear Lord God, I ask for your help. Lead me to her today. I ask you protect her and keep—

He felt a tap on his shoulder. He looked up into the face of a Denver police officer.

"Are you okay, sir?"

"Yes, I'm fine— I was just— um, I was just trying to wake up. I recently started working the nightshift. You know how it is." Derry shook his head a little to show he was trying to stay awake.

"You need a ride home? Don't want you falling asleep behind the wheel."

"If I had a car that might be a problem. I'm waiting for my bus."

The officer looked out the window and back. "Okay, as long as you're not driving anywhere."

Hearing the deep engine sound, Derry glanced outside to see a bus approaching. He grabbed his coffee as he excused himself. The policeman stepped out of his way and Derry headed toward the RTD bus stop out front.

That was close.

39

"We have no more use for him and he is a risk to our operation." Nasir sat in one of the folding chairs that surrounded the large piece of chipboard sitting on top of boxes that served as a table. John Motova glared at him from the other side.

"Rostislav is family, not rubbish. He is not something to throw away because you don't feel he's needed any longer." John looked down and began to carve into the wood with his pocket knife.

"You are part of the *umma* and that is more than family. As a follower of the one true faith, you must put family aside for Islam as the Qur'an orders. He is a man of no faith, as low as a Jew. He believes only in himself. And a man who only believes in himself is not a man. He will talk. He could jeopardize the whole operation."

Nasir waited quietly while John worked on the carving. He knew this would be a hard thing for John. He understood how Russians valued family connections. It was something his people had once believed in before they learned the truth. Now they knew the community of believers was the only community that mattered. Nasir had one objective, to promote Islam. And anything that got in the way was to be removed. America, a land of nonbelievers, stood in the way every day with its big powerful weapons. So much might, in the hands of depraved infidels. But anything not protected by Allah could be destroyed, and America was not of Allah. It would be destroyed. While America was busy rebuilding its cities, the Arab nations would unite as one behind the call of Islam and fulfill their mission to Allah.

"I was without faith three years ago, and now I am a strong follower. Give me time to talk with him, to help him understand. I'm sure he'll come around." John carved as he talked. This showed Nasir that John did not fully believe his own words, but was not ready to accept the truth either.

"Rostislav only loves money and believes he will soon be a rich man. He does not think he needs anything else. You came to Islam a broken man, a drunk. Your family was falling apart and your wife had filed for divorce. You understood that only through Allah and his one true Prophet Mohammed, could you find a reason to live."

"How do you know this about me?"

"I know a lot more about you than you think. Do you believe that I would place so much confidence in a man without learning who he is? I also know your two sons refuse to listen to your words. If you cannot convince them, how much hope is there that you can change the heart of your wife's cousin, a man you have not seen in years?" Nasir studied John's eyes as he stared at the scratches he made in the table. John was like a child when it came to the plan he had helped design. He did not understand to what extent America would go to find the men behind the attacks. Nasir did not want to end up in a deck of cards with a ten-million-dollar bounty listed under his picture. He would not take any chances.

"He may not ever be a follower, but his skills are needed, and he has done what you've asked." John laid the knife aside. "When I gave his name to you, it was to help him. My wife's family and his are very close. She will not forgive me if I let him die."

"Who is the leader in your home, you or your wife? Have you not learned your place in your own house? Have you not read the words of the Prophet? Your wife is to submit to you and obey you, to learn her place. You sound more like a woman." Nasir spat on the ground.

John's body stiffened before he raised his shoulders and straightened his back. "I am the head of my house. She listens to me."

Nasir did not believe him, but now was not the time to disagree. "Then why are you risking the outcome of this great mission because of your wife's feelings? You have already made one mistake that cost us five hundred thousand dollars. How much more are you willing to risk?" Nasir could have killed Rostislav at any time, but he wanted Motova to do it. First, it would prevent John from blaming Nasir or the team for the death. Second, it would bind him to the undertaking. Motova's resistance reinforced the need to have him carry out the task.

John picked up the knife and gripped the handle. He looked into Nasir eyes. "I am no one's dog, not hers and not yours. I will do what I believe to be in Allah's will." John half rose from his chair.

Nasir grabbed his wrist, pinning John's hand against the table. "You are saying you know Allah's will better, after three short years, then a learned man who has studied the Qur'an and other sacred writings his whole life?"

John pulled, trying to free his arm. "No." The man was weak inside and out. "You have spent more years studying than I."

Nasir went on. "Are you not willing to do the will of Allah?"

"I will do what *Allah* demands, if Allah demands it."

"Am I not an *Ulama*? A student of Mohammed's words? Do you know a man that understands the words of the great prophet better than I?"

The muscles in John's arm stiffened. He looked deep into Nasir's eyes. Several seconds passed before he relaxed and leaned forward, putting his weight on his flatten hand. "—Yes, you are an *Ulama* and know the prophet's words. And no, I do not know of anyone more knowledgeable in the studies of the Qur'an than you." *Full and complete submission, finally.*

"I am telling you what Allah *demands*." Nasir stared back, waiting to see if John would be able to overcome his Russian heritage that fought against what Nasir was asking of him.

"—Yes, I will – do as Allah requires." John's eyes shifted away, as he waited for Nasir to release his grip.

"Allah requires the death of Rostislav." He released John's arm.

John peered down at the table. "If that is the only way."

"Is it not better that this message be delivered by a family member?"

John sat back down, motionless for several seconds. Taking his knife, he folded it and slid it into his pocket as he stared at the door that led to Rostislav. He bowed his head for several seconds before he rose to his feet with tightly clenched fists and white knuckles. His back stiffened as his head came up. "May Allah's will be done."

———

Sara rubbed her arm as she stood on the corner of Lincoln and 16th. Her stomach was doing its morning somersaults again. She needed something light to put in it, but she was penniless after having been mugged.

The light changed and she moved across the intersection with the crowd that ignored her. To them she was nothing more than an obstacle to get around before her dirt rubbed off on them.

Someone bumped into her sore arm sending a sharp pain deep inside. Two days ago she would have gone to the doctor's office after being smashed with a wooden broom handle. Now, even the free clinic was off limits. Lightly rubbing just below the pained area, she was thankful the person who swung the weapon had less than a foot in which to maneuver.

With no place to sleep indoors last night, Sara had found a half-way clean corner in a mostly empty parking garage. She learned quickly that location belonged to others. They grabbed her bag as payment for trespassing, and when she would not let go, they hit her. Everything she had was now theirs. Rules of the street were harsh. No longer pretending to be homeless, she was literally broke and hungry.

Passing a restaurant, the smell of coffee took her mind away from the pain in her arm. She turned into the coffee shop as a paying customer stepped out.

The young woman working the counter gave Sara a look of disgust before talking to the next person in line. Sara did not blame her. She should leave, but the sweet smells held onto her. She took one long inhale before turning for the door.

"Are you hungry?"

She was not sure where the question came from. She turned toward the sound to see a young woman looking at her.

"Excuse me?" Sara's voice was weak in case she was wrong. She did not want to look like a bigger fool than she already felt.

"Have you had anything to eat today?" the woman asked with understanding blue eyes. She stepped closer to Sara.

"Ah, no. I don't have any money. I was robbed last night."

The woman nodded. "Oh, I'm sorry to hear that." It almost sounded like she believed her, but not quite. "I can't give you any money, but I can buy you something to eat. What would you like?" The woman smiled as she glanced at the glass case filled with pastries and other morning delights.

Sara stared at all the sugary products. They smelled so good, but they would only serve to fuel the storm raging in her stomach. "A plain yogurt would be great." This woman was being so kind to her and she was coming across as finicky.

The woman gave Sara a sidewise glance. "You sure you wouldn't rather have one of the pastries? I just finished one and they are really good."

Sara placed her hand on her midsection. "No, maybe just some coffee then."

"No yogurt or pastries? I can't have you starving. Yogurt it is." The woman motioned for Sara to step up to the counter with her, where she received another hash glare from the cashier.

The kind woman paid for two small containers of fruit filled yogurt and a large coffee with extra cream. Handing them to Sara, she said, "You know, there are lots of places looking for help right now. If you just cleaned yourself up a little I'm sure one of them would hire you."

Not if they knew I'm hiding from the Feds. "Thank you, I'll check into it." Before the woman could corner her into looking for work, Sara turned and stepped out.

———

"Yes, I'm with The Department of Homeland Security. I need to talk with you about Sara Beckwith." Alex stood on the stoop of the Knight's home. She showed her identification.

"What about her?" Kevin stood behind the screen door. He pushed the lock down. *Interesting.*

"I understand she rents a room in your home?" Alex used her sweetest accent, hoping to disarm the man.

"If you're with Homeland, you already know that."

"Yes, we do. I would like to ask you just a few questions."

"Go ahead." He crossed his arms.

Her charms did not seem to be working, he was not giving in. "I don't mean any harm, but someone at the FBI wants to question Sara in relation to an agent's murder."

Kevin's shoulders dropped a little. "I met Todd once. He seemed like a really nice person, once you got past his neediness. I know she could not possibly be involved in his death."

"Is she at home? Can I take a quick look around?"

"The last time I saw her was last night when she left to go back to work." His frame straightened back up, as he moved forward a small amount.

Alex stepped a little closer to the door. "Yes, they said she never made it. I hope she's not hurt somewhere."

"Someone from her office called an hour ago asking me questions. They told me if I hear anything from her to call them immediately. She never should have gone in last night, not after losing a close friend."

"Well," Alex turned up the sweet part of her southern accent, "one of the functions of Homeland is to monitor and coordinate with the other law enforcement branches. Because Sara works for the FBI, my department has been asked to— help out. To make sure everything is done fairly for all involved."

"Are you saying you don't trust the *FBI*?" He almost smiled.

"No, not at all. We just want to make sure emotions don't interfere with the investigation. We really have Sara's best interests in mind. Would you mind if I look around her living area?"

"You have a warrant?" His tone was flat. Said with a degree of certainty.

She reached into her bag and pulled out a fake warrant that she made that morning. Almost everyone thinks to ask but few even know how a real one looks like. Hers looked real enough, just in case. She held it out. He unlocked and opened the screen door to retrieve it. After taking a quick scan he handed it back. "I guess I can't stop you." Kevin stepped back allowing her to enter.

"Thank you; I will only be a minute." As she slipped the warrant back into her bag, she pulled a small envelope containing a jump drive out, palming it as she made her way around the kids' toys that were scattered across the floor. He showed her to Sara's small apartment. It was tiny, much smaller than she'd expected. Kevin stood at the doorway, eyeing her. In the background, a baby started crying. When Kevin turned his head, Alex allowed the jump drive to slip out of the envelope onto the floor under the coffee table.

She pulled out her phone and took half a dozen pictures. "Everything looks fine. I said it wouldn't take long. Thank you for your time." Alex stepped around Kevin and headed for the front door. She heard him moving off in the other direction, toward the sounds of the kids.

40

Faircloth stepped into Lamar's office without knocking. "I've got to hand it to you. You trained her well."

"Thank you. Now what are you referring to?" Lamar stood at Faircloth's accusation.

"I'm talking about Sara."

"I figured that much out. What about her?"

"Sara's tried to send us on a wild goose chase. But we've found her on one of the city cams in Denver." He knew Lamar would not give up information about one of his own easily.

"Last I heard, she left Denver. Was on her way to London."

"The trail she left last night was a setup to throw us off. Another sign of how good she is. She never left Denver."

"You're sure?" Lamar studied Faircloth's face.

"Absolutely, we caught her on a city cam. She's here alright."

Lamar's glare bore into Faircloth. "If I were kept in the loop, maybe you wouldn't spend all your time running in circles. You're treating Sara as if she has already been found guilty of murder, and we are not even sure if Todd was murdered."

Faircloth took the iPad from under his arm, and handed it over to Lamar. "It took some work but I've got the preliminary report from the medical examiner. It's definitely murder disguised to look like food poisoning. The toxin entered Todd's bloodstream through a small puncture wound in his side."

Lamar picked up the iPad and looked at the report Faircloth had brought up. "This is just Dr. Carpenter's preliminary report, not even filed. It doesn't say that Todd was murdered, but that botulism bacteria were found in his blood stream and may have entered through a puncture wound in the skin. It also states that the food he was eating that night has not yet been tested."

"But his stomach contents were tested and they came up clean. You still believe she's innocent. She could shoot somebody right here in front of you and you wouldn't believe that she's a murderer."

"I know she wouldn't kill someone. She's not that kind of person. No matter what evidence you show me, I won't believe Sarah's capable of killing an innocent person, especially Todd."

"That's why I won't ask for your help to find her."

"But I do believe that the only way to clear her name is to bring her in."

Faircloth mulled over Lamar's response. "I'll go with that for now, if you're really willing to help us find her."

"I am, but Sara knows better than to get caught on camera."

"What? Are you just saying that to protector her, or are you surprised she messed up?" Faircloth took the iPad back.

"She's very smart and doesn't make dumb mistakes. She wouldn't leave a trail out of town only to get caught on a camera in Denver."

Faircloth shrugged. He was not about to let Lamar rain on his parade. "Maybe she slipped up. All I know is we got her image this morning."

"You sure it was her?"

Faircloth tapped on the screen a few times, and showed Lamar the image of Sara. "Are you telling me that's not her?"

Lamar examined it. "Something is not right." Taking the iPad out of Faircloth's hand, he dropped into his seat, setting the tablet on his desk as he leaned over it to study the image. "This picture, I've seen something like it before. It's from—" He lifted the iPad, raising it closer to his face.

Faircloth reached across Lamar's desk and ripped the tablet free from Lamar's hands. "What are you trying to say?"

Lamar dropped back against the rear chair. "It might be her but I know I've seen that picture before. It's a plant and you're being played."

"You're telling me that Sara planted this picture? That she broke into the city cameras and put a picture of herself on our system, while she was really on a plane to England? Why are you trying to derail my investigation?"

"Your investigation is to find and catch a murderer. I'm only trying to help you find Todd's killer, and clear Sara's name. The only thing you are doing is letting your bias get in the way of the truth." Lamar was back on his feet, fists clenched, pushing into his desk.

Faircloth took a step forward as he tried to stare Lamar down. "I go where the evidence leads. It points to her. Why would she run if she wasn't guilty?"

"Maybe because she wants to find Todd's killer, and she knows if you catch her you'll quit looking and she'll end up behind bars."

"If she's so innocent, she would know the best thing she could do is come in and tell us what she knows. She should help us do our jobs."

"When you've already made up your mind that she's guilty? You're right about one thing. She's smart. And maybe staying free is the only way she can find the real killer. You sure aren't looking for anyone else."

Faircloth stepped all the way to Lamar's desk and placed his fists on top, glaring into Lamar's face. "I'm the best homicide investigator in the western region. Unlike you, I don't let my personal feelings get in the way. I go where the investigation leads, always."

Lamar pulled back and stood straight. "Even when the evidence doesn't make sense? Too many things are out of place," Lamar insisted.

Faircloth was relieved this encounter wasn't going to come to blows. He would lose. "They're not out of place. We just don't have the full picture. But when we do, I'll do everything I can to bring the murderer in, no matter what my relationship is with them."

The seconds between Faircloth's words and Lamar's response lasted an eternity. "Your statement proves you believe she's the one who killed Todd. Do you think she also killed the senator and his brother? You'd be better off spending your resources looking for their murderers."

"We've followed up on all of the leads we have for both of the Henderson murders. Sara's our only active lead right now. She obviously did not kill Senator Henderson or his brother. She has alibies for both days. But she could be working with the people who did kill them. We have to bring her in if we're going to solve any of these cases."

"But you *do* believe she killed Todd?"

Faircloth needed to defuse the situation. It was getting out of hand. He turned and walked a few steps away from the desk as he spoke. "With the eyewitness testimony and the picture of her at Todd's apartment, I'd say we have more than enough evidence to bring her in for questioning."

"Yeah, I tried to get ahold of this so called eyewitness. The number she gave goes to a burn phone. Doesn't that make you question just how real this evidence is?"

"That doesn't matter. We have the picture placing Sara at the crime scene. Maybe the woman who talked with the police had her reasons for using a phone not registered to her."

"Pictures can be doctored. Unless you can find that witness, it means nothing."

Faircloth turned to face Lamar. "There's more."

"What?"

Faircloth hesitated. Emotions in the room were high. "Kent's at her home as we speak. He found a jump drive that looks identical to the one Todd brought back from Texas."

"That means nothing. I've got dozens of them between here and home. They're government issue."

"You're allowed to have them, she's not. It's against the conditions of her probation to touch computers outside of work."

Lamar interrupted. "A jump drive is not a computer. So she didn't break her probation."

Faircloth held up a hand. "That's not all. Kent stuck it in his laptop and found several encrypted files, using the bureau's naming standards."

"This is crazy, maybe the craziest thing I've ever heard. I may not be the top *homicide investigator* in the world, but even I can see that the evidence is lined up too neatly. Someone's setting Sara up."

"You're too close to her to be objective on this investigation."

Lamar stood defiant. "I may be too close to be objective in your eyes. But I'm also close enough to my team to know what they're capable of, what their strengths and weaknesses are. I know my people. And I know Sara didn't and couldn't murder anyone."

Faircloth knew his men, too. He looked into Lamar's face. "I can't trust you on this one. You'll spin and twist the evidence to make your person appear innocent. I only want those that'll do the job, and that's not you."

"Have you ever known me to disobey an order— without good cause?" Lamar relaxed his glare. "I need to be on this case to keep things fair. Otherwise, between you and Booker, Sara could end up being railroaded."

Faircloth did not trust Lamar. He might try to inform Sara or interfere. Lamar could not be allowed to be part of this investigation.

"I'm sorry I stepped in here. I was hoping to get some insight into finding Sara, but all I got was an agent willing to cross the line to protect his own."

"Insight? You came in with guns blazing, looking for a fight."

Faircloth realized he could have handled this better, but that dog had already left the gate. "I am going to recommend you be pulled completely from the case. I will take over your team, what's left of it."

"And what am I supposed to do? Sit around and surf the net?"

Faircloth stepped forward and looked his coworker in the eyes. "What you do with your time is none of my business as long as you're doing it a long way from my investigation." Before Lamar could protest Faircloth exited the room.

———

Tony's phone rang. It had to be Booker.

"Hello."

"I've got something new I need you to work on. Since everything is in the open about Sara, you no longer need to work covertly. I need you to come into the office right away. We found an encrypted jump drive at Sara's apartment. It'll be waiting for you when you get here. I need to know what's on it ASAP. Get in here and work in it."

"I may need some help. I'm not the encryption expert, that was— Todd. I'll call Lamar and see about getting some help."

"He's out of the loop. You'll report to Agent Faircloth now. — I'll see about pulling resources from other parts of CART to help you."

"There's not a one of them as good as Todd or Sara."

"We'll have to work with what we have. Get here as soon as you can."

41

Sitting in the car, Sam considered the computer store. "You sure this place is secure?"

"It has the type of security we need, I hope. —And the owner is an old friend, sort of. I called him the other day and told him I might come by. If anyone in town has a system that can run the decryption algorithms, he will."

"I don't like it." The two sat about fifty feet from the large glass windows that spanned the front of the store. Sam gripped the jump drive in his hand.

Kai turned toward him. "If you know of a better place, we can go there. What about all of those *CIA assets*?" Sarcasm was written all over her face.

He turned his head to her. "You know as well as I do, we can't use them. I do not know how deep the infiltration goes." Sam partially opened his fist and observed the drive before looking back up. "Would you stake your life on his trustworthiness?"

A look of disbelief come over her face. "It's not like we are going to show him what we find."

"No, but he could have tracking and logging software hidden on his systems."

"Good point. I'll check before we start. And when we're done I'll wipe the system clean." She crossed her arms, showing more confidence than Sam thought she should.

"Are you sure you can find hidden software?"

"Unless he's taken a whole ton of classes or had an intelligence transplant, yeah, I'm sure I can find anything he might have on the system."

Sam smiled. "Getting a little uppity, are we?"

She kept a straight face as her eyes twinkled. "Nope." The twinkle disappeared. "But I've learned a lot while working for Homeland. I'm sure I can find anything he would come up with."

"Okay, I trust you, not him, to keep this safe." He reached for the door handle. "Let's get this over with."

They entered the store and found Ted stocking shelves in the second aisle. His dark hair and pale skin stood in sharp contrast. At five foot nine, and only one hundred and twenty-five pounds, he did not pose much of a threat to anyone. He looked up when they entered the aisle. Shock crossed his face. "Long time no see, Kai." Ted turned back to hang up the cables in his hand.

"It's nice to see you, Ted." Kai smiled at him as she and Sam approached.

"It's nice to see you, too. Who's this guy?" The distrust between the two men was mutual.

"Sam's an old friend of the family and just got in town today." She moved a little closer to Ted.

Sam shook Ted's hand. Ted had a weak grip. "She's like my little sister." It was clear Ted was experiencing a hint of jealousy.

"A friend of the family, huh? You knew her in Hawaii?"

"Yes, I was friends with her father."

"Did you work with him? Were you in the same field?" Ted's eyes flashed from Sam to Kai and back as he smiled. He was fishing for the truth. He wouldn't get it.

Sam answered seriously. "We worked at the DOD together. I'm an accountant."

"At the DOD?" Ted looked at Kai for verification.

"Yes, my dad worked for the DOD."

"What about all those stories?" Ted carefully regarded Kai. Disbelief covered his face.

Kai chuckled. "You mean the ones about Dad being a spy?"

"Yeah." Ted felt a little sheepish.

"I don't know who started those stories, but I couldn't have come up with a better lie to make people leave me alone." She gave Ted a disarming grin.

Shaking his head, he continued, "Well, it worked. It kept me from—" Like he ever had a chance with her.

Sam hoped his grin was not obvious. "You mean you would have been hitting on my little sister?"

Ted shook off his regret before speaking to Kai. "So, why are you contacting me now?"

"We stopped by because we need to use one of your high-end computers." Kai looked a little embarrassed.

"So lunch is off?" Ted said jokingly.

"Maybe we can do it another time, now that I'm back in town."

"Sure, that's fine. What do you need a computer for?" He sounded disappointed, but not surprised.

Sam stepped in. "Can't say. It has to do with a government contractor I'm auditing here in Denver."

"Really? Who?"

Sam smiled at Ted's typical response.

"Oh, yeah, you can't say." Ted glanced over at Kai with a smirk. "You sure your father wasn't a spy?"

Kai laughed. "It felt like it sometimes. Government and its money. Anyway, got a system we can use?"

"Can you give me an idea of how much power you need? I rent systems according to memory, disk space, and CPU cycles."

"You're not in the business of selling computers anymore?" Kai glanced around the store at the shelves of hardware.

"I still sell a few, but most of my income is from renting. I had to change strategies about two years ago. I just can't compete with Internet pricing. People come in, spend hours looking at what I have, ask me questions, then buy online." He shook his head and stared at the floor. "They think my time should be free. It's so wrong."

Sam cut into Ted's brooding. "Sorry to hear that, but we are in a hurry."

Ted looked up. Sam stood about five inches taller, with broad shoulders. "Sure, who's going to pay?" Ted pointed to a sign on the wall behind him. It listed hourly rates along with CPU cycles, and other parameters.

"DOD will cover it." Sam said.

Ted motioned toward the back wall where four large black racks stood filled with equipment. In front of the racks were four small cubicles containing tables with keyboards and monitors. "I have twenty interconnected servers, fully encrypted, and backed up. I'm tied into a 10 gigabit backbone and each system is fully backed up both in the cloud and locally on hot swap redundant hard drives. All my systems have battery backup and I have a generator out back in case of long term power failures." His sales pitch showed he was proud of what he had. "I have customers all around the world."

Sam stepped forward and looked at the setup. "What if your customer needs a more *private* solution?"

"As I said, the systems are fully encrypted, each customer uses their own encryption key. I have no master key for anyone's work, making it almost impossible for someone else to steal your work once it's encrypted."

"The company I am auditing has a— solution for many of our defense issues. If it were to fall into the wrong hands, the ramifications to both our defense systems and the economy could be catastrophic. I can't take any chances of even the name leaking out."

Ted looked impressed. "Are we talking about protection from the Chinese?"

"Among others. Are some of your customers from China or that part of the world?"

"Not sure. I've heard the Chinese have whole teams of people working on hacking into our government."

Sam stayed quiet and let Ted's imagination take over.

"The only sure way is to let you use one of my brand new systems in the back. I just got them in and formatted. I can unplug them from the Internet."

"And reformat the hard drives when we're done?" It sounded like a question, but it was not.

42

Ted showed them the rear storage room that he used as a staging area for new equipment. On walking in, Kai took charge of the computer while Sam walked around and unplugged the cameras. She disconnected the internet and made sure the system did not have wireless or Bluetooth connections. It took about five minutes before she turned to Sam. "Okay, we're clear. The system is completely isolated."

"This is so cool." Ted beamed.

Sam moved in next to Kai as he nodded toward Ted. "Thank you for your help. We will let you know when we're done."

"Can't I stay and watch? I won't say anything."

"You're joking, I hope." Sam stared him down. Ted turned and left. Once he was gone, Sam whispered to Kia. "I may have to kill him after all."

She turned to see Sam smiling, but the smile did not reach his eyes. "If he shows up dead, I'll never forgive you."

"Then I guess you'd better make sure I don't need to kill him." His tone was lighthearted, but Kai was not sure how serious he was.

She held out her hand. "Just give me the drive and tell me your little CIA secrets for reading the data."

He took a quick peek out the one-way mirror window that looked into the store before handing it over.

She slipped the drive into the computer and opened the directory which contained five files.

Sam stood behind her. "Let's see if Henderson used the same tricks I learned. Take the files and flip them."

"Flip them? What exactly do you mean?"

He held up his hand, fingers spread and twisted them around, front to back. "Picture the file as a string of ones and zeros. Flip each file front to back, making the end of the file the beginning and the beginning the end. But keep the null byte at the end."

"Should I flip it byte by byte or bit by bit?"

"Bit by bit."

"Okay, it will take a few minutes. I need to write a script." Minutes later she announced, "Done." She then proceeded to run her script and flip the files.

"Now, invert each file except the last byte. You know, change each one to a zero and each zero to a one."

"Yeah, I got it." She did. "You know I tried this and a thousand other variations."

"I'm sure you did, but you have to do both before you can decrypt them. And then you need the right key." He pointed to the much smaller file. "The key should be in there."

"And then what program should I use for the decryption?"

"The ones in front of you. You have five files. Only one contains the information we are looking for. The smallest file is the key. The three largest ones are the encryption-decryption programs."

She turned in her chair, smiled and looked up at Sam. "Really? You guys are very sneaky."

He straightened up and crossed his arms. "We have to be. In the field we don't always have the luxury of storing or sending information a hundred different ways, breaking it apart to be reassembled by the right people."

"But this is so simple. Everything is right here. But if you always do it this way, can't anyone with a computer learn what you have done?"

Sam, leaned back in his chair, "There are only a handful of people who know about this method and it is only used in extreme emergencies. I worked with Ryan Blinder a while back. Part of our chain of command was corrupted. He showed me this method for transmitting data and it worked. He said he learned it from an old friend and teacher." Leaning forward he added, "Let's go. Ted's charging me by the second."

He nodded at the screen as he pointed at the three largest files. "Change them to executable."

"Okay." She did.

"Let me see the key file in text format."

She opened the smallest file and both of them read the short paragraph.

"It's impossible to know which groupings of letters he used for each of the three programs. This is why I said we needed something with a little power behind it."

There are three sentences so let's assume a phrase from the first sentence is the key for the first program and so on. But I don't know what part of each sentence to use."

"I can write a script to try all the possible phrases for each sentence, starting with the whole sentence and going down. I will have it feed the groups of letters into each program."

"How long will that take?"

"On this system, it should not be long. A lot depends on how fast each program runs."

Sam nodded. "Let's get started."

It took about ten minutes to get the script set up and going. "You know, this could create hundreds of output files, right?"

"Maybe."

They watched as the programs ran. Soon several output files were produced.

"You hungry?" Sam's question surprised her.

She looked at the time, ten minutes past two. "Don't you want to see what we have?"

"Yes, but I need to go through them alone first."

"So, I'm only kind of on the team?"

"No, you are fully on the team, just not part of the CIA." He reached over and reassuringly rubbed her shoulder. "Once I read through the data, if it looks okay, I'll let you read it."

She stood and held out her hand. "I fly means you buy."

———

Returning from the food run, Kai saw Ted talking with a man near the hall that led to the rear of the store. This new person did not need to know about the work going on in the back. Kai wandered around the store, staying close enough to hear what they were saying.

"You sure you have not seen Sara? I thought for sure she would come by here and ask to use one of your computers."

"I haven't seen Sara in over two years. I thought her punishment was to work for the FBI, as if that was some sort of punishment. What happened? Did she do something else wrong? Is she on the run?"

The man looked around the store. Spotting Kai, he shoved his hands into his pockets and quickly turned away.

Kai moved a little closer. "Are you a friend of Sara's?"

He glanced over at her then started to move away without answering.

"Sara Beckwith? You said you were looking for her. Are you a cop?"

He shook his head. "No, I'm not a cop. I was just looking for a friend and thought she might have come by here. That's all." He again turned to leave. Speaking to Ted, he added, "If you see her, can you tell her Derry stopped by and have her call this number?" He handed Ted a slip of paper.

The moment Kai heard the name, she remembered where she had seen the face. It was in the news. "You're Sara's boyfriend, Derry something or other. An Irish name."

He stopped and examined Kai a little closer. "Maybe."

Kai took a step forward. "I used to work with her. I knew her—we were friends, before she was arrested."

The man was thinking hard but not saying a word. He was very guarded.

"My name is Kai Luana." Kai needed him to trust her. She did not want to see Sara in jail for what Alex had done. "I worked with her when Levy was blackmailing her."

"I remember hearing about you. I thought you left the state."

Kai felt a little ashamed for letting everyone else take the fall. "Sara protected me back then. Now I want to return the favor."

Derry stood his ground, unmoving. "And just how do you plan to do that?"

"I know she didn't kill that agent."

"How do you know anything about what is going on with her?"

Kai walked up and whispered in his ear, "I know she was set up, and I know who did it."

After examining several files, Sam found the successfully decrypted one he was looking for and began reading through it. It did not have as much information as he had hoped. Ryan had found two of the leaks and was building an organization chart for a terrorist group. Several other names were in the file as possibles, but the two names he had come up with confirmed what Kai had said. Sam read about them.

Agent Patrick Landry of Homeland Security, aka Dace Roux. He had been a DGSE agent for the French Government, their external intelligence agency, before becoming a Muslim. After turning in a letter to his upper management accusing them of illegal actions against French citizens of Islamic beliefs, he deleted as much information as he could on Muslim terrorists and left the force. He was wanted by the French government in connection with several terrorist acts committed against French citizens.

The next was Agent Curtis Hewitt, also of Homeland. His real name was Jonas Hahn. He was a German citizen who had become disillusioned with Germany's loss of world power. He was very vocal about his dislike and distrust of the EU. He had lost his job as a computer analyst in the government because of it. Shortly afterward, he turned to Islam. He now earned his living as a terrorist for hire.

The third person, said to be working with the other two, was missing a name and picture. But this person was also a computer expert. After his talk with Kai, Sam was sure this was Alex aka Gabriele. A cold-blooded killer. It would be easy to find her picture in the Homeland computer system and add it to the file. He would do that later.

Hearing muffled voices through the glass he stopped his work and glanced into the store. Kai was talking with Ted and another man. He studied the new member to the store. After determining the man was not a threat Sam went back to the file.

Much of the information was long on the seriousness of the upcoming attack, but short on the actual details. The type of attack, when it would happen, and where, were still unknowns.

Before he made it much further the voices grew louder as the room filled with the smell of food. Sam closed the file and looked up to see Kai walking into the room with the unknown man.

Sam stood. "Who's this?"

Kai pointed to Derry as she set the carryout bag on the edge of the table. "This is Sara's boyfriend. His name is Derry Conway."

"Sara's boyfriend?" Sam could not believe this. "What is he

doing here?"

Kai hesitated. "He is looking for Sara. I owe Sara a lot. I told him I know who set her up."

"Do you know what we are up against here?" Bringing an unknown person into this operation could jeopardize the whole thing. "You should know better than to share that information."

Kai stood halfway between the two men. "We might need Sara for this."

"I decide who we need and don't need."

Derry shifted his weight to a more defensive position. "Hey, I don't know what's going on here, or who you are. I'm just here to find Sara, to save Sara. Kai said she had information that could help."

Both Kai and Sam looked at Derry. Sam needed to keep things under his control. He looked out into the store for Ted. The man was working with a customer. Good. He turned back to Kai. "Why do you think we might need Sara's help?"

Kai moved a little closer to Derry. She needed Sam to trust Derry. "Sara is the best computer hacker I have ever seen. If anyone can follow the terrorists' electronic trail it will be her."

Sam listened. When Kai finished, he studied Derry. "Sara could be an asset to us. Do you know where she is?"

"Not yet. But I won't stop searching until I find her." The man shifted back and forth. He wanted to get out of there.

"What makes you think you have a chance of finding her if she does not want to be found?"

"I know her better than anyone. I—"

"Know how she thinks? The FBI has trained agents who study the way a person thinks."

"I was about to say, I know how she feels. Her thinking is very logical most of the time. But that still leaves hundreds of possibilities for where she could be hiding. I know how she feels about places, not just physical locations, but types of places. That gives me an advantage in knowing where to look or places to avoid."

The kid was no dummy. That type of understanding about a person could be a real edge.

Sam continued to size up Derry. "How do I know I can trust you? How do I know you won't crack and run at the first sign of trouble?"

Kai took a deep breath, then she told Sam about all that Derry had gone through to save Sara from Levy.

Sam listened closely. His opinion of Derry was quickly changing. Standing, Sam walked over and shook Derry's hand. "It looks like you are now part of the team. I am recruiting you to work for me as an agent of the U.S. Government. Are you willing to do as I ask?"

Derry studied Sam. "Will it help save Sara?" Derry's eyes did not flinch as he waited for the answer.

"Her, and thousands of others."

"Then I'm in, as long as you know Sara comes first for me."

"I understand." Sam turned to Kai. "Sara is going to need a high end laptop. Can you take care of that while I fill Derry in on the details?"

43

"I need an update." Faircloth stepped into Kent's office. Ernest Reeves was in there, helping out, doing whatever Kent asked. He was from the part of CART that ran traces on bank transactions, looking for bank fraud, money laundering and now, terrorist funding.

Ernest spoke first. "Sara's boyfriend Derry was very busy last night. He must have had this planned out well in advance. He maxed out his credit cards, acquiring cash and other items."

"What type of items?" Faircloth stepped in and took a seat. Rubbing his face, he worked on listening. Short nights and long days were hard on this old agent. In the back of his mind, he knew this would be his last case.

"He mostly bought a few burn phones, ready-to-eat meals, and snack foods."

"Do we have the info on the phones?"

"I'm still working on that, but we do know they were smart phones. He can hook up to the internet anywhere he has a signal."

"Keep working on it." Looking at both men he asked, "Does it appear that her boyfriend thinks Sara is still around?"

Ernest shrugged. "He could be planning on meeting her somewhere."

Kent piped in. "Or, if he's trying to help her escape, he could be a decoy to throw us off."

"We have camera footage of Sara in Denver. I don't think she is planning to go anywhere." Faircloth rubbed his eyes. "I believe this Derry fellow is going to meet up with her. If we find him, we will find her." Faircloth swiveled his chair toward Kent. "Add his image to the search and—" looking at Ernest he added, "keep an eye out for any more credit card transactions."

"Sure thing," Ernest replied.

"Anything else?" The question was to both of them.

"I've had a lot of false hits on facial rec but nothing to latch onto," Kent supplied.

"Ernest, I want both of their pictures in every cop's hands within fifty miles of Denver. I want them at the bus stations, train stations and at the public and private airports in case they try to leave the area."

"Hers was sent out last night. I'll get his added right away."

"This gal is slippery, and her escape was well planned. Keep me posted if anything pops up." He rose from his seat and left.

———

Kai slowed as she approached the door to her apartment. Alex had never called about the results on the decryption program, which worked out fine for Kai, but it felt out of place. Opening the door and stepping in, Kai saw Alex at the table, sitting in the same spot she was in when Kai had left that morning.

"Welcome back, stranger." Alex looked up from her seat. "You don't look very sweaty for spending the day running."

"Oh, after my morning workout, I went to the gym to work on some different muscle groups. I cleaned up there before heading over to sign up for that triathlon."

"So you're really going to do it? Remember, this is only a temporary assignment. I don't know how long Hewitt's going to want you around."

Alex's words sent a chill down Kai's arms. Once done with the decryption, was she going to end up like that FBI agent? "It doesn't matter, the registration was full."

Alex closed the laptop and set it aside. "I ordered us some dinner. I thought you'd be back earlier. Yours is in the fridge."

"Thanks." Kai went to her room and dropped the pack off. Returning to the kitchen she went straight for the food. "Pizza. Is this from that place you told me about?" She took it out and slipped it into the microwave.

"Of course, best pizza in Colorado. You deserve it for all your hard work." Alex took her computer to the living room before dropping onto the couch. "You made it back in time to watch a movie with me."

She turned on the TV after inserting a DVD into the player.

With the hot pizza in one hand and a drink in the other, Kai took a seat next to Alex.

Got to act like everything is fine.

She nibbled on the food as they watched the movie. The pizza was good but sitting this close to a murdering-terrorist was not good for the appetite. After most of a slice, Kai set the plate down.

"You feeling okay?"

Kai rubbed her stomach. Her digestive system was complaining loudly. "The pizza is just not sitting well with me tonight."

"That's some really good pizza. You sure it's not because you're low on sugar. I would think after spending the day working out you would need lots of food."

Kai picked up the slice and took another bite. It only took a few seconds for her body to tell her that was a mistake. Running to the kitchen, her body rejected the meal. She stood over the sink as the room around her weaved back and forth. Her mind worked to stop the ever increasing spinning in her head.

"Are you okay? You look really sick."

"Something didn't sit right. I think I need to go lie down."

Alex went to her side to support her. "Maybe we should call a doctor or something."

"No, I'm sure it's nothing. Just let me sit down for a few minutes. I'll be fine."

Alex helped her to the table where Kai dropped onto a chair. As her bottom hit, her burn phone pushed hard into the rear of her hip. She wanted to pull it out of her pocket but not in front of Alex.

Is this how that agent felt?

"You sure we shouldn't go to the hospital? You really don't look very good."

"I don't feel very good either." The room stopped its sideways spinning and started dropping. She tried to stand but she didn't have the strength. "I need to lay down. Can you help me to my room?"

I need to call Sam.

Kai's arm lifted as Alex tucked her shoulder in under it.

"I'm taking you to the hospital."

44

Tazeem pulled into the trailer park south of Atlanta. He hated this place, but it was all he could afford. Soon that would improve. It was a promise he had made to himself and his family.

Stiff muscles turned the wheel as he weaved through the park. Three hours of training in Detroit followed by over eleven hours on the road made for a long day. He had missed his evening prayers, a sin, but stopping in the middle of Atlanta could have brought suspicion. If questioned, it could have cost him the device that sat in the van behind him. That made his sin excusable.

Driving slowly, he looked into the windows of a nice new doublewide. One day soon he would have such luxuries to enjoy. His home sat near the back of the park, where all the older trailers were. Several of the streetlights were out. He pulled in beside his nineteen-year-old single-wide trailer.

Reaching for the keys to shut down the engine, a small ache shot up his back. He reached up and kneaded his shoulder muscles.

The review session that morning had been necessary. It was a chance to practice setting up and using the device. But to be questioned by a Russian was humiliating. Working with a pig of a man without faith had destroyed what would otherwise have been a time to praise Allah. Tazeem may not be as learned as Nasir, but he knew that the Qur'an said being without faith made the Russian lower than a Christian or a Jewish dog. As misguided as Jews and Christians were, they were still people of the Book. He had more respect for a dog than he did for the Russian. A man without any faith was a man without a soul.

Tazeem had been born in Atlanta, Georgia to Sunni Iranian parents. His parents had left Iran when the Shia Ayatollah took control.

They should have stayed to fight the heretics. But they had run. They put their comfort above the law.

His father filled him with lies when he was young, telling him America was a good place to live, full of good people. How could his own father be so blind? How could he spend time every day reading the words of the one true prophet, Mohammed, and not see the truth?

America was not a great nation. America was a land of depravity, a place that would never accept the words of the one true prophet without force.

His father believed the lies of this filthy country because it made him rich. He had a big house and three cars, three cars for two people. He was owned by the infidels and no longer a man to admire. His father has left the true faith, and the punishment for that was death. The law left no room for exceptions, and die he would. It would either be by his hands or the hands of the Americans once they learned he was Muslim. This country had turned anti-Muslim for a short time after 9-11. But that was nothing compared to what would happen soon.

Turning in his seat, Tazeem peeked under the blue plastic tarp at the device that would bring such pain. His heart swelled with pride. He was one of the chosen to lead in the war.

Dropping the tarp and making sure it covered the unit, he reached down and grabbed the Russian manual. He couldn't read it, but the Russian Army always assumed their military could not read and made everything doable by pictures.

Grabbing the door handle, he glanced at his home. His oldest son was at the door, waiting for him. He, too, would make a good leader someday.

———

Kai forced herself into a sitting position. She was in the backseat of Alex's car. Her eyes tried to focus on the passing scenery as Alex drove. Kai did not believe they were headed to the hospital, but was too weak to force the car to a stop or even open the door and jump out. The lump in her rear pocket was barely noticeable as more of her body was shutting down. But she had to do something.

Pushing her hand back, she slipped the phone out. Alex paid little attention to her. Sam had given Kai a number to call in case of an emergency and this was definitely an emergency. She pulled the phone around and held it close to the back of Alex's seat.

The sun dipped behind the mountain peaks as the land took on a deserted feel. Making sure the sound was off, Kai hit the speed dial.

On the first ring, Sam answered. Kai spoke over his voice. "This doesn't look like the way to the hospital. There aren't any houses around here. Are you sure this is right?"

"So, you are still able to talk. I am impressed. Todd had passed out by now." Her southern accent had been replaced by the one Kai heard on the other side of Landry's door. "But you did eat the poison and then throw up. I put it directly into Todd's bloodstream. You may live a little longer than he did. But the end will be the same."

Kai held her thumb over the speaker. "What are you talking about? You said you would help me. Take me to a doctor. This is in the middle of nowhere."

"Which makes it a perfect place to dump your body. This area of Rocky Mountain Arsenal is off limits. No one will find you for weeks, maybe years. By then, no one will care."

"Why won't you help me? I'm— sick." Kai was having trouble concentrating.

"Why would I help you? I'm the one who poisoned you."

"You need my help, — for the — fiilesss" The pain that had started in Kai's belly ran through her whole body. Her words were beginning to slur.

"Bringing you to Denver was a mistake. You took up too much of my time and gave us nothing." The car pulled to a stop.

Kai clumsily slid the phone back into her pocket.

Alex got out and opened the rear door. Kai's head fell back against the seat. Alex pushed the woman. Kai had passed out. Good, she would not resist. Grabbing Kai under the arms, Alex roughly pulled her out of the car.

"Mmmm, in—lake?" Kai mumbled, but did not put up a fight.

"I would dump you in the lake, but your body would float to the top and could be spotted by someone flying over. Nope, you are to become part of the wildlife refuge. I'll drop you where only the coyotes will find you." The short blond dragged Kai's body behind some scrubby bushes, pushed her under as far as she could and walked away.

———

As the sun was disappearing behind the Colorado mountains, Derry stood at a crossroads. After meeting with Kai and her friend Sam, he'd spent the day wandering the streets of downtown Denver. It was crazy to think that by aimlessly roaming he could find Sara. Especially since she didn't want to be found. He would have better luck finding a three legged horse at the racetrack.

Looking around, the thought of sleeping on the street did not appeal to him, but the homeless shelters held even less attraction. Maybe a different hotel, but any that were not filled with crawly things would require a credit card. Twenty-four hours was more than enough time for the FBI to get his name out there alongside Sara's. He couldn't take the chance.

He glanced to the right. Something about the place was familiar. Stepping in that direction, his mind worked to pull up memories. When it did, he regretted it. Cloaked in darkness, the edifice turned back the clock.

The night came back to him. He could hear Sara's screams, see the blood. But as much as he hated the structure, it drew him in one step at a time. He replayed the night over in his mind. Levy, a truly heartless man, had tortured and tried to kill Sara and him. Realizing his hand was rubbing the scar left by the knife that had nearly ended his life, he pulled it away.

Whatever happened to the electric chair? Did the FBI still have it or had it been destroyed by now? A chilling breeze hit the back of his neck. He twisted his shoulders and head, trying to push away the tingling sensation that moved down his back. Evil poured out of every boarded up window, as the hidden demons sucked the light out of the air. Yet it lured him in.

The last time he had been in that building, he and Sara had both almost died. Was that really almost three years ago, or just last week? If not for the grace of God, they would both have had their final minutes on this planet. Some say you cannot remember pain. Those who say that have never experienced the worst kind of pain, the type that changes you for life. The pain was there, rising up from just below the top layer of skin. His body gave a slight, involuntary shutter.

Stepping closer, he examined its entrance. The boards that kept the world out were covered with graffiti. It was a good indication that no one was allowed in, as it should be.

"Derry?"

Was he hearing things? The agony from that night was playing with his mind.

"Derry, is that you?"

He spun around to see someone in rags. "Sara?" It was her voice, her eyes. He took a step forward. She moved toward him. "Sara, you're safe." His arms flowed around her as she rushed in. He held on tight. He wanted this moment to last forever. Somehow she'd found him.

Pulling away, she stared up at him. "How'd you know where I'd be?"

"I've been looking for you—"

She pulled back, breaking the grip he had on her. "Does anyone else know where you are?" Her head went one way, then the other. "If you found me, so can they."

She turned and took three strides. He shot forward to cut the increasing separation in half and grabbed her arm. "No, wait. I'm alone."

"Ouch. Let go."

He released her as he stepped around to block her path. "Sorry. I didn't mean to grab so hard."

She rubbed just above where his hand had been. "Just don't touch me there."

"I said I was sorry. Are you hurt?"

"Move out of my way." Her eyes looked straight ahead, not up at him.

"Please, wait, just hear me out."

Her head snapped up where he could look into her fearful eyes. "How did you find me?" Her question demanded an answer.

"I didn't. I've been looking all day. I have wandered all over Denver, hoping to find you. But you found me."

Her doubt came through despite the disguise and low streetlights. "If anyone asks, you've been looking, but you didn't find me." Her head dropped. "Now, move."

"No."

"If you don't get out of my way, I'll scream."

"For who, the police?"

Her face was stone. Brown icebergs glared up at him. But he did not waver, and he was not going to. He would not lose her again, not tonight. He refused to look away. "I came here to help you."

"And I told you not to, you bullheaded jerk."

"That may be, but you are in deep trouble and you need help."

"From you? What can you do to help?"

He knew she was hurting and scared, but her words stung.

"I told you I would never leave you. I meant it."

Her eyes softened as she lost herself in his gentle look. An eternity passed before she spoke. "Okay, you win—for now. Can we at least move away from the streetlight?"

They stepped into the alley, toward the abandoned building. Once out of the road, she turned toward him. "I told you not to look for me, but I should have known better."

He moved closer to the building as he talked. "I love you. What'd you expect?"

"You've always got to play the hero." Her tone changed. "I'm glad you're here."

He realized she was standing near a green dumpster, the same one he had hidden behind almost three years ago. He walked toward it and checked behind it as he spoke absentmindedly. "This is where I hid from Levy's men."

She did not move or speak.

He looked over at her before turning back toward the building. As he walked around, examining the boarded windows and rear door, she remained quiet and unmoved. All the boards were solidly intact. It was strange that an abandoned building would sit untouched for almost three years with no one breaking in. "I think we could hide out inside here."

"Are you out of your mind? No one would spend a night in that place. Not after what happened there." She faced away from the streetlight so he couldn't make out her expression.

"Exactly. What happened here was all over the news for months. No one would spend a night here. That is exactly why we can." Without another word they both turned their eyes toward the doorway that led into Levy's building. The wood planks that covered the passageway where a steel door once stood was covered with gang artwork and filled with small holes and dents. They stepped toward it.

"There is a reason no one has broken in. The place is filled with evil."

He glanced at her. "Evil that we stood up against and defeated with God's help." Reaching out, he grabbed the edge of the covering and gave it a yank. It barely moved.

"Maybe no one broke in because they can't."

Walking a few feet, he grabbed a panel that covered one of the windows and pulled. It held tighter than the covering on the door. He walked back. He examined the doorway more closely. "There is always a way in, a weak point that we can leverage."

"What if someone else is keeping this place closed up tight for Levy?"

"Who would do that?" But it was something he hadn't thought of. "Is Levy out of jail?"

"Not that I know of. Everyone who worked for him has at least three more years in jail and Levy's in for a minimum of fifteen." Her voice dropped. "Not long enough if you ask me."

He contemplated her words. There was a lot more hidden behind them than she was saying.

"I keep tabs on them. One of Levy's guys may come after me when they get out. I want to know when that might happen," Sara continued.

This was something she had never talked about with him. "Then I guess you had better be with someone who can protect you."

"Or be where no one can find me."

What? "That would be impossible and you know it."

"Maybe." She shrugged and moved toward the building.

––––––

The drive that was found under the coffee table at Sara's home contained several files, all encrypted. Tony ran a few tests to see what algorithms had been used on them. The tests would not necessarily name the programs that encrypted them, but it would say what family the encryption fell into. They returned a mixed bag of results, but one caught his attention. One file used the Bureau's standard protocol and encryption algorithm. It would not take long to open that file. Using the master key, he decrypted it in only a few minutes.

Opening it, he planned to give it a quick scan before sending it to Faircloth. The subject of the file changed his mind. It was a lengthy report on Agent Booker, containing pictures of her and her family. The text included schedules and routes they took to work and school. He reached for his phone.

"Agent Booker, I have opened the first file from the thumb drive found in Sara's home."

"I'm in the middle of dinner with my family, this better be good. What did you find?"

"It's about you and your family."

"What do you mean it's about me and my family?" Her voice rose a notch.

"The file has pictures and schedules for you, your husband and son. Are—"

"I'm on my way in. Don't show that to anyone. Am I clear?" The line went dead.

While he waited for Booker to arrive, Tony tried to come up with a reason why Sara would have this file. It was assumed the drive was the one Todd had brought back from Texas, which had originated at the senator's home. Why would Senator Henderson have a file on Booker? Why would someone kill him for it, and why would he send a copy to his brother?

Things were not adding up.

45

Derry watched Sara eating slowly. The only light in the room consisted of a few beams of streetlight that slipped through the holes in the boards that covered the windows. She stopped with her hand halfway to her mouth, then lowered it back to the table as she pushed her chair back.

"What's wrong?" He was worried.

"This place."

"It's safe." He had only spent one torturous day here. Sara had been forced to work here for two years by a cruel, inhuman, blackmailer and murderer.

"It's filled with nightmares. I can't believe I let you talk me into this."

"Kai's old apartment isn't filled with those memories. This was Kai's home. Those things took place somewhere else."

Derry knew all too well the reasons why Sara hated this place. Kai and Sara first met when they were both forced to work for Mr. Levy. He blackmailed them both into writing code for a major credit card scheme. Levy had forced Kai to live in this building, in this makeshift apartment. He wanted Kai under his control twenty-four hours a day. He wanted the same for Sara, but she refused. She knew that she was the key to making the credit card program work and used that leverage to force Levy to allow her to live in her own apartment. She knew what went on in this building and it was far more than just stealing money. Levy had his own little torture chamber in the basement. One day he had forced Sara to watch what happened to those who betrayed him. He had killed Sara's friend Steve in an electric chair. Later, when Sara tried to run away with Levy's money, Levy had tried to do the same to Sara and Derry. Even if the evil was gone, the nightmares were still here.

"Those things still took place in this building."

"We will only be here for a night or two. Tomorrow we can look for someplace else." He didn't like the place either, but right now it was the best option.

"Sure." She stared at a spot on the table, unwilling to look at him.

He reached over and rubbed her shoulder. "No one will ever come here looking for us." He looked around in the dim light. Kai's place or not, tonight's sleep would be light if he got any at all. Nightmares were not the only things that hid in every corner.

She pushed her food a few inches away. "What if we call the police and tell them what you told me?"

"You mean that Kai and her friend Sam believe they know who murdered Todd?" He couldn't picture local police being willing or able to stand up against Homeland Security.

"Sure. It could buy us some time to get the proof we need."

"While both of us are locked up? Do you really believe the police will let us go looking for proof that some people in Homeland are murderers?" Derry shook his head before taking another bite. He glanced at the energy bar and wondered what they put into it. The only flavor it had was sugar. "We need proof before we call the cops."

"What do you think we should do? Go find the woman who murdered Todd? You can hold her while I beat her up and ask her questions. We just need to make sure it's recorded."

"I can go for that, if you think it would work." He smiled just a little.

Her worry was manifesting itself in her sarcastic comments.

Sara dropped her head onto the table for half a second. Lifting it, she flung her hair back. "Kai is our only witness. We have to get her to go to the FBI."

"She can't go. At least not yet. She is the only one on the inside at Homeland. She has to stay to help uncover their plan." Derry chewed on the overly sweet "health" bar.

"I haven't seen or heard from her in nearly three years and she pops up in the middle of all this. How strange is that?" Sara shook her head wonderingly. "How does she look?"

"Tall, skinny, like a runner."

"Skinny? Kai's a runner again? She said she ran before she worked for Levy. I'm glad she took it up again. But that's not what I mean."

"Having never seen her before, I don't have anything to compare it with. She seemed scared." He wasn't exactly sure what Sara was looking for.

"Then the danger to the country must be very real. Kai's not one to scare easily. Her carefree attitude bothered me when we worked for Levy. I think she spent more time worrying about me than herself." Sara sat up a little straighter. "So, you said she was working with a CIA agent? Sam?"

"Yes, she said he was an old friend."

"How do you know he was CIA? Did he tell you?"

"Kai did. He wouldn't say anything about himself. About all I got from him was that if I wanted to save the world I had to do what he said."

"I guess the rumors about Kai's dad were true." Her tone was flat. Sara was controlling her emotions, trying to think things through.

"Kai said she overheard the murder confession in a conversation behind a closed door at Homeland Security." Derry was trying to help her sort things out.

Sara stood. "Legally that is just hearsay." She folded her arms around her midsection and paced just on the other side of the table. "So, as far as the courts care, we really have nothing."

"Maybe not in a legal sense. But we know who killed Todd and the terrorists don't know we know. Now we need to find out why Todd was killed and why they felt the need to blame you." Derry inspected the sickening floor, covered with trash and animal droppings from years of abandonment. Rats were the only living creatures brave enough to move into this structure. The room reeked, but it did not seem as bad as when they had first stepped in.

Sara stopped. Her attention was on him, waiting. Even in the faint light Derry could see Sara's face changing. She was beginning to look like his Sara again. "Did Sam say anything about Todd's murder being connected with the senator's murder?"

"Yes, and with Henderson's brother's death as well."

"We are fairly sure the senator was killed by at least two men."

"We?"

"The FBI. So the woman who killed Todd must be working with the men who killed Senator Henderson. For anyone to kill a senator and an FBI agent they would have to be out of their minds."

"I know. Sam and I talked about this. The FBI will not stop until they are found. The terrorists are being very brazen to leave such a trail.

"Which means that whatever they are planning will happen soon enough that they are not worried about being found out beforehand. What else did you learn?" Sara only looked in his direction when she had a question. Other than that she studied an unknown spot on the floor.

"Kai said that in addition to this Alex woman there were two men in the conversation about Todd's death. They also work at Homeland. It is likely they are the ones who killed the senator." Derry pulled a laptop from his pack and turned it on. "Sam gave me some information on them."

She eyed the computer. "That's a nice system."

"Kai picked it out. She said you would like it."

Sara took her seat, scooted the chair next to his, and pulled the laptop away from him. She wanted to drive. "Where is this information?"

"There's a document under the main directory."

Sara tapped the touchpad lightly a few times and brought up the file.

She scrolled through it, going faster than Derry could keep up. "Slow down a little," he said quietly.

She pointed to the battery life indicator. "You should have charged it before you left Ted's store if you wanted me to go slow." Stopping on one of the images, she added. "I know him. That's Agent Hewitt. He's been helping us with the senator's investigation." She moved farther down the file and stopped on another image of a man. "They work together. This guy is Hewitt's boss, Landry."

The computer shut down before they could get any further. They again sat in a room draped in darkness but for a few slivers of streetlight coming through.

She stood again. "The FBI is always complaining about Homeland sticking their noses in places they don't belong. They take credit for investigations while we do the work. They withhold information from us. They have too much power. But now you are telling me these men are terrorists? Going up against them is risky at best and deadly if caught."

Derry stood and moved around the table. "But they killed Todd, your friend."

"Don't you think I know that?" Stress caused her voice to be louder than she intended.

He moved toward her, to comfort her. He reached out his hands and gently placed them on her arms, carefully avoiding her injury. She shifted, moving that tender area farther away from his hands.

"We have to do this. I believe we can do this. Remember, we have the one ally that can't be beat." Derry reached up and gently stroked her hair.

She was silent for several seconds. "I sure hope so. Todd didn't have many friends in this world. Someone has to stick up for him." She leaned in. Slipping her good arm around him, she placed her head against his chest. "I'm just scared. So many people have died, and I don't want to be one of them."

"I know. It would be foolish not to be scared." He kissed the top of her head. "Do you know what bravery is?"

She nodded. "Standing against your fears and doing what is right."

He let her rest in his arms as long as she wanted.

After a minute she pulled away. "But what can we do? I'm not an agent and neither are you."

"No. So we have to use our brains."

"Agents are smart and trained. I'm just a programmer. I don't think the way an agent thinks."

"No, you don't, which is our real advantage. The people we are up against have shown they can outsmart most agents because they know how law enforcement agencies work. We need to attack this problem the way a programmer would."

"What makes you think a programmer can solve it when agents can't?"

"I am just going by what I believe the terrorists think. Why else would they want you out of the way?"

"If they wanted me out of the way, why not kill me like they did everyone else?" She stared into his eyes.

"Because not killing you must have some benefit for them. What advantage would they have in keeping you alive?—Sorry that came out kind of cold."

She didn't seem to notice. She was in business mode. "It makes the Bureau mount a massive manhunt. It diverts their attention." Sara took a seat at the table. Pulling one leg up, she rested her chin on her knee as they talked.

"Massive? How massive?"

"I am sure it is tying up most of the FBI's resources. Not only that, the FBI would pull in the local police, airport security, plus anyone else they can think of. It won't stop day to day activities, but all other long term and lower priority projects would be set aside."

Derry took a few steps toward the table. "Sounds like a magic act."

"What do you mean?"

"The trick in a magic act is to have everyone looking at the beautiful woman, while the real action is happening just out of view."

She lifted her head. "So I'm the blonde bimbo?"

"In a manner of speaking." He snickered with her. It was good to share even this tiny bit of humor.

After a moment of silence, she added. "So, while everyone is looking for me, the terrorists must be feeling safe to do whatever they want."

"And we need to find out what that is." This was the big step Derry had been waiting for Sara to take. She had to become determined to not run, or hide, but to solve the crime.

"How do we do that?" Sara wondered.

The phone in Derry's pocket buzzed.

"You brought your phone here?" She stood, ready to bolt.

"No, it's a burn phone." He pulled it out. "Sam is the only one who has this number."

He answered. "Hello?"

"This is Sam. I need a favor." He sounded worried and his tone was hushed.

"Shoot."

"Kai's hurt badly. Her roommate tried to kill her."

"Hurt? How bad?" Derry's eyes shifted to Sara. She was studying him intently.

"The doctor said I got her to the hospital in time. She'll live. But she needs time to recover. I need some place safe to hide her. If they find out she's still alive they will come after her again."

"Can't you admit her to the hospital under a different name?"

"I can change her name, but not her description or what happened to her. I convinced the doctor not to fill out a report as long as Kai is gone before his shift is over."

"My house is empty right now. You could use it."

"Out of the question. The FBI is watching it. Homeland is probably watching it, too. You know people around here. How about a friend? Someone you trust with your life?"

———

As his wife cleared the table after their evening meal, Tazeem remained seated, studying the writings of Al-Shafi'i. It was late and he should be going to bed, but tonight he stayed to tell her part of the plan and how it aligned with the words of the great Imam. Tazeem was proud of his role in this great venture and he wanted his wife to be proud also.

He was excited as he spoke. "At the training session those of us assembled with Nasir praised Allah for giving us this great plan. In less than a week, deadly poison will be pumped into the air in five major cities. These highly populated targets will taste Allah's sting. Millions of Americans will die and this nation will be devastated beyond anything it has experienced before. They will see that the power of Allah can reach deep into their weak, little world. The land in and around these cities will be poisoned for years and the self-righteous Americans will never again have the strength to attack the Islamic states. Then Islam can spread across the globe like a wind driven brushfire."

Nina stopped working to listen. When Tazeem leaned back to take a sip of coffee she spoke. "I still do not understand why you want to destroy this country." Her tone was quiet yet harsh.

That same stupid question, again. Why can't she accept that it is the will of Allah? All infidels must die. "How can we continue to live in a country that does not follow the will of Allah? America is a lawless country where our own children are treated as outcasts because we choose the true path." Tazeem flipped back a few pages in the book in front of him and pointed to a paragraph at the top of the page. "Right here, Al-

Shafi'i interprets the great prophet's words for us. Mohammed says all infidels that are not under our control and paying the jizya, shall come under the sword." He looked up at her. "Allah wants us to kill them."

"You believe destroying Atlanta will change this?" She barely glanced at the book, one he told her to read one hour every day.

"Not just Atlanta. We have men willing to die for this cause in Chicago, New York, Denver, and Los Angeles. When these five cities fall, this nation will see the power of the one, true god." Nasir had told them not to speak about this to anyone, but his wife needed to understand, to see the truth. Mohammed's words were very clear to those who understood them, and Nasir was only doing what Al-Shafi'i ordered them to do.

Tazeem closed the book and rubbed his hand across the cover as he glanced around the kitchen where several dirty dishes sat next to the sink. He hated this place. Thirty feet out any window were the homes of unbelievers, pigs. He looked back at his wife, into her eyes. What could he say that she would understand? She was not as smart as he had hoped. Maybe she was just too simple after all. Before they met, she had been an infidel, like the rest of her family. He had showed her the true path to Allah. It was through these studies that they had grown close to each other and were married. She was a slow learner and only in the last couple of years had she truly started to understand Islam and the sacrifices it demanded. But understanding what is required and living it are not the same thing.

"You like living like this?" He waved his hand around the tiny kitchen. "The roof leaks. We freeze in the winter and burn up in the summer. We are barely getting by, and each month is harder."

"You blame America for our lack of money?" Her hands were on her hips.

He hated the way she looked down on him. Only in the Western world could women get away with thinking they were equal with or better than men. He wanted to put a stop to this, but now was not the time for a lesson in respect.

"If you did not spend so much time in your meetings at the mosque, learning how to hate, and took the overtime they are always offering you at work, we could live better. Even your own father has offered you a better paying job, a good job." Her eyes bore into his.

He would not flinch, not this time. She should be slapped, for the Qur'an says it is right to beat a disobedient woman. "I would never work for him. He only makes the offers out of pity." How could she know what his father really thought of him? The two had only seen each other a few times, and not at all in the last three years.

He continued his lesson. "You feel it is okay for our children to be harassed at school? They follow Allah and his teachings and they should be respected for that, not made fun of. It is an insult to Allah and to Mohammed, his prophet."

"Our children are no more harassed than any other children. It does not matter whether your child is Christian, Muslim, Jewish, or atheist, they are all picked on."

"Do not put my children in the same group as Jews, Christians and nonbelievers."

"Why, because their parents don't take everything personally?" Her knuckles turned white as she leaned forward. She was not backing down.

He stood. "Because none of them have true faith. They do not follow the Qur'an."

"You mean because they are not out there killing everyone that is different from them? Shafi'i is not the only caliph we have studied. Not all say to kill every nonbeliever."

"These others are wrong. We follow Al-Shafi'i's teachings."

His words made her hesitate. "What you are planning will make us enemies in our own land. All Muslims will have to leave their homes. And if they find out that you took part in this, they will kill all of us, including our children."

He had had enough. She was showing too much disrespect. It was the teachings of this nation that encouraged such attitudes. She needed to move past what she learned as a child. He had no choice but to show her what her own actions had brought. The first five steps he took around the table she stood her ground, defying him. But when he raised his hand, she saw the error in antagonizing him.

Is threatening to strike her enough of a lesson? No. She needs to learn that only the words of Allah, as spoken by his one true prophet, matter.

His fist flew quickly, before she could duck.

Her head bounced against the wall behind her. She twisted her face away as she let out a scream. Her eyes opened wide. Reaching out to grab her, he kept her from falling to the ground. He pulled his fist back to strike a second time when he heard a second scream behind him. He stopped as he felt one of his children grabbing his leg. Looking down he saw his oldest daughter beating on it. Tears streamed down her face. Smacking her on the side of the head, he demanded she go to bed.

She pulled away, terror in her face.

"Go back to your room! Now!" He released his wife and raised his hand toward his daughter again.

She jumped back before backing through the living room, her fear filled eyes never leaving his face. When she entered the hall, he saw his other children, all staring at him in horror. "All of you, get into your rooms and don't come out!"

Quickly, they obeyed. He turned back to his wife. The side of her face was red and swollen with a trickle of blood forming at the corner of her mouth.

"You know you brought this on yourself." He stepped back. He wanted to hit her again but resisted the urge. This was enough of a lesson for now. "Women are to obey, not disagree with their husbands. Go take care of yourself. You have blood running down your face."

Her stare dropped to the floor before she stepped away. Grabbing a dishcloth, she filled it with ice and held it to the side of her face. She looked up at him for only a second, but he saw her eyes were lifeless, without disrespect. *Is she finally learning her place?*

"I am worried about our children. That is all. We have to live here after the attack." She shook a little as she spoke.

"And it will be much better afterwards, you will see." He walked to the other side of the table. "This godless nation loves money, alcohol, and sex. That is what they worship and that is what must be destroyed. America must be shown the truth."

She relaxed a little, but kept her eyes lowered. Uncertainty filled her voice. "Not everyone is that way. There are millions of Christians and Jews that follow their beliefs. They may be confused, but you have even said we all follow the same god."

Tazeem spat. "Jews, may they be the first to die." She knew so little of the Qur'an. "They are like all the others that worship money. They are like my father. The only way to bring change into this nation

Deadly Infiltration

is to bring in Sharia law, the law given to us from Allah. Then this will be a country we can live in."

She leaned against the counter, staring at him now. He scanned his neighbor's trailer across their narrow yard. A figure stood at the window. Had they seen him hit his wife? The people who lived in this park spent too much time sticking their noses into other people's business.

His wife glanced down the hallway where their three boys and two girls should have been sleeping. For all her faults, she was a good mother. "Do not worry about them. Here, in our trailer, you will be too far away from where I will release the poison. Just make sure you stay home this Friday. If you are worried, stay inside with the windows shut."

"What about your own family, your mother and father? Or my sister and her kids? They live in Atlanta. You cannot let them die in your quest to destroy the nonbelievers."

Again she was thinking with her emotions. She was so weak. "We cannot tell anyone, do you understand? No calls, no emails, no texting. I am sorry, but your sister must die for her sins. She is married to an infidel, a nonbeliever. She has sealed her fate."

Nina's eyes glistened with the tears she held back. "And your own mother and father? They are believers. Are you willing to let them die in this attack?"

"They are believers of Islam in words only. What they love is money. They are not true followers." His parents said they followed the great prophet, but with their nice house and well-paying jobs they deserved to die. You could not tell them from the Christians or Jews that lived around them. They had even had Jews in their home. It made him sick.

Her eyes shifted to the Russian book on the edge of the table. "What is this book?"

"It contains instructions for how to set up the device that will be used to make the poison."

"Is this device still in the van? Will our children ever be able to ride in it again?" she asked faintly. The side of her face was starting to swell.

Her defiance was still there, weaker than before, but not gone. Maybe after Islam had come to this land he would get a second wife to raise the children. "The van will be safe once I remove the device."

"When will that be?"

"You ask too many questions. What I do and when is none of your concern. Your life is simple, you are to care for our children and do as I say."

"Of course."

Did she really mean it? "I want you to swear on penalty of death, that you will not call or tell your sister or my parents about this."

Her eyes shifted back to him. "I told you I would obey you. Isn't that enough?"

"No, I want to hear you say it."

"You have my word that I will not tell them about the device or your plans." Her eyes glazed over.

————

Luca Clayton had had the feeling of being watched since lunch, but every time she looked around, the world appeared normal. It had to be her job. The project she had been working on had her imagination going in all different directions. She saw a terrorist in every person who spoke, acted, or looked different from what she was used to.

Her dad was right. This wasn't the right job for her.

After a late dinner and a few drinks with a couple of her friends, she felt better. It was therapeutic to spend time doing normal things. She took a taxi back to her apartment. It wasn't located in the best part of town, but according to the police records it was the safest neighborhood in her price range. She paid the cabby and took the stairs to the third floor to work off some calories from dinner.

On entering her apartment, she flipped the light switch. Nothing. Did she lose another bulb? She headed for the table lamp a few steps away. Reaching her hand out, she felt something touch the side of her neck. Her hand flew up to brush it away, but was blocked as someone covered her mouth.

Before she could move away, she was pulled back against a solid form and her head was lifted up slightly. She let out a muffled scream. Taking air in through her nose, Luca kicked and screamed as a sharp pain slid across her throat. The air in her lungs made a gurgling sound as it escaped through the hole in her windpipe.

46

Sunday

Opening his eyes, Lamar listened as the sound of creaking wood made its way into his bedroom. He reached for his housecoat and the gun that he kept beside the bed. Someone was on his front porch. He knew the sounds of this old house all too well. Turning, he told Mary to stay put while he went and checked things out.

"It could be one of my kids." Mary whispered. She was referring to the kids in the youth home next door. Her mother had started taking in troubled kids when Lamar was sixteen. He had been the first. That was how he met Mary. Now twenty-seven years later, Mary ran the home with the help of a full time live-in social worker. Lamar helped out when he could.

"If it is, I'll try not to kill them. But they've been warned about waking me." As quietly as his massive size allowed, he traveled out of the bedroom and down the hall. Before he made it to the door, the intruder knocked.

It must be one of Mary's kids. Lamar didn't want to give the kid a heart attack, so he slipped the pistol into a drawer next to the front door and flipped on the lights. Looking out the peephole, he saw a dark haired man carrying a woman in his arms. Her black hair hung almost to the ground. They were both too old to be from the youth home.

Lamar reached back into the drawer and withdrew his gun. Opening the door, he held the weapon just out of view of his visitors. "Yes?" Not a polite greeting, but it was the best they would get in the middle of the night.

"Are you Agent Stover, Lamar Stover?"

"I'm sure you knew that before you started up the walkway. What's wrong with your friend?" Lamar had heard about ploys being played on law enforcement like this. As soon as they let their guard down the assailants pulled out guns and killed them.

"Your friend Derry said you would help us." He nodded down at the woman in his arms. "She was poisoned. She needs help and a safe place to stay for a few days."

"I don't know you from Adam. How'd—" The door was yanked out of his hand.

"Let them in, you brute. You know we are always available if someone needs help." Mary pushed the big man aside.

"Honey, what are you doing? We don't know these people." Lamar tried to stop Mary.

"They're in need of help. You've got your gun if he tries anything." She stepped around Lamar, as she pushed the screen door open. "Bring her inside, the poor girl. What happened to her?"

"Thank you. My name is Sam Freymen and this is Kai. Someone tried to poison her. She has been treated by a doctor, but she needs a safe place to stay for a few days." Sam stepped in and took Kai to the couch. He laid her down very gently.

Mary stayed by her side as Sam moved away.

Lamar stayed back, keeping an eye on Sam and his pistol ready. Every time Mary took in another needy, unknown person, he feared for her safety.

"She's as white as a sheet." Mary placed her hand on Kai's forehead. "She's warm, but not burning up. How did this happen to her?"

"Yeah, and how did you get my name and address?" Lamar did not trust the situation or this man.

Sam watched as Mary mothered Kai. "As I said before, Derry Conway gave me your name and address. He said I could trust you to help. I work for the CIA and –"

"I hope you can prove that."

Sam held up one hand as he used the other to reach into the side pocket of his cargo pants. Taking out his wallet, he handed his ID across to Lamar.

Lamar opened it. It looked real enough. He lowered the pistol. CIA were not always to be trusted. "And what's her story?"

Sam sat on the couch at Kai's feet. "She was poisoned by a co-worker whom I believe to be a hired assassin." He looked up at Lamar. "What I am about to tell you is part of an ongoing investigation and needs to be kept among us only." Sam told Lamar about Kai working for Homeland Security. "I believe a terrorist group is operating out of the Denver office. I needed more information to prove it and to identify everyone involved."

Lamar did not interrupt.

Sam looked at Kai again. "This is my fault. I told her she needed to go back into work, to try to get that information. But it turns out we were too late. Her roommate had already decided to kill her."

Lamar had taken a seat in his easy chair, gun in hand resting on his leg.

Sam seemed undaunted by the pistol. "I didn't think they had caught onto her. I don't know how they could have known she was working with me. But about eight hours ago I got a call from her. She dialed the phone without her captor knowing. I couldn't hear everything that was said, but I knew she was in trouble. I ran a locator on her phone. It led me to a restricted area of Rocky Mountain Arsenal. I found her body stuffed under some bushes. She was almost dead. At the hospital a doctor pumped her stomach and filled her with antitoxins. They also ran her blood through a filter. The doctor said she'll make it, but she won't be on her feet for a couple of days."

So this is Kai, Sara's only friend from her past. Lamar rubbed his face. "Why not stay in the hospital under protection and better care?"

"The ones who tried to kill her are in our government. I was able to keep her name out of the database, but if she took up a bed, they would find her." Sam wavered for a second. "I suspect she was poisoned with the same toxin that killed your Agent Jenkins."

"You know who killed Todd?" Lamar started to get up, but resisted the urge.

"She overheard a conversation." Sam nodded at the unconscious woman.

"If you know who murdered Todd, Sara can come home and we can go after them." Lamar leaned forward in his chair. He wanted to get up and find the killers.

Mary's face brighten a little with hope. "Does this mean Sara will be cleared?"

Sam glanced down at Kai. "Derry was right about you two. You are good people." He looked up at Mary. "Mrs. Stover, would you mind making Kai some very watery soup, no solids? She should eat something."

"Tomorrow I'll start her off with some clear liquids and see how she does. Tonight she needs rest without a couple of men getting all agitated around her. If you boys have more secrets to tell each other, maybe you should take your talk outside" Mary placed a pillow under Kai's head and looked around for a blanket.

Lamar stood. "Let me get dressed." He left for his room as Mary asked Sam more questions about what the doctor had said about Kai's condition. When Lamar returned they were talking like old friends. Mary had that effect on people. Lamar stepped toward the door. "Well, come on. It was your idea to get me out of bed in the middle of the night."

They stepped out as the early morning light was beginning to make its presence known.

Lamar looked seriously at the younger man. "What's really going on?"

"What I am about to tell you cannot find its way into any FBI reports anywhere. In fact, nothing about tonight can, not my visit, not Kai, and not anything about knowing who killed your agent." Sam stopped and stared into Lamar's eyes.

Lamar studied the man's face. Everything about him had changed the minute they stepped out of the house. He went from a caring friend, to a stone cold, hardened leader. He was CIA all the way through. "Is this a personal or business request?"

"Business, at the highest level."

"Not that it matters, I've been asked to take some time off. The FBI thinks I'm too close to Sara to be of any help. I won't be writing any reports anytime soon."

Sam gave a very slight knowing nod. "That's good for now. That can actually work to our advantage. Before I tell you any more, I need you to swear that you will not share this information with anyone."

"I have sworn to defend this country, and I will do everything in my power to fulfill that obligation. If you can convince me that keeping this all a secret is necessary, I will do so."

Deadly Infiltration

"It is." Sam scanned the street before starting. "The group that tried to kill Kai is also behind the murder of the senator, his brother, your FBI agent, and a CIA operative." Sam told Lamar everything he knew.

By the end of the hour, Lamar was fully committed to helping Sam and caring for Kai.

———

Derry paced the living area while listening for movement on the other side of the door. *How could she still be asleep after all the racket I made?*

He had been awake before sunrise, not that he had slept much during the night anyway. He moved toward the door and placed his ear against it. The gravity of what they were up against weighed heavily on him. He tapped and waited.

"Yes."

He opened the door to see the sleepy-eyed love of his life. "I didn't wake you, did I?"

She sat up. "You mean just now or earlier, when you were making so much noise out there?"

He gave what he hoped was a sheepish smile. "Sorry."

"Really?—doesn't matter. I don't think I got more than three hours of sleep anyway." She sat up and leaned against the wall of Kai's old bedroom, pushing her dark brown hair back off her forehead. Lifting one knee, she used it to prop up her elbow as her hand held her hair up. "Something is bugging me."

"Besides the bugs?" He smiled.

She didn't. "I know you have met this CIA Sam, but I haven't."

He shrugged. She was right. "Yeah, he was with Kai. What about it?"

"I don't trust him—completely. How do I know he won't give that phone number to the FBI if he finds it can buy him something? He's CIA. They have their own agenda."

"Sam? I don't think he would ever—"

She tilted her head into a *"really?"* pose.

"Fine, you win." He pulled the phone from his pocket and completely shut it down, removing the battery. "Keeping it on was just running the battery down anyway." He stepped into the room.

For the first time there was enough light to see the discoloration on Sara's arm. The skin was a sickening, dark purple. He nodded at it. "Are you going to be okay?"

"I don't think it's broken." She rubbed it with the lightest touch as she examined it.

"Should we wrap it? Maybe a sling or something?"

She glanced at him. "Wrap it? Why? What good would that do?"

"Help it feel better? Protect it from getting hit?"

"Do I look like a helpless, little female? It looks much worse than it actually feels this morning. How about we use our time looking for a better place to stay, one that doesn't stink and is not full of ghosts?" She stood and walked past him out of the room.

He followed her toward the table where his pack sat. "You mean one that other homeless people live in?"

She stopped dead and slowly turned toward him. "—*No*, not with other homeless people." Some of the color drained from her face. She moved to the table and took a seat, resting her elbows on it as she leaned forward. "Maybe if you cleaned the place up. Paint some of the walls." Her face had a silly grin.

He grinned back at her. "That would cost too much, but I've been thinking. I was looking around this morning and I have a few ideas."

———

Getting to the conference room three minutes ahead of Booker gave Tony just enough time to review the newest copy of his file. He reached for his coffee, which was pumped full of sugar and cream, and forced a sip down. After seven cups throughout the night the taste was growing on him. Coffee wasn't his first choice for keeping his body moving, but it was free around the office. What he really needed was a few hours in the sack and a shower.

Booker had kept him here all night, running traces on Sara's system, and working to decrypt the remaining files on the jump drive found at Sara's apartment.

While he fulfilled her commands, she had called in several agents to shadow her family. Two were assigned to watch her home even when the house was empty. This normally rational woman had been transformed into a hyper-protective mother and wife.

The file that Tony had decrypted was far too detailed for one person to have gathered alone. Tony doubted its legitimacy. He did not believe it was compiled by Sara or a radical extremist group. If it were, why would the senator have it, and why would he send it to his brother in Texas? There was a lot of evidence against Sara, but none of it made any sense.

He had voiced his concerns to Booker a few times during the night, but she never heard them. She was focused on her family's safety. He took another sip. The energy liquid was cooling off. He finished it off before it went south. Lukewarm coffee was bad no matter what you added to it.

"You have everything ready?" Booker, red eyed and looking ten years older than the night before, approached him.

"It's all ready to go." He hit the button on the remote to bring up the first image.

"Good." She turned to the room. "Time to get this meeting started."

———

"Thank you all for coming in on a Sunday, especially on such short notice." Agent Booker stepped away from Tony as she looked around the room. All of Faircloth's team were here plus several other agents. She was a little surprised to see Agent Hewitt of Homeland Security included in the mix. "Due to new information that Tony uncovered, I'm taking the lead in this investigation. It appears all of us are potential targets."

Chris motioned with his hand to get her attention. "Potential targets? From whom? I thought this meeting was about finding Sara?"

Booker stepped closer to the table. Placing both hands on the end of it, she leaned in and looked Chris square in the face. "*We are* talking about Sara, the person whom *we* believe murdered Todd." She studied his face before continuing. "Don't let the game she played on all of us fool you."

Booker straightened up and took a deep breath as she stepped back. "It appears Sara has been gathering intel on us. So far we have decrypted one file from the jump drive found at her apartment and it contains extensive information on me and my family." She nodded to Tony as she stepped to the far side of the room, close to the windows.

"You're up." Looking around the room, she saw that most had their eyes on her, not Tony.

He hesitated, "You sure you want everyone in the room to see this data?" His eyes shifted toward Agent Hewitt.

He has a point. "Just bring up the summary."

He tapped his screen and a slide popped up on the display in the front of the room. "The drive that was recovered from Sara's apartment contained several encrypted files. We have only decrypted one so far. That file held details about Special Agent Booker, including her family's schedule. The file also contained pictures of Agent Booker and her husband at various locations around town." Pictures of Mr. Booker with his son lined the right side of the display.

Booker stepped in and took over. "Sara, or one of her accomplices, has been following me, my husband, and my son. These pictures date back at least a year. The file also lists the times I and my husband go to work and the different routes we take, along with information about my son's school."

She turned from the display to face the room straight on. "Sara has made this very personal. Tony has not decrypted the other files yet, but is working on them. We do not know for sure, but we can assume they contain similar information on others in this room. All of us need to change up our routines. You need to watch for people trailing you. If you have loved ones, send them out of town or to a friend's house for a few days. Remember, you can't be too careful."

Faircloth spoke up, "We believe that all of these cases are connected, the murders of the senator and his wife, the senator's half-brother, and Agent Jenkins. We also believe they are tied to the mole who is sending intel to groups in the Middle East. It's all the same case."

"You're saying you think Sara did all this? I find that somewhat impossible to believe." Kent shook his head.

"Tony, give a short summary of what you found that makes you think Sara killed Todd." Booker moved to the side of the room.

Tony stepped to the front. "Like many in this room, if you would have asked me two days ago if I thought Sara could be a saboteur or extremist, I would have said you were crazy. But with each step I take, I'm finding more and more evidence that indicates that Sara is involved in this case and probably working with the terrorists."

His opening statement gained the interest of everyone in the room. "I found evidence that Todd had learned that Sara meant to destroy the senator's hard drive. She deleted emails that he was going to send to Agent Booker and others. I also checked the system Sara was using in the lab. The values she entered into the hard drive test were way off from the values she used in her previous tests, forty times higher."

Kent asked, "So you think that would give Sara the motive to kill Todd? Sounds really thin to me. I mean, I never worked with her before this case, but most killers need a better reason than that."

Booker looked around the room. Other faces also held doubt. She took a step forward to bring the attention to her. "At this point we can't say how closely she was tied to the murders. What the evidence does show is that she is involved, feeding information, or at the bare minimum, tampering with evidence in a murder case of a U.S. senator. We know for a fact that she has been gathering information on me and my family and most likely others in this room. We can make a logical, educated guess, based on this evidence and the fact that she ran, that she is deeply involved in both Todd's and the Senator's murders. These reasons alone are enough to put her at the top of our search." Booker nodded to Tony.

The doubt was gone. Tony went on with his report. Parts of it were redundant with Booker's speech. "The data I recovered, the encrypted files and links plus activities on her system, all show she is working against the interests of this country. And the timing of her leaving make even me believe she is an accessory to Todd's murder and most likely, to the senator's as well. A single person could not possibly be behind all of the murders, so Sara is not working alone."

Booker moved back to the center of the room. "Sara had access to our procedures, our methods, the types of surveillance we used, and through our computers, the whole law enforcement community. Her position here is perfect for a mole."

"We all have that access. That does not make her guilty. Do you really believe she masterminded all this?" Kent shifted his eyes between Booker and Faircloth. Faircloth was looking down at his notepad.

Booker studied the floor before answering. She did not call this meeting to start a debate. "I'm not sure who is controlling the activities of this radical cell, but I do believe Sara is fully involved with them. And when we find her, she will lead us to the rest of the group. She is the only name we have at the moment and therefore the best lead and our top priority." The meeting had ceased being productive. They all needed time for the information to sink in, but time was not something they had an abundance of. "Now, if there are no more questions, we need to hit this hard."

Everyone grabbed their belongings and started to get up. "One more thing. This information is only to be shared with those on the case. If I learn that any of you are in contact with Agent Stover on this, I will have you up on charges. Am I clear?" She glared over at Tony.

———

Sara sat across from Derry with her arms crossed, her eyes boring into him. "So what are your great ideas?"

"I found the water main, and I think I can turn it on. I also found some electrical wire. If I get some power in here, we will have everything we need for a while. I don't think we will be able to do better than this anywhere else."

Sara looked around before adding, "I still don't like this place. Did you know Levy wanted me to live here too? I said no way, I'd rather die. I guess he wins in the end." She rubbed her hands together, trying to rub the dirt off. "Water would be nice."

He knew the stories. She had shared all that happened here with him. "It's been off for a while, but I'll work on it." He sat next to her. "Think of this as camping."

"Whoever said I wanted to go camping? We build houses to live in for a reason." She turned in her chair and leaned back. "Once you do all these miracles, water, power, then what?"

He leaned against the back of the chair in front of him. "I would like to see what's in the rest of that file."

She stood and walked over to the boarded window and peeked out between the window edge and the board. He waited. After a minute or so she turned toward him. "Let's go get some water and power. Just sitting around is driving me bonkers."

"It's all in the basement."

"Of course. In the basement," she mumbled, then froze in her spot.

He didn't much like the thought of being down there either. It was the one place in this building that they would both avoid at all costs. It was the place where Levy had tried to kill them. Derry debated whether to make her stay upstairs or not.

She gave a slight shake of her head before stepping through the apartment door. Stopping just inside the hallway, she turned to Derry. "You said you found wire in the basement for us to get power?"

"Yeah, I plan to tie it into the power pole in the alley."

"Can't you just turn on the electricity like you turn on the water?"

"That was my hope. But someone cut the outside wires and took them. Copper is worth a lot of money these days."

"I'm surprised they didn't strip the inside too." Suddenly her hand grasped for her stomach as she fell into the wall.

He reached out to steady her. "You okay?"

"Yeah, I'm—" She moved back through the door and dumped herself into a chair. "I—just need to rest a minute. You got anything to eat that is easy on the tummy?"

He was already reaching for his backpack. He emptied its contents onto the table. "Grab whatever appeals to you."

She reached for a plain rice cake and a bottle of water. "You go on down. I'll be fine in a few minutes."

He added an energy bar to her selections. "You sure?"

She took a bite of the rice cake as she looked up at him. Even in the dim light, her expression answered the question.

"I'll turn on the water and be back to check on you."

"Just go. I'm fine. This isn't the first time I've felt this way." She reached for the bar and opened it as he turned away.

Once in the basement, it took several attempts to get the water on. Once on, he heard water running through the pipes, longer than it should to fill the empty lines. He ran all over the building turning off valves in sinks and other locations. By the time he got back to Sara, she was in the kitchen with the water running. "You know, water that sits for three years gets really disgusting."

"Feeling better, I see." He glanced at the table. Two empty wrappers sat near the middle. *Good, she ate something.*

"Of course." She observed the flow, checking the color of the water. Once she decided it was safe, she put both hands under the water and rubbed them together before splashing some on her face. Turning, she grabbed the back of Derry's shirt and dried her face. "You don't mind, do you? Didn't think so. Ready to get the electricity turned on?" She was much perkier than she had been twenty minutes before. "How bad is it down there?" She stopped and looked back at him.

He stepped past her. "The place is empty. It appears the police took just about everything as evidence." He headed down to the basement with her following right behind.

Along the east wall were several small windows covered by bars. "Looks like almost any basement in America now. It even has a workbench against the wall." He walked over to the wire hanging from the ceiling. "I'm hoping this wire is long enough to make it to the power outside." He yanked on it as wire staples popped out of the wood floor joist.

"Looks like someone did half your job for you."

"Yeah, me. I started on it this morning while you were asleep, but didn't finish it. I was afraid I'd wake you."

She walked over and tried to help. "You sure pulling on the wire like this won't damage it?"

"I—hope—not." One word between each pull. As a few staples popped out altogether, his elbow jerked back, hitting Sara.

"Ouch." She stepped away.

He stopped and turned.

She was rubbing her ribs. "What can I do to help that won't endanger my life?"

"Sorry, I didn't mean to hit you." He dug into his pocket and pulled out a Swiss army knife. "I need that end," he nodded toward a subpanel mounted on the post at the back end of the stairs, "loosened up. Do you think you can undo the screws holding the wire in?"

She took the pocketknife and walked over to the breaker box.

The last several wire-staples popped out easier than he'd expected. Now the wire disappeared behind the workbench. He grabbed one end of the bench and yanked it away from the wall a few inches. It was heavier than it looked. After several more tugs he had made enough room behind it to work. The wire was not attached where he had expected.

"What in the world?" He looked across at the subpanel before looking back at the wall. Bending down, he peered at the wire disappearing into the wall. He pushed his finger in beside it. The wall was softer and made from something smoother than cement. He twisted to look at Sara. "Hey, what's next door?"

47

Derry grabbed a short piece of wood left in the corner of the basement and used it to break away the plaster that surrounded the wire. Sara stood back a couple of feet, staying clear of his jabs and the flying chunks.

As the hole grew, it revealed a ten-foot-long tunnel that connected the basement to the U-Store-It building that hugged up against the north wall. At the far end of the shaft, it took a ninety degree turn then went up to ground level and stopped at a steel hatch. The wire had been used to power lights in the tunnel.

Using the flashlight on one of the phones, Derry located the handle on the trapdoor. He turned it and pushed the lid up. It fell back against the wall of a room. Entering, he found a switch next to the door. He flipped it. Lights flickered to reveal an eight by ten foot storage room filled with filing cabinets along one wall. Next to the door was a large canvas bag and a leather briefcase. Sara joined him. He opened one of the file cabinets. It was filled with accounting records in Levy's name. Here was information the police would be interested in. But they would have to deal with that later.

This building had never been searched by the police. Levy must have rented the storage space using an alias.

Sara's find was far more interesting. She opened the bag and started pulling out bundles of twenties, fifties and hundreds wrapped in plastic. She also pulled out a change of men's clothes and handed them to Derry. They were a little bigger than he wore, but might come in handy.

As she reloaded the bag Derry grabbed the briefcase and opened it. It housed two new identities for Levy, including passports, driver licenses, club memberships and two different sets of family photos. The man knew what he was doing. Setting the false identities aside, he retrieved a Springfield XD pistol with three magazines filled with ammo. He slipped the pistol into his belt and the extra ammo into his pockets.

"Is that necessary?" Sara was gawking at him.

"We don't know yet. Besides, I can't just leave it here."

"Yes you can. If no one has bothered this place in three years, there is no reason to think that will change."

He didn't want to argue about this now. "I think we can get some power from here." He walked over to a wall plug. "We can at least charge the laptop."

Her look told him he wasn't fooling her with his attempt to change the subject. Jumping back into the hole, he yanked the wire loose and pulled it into the storeroom. Retrieving his knife he got ready to tap into the electricity.

"You sure this will work? What if we blow the breaker in this building?"

"Good point. I need to isolate Kai's apartment from the rest of the building before we hook up the wire. That will only take a few minutes."

"I'm not staying here while you do that." She peered down at the money, tapping the bag with her foot. "If you're taking the gun, I'm taking the money."

"Uh, I—"

She spun toward him. "You what? You think we should leave it here?"

Derry had to ask himself why taking the gun was okay, but taking the money bothered him. Was it because taking the money felt more like stealing? *What a hypocrite I am.*

She turned back and reached down, placing both hands on the bag to pick it up. She carried it to the hole. "Help me with this and stop looking at me that way. Think of this as back pay for working for him for two years with nothing to show for it."

———

After some rewiring of the breaker box and making sure the electricity would only power one circuit to the apartment, Derry connected the wire to the circuit in the storage room then headed back upstairs. He found Sara peeking out the crack between the building and the wood covering the window again. "We should have power," he announced.

"I know. One of the lights came on a few minutes ago. I plugged in the computer but it was too dead to come up." She walked over to the table and pressed the power button again. "Looks like we have lift-off." She took a seat and brought up the file they had been looking at the night before.

As she started going through the file, he asked her to go a little slower this time. After a complaint about always having to cater to the slowest student, she promised to suffer through it.

Derry read Agent Landry's information. "So these guys are Muslim."

"That's what I would have expected. Islamic terrorism is on the rise, increasing every year. And there have been rumors around the office of a huge leak somewhere in the government. Someone has been sending information to the Middle East about every operation we have over there. So we were pretty sure whoever was providing the information would be Muslim."

"It seems like Muslims are popping up everywhere."

She gave him an inquisitive look.

"I mean almost anywhere you go or look, inside our government and out, you run into people of Islamic faith."

"You sound surprised." Sara lifted one eyebrow.

"I know we can't show any discrimination based on one's beliefs, but—"

"But what? Do you think we should?"

"If you studied the different schools that follow the Qur'an, you wouldn't be so eager to open your doors to all Muslims. At least not all doors, that is."

She pulled away from him. "My fiancé's a bigot. I'm a little surprised." She looked deep into his eyes.

He stood and walked across the room. Just sitting around was hard for him and he wanted to move. "I'm not a bigot. It's just—"

"Just what?" Her gaze followed him around the room.

"It's just common sense. Do you know what the Qur'an says?"

"Not really, but I'm sure you do. You have certainly taken enough classes lately."

He smiled at her. She was talking about the elective classes he had taken at the college. He had taken the first class just to fill a requirement. But after that first class, he became fascinated with the whole topic of various religions. The professor who taught the classes had lived in the Middle East for a couple of years and really understood the three main religions, Judaism, Christianity, and Islam. These people groups had quite a history together. Derry had taken every class this professor taught and had become quite knowledgeable. "How much do you really know about the Qur'an?"

"I've never read it, but I can't believe it's that much different from the Bible. Muslims worship God like us."

"Not like us. That is propaganda." He looked down, trying to organize his thoughts so he could convey what he'd learned without spending three hours talking about it. "First, you have to understand that almost no one reads the Qur'an alone. They all have other books to help them understand it."

"So? I read commentaries on the Bible to help me understand it."

This wasn't coming out right. Lightly pinching is lip between his thumb and index finger, he slowly paced. "It's not the same. The Bible is a complete story. It can stand alone. The Qur'an is more like parts of a sermon. But if you don't know the stories behind the sermon you can't really understand it."

"Why would this Mohammed person write it like that?"

Derry stopped and smiled. "Muslims believe that the Qur'an is the eternal speech of Allah, so that is not Mohammed's fault, but that's a whole other issue. In the early days of Islam, whenever someone didn't understand the Qur'an, or didn't know the background story, and asked for more information they were told to go ask a Jew or a Christian, someone who was a reader of the 'Book'. Many parts of the Qur'an are based on characters from the Bible. This lasted for about a hundred years or so. Then different religious scholars, called *Ulama*, started coming up with their own interpretations. They did not want their followers depending on the Jews and Christians. Over the centuries there have been many interpretations, and there are at least ten significant different schools of thought today."

Sara winkled her forehead. "More than just the Sunni and Shia?"

"Those two groups cover many of the different schools I was talking about. But we are getting way off track. We should get back to work." He stepped closer to her.

"In a minute. I want to understand why I am so confused all the time when it comes to Islam. For example, one group of Muslims works with us, at the Bureau, to fight against a different group. But both groups say they are following Allah's will. So are you saying that none of this killing of nonbelievers stuff is in the Qur'an? That it is only in their commentaries?"

He backed up against the wall, trying to remember what his instructor had said. "I'm not saying that at all. Not only is the killing of infidels in the Qur'an, but so is lying to further Islam, turning Jews and Christians into slaves, or making them pay a tax to stay alive, and—" He stepped forward, pulled on a chair to place one foot on the seat, as he leaned toward her. "So is protecting all women and children, being honest in all your business dealings, and helping those in need."

"You're not helping me any. What you say makes no sense. Does it say to kill women and children or to help them?"

"It says both in different parts of the book. That is where the different interpretations or different schools come in. Each one of the *Ulama* varied in what they believed to be the true meaning of Islam, as well as what the Qur'an and the sayings of Mohammed actually mean. Some of them were much more peaceful than others. So the different groups do not interpret the Qur'an the same way. The whole world of Islam is very splintered."

"So, if I want to know if a Muslim wants to kill me, I would need to know which school he follows?"

"That might help. Unless he belongs to a group that is okay with lying to further their religion. Then he might lie about what group he belongs to." Derry moved back to the table. "You can't always know for sure. That's the problem."

Sara looked distressed. This subject was hitting a nerve with her. He moved into the seat next to her and reached over to give her hand a light squeeze then turned his head toward the screen and started reading again. "It's going to be okay. But we need to get through this. Have you read anything about an attack?"

A few seconds went by before she pushed her hair back out of her face and refocused on the document on the computer. "Only that the writer of this document thinks one is coming soon and several cities are involved. It might be a chemical attack or an explosion of some sort. He's not sure. Most of the information is about the people involved, who they are or who he thought they might be. He's not sure how many are behind it, but he knows there is a group in each city." She moved farther down the file. Coming to the end, she looked up. "There aren't any more details here."

Derry stepped back from the table. Sara returned her focus to the laptop. Pulling one leg up, she tucked it under her chin. "I was just thinking about your comments on the Qur'an."

"What about it?"

"So, are you saying that according to some groups any terrorist act committed by a Muslim is fine in their eyes, no matter how many people they kill?"

"Not exactly."

"But don't they believe that killing millions of innocent people is wrong?"

"You have to understand that our definition of innocent and theirs is very different. Unless someone believes in Islam the way the terrorist does, that person is not considered innocent. They are considered an infidel. Killing millions of infidels is not wrong in their eyes. In fact, it is required."

"What about all the fighting that is going on right now in the Middle East? Those are Muslims killing each other. Isn't that against the Qur'an?"

"In the eyes of those on each side, the other Muslims are not following the true path so they deserve to die."

"This is crazy. Maybe once this is over, I should take some of those classes. If we are still alive, that is."

Her words sparked something in Derry's mind. Even after taking the classes on Islam, the truth of what they were up against had not become clear to him until now. "This is not a battle of man against man, but a battle of good versus evil. We are not fighting this battle alone. God is on our side. That gives me hope."

They sat in silence for a while.

Finally, Sara looked up. "It gives me hope, too. Let's see if we can stop some terrorists. To do that, I will need a few things."

48

Monday

Booker had given Tony part of Sunday afternoon off, which he used wisely. He spent it cleaning up and sleeping, but everything came with a cost. At 3am, he woke up, his mind refusing to let his questions go. They stuck in his gut, and he couldn't get back to sleep. He eventually gave up and went into work before the sun came up.

Everything Sara had done over the last two years was now suspect, but that would have to wait. He needed to know what she was up to right now. Tony had spent all weekend hitting a brick wall. He could not figure out why Sara would add Halter's name to the DEA watch list, but after lying awake for two hours he now had some new ideas.

Tony checked Sara's system to see if there were any unaccounted-for time gaps. A gap could indicate that she might have been doing something she did not want other people to see. He found a two hour gap.

Sara was smart, she had hidden what she did well. Which is why Tony had such a hard time finding anything. But everything still went out through the government's routers, even if it did not appear to come from Sara's computer. Tony grabbed the chunk of data from the router for the missing time period and looked for anything that was not assigned to a particular computer. He found what he was looking for. The unassigned routing took him to a bank where half a million dollars had been moved. The money had then been split into several smaller amounts and moved through half a dozen banks and three times that many accounts, before being joined in an offshore numbered account. The bank was in a country that was unwilling to work with the U.S. government. He sent a message to Booker.

Two minutes later his phone buzzed. "Tony here."

"It's Booker. What have you found?

Tony filled her in on the details.

"Tell me more about the money. Can we move it or put a lock on it?"

"No, not in the country she picked. They have no love for us." The line was silent for a second or two.

"You're sure it was put there by her?"

"Ninety percent sure. She tried to hide her tracks and it was a little tricky at times, but I'm as sure as I can be."

"You know her. You've worked with her for two years. Tell me what you think she's up to."

"It's completely out of character for the Sara I know. But if I ignore that, I can think of only two reasons."

"Enlighten me."

"Either she's working with this Brian Halter, whose real name is Motova, and did this to hide money from the U.S. government, or she stole it from him."

"What do we know about him?"

"He was born and raised in Russia. He came to the U.S. with his wife after graduating from college with a chemistry degree. He's now a U.S. citizen. He's been in trouble with local law enforcement twice, but nothing serious. Sometime in the last three years, he became a Muslim. His wife went back to Russia about eight months ago."

"So he was in the clear until Sara brought attention to him?"

"Which begs the question, why would she do that?" Tony pushed his chair away from his desk. "She added him as a medium priority on the DEA watch list."

"How could she do that? Never mind—. We'll find out once we get her. Anything showing a tie or connection between them? Something in their past?"

It took Tony a minute to find it. "Maybe. Several years ago Motova and his wife were foster parents. The children they fostered are not listed, their names are protected by child services. But Sara spent several years in the foster care system."

"That's got to be the connection. She must be working with him."

Deadly Infiltration

"Maybe. But *the little I know of her time in foster care, she hated it.*"

"She told you that?"

"Not to me. A while back, Todd asked her about it and she turned white before getting up and leaving the room. When she came back, her eyes were red. We never asked again."

"What a great way to cover something."

"You think she was faking it?"

"That's how I would do it. Once the tears card is played, no man in the world would ever ask again. Can you tag the money and see when it's accessed?"

"That should be easy enough. But if the bank finds out, there could be repercussions."

"I'm willing to take that risk. We don't have time to go through proper channels. We need to know where she accesses the money from, her physical location."

"We have a program that will do that. But there's one problem."

"Which is?"

"Sara did a lot of work on that program. Banking's her baby."

"You're saying the program's no good against her?"

"It may not work. She knows her way around it."

"Do you know of a way to fix this problem?"

"Maybe. If I trap each IP node she routes through, I might be able to reconstruct the path and look for false trails, but that takes time."

"Do you have something more important to be working on?" It wasn't really a question.

"I'll get right on it."

"And don't screw it up, understand?"

———

Lamar stared out the front window at an old man walking a disobedient little dog. *It's not like that size of dog offers any protection, there must be another reason why people are willing to put up with them.* Turning away, he went into the guestroom to check on Kai.

She was partially sitting up. Most of her color had returned.

"How are you feeling?"

"Like death warmed over." She pushed herself up a little more. "You guys are great for letting me stay here."

"Yeah, wait 'til you get the bill." He had a wide smile. His phone sang a tune. He did not recognize the number and he started to hit reject, but stopped. "This could be Sam." He stepped toward the door as he answered. "Yes?"

"Hello, Agent Stover?" It did not sound like Sam.

"Speaking."

"I understand Sara Beckwith works for you?" Clearly not who he was expecting, and other than those on the case or from the office, there was no one he wanted to speak with.

"Who is this?"

"My name is Colby—"

"How'd you get this number?" His phone was unlisted, as were all FBI agents'.

"I'm trying to find out about Sara Beckwith."

Someone at the Bureau must have slipped up. If Lamar found out who, it could cost them their job. "This is an unlisted and classified number. You should not be calling it. If you want to learn about any one at the Bureau, go through our PR department. That's what it's there for." Pulling the phone away from his head, he punched 'End Call' before searching the number online. The results popped up just as the phone sang again, same number.

This man had way too much gall, or maybe he was just plain stupid. Either way, this Denver Post reporter needed to learn his lesson.

Lamar spoke before the caller could get a word in. "I know you are calling from the paper. What is the name of your manager? I will be calling them to report your misconduct."

"First off, Agent Stover, I have done nothing illegal or unethical, and second this is a private call to ask about my—"

Enough was enough. Lamar did not have time for this and at this point he really didn't care. He killed the call and blocked the number, before heading back into Kai's room.

"Was it Sam?" She sounded hopeful.

"Sorry, just some reporter who wants to lose his job."

———

Gabriele sat at her computer, thankful to be able to work in her own office again instead in that tiny room with Kai. Jonas opened the door without knocking. "Is everything taken care of?"

She turned in her chair to face him. "You mean, is Kai dead? Yes."

"Dace wants know where the proof is. He has not seen any reports about someone finding her."

"I dumped her body where no one will find her. I didn't think you wanted the police asking questions." Gabriele was insulted by his attitude. He shouldn't question her work.

"Did you take some pictures to prove she was dead?"

"And have that kind of evidence on my phone? Are you out of your mind?"

Jonas stepped in and closed the door. Her office suddenly began to feel crowded. "Dace also wants to know about the money. Have you recovered it yet?"

"I'm working on it, but it takes time." Maybe she had killed the wrong person. Dace should be the one left out for the animals to feast on.

49

"If you are so scared to go out in public, why don't you hack Homeland from here? We can turn one of the burn phones into a Wi-Fi hot spot again." Derry stood outside of the bathroom, studying Sara.

She worked in front of the mirror, putting on some of the costume makeup that Derry had found at a thrift store the night before. "A burn phone only means that they can't trace who the phone belongs to. When in use or even just turned on, its location can still be traced. And as much as I hate this place, I don't want the FBI showing up uninvited."

Derry stepped in beside her and checked his gray hair. The changes in his appearance were not as dramatic as hers. She had darkened her skin, dyed her hair red and flared her nostrils with little plastic inserts. He wasn't sure if he would recognize her if he passed her on the street. "Can't you hack into any place without being caught? Isn't that why the FBI wanted you to work for them?"

"We are talking about hacking into the Department of Homeland Security." She pushed past him and out of the too small bathroom. "The laptop Kai picked out is great, but it doesn't have any of the needed programs on it. And unless you want to wait a few days or weeks for me to rewrite or download everything we need in order to tap in invisibly, we need to go somewhere else just in case we get tracked. We need some place with public Wi-Fi. If I see we've been spotted or if the cops show up, I want an escape route."

"I looked at satellite views last night. There is a branch of the Denver Public Library nearby and it is near a park. The space is pretty open around it, but there is a bricked off area right next to the building. We should be able to tap into the Wi-Fi from there." He followed her out and headed toward the backpack. They had two computers to work with, his laptop and the high-end Linux computer he had gotten at Ted's store. He placed both in the pack. "I'm thinking we can work inside the bricked-off utility area and if the police show up they will think we are inside the building. When they go inside we can just walk away."

"I'll see how it looks when we get there. We can always go on downtown to the main branch if it's too much in the open." She grabbed some money out of the duffel bag. "In case we want some real food." She looked over at him and added, "Old man."

"Sure you don't mind being seen in public with someone twice your age?" He hoisted the pack onto his shoulder.

"We're homeless." She spread her arms a little and twisted to show off the rags she wore. "No one will give it a second thought." She let Derry go first.

"We have to go out through the basement. Are you okay with that?"

"I will always despise that place. But I am ready to go." She followed close behind him the whole way. They crossed the basement and walked behind the workbench. The tunnel was low. Derry dropped to his hands and knees and made his way through. Sara bent very low at the waist and followed. "Told you shorter is better."

He answered her snide remark as he went up the ladder at the end. "Tell me that next time you need something off the top shelf."

"I only ask for your help to make you feel important." She followed him through the storage unit.

Stopping at its entrance, Derry took a piece of paper and folded it several times before placing it in the space between the door and the frame. It made the door hard to close and hard to open. "Just in case anyone checks the locks on all the storage units while we're away."

The building exit was at the opposite end of the hall from their storeroom and exited on the opposite side from the building they had been hiding in. Stepping out onto the sidewalk, Sara turned north.

"The library is this way." Derry pointed.

"But the bus stop is this way. Remember, I used to work here."

He reached over and grabbed her hand, pulling her toward him. "People on a bus have the opportunity to really look at each other." He examined her makeup in the bright sunlight. "You did good work, but it's still only costume makeup. We don't want to spend too much time being scrutinized by other people."

"We could tell them we are actors in a play." She smiled before following him.

"And they would want to know what play."

———

Excitement filled Tazeem as he pulled the van up in front of the warehouse. Two men slid the large doors of the warehouse aside. Pulling in, he spoke to the one on his side of the van, "Get some help to unload the equipment. It is heavy."

The other man closed the large doors behind them. Getting out of the driver's seat, Tazeem stood back and let the others do the hard work. He was their leader and as such had the privilege of supervising.

A large man approached Tazeem. They called him The Chemist. It would be his responsibility to use the machine they were unloading. The device would combine the chemicals that Tazeem had delivered earlier, into the poison that would be used to kill the infidels. "Welcome back. Did the trip go well?"

Tazeem nodded. "Yes, of course."

The Chemist moved around to the rear of the van, where the unit was being pulled out and set on a large industrial cart. "This is much larger than I thought it would be."

Tazeem joined him. "Yes, it's Russian military. They think the bigger the better. We must get this set up in the air tight room and get it running. I will show you how it works."

The Chemist turned toward him. "It should not be too difficult."

"It is not difficult, but I have been trained."

"Are you sure it works after all the bouncing around in the back of your van?" He stepped back, aloof from the others.

"Yes, it was secured well. If it does not work, it will not be my fault."

"It should have been me at that meeting. I am the one with the right education." The Chemist spit on the ground. An insult that Tazeem would address later.

"You do not think I can learn how to do this task? You believe your time in an American college has made you better than me?"

The Chemist glared at Tazeem. "Yes. I was asked to be part of this team—"

"My team, you are part of *my* team."

"Yes, your little team. But I only agreed to help because my Imam approached me in Nasir's name."

If this arrogant overweight pig of a man had not been needed, Tazeem would have killed him where he stood. But the truth was he was the only one who could do his job. His death would come later. "That is not important right now. I am the leader of this group. If you have any questions about that I will put you in touch with Nasir." He stared until the fat man turned away.

"We will see if you learned enough," The Chemist said under his breath. Turning to the man next to the cart he instructed, "Take the device to the corner room. Make sure you handle it carefully."

"Are the timers and drones ready?" Tazeem spoke to the back of the Chemist's head.

He answered without turning. "Ask the man you assigned to them. I am here to make the nerve agent, nothing more."

Tazeem looked around for Ghazi, who was working in the far corner of the warehouse. He walked over to the long wooden table where four drones sat. Each had a wingspan of six feet. "Will these be ready on time?"

"Yes, but I have looked at the canisters you want me to attach. They are made out of aluminum."

"Yes, strong and lightweight."

"And visible to active radar."

"Only if the military is looking for us." Tazeem examined the fiberglass and ceramic drone bodies. "Won't the engine and electronics also show up with active radar?"

Ghazi gave a short shrug as he placed a circuit board into the body of one of the drones. "Yes, but the bigger the reflection, the easier it will be to see. And I will—"

"I want to test the powder when I have some made. To make sure the machine is actually working." It was The Chemist again, interrupting him.

Tazeem held up his hand, telling The Chemist to wait his turn as he glanced back at Ghazi. "You were saying?"

"Yes, I will need to do a test flight for weight and range." Ghazi turned to The Chemist. "Can you give me the weight for one point five cubic liters of the poison?"

"Not until I make some." The Chemist grabbed Tazeem's shoulder, spinning him around. "That piece of junk you brought in here was not designed for this. I read through the booklet."

Tazeem knocked the hand off his shoulder. "Now you are telling me you read Russian?" He wanted to ram his fist into the man's face, but it would only make things worse and they didn't have time to find a new chemist if he walked off.

"Well enough, yes. I do not believe it will work."

"It will. The man who trained us has made changes to the equipment. He has assured us it will work."

"We are trusting this operation to a Russian defector?"

"Who is also a family member of John—" The Chemist was not to know the names of members on other teams, no one was. "He can be trusted."

"As I said when I walked over here. I will need to test this agent. If it doesn't work, then Ghazi's drones will be doing nothing but dumping a harmless fine powder on Atlanta. No one will notice or care."

The team was falling apart and they were so close to completion. "If you follow the instructions, his drones will rain death down on the city. Allah be praised."

The Chemist faced Tazeem, attempting to stare him down. The room was quiet, as if the poison had already done its work. After a couple of seconds, the Chemist added, "Allah be praised— *if this works.*" He turned and moved farther away from the workbench.

Tazeem wanted to grab him and show him what that bit of disrespect deserved. He chose to wait, however. "When will you be ready to test the agent?"

"I will be ready to test it tomorrow morning. I will need some mice or maybe a stray cat." The corners of his mouth turned up ever so slightly at his victory.

"Go buy yourself some mice or some pigs, if *you* prefer. That might be more fitting. What time will you be running the test? I want to see the results."

The Chemist looked into Tazeem's eyes. "Tomorrow morning at seven, before everyone else arrives. I will run the test whether you are here or not."

Tazeem nodded and turned away.

50

The area of town where the library was located was not a homeless hangout like many public libraries seemed to be. Derry wondered how much he and Sara stuck out. There were some older kids shooting hoops, but otherwise the park looked empty. He speculated that most people in this older middle-class neighborhood were at work. He and Sara ate breakfast under a tree on the building's west side.

"Is that the walled-in area you suggest we use?" Sara scanned the building and its surroundings.

The mostly warm food that they had gotten at a local supermarket would have been barely passable on any other day. But today it tasted great. Derry took another bite as his gaze followed hers. The alcove's wall was about six feet high. It surrounded the air conditioning unit as well as a large electrical transformer box, screening them from view. There was a narrow walkway between the brick wall and the wall of the library.

"We could try someplace else." He finished off his meal with a long drink of Coke.

Sara looked around the park. "Nice community. It probably doesn't have tons of cops driving around it." She wiped her hands and stood. He grabbed their belongings as they started walking across the small parking area.

She headed toward the structure, but stopped just outside and looked out toward the street. "This area's pretty dead. Hopefully no one will notice us ducking into your hideaway."

Derry walked ahead of Sara into the closed off area. "I don't think anyone will care." He moved around to the rear of the large green box. The transformer gave off a low hum.

She followed him in. "I'm only willing to try it here because I don't want to walk all the way downtown."

"So, I win because you're lazy?"

"It's hot and getting hotter. Why walk all the way downtown if we don't have to? I'm practical."

"Call it what you want, Miss Practical." He set the pack on the ground and pulled her laptop out first. After handing it to her, he reached for his.

She set her computer on top of the cooling unit.

"Umm, I wouldn't put it there."

"Why not? It's just the right height." Its surface was just above her waist.

The unit kicked on, making Sara jump. The laptop started to slide off as the blast of air pushed upwards.

Derry reached over and grabbed it before it hit the ground. "That's why." He set it down on the ground.

"That was close." Sara turned and looked at the unit. "I always thought those things blew down, sucking air in."

"I told you not to put it there." He sat on the ground with his back against the bricks and grabbed his computer.

"I thought you meant because of the electrical field or something. How did you know it was going to do that?" She looked closer at the fan that had almost ruined their plans and her computer.

"It's summer, it's hot, so the air conditioner will be on all day. And all cooling units blow upwards, no matter the size. That's why you have to keep the area above them clear."

"Something else you learned in college?" She joined him on the ground and picked up her computer.

"No, I had one installed in the guest house after you moved out."

They both logged into the Denver Library Internet system. "You could have done that when I lived there. And don't forget to run your VPN."

"I would have installed one if I had had the money then." He checked the link properties. "My signal strength is okay but not great." He brought up his 'virtual private network' before leaning over to look at her display. She was already three steps ahead.

"Yeah, it's fine." She responded absentmindedly.

"You sure this VPN will keep us hidden?"

"Only from the Library's filters. It was a freebee and not the best. Any hacker worth their salt will be able to punch through it."

Feeling a little useless, Derry ran a search on Jonas Hahn and Dace Roux. As he expected, nothing popped up on his Google search. He changed to a different search engine and expanded it to include the rest of the world. It was much slower, but their names did show up a few places. He read the websites, but did not learn anything that wasn't already in the file from Sam.

However, this gave him another idea. Using the login and password he used at his job with an accounting firm, he went through the office computer and posed as both men's accountant. He tapped into the European Union network and ran a financial background check on each man. Some new records showed up within the French and German systems. He was able to retrieve records of employment, tax returns, credit cards, savings, and addresses of where they had lived. The information was from several years back, but Derry hoped it would give him a lead to follow.

Derry tried to pick up the trail from their last known addresses in Europe. Jonas Hahn's flat had been rented several times and sold twice. It appeared he no longer owned any property in Germany. Dace Roux's home, on the other hand, had never been sold.

Interesting, he must be planning to come back.

Derry checked to see who was living in it now. The search came up with the name Philippe Sauvageau. He ran a search on that name but came up empty. The person had no past and, it would appear, no life at all. Derry tried several ways to hack into the French Government databases to learn more, but after more than an hour, he knew he had a lot to learn before he would be as good as Sara.

Hearing voices, Derry stuck his head around the wall. The park was filling up. He checked the time. They had been there most of the morning. He leaned over toward Sara and looked at her screen. "How's it coming?"

She jumped at his voice. "You startled me." Looking around she added, "I felt like I was back at work." She hit a few more keys before closing the lid. "I got tons of stuff downloaded, including both government and private emails. Hewitt's stuff was easy to find, at least what he had on Homeland's database. Landry is trying to hide something." She handed the laptop to Derry, who packed it away.

"What type of stuff?"

"We need to go. I'm not sure, but I think someone tried to ping my system."

Derry stood and looked around before helping her to her feet.

"My legs are stiff."

He stepped out first and scanned the street and park. "I don't see anything unusual."

She followed. They headed away from the road, through the park.

"You never said what type of stuff you found on Landry."

She kept her head down as she talked. "He had several email accounts, but there was one that he only accessed one time from work and that was awhile back. I copied over everything I could from it, but it's all encrypted. So I copied all of Homeland's decryption tools. I hope we can open the files."

"Do you think we can do that?"

"If we can find the decryption key we should be able to decrypt the files with the programs I downloaded. Without it, we would need some high-end programs that we don't have." Sara and Derry kept their heads down as they passed a new group of kids playing basketball.

"We should stop and get something to eat before we head back to the apartment."

Sara giggled. "In the middle of the world coming to an end all you can think about is food?"

"Food could be hard to come by if the attack happens. I'm just planning ahead." As they made their way to the other side of the park, Derry took a quick peek over his shoulder. "Oh boy. That was close."

Sara paused as she turned back to look.

Two Denver police cars and a black FBI SUV were in the library parking lot. Men were getting out.

"Turn around and keep going." Derry reached for her hand.

———

"Well, that was harder than I thought it would be." Gabriele spoke out loud even though no one was around to hear her. "Maybe I should have let Kai live and made her do this."

Gabriele had spent the morning tracking down what had happened to the missing money. With the information that Dace had received from Nasir, she was able to find the money in an offshore account. She had just finished transferring the missing money into Nasir's account in Egypt. She was still not quite sure who within the FBI had done this, but there did not appear to be any ties between the money transfer and their cover at Homeland. Dace would find that reassuring. She called him and reported that the money was now available and she expected payment immediately.

———

Jenny had been working in IT at Homeland Security for three years. In that time, she had seen the number of attempts to hack into government databases skyrocket. It was sometimes a weekly or even daily event. And most attempts were unsuccessful. But this person was good. They had made it past all the firewalls and traps. They were inside the system, snooping around. That did not happen every day. Jenny put in a call to the FBI. This was serious and the FBI had the resources to investigate such a breach.

The information about the breach reached Booker within minutes. For some reason, she felt it could be Sara, so she had Tony take over the investigation.

It took some doing, but he eventually found the hacker's location.

Faircloth was now on the scene at the library. Tony listened as Booker talked with Faircloth on her phone. Faircloth reported that no one matching Sara's or Derry's description had been seen in or around the library. As the link was now broken there was no way to learn who had been behind the hack. Booker shoved her phone into her pocket and stormed out of Tony's office.

No sooner had this wild goose chase ended, then a flag popped up on Tony's system. The money was on the move from the offshore account. The trace started automatically, and with a little luck and a slipup on Sara's part, he would catch his prey.

The new home for the money came back after only ten minutes. It had been a direct move, very straight forward. This was not the action of someone trying to hide their work. The money went directly from island currency to Egyptian Pounds.

Tony had the routing and account numbers for the new bank in a matter of seconds. Sara must be in a hurry. She had slipped up. Or maybe she believed no one knew about her theft so there was no need to hide the transfer.

Is she really that naïve?

Nasser Social Bank, Egypt.

This did not feel right. Sara was too smart for this. And why Egypt? *Is she working with terrorists? Is she one of them?* Tony could not accept that possibility.

The FBI's latest report on the bank popped up. It was a Sharia law bank and was suspected as a front for terrorist activities.

Booker's words came to mind, *"Her conversion to Christianity was just a lie to keep her out of jail."*

The money had been moved to Egypt, a place where the U.S. government could never touch it. If Sara was a terrorist it all made sense now, but he just couldn't picture Sara in a burka.

Tony started another trace to find out where the commands to move the money had originated. His second trace ended quickly. Again he was not required to follow tons of loops and false paths. He reached for his phone and put in a call to Booker's office.

"She moved the money."

"Did you find her location?"

He knew it was wrong to admire Sara, but he felt the smile form despite himself. "Maybe."

"What do you mean, 'Maybe?'"

"The commands originated from a Department of Homeland Security computer."

"So when she hacked in earlier she was setting this up."

And he had thought someone was just snooping around inside their database. "It sure looks like you were right. I'll start a facial-rec program for the area around the library. It's not an area with lots of cameras, but we might get lucky."

"See if there are any private security cameras in the area, too. And keep me informed."

———

When Tazeem's wife, Nina, picked up their three oldest kids from school, she looked at some of the other mothers and fathers who were there. Each one of them loved their children just as much as she loved hers.

She knew the families in Atlanta were no different. Her sister was no different. Her sister loved her son and daughter just as much as Nina loved her kids.

And soon they would all be dead. Why? Because of her husband. Because he felt they were not worthy. Because he felt he was better than them. Because he felt their god was not the same as his god. Nina thought about what she had read a few days ago and had reread every day since. *Even Al-Shafi'i could not deny Mohammed's words. They were not to kill women and children of nonbelievers.*

Nina put her children in the car and headed home. Something had to be done, but what? She'd promised her husband she would not tell anyone about the attack.

51

Derry stood over the kitchen sink in Kai's apartment. Using one of the old towels he found lying around, he cleaned the makeup off his face and rinsed the gray out of his hair. The gray didn't bother him, but Sara kept making comments about him being so much older than her. She was still in the bathroom, scrubbing every tiny bit of her makeup off.

While she worked on her face, he sat at the table going through Hewitt's files. He noticed she stopped a few times to rest. Her health was not good and all this hiding out from the police, eating processed foods, and lack of sleep was taking its toll. He would ask her if she needed help, but every time he brought up anything about her weight loss or health, she got mad. He turned back toward the computer and continued to read then finally spoke up, "Something seems a little weird. I'm reading through Hewitt's emails and—"

Sara stepped out of the bathroom. The red was not coming out at all. She rubbed her hair with another towel. "And what?"

"It might be nothing, but he has a lot of travel information on his computer. He has flight information for four different men flying to four different countries this Friday." He peeked out the corner of his eye at her, "Red."

"Is that going to be my new name? Can't think of anything more original?" Sara took a few steps toward him and flicked the wet towel at him before returning it to work on her hair. "Who are these men and where are they going?"

"The destinations are all over the world. As for who they are—," he shrugged. "All I have is their names. I can't find any other information about them in any of Hewitt's files."

She dropped into the chair next to him. "Let's see what else we can find out. Are they all leaving from DIA? If so, maybe they all live around here somewhere, unless they are visiting from out of town." Sara set up a Wi-Fi hot spot using one of the unused burn phones. "Let's run a search on each name."

Derry did as she asked. "Even though they are all leaving from DIA, I can't find any records for any of those names in Colorado. I got two hits for one of the names, an eight-year-old living in New Jersey and a seventy-three-year-old in Kansas. I don't think this airline ticket is for either one of them."

"Nothing on any of the names in New York either. If these men were working for Hewitt they should show up either here or there."

"Maybe they all belong to Hewitt. Maybe they are aliases." Derry studied Sara's face to see if she agreed. She did.

"If that's true—" She reached over and turned his laptop toward her. "Then he's got to have a reason for making four different airline reservations at the same time. But what?"

"Insurance."

Sara leaned back and looked at him. "Why would he do that? If someone learned about them it will just bring suspicion on him."

"Each name has travel arrangements for a different country but all for the same date. If for some reason the attack is stopped and the FBI goes looking for him, they will have to spread their search out to four different places. It would make it harder for them to find him. I think it's pretty smart."

"You could be right. And if he has other identities to change to once he is outside the country he'll be able to disappear."

"I think we now know when the attack will happen. It will be sometime after eight in the morning on Friday." Derry turned the laptop back toward himself.

"More likely after noon on Friday. He will want to be past our borders when it goes down. After it happens all planes could be forced to land for fear of more attacks." Scrolling through the files one more time Sara finally looked up. "I don't see anything else of use in Hewitt's files. Let's see what we can learn from Landry's files."

"We have less than five days to stop this. Those files are encrypted. Do you think you can decrypt them quickly?"

Deadly Infiltration

"Give me a few hours to work on Landry's files. If we still don't have anything in four hours, we will call Sam with what we have."

———

The facial-rec program failed to find anyone that matched Sara or Derry, yet after the bank transfer through Homeland, Tony was sure Sara had been at that library. He picked a few city-cams around the library and started going through the images himself from around the time the connection to Homeland was lost.

He almost went right by the homeless couple, but the older man holding the younger lady's hand seemed out of place somehow. He brought up a picture of Derry and compared it to the face of the gray haired man.

"Got you. Now I just need to see where you went."

———

Sara slapped the keyboard for the fourth time. "I am so close."

Derry stepped near. "Anything I can do?"

She looked up at him. "You wouldn't happen to have the decryption key in your pocket, would you?"

He sat down next to her. "How about taking a break?"

"No, I am this close." She held up her fingers about an inch apart. "I am sure I have the right program. I just need the key. Without it I may have to run every conceivable combination there is."

"How long would that take?"

"On this thing? Let me see, what year is this?"

"Okay I get the point. Maybe I could help by looking through Landry's non-encrypted files. Just tell me what to look for."

"It would most likely be a name of a place or person, something he could remember, but I doubt you will find it in there. He would keep it well hidden."

"Hold on for a second." He brought up the research he had done on Landry or Roux, his real name. "Try Philippe Sauvageau."

She leaned over her keyboard as her head turned toward him. "Where'd you get that name?"

He explained his morning's work.

"It's worth a try." Her first pass failed. She flipped the two names, first for last. It worked. She leaned over and kissed him. "You're a lifesaver."

"Let's hope so."

After the emails were decrypted, Sara transferred the files to Derry's computer so they could both search through them. Derry began at the top of the list and Sara began in the middle. An hour later they compared notes. "What have you got?" he asked.

She brought up her notes. "I found a lot of emails about different groups around the country, five groups in all, I think. I also found several dates, but they don't make sense."

"Anything to say where these groups are at?"

"No. They use names like 'city of five' or 'city to the north.' My guess is it has to do with the group in that city or a characteristic of the city compared to the others cities that will be attacked, but there are not enough details to know for sure where any of these cities are."

Derry moved his finger around on his touchpad as he thought. "You said the dates didn't make sense. The Muslims don't use our calendar. Their year one was when Muhammad received his revelation or something like that."

"I know that." She smiled as she nodded her head slightly. "I looked it up. But that still does not help. The date of the attack is happening in 'Carry.' Carry what?"

"Well, whatever it means, it means now. We know that from Hewitt's travel plans."

She shrugged. "Okay. You're right. And I think it will be a chemical attack of some type."

Derry looked over at his monitor. "That's what I got, too. Except the chemicals they have listed are all harmless. Unless they're also in code." He moved his mouse through the list.

Sara scrolled down to the next page of her notes. "I found two chemical names so far. I did a search on them. I couldn't find any harmful compounds that they are both used in. So, it has to be a code."

He leaned forward to read along. "Those are the same as the ones I found. But I found one more. I have iodine, arsenic and silicon." He brought up a web page that talked about two of the elements. "Arsenic and silicon are used in the making of integrated circuits and I think iodine is also used somewhere in the process. And arsenic is a poison but—"

Sara cut him off. "But not something you would use in a chemical attack. It's not a gas and besides, it's used everywhere."

"So if the chemical names are coded, how do we learn what they really are? It could be something simple, like maybe, black means blue and red means yellow. All the color code names are still colors." He glanced at her work. "So maybe 'Iodine' means 'Oxygen' or something like that."

"Makes sense, but how do you propose to find the real names? Try every combination there is?"

"No. It would have to be something simple enough that the members of the cells would know what they mean." Standing, he walked around the room as he munched on an energy bar. Their late lunch was not enough to carry him through the evening. "There are lots of ways to transpose the names. They could be offset on the periodic table or the atomic weight in whole units could be their element number."

"Or a hundred other methods." Sara moved to the kitchen counter and jumped up. She gently swung her feet against the cabinet door, making a rather loud bang. "This is impossible."

Derry looked at her swinging feet. She slowed them down, making less noise. "I'm going to play around with a Periodic Table. See what pops up."

"Good luck, but it would be faster to write a program and try all the different possibilities."

"For you maybe." He took his seat and pulled up a Periodic Table of Elements on his computer.

She dropped down off the counter and joined him.

He tried several possibilities. The first one was to use the atomic weights as the new element numbers. Silicon gave him nickel, and arsenic gave him tungsten, which was okay but iodine has the weight of 126.90, a number off the chart. No good. Doing the reverse did not work either as it produced weights that were not on the chart. He rubbed his hands on his pant legs and peered over at Sara. She was studying him. "What?"

"Nothing." She turned away, then got up and wandered aimlessly around the room.

Derry went back to work. *What if it is a pictorial translation?* Looking at the table he mentally folded it in half in both directions. Taking the names of the elements that touched his, he ran a search for possible combinations. None of them came up with a usable result.

Sara stopped walking and looked over his shoulder. "Running out of ideas yet?"

"Almost, but not yet."

He had one last idea. He looked at the elements touching those they found. He looked at the elements on the right, left, top and bottom of each one. The elements touching on the top showed positive results. They were bromine, phosphorus and carbon. In the right combination with other elements, they could form a binary agent, commonly known as a nerve agent, the worst of which was in the Novichok family. The article he found on nerve agents said it produced a powder that was seven to eight times deadlier than nerve gases and not detectable by standard means.

"I need to get this to Sam right now." Grabbing the phone, he reinserted the battery and punched in Sam's number as he stood to pace. He couldn't sit, not with the world coming to an end.

Passing by the boarded window, something grabbed his attention. He backed up and peeked through the narrow slit. A newer black car sat half a block away. He killed the call.

———

Dace Roux sat in his living room, planning his soon departure from this godless country when his phone rang. It was a secured number, one he knew all too well. "What do you need at this hour, Jonas?"

"We have a big problem."

"What do you mean *we* have a problem?"

"I just got off the phone with Gabriele. Someone in IT failed to inform us, but it appears our systems were hacked into today."

"That happens on a regular basis." Roux stood and moved to the window that looked out over the city. He would miss the view.

"Gabriele followed it up. This time the hacker actually got in and now the FBI has taken over the investigation. They are sure it was Sara Beckwith, and Gabriele thinks she downloaded our files."

"I do not keep any documents at work that can incriminate me."

"She also went through our key logs. Gabriele is retracing her footsteps. We will know more by morning."

"Fine. You may approach me then if Gabriele is able to discover something that could possibly turn out to be a problem." Dace did not appreciate phone calls to do with work in his off hours, but he understood how Jonas might be getting nervous as their important date approached.

52

Chris sat in the car scrutinizing the red brick building. The first two locations on the list of Sara's old work places and former residences had come up dry. Based on camera images, Tony was convinced Sara and Derry had headed toward this part of town, but Chris did not hold out much hope for this location. The FBI report on the crimes committed in this building were extensive. He knew what had happened here. He could not imagine Sara spending a night here. He certainly wouldn't. People avoid places filled with painful memories. Then again, if Sara was who Booker described, she was not most people. The report said Faircloth had been part of the task force that had saved Sara and her boyfriend that day.

When Tony mentioned this location as a possible hideout, Faircloth said that given how smart Sara was and what she had gone through, it would be a perfect hiding spot. So he had sent Chris to watch the place.

The sun had set and this part of town had few working streetlights, making his black government issued car all the harder to spot. The object of his attention sat a half block away in a ghostly darkness that enveloped everything on the street. He closed his eyes in hopes of speeding up his night vision. Kent always told him it was stupid, and the eyes adjusted to new conditions at the same rate no matter what tricks you tried. That didn't matter. He did it anyway.

On opening them, he peered into the deep shadows at the boarded windows. One of the panels had a faint outline. A small amount of light escaped past the board. Staring at it made it disappear. He closed his eyes again, this time a little longer.

When he reopened them he was sure he detected a faint whitish light glowing around the window before dimming once more. Two seconds later it went out. Someone was in there, moving around, and may have seen him.

Reaching for his phone, he made a call.

———

Derry rushed to the laptop and pushed the lid down.

"What are you doing? I'm not—"

"Grab your stuff." He pulled the plug from the wall.

"Is it the cops?" She turned for the pack and opened it.

He took it and started shoving everything on the table into it. "There's a shiny black car out there. I'm sure it's the FBI."

"A black car?" She walked toward the window. "Where?"

"Down the road a half block or so." He headed into the bedroom without turning on the lights. "Is there anything in here you need?"

She joined him. "Not now." Turning, she reached for the duffel bag from Levy's storeroom. "But we will need this." She handed it to him. "What about your call?"

He went over to the counter and grabbed the food bars that were sitting out along with the other electronics. "I'll call Sam once we're safe. Come on." He headed out the door for the basement. She followed close behind.

———

Faircloth had told Chris not to go into the building until backup arrived. He was less than five minutes away. Chris decided to wait outside of the car where he had a better view of the building.

Chris closed his eyes as he opened his door. He did not want to lose the little night vision he had to the dome light. He walked toward the rear of the building. Odds were that would be their escape route. He took up a position behind a dumpster. It gave him a field of view for both the side and back. There he waited. A black SUV, along with two Denver Police cars, pulled up.

Faircloth had never been much on wasting time. He stepped out and told Kent to grab the pry-bar. He then sent two police officers around front. Without waiting, he headed for the rear door. All the entrances to the building were now covered. Kent was prying loose the wood that covered the rear door. On the fourth yank the panel broke free.

Faircloth charged in first, with Chris, Kent, and two police officers following behind.

———

Derry grabbed the wire leading into the tunnel and pulled. The one small light in the basement went out.

"What are you doing?" Sara's voice came from behind him. "Now I can't see a thing."

"Where's one of those phones?"

He heard her fumbling before the soft glow of the screen showed her standing two feet away. The flashlight mode quickly followed. She stepped past him, and headed for the tunnel. "Why'd you kill the lights?"

He pulled the wire the rest of the way out of the tunnel. "To hide our exit." He tossed the wire as far as he could across the room and followed her into the hole. The light was disappearing quickly as she headed to the opposite end of the tunnel. Turning, he grabbed the workbench and yanked it back into place.

"Are you *trying* to tell them where we are?" Sara's voice was a harsh whisper. The light started to move up the short ladder as he heard her groan softly.

He knew her arm still bothered her, even though she tried to hide it most of the time. Derry mumbled his response, it wasn't intended for her. "Nope. Just trying to save us." He gave the workbench one last pull to secure it against the wall. With the hole covered he turned to follow her as he heard voices entering the room behind him. As he started up the ladder, a tiny flash of light passed across the edge of the hole. He froze. Once the beam was gone he climbed as quickly and quietly as he could.

Once in the storage room, Sara closed the hatch behind him. "Now what?"

"They're in the basement and might be right behind me." With the light from her phone to see by, he grabbed one of the filing cabinets and pulled it over gently to rest on top of the trapdoor.

She had moved to the door leading into the hall.

"Kill the light." He stepped closer to her. "Are you ready?"

"Not really, but we don't have a choice in the matter." She slipped the phone into her pocket and picked up the duffel bag with her good arm, while he picked up the pack.

He then reached over and took the heavy weight from her shoulder. "In case we have to run." She didn't resist. He led the way into the hall and out of the building. Two police cars passed them. The second one slowed just enough to send chills down their backs. "We need to get off this road." Cutting behind one of the building on the next block over, they made their way through the alleys. After traveling four blocks in a northerly direction, they came to the railroad yard.

"We could hide out here," Sara suggested.

"Too obvious. They will cover this place as soon as they know we aren't in the building."

They turned east, toward Five Points.

"Hey, hold up." Derry dropped behind.

"What? You're not hurt are you?"

"No, but I need to call Sam."

"Now? Can't it wait?"

"This information is too important to wait." He hid behind some parked cars as Sara joined him.

53

Tuesday

Agent Booker stood behind the desk in her home study scrutinizing the man sitting before her. Agent Sam Freymen of the CIA had shown up 20 minutes earlier and gotten her out of bed. He told her he had new information concerning the murder of Todd Jenkins. He also told her it was a matter of national security and that millions of lives were at stake. He then insisted she call in her lead investigator before he would share any details. Reluctantly she called Faircloth and told him to come to her home immediately. While they waited for Faircloth to arrive Booker went over the details of the case in her mind, trying to see what they could have missed.

"How do I know you are not telling me a pack of lies? CIA has not been known to be the most honest organization."

Sam reached into a pocket and produced a piece of paper. "This should help explain things."

Booker quickly scanned the words. "Are you saying this letter is legit, and that it gives you the authority to take over *my* investigation?"

Sam sat there as if this was a cozy meeting between two friends, but it was not. "That is correct. I would rather not remove you, but I will do what it takes to complete my mission."

What a smug little arrogant excuse of a CIA agent. Her fingernails dug into the palms of her hands as she leaned harder onto her fists. "You have broken every code of ethics and respect that our two agencies share by showing up here in the middle of the night. I should have you arrested."

"On what grounds? Bringing you new information that could save millions of lives, or the fact that I disturbed your beauty sleep?" His tone was almost flat, without emotion.

"Don't get cocky with me. You haven't shown me any evidence of a life or death situation."

"I will." He looked at his watch.

"My investigation is an FBI matter. What gives the CIA the power to interrupt it? You're not law enforcement, at least not inside U.S. borders, and you only have power to work inside the country under a few very special circumstances." She was worked up and needed to calm herself. If this man and this case were what he alleged they were, she needed to stop listening to her emotions and her hurt pride and find a way to work with him. But if he were lying she would do everything in her power to ensure he spent as much of his life in jail as possible.

"The CIA has the authority to work inside the U.S. when the case involves international crimes against our country, and if the suspects are not U.S. citizens. It is debated if both requirements have to be met, but that is irrelevant in this case."

"Our suspect, Sara Beckwith, is a U.S. citizen."

"You are driving your camels to the wrong oasis."

"What?"

"It means—"

"I know what it means. Are you saying Sara is innocent or that she's not a citizen?"

"She had nothing to do with the murder of Agent Jenkins." He checked his watch again. He obviously did not want to say too much before Faircloth arrived.

They could hear sounds of footsteps coming down the hall. Both heads turned at the sound of the pocket doors sliding open. Booker's husband stuck his head in. "Agent Faircloth is here." Jeff Booker stepped aside as the older agent moved past him.

Faircloth's hair was disheveled and his face was covered with gray stubble. "What's all this about?"

Booker nodded to Jeff. "Thank you for letting him in." She glanced at the clock on her wall. "Would you please take care of Foster this morning?"

He gave a knowing nod. "No problem. Do you want any coffee?"

"I sure could use some." Faircloth's voice was gruff.

"Better make a full pot."

Mr. Booker stepped out and closed the doors.

"How long before he leaves?" Sam sat up a little straighter.

"I'm sorry if my husband's presence in his own home is a problem for you. He's not the intruder here. And if that bothers you, you should have thought about it before you came to my private residence." This man never smiled. His face was made of stone.

"I apologize for upsetting your routine. It's just that what I am about to share can't make its way out into the public under any circumstances." Sam's gaze went to the closed doors before coming back to rest on Booker's face.

"As I said before, if he's a problem maybe you shouldn't have come here. If there is anyone in this house that I don't trust, it's you."

Sam stood and walked the three short steps to her desk. Pulling a phone from his pocket he handed it over. "Hit speed dial two."

"Why?"

"It will help alleviate your uncertainties."

She took the phone. "Who am I calling?" She hit speed dial two.

"Director Comey's office, may I help you?"

Is this guy for real? Did he actually have me call my own boss? "Um, yes, is the Director in?"

"He should be in within the next half hour. Would you like to leave a message?"

She knew if this CIA agent was telling the truth this call could cost her, but she had to be certain. "Yes, this is Special Agent Booker of the Denver office. Could you have him call me at his earliest convenience?"

"What shall I tell him this is to do with?"

"Agent Samuel Freymen of the CIA."

There was a long pause. Booker studied the man standing near her desk while she waited. If this was a bluff, it was a very good one. His eyes never wavered as he returned her gaze.

"This is Director Comey. What appears to be the problem?"

This was not going the way she expected. "This is Special Agent Booker, Special Agent in Charge of the Denver Office. I am verifying Agent Freymen's authority to— assert his power over the FBI." There. She'd said it. It did not come out as graciously as she had intended, but it was out.

A long slow breath filled the line as she gripped the phone tighter.

"We have no choice in this matter. You are to give Agent Freymen your full and complete cooperation. — I have been talking with his boss and the President for the last twenty minutes. Do as he asks. This is not a request."

"Yes, sir. I will." The line went dead. She tossed the phone back to Sam. "I guess we are to answer to you for now."

Faircloth's head snapped up from the half slumber he'd fallen into. "What do you mean, he's in change? Who is this guy and why am I here?" His glare shifted from Booker to Sam and back.

A tap at the door broke the tension.

"Come in."

Jeff stepped in with a pot of coffee and three mugs. "I'm taking Foster to Mickey D's for breakfast." He headed back out.

"Thank you, and I'm sorry about this. I—" It was her turn to take their son to school, not Jeff's. She'd make it up to them once this was over.

"It's important, I know. I got it covered." He backed out and closed the doors.

No sooner had the doors touched than Faircloth brought the room back to business. "Well? I'm waiting."

Sam began to speak, but Booker stepped around her desk and spoke first. "Agent Freymen has the authority to take over our investigation by order of both our director and," she turned her head toward Sam, "the President?"

He gave an affirmative nod.

"Now, tell us what in the world is going on." She poured a cup of coffee for herself and moved back behind her desk. Reaching into her desk, she retrieved two packages of sugar and one of cream and added them to her cup.

"So it's the power of the White House that made me get out of bed after only three hours of sleep. Knew I shouldn't have voted for him." Faircloth looked at Sam. "Do you know I was up most of the night—,"

"Chasing Sara and Derry. I heard all about it from Agent Booker."

"We almost had them." Faircloth was fully awake for the first time since entering the office.

Sam stood and got two cups of coffee. Turning, he gave one to Faircloth before moving to the side of the room where he could see both of them.

"The case you have been working on is so much bigger and deadlier than either of you know or can imagine." They sat and listened. He addressed Booker. "I am sure you know about the leak inside one of our agencies?"

She nodded toward Faircloth. "He also knows. We believe Sara might be part of it."

"You still think she is behind your agent's death?"

"That is the way the evidence points."

"It's all fabricated. The person who killed Agent Jenkins framed Sara then tried to kill a friend of mine as well."

"How do you know it wasn't Sara?"

"Because I know who it was. It was not anyone in the FBI. The murderer used the same poison on my friend that was used on Jenkins."

Booker nodded. "I'd like to see the report on that."

"There isn't one, and there won't be."

Another reason not to trust the CIA. They never feel reports are needed except when it serves them. "Tell me why the CIA wants to take over my case."

Sam took a sip and set the cup aside. "To date we have lost Agent Jenkins, Senator Henderson and his wife, the senator's brother, a CIA officer, and a family in the Middle East. All of these deaths were committed by the same terrorist group. And all these deaths are nothing compared with what will happen if we don't stop the impending attack."

"What impending attack?" Faircloth finished his coffee and stood to get more.

"Are you telling me this is just the beginning?" Booker was listening now.

"Todd was murdered because the terrorists wanted to retrieve the files on the jump drive that was found in Texas. The enemy did not want us to know what was on that drive."

"That was our assumption as well. The same for the senator and his brother."

"That file had been put together by the CIA, but was lost when the author of it was killed. However, we now have a copy of it, fully decrypted."

This was good news. "What's in the file?"

"It contains information on a group of terrorists that have infiltrated Homeland Security."

"Homeland?" Booker and Faircloth asked as one.

"Yes. Not the FBI."

"Are you going to arrest them?" Booker leaned in.

"In due time. But they are planning a major attack on U.S. soil. This attack has been in the works for at least three years and goes way beyond just the few moles working at Homeland Security. The terrorists working for Homeland are not the masterminds. So going after them now will—"

"Only alert the others." Sam had Booker's complete attention now. "I have to know something before we go on. Who in Homeland are we talking about?"

Sam reached for his coffee and stared into it. He took a long sip. Setting his cup aside, he pulled a jump drive from his pocket and handed it to Booker. Faircloth moved around to stand behind Booker's chair as she inserted it into her computer. "Here is the file that has caused so much trouble." Sam took up residence next to Faircloth.

The three read through the file. Half way through Booker whispered. "So, Sara is innocent and Landry and Hewitt at Homeland are guilty of terrorism?"

"Yes." Sam answered.

"Where is all the information about the attack? When? Where? How? Everything in here is just guesswork and a few names." Faircloth was clearly disappointed.

Sam stepped back around the desk where he had a clear view of their faces. "Up until a few hours ago this was all we knew."

Booker sat up. "But now?"

"One of my operatives acquired new information that the attack will be this Friday, and it will be a chemical attack. This aligns with our other intel."

"Who is this operative and where did they *acquire* this information?"

Sam gave Faircloth a quick glance. "Does it matter?"

"If you want us to pull every field agent in on this, I want to know how good your information is." Booker was still skeptical.

Sam shrugged. "Sara and Derry broke into Hewitt's and Landry's computers."

Booker was on her feet with the words right at the edge of her mouth.

Sam never gave her the chance. "They discovered that the terrorists are planning to make a very deadly nerve agent."

Booker crossed her arms. "So Sara is your trusted spy?" It was difficult for Booker to get past her prejudice against Sara.

"I still don't see, if we have all this information, why we don't just go arrest Hewitt and Landry. I'm sure we can get something out of them and if they are out of the way, the others will scatter." Faircloth preferred a direct approach.

Booker saw the fallacy with this immediately. "None of the evidence we have can be used. What would we arrest them for?"

Faircloth walked back over to his chair and dropped into it, spilling some of his coffee on Booker's nice rug.

Sam continued, "And arresting a few ground troops is not our objective. If we put a stop to the attack today, what do you think will happen to all the preparations that have been made? The cells that have been set up? The chemicals they have as well as the equipment? An arrest now may delay the attack, but it would certainly not stop it from happening in the near future."

Faircloth mumbled into his cup. "Doesn't the CIA have someplace they can beat the answers out of them?"

Sam left this comment unanswered. "The terrorists will either wait a few months and set up in different cities or jump the gun and attack right now. Either way, we lose."

"Anything else we should know?" Booker looked back at Sam. He was the opposite of Faircloth in many ways. He was soft-spoken, very articulate, patient, and extremely well fit.

"We believe five cities will be hit. Because our only leads have come out of Denver, your office will be designated as the central command center for the country."

Faircloth stood. "And we're betting the survival of this country on the word of a convicted felon, who an hour ago was wanted for murder." He shook his head as he headed for the door. "I need to call my team in. They thought they had the morning off."

———

Lamar's phone rang, waking him from a deep sleep. He fumbled for the noisy box and answered the call. "Stover."

"There have been some new developments in the case." It was Booker's voice.

Lamar was instantly awake. "What's up?"

"We have new information that I cannot share over the phone. But suffice it to say I now know that Sara was not involved in Todd's murder and I need you back on the case. Meet me at the office ASAP."

This was the Booker that Lamar was used to. "I will be there as soon as I can." He hung up the phone, shaking his head.

"What was that all about?" Mary was awake now, too.

"Booker has finally come to her senses. She says she has new information proving Sara is not involved in the murder. I have to get into the office right away."

"Oh, thank the Lord."

54

Jonas and Dace stood behind Gabriele as she worked on Dace's computer.

She had given them a full report of her findings on the cyber break-in about an hour before. Someone had discovered Dace's private email account. For twenty minutes he maintained that what she said was impossible, telling both of them that he had only logged into that email account from the office once. So no one could even know about it, much less hack into it. When Gabriele showed him the account login information that she pulled from the same database, he agreed that maybe there could be a possible problem.

"When was the last time you logged into this account from home?" Gabriele pointed to the screen which displayed information about Dace's email account.

"Three nights ago."

"Not last night?"

"I just told you when. This is a complete—"

"Well, according to this, someone logged in yesterday and read, or downloaded every file."

"That does not matter. I delete every message once I have read it. And every email is fully encrypted."

Gabriele brought up his trash folder. "You mean these emails?"

Jonas walked around the desk to look Dace in the face. "I told you, you have to empty the trash folder or the files stay around." He shook his head. "Of all the stupid, beginner mistakes you could make."

Dace moved in a little closer. "Open one and see if you can read it. See, you cannot. As I said, it does not matter if some emails were downloaded. No one can read them."

Gabriele pushed her chair back, almost hitting Dace. Standing, she turned and faced the two men. "Unless you used the same encryption algorithm as the one used by the senator, the FBI will most likely have them decrypted by now."

"Again, even the plain text is coded. Nothing says what it means."

Jonas turned away. "You are a fool."

"No one calls me such a derogatory term and survives." Dace's head snapped toward Jonas.

"I warned you about this. I—"

Gabriele cut him off. She turned to face him. "Do not think that you are unblemished in this. You have half a dozen airline reservations for this Friday on your computer. That is a dead giveaway of when the attack will take place."

Jonas looked down at Gabriele. "We have to destroy all our files, emails and anything else that can be traced to us." Looking over at Dace, he added. "And we need to notify Nasir."

―――――

Jonas studied Gabriele as she busily wiped out every private, then public email account that any of them had. Dace stood across the room talking on the phone.

Nasir was calm but his irritation was clear. "And if someone is able to decrypt your files, what will they learn?"

"I do not feel that is possible— But the files contain code names for the chemicals and for the locations, plus schedules for when they were brought in and delivered. But everything is in code so no one will know what the files mean even if they can read them."

Dace's self-confidence was beyond belief.

"The FBI is not as incompetent as you might imagine. Your incompetence, however, has cost this operation heavily. It will be your downfall. I do not want it to be mine."

"If you read over the files you will see that I am right. I believe the only fact they will be able to get from them is how many cities we plan to hit. The names are too general for them to deduce any more than that."

"You had better be right— I have put years of planning into this attack. Our teams are very close to completion and now it could all be for naught."

"We could delay the attack two or three weeks and move to different cities. Three weeks would give us time—" Dace was looking for a way out.

"Time to be caught. The Americans now know the date, several of our members, and the type of attack. And you want to delay it to allow them more time to find out the rest?"

"We have suffered several setbacks and the time—"

"No."

"But, if—"

"We will not delay the attack. Too much work has gone into it. We will do what they do not expect. We will move the attack date up. But in order to make that happen I will need you and Jonas to help Motova. When his bank account was discovered I had him move the operation. They are now behind schedule and you will help him make up for lost time. I will send you the new location. I want both of you out there today."

"But—" Dace protested.

"What is the problem? You cannot stay where you are. Your positions have been compromised."

"Yes, we know that is a strong possibility. We are in the process of destroying all documents that can lead to us, and we have moved our travel arrangements up to today.

"You will leave your positions as I have stated, but not to run away and hide like cowering Jews. You will stay in Denver and help that team get ready. I am moving the date up to tomorrow."

"That is impossible. That timeline would mean we have to—"

"Be there for the attack. Yes, and if you are as smart as you have told me, you will find a way to survive."

"That was not the agreement we made with you. We were to assist you and your teams in all areas of security, transportation, and information. We were not to be part of the actual dispersal team."

"You and Jonas have brought this on yourselves. You have no choice in this. The Americans know who you are. They have your pictures, fingerprints and DNA. The only way you can survive is if the Americans are too busy fighting for their own survival to hunt for you. If this attack fails, they will find you no matter what country you try to hide in. And once they do, they will not waste their country's time and money bringing you to trial. Their CIA or one of their Delta Force teams will ensure this."

Dace knew Nasir was right. His arrogance seemed to vanish. "We will do our part to spread the one true belief. Allah be praised."

Dace ended his call and turned to Gabriele. "How is the file deletion coming?"

"I just executed a program that will delete all of the files from the system that any of us have ever touched. There will be no electronic trail to link us to anything."

"Good. We must leave immediately."

————

Derry and Sara had spent a restless night on the streets, hoping to evade the FBI. Finally, they decided to hide in plain sight with the crowds that were shopping.

Sara took a seat on the planter ledge. "I'm wiped out. I can't spend another night like that. We need to find a better place to stay tonight."

Derry looked at Sara, her hands were shaky. Her strength was almost gone. He dropped the duffel bag next to her and retrieved the pack off her shoulder. She gave him a slight smile as a thank you.

"Can I go to sleep right here?" She leaned back and closed her eyes.

"First, we should change. I'm sure every cop in the city has our description by now."

She looked up at him. Her expression displayed a weariness that he felt as well. He dropped down next to her as he slid one arm around her bony shoulders. She placed her head against his chest. He leaned down and whispered, "We have several hundred dollars in the front pocket of the pack plus all that money Levy left behind." He tapped the large duffle bag with his foot before nodding toward the shopping area. "How about we go buy some new duds?"

She peeked up at him. "Duds? I don't wear duds, but a new outfit or two sounds great."

He pulled out a roll of bills. He gave her most of it. "Shall we?" He stood and helped her up before they headed across the mall.

After changing into their new clothes, complete with hats and sunglasses, they grabbed a bite to eat at the food court. Hot fresh food helped Sara's energy level and attitude immensely. Leaving the mall, they dropped off the old clothes at a Goodwill box in the parking lot.

"I feel much better. Where to now?" She smiled up at him.

"We need high-speed internet and a place we won't be disturbed."

"The main public library is just a few blocks away. I'm just not sure it's safe. What are you planning to do?"

"You need to rest and I just want to check on a few things. I'll keep an eye open for the cops."

As they crossed Bannock Street, just outside of the main Denver library, Derry let his eyes skim over Sara. "That *outfit* makes you look like a kid."

She turned away, toward the cars waiting for the light to change. "That was the idea. Most people don't really notice college kids."

Once inside the building, he examined the layout. The place was huge. He looked over the map at the entrance before leading her to the elevator. They got off on the fourth floor and found an empty room. Derry closed the door as Sara dropped into a chair and plopped her head down on the table.

"Got any of those granola bars left?"

After pulling out his computer, Derry rummaged around the bottom of the pack before tossing her one.

She placed it beside her head and closed her eyes. He was tired too, but they couldn't both fall asleep.

One word was stuck in his mind. Novichok. He wanted to learn more about the nerve agent that was seven times deadlier than the others.

He brought up a webpage on it and read all he could find. There were a lot of unknowns about it. But he did learn that Novichok was a fine powder, not a gas. Bringing up a text window he started a list of questions and thoughts.

Is a powder good or bad? - A powder would have to be dispersed through the air.

To do that they would need a plane or could they do it with drones?

Drones that have larger payloads are expensive and hard to get ahold of. Plus you would need a pilot to control each one, more people.

How many drones would it take?

How deadly is seven times deadlier and what does that mean? By weight? By volume? By what?

How much do they have?

How much do they need to kill half of Denver?

How long does it stay deadly?

He went to all the links he could find but could not find any consistent answers.

Sara raised her head. "Aren't you tired?"

"No, not really." Whatever was pumping through his body, adrenalin, fear, or both, kept him awake. He checked the time. It had been almost two hours.

Sara sat up and moved in beside him.

He slid the mouse over to kill the window.

"Don't." She reached for his hand.

He stopped.

She took the mouse from under his fingers. She quickly read through his notes and several web pages. Sara was a fast reader. After ten minutes she probably knew almost as much as he did. "Did you know this last night?"

"Only the possible name for the nerve agent."

She dropped back and crossed her arms. "This stuff sounds wicked. Why would anyone ever invent something like this?"

"It came out of Russia."

Her head turned slowly toward him, as the word came out. "So?"

"They developed it toward the end of the cold war. They—"

"Wanted to destroy the planet?" She leaned back, grabbed the granola bar and started eating.

He reached for the mouse. She pulled it away. "I'm still reading. I just needed something for my low blood sugar." Part way through the page she leaned in. "What?" She pointed to a list of the compounds that made up the agent. '2-Methylpropyl'. "I've seen that somewhere before. I'm sure of it."

"You have? Where?"

Tilting her head, she looked into the distance as she tried to recall. "It was—"

He waited.

She turned toward him. "It had to do with some money I took."

55

She knew that what she was about to do was against her husband's orders. But some things were more important than what one man wanted. She held the phone in her sweaty palm. "Hi. This is Nina. Do you think Bill can get off early this Friday? I am planning a surprise party for Tazeem and I really want you and your whole family to be here." She licked her lips. Cotton filled her mouth as the words tumbled out too quickly. Would her sister notice?

If Tazeem learned about the call he would be furious and would hit her again, more than he had the other night. But a little physical pain was worth the lives of her family.

She waited for the response that was slow in coming. "You're having a surprise party for Tazeem and you want us there? He hates us. He told me he never wanted us in his home again."

"I've talked to him about that night. He said he was in a bad mood because of his job. It's all better now. In fact, that's what the party is all about. He got a big promotion. He wants you to understand that he's not mad anymore and the kids miss seeing their cousins. Please tell me you'll come." *I need to slow down.*

"It's been over a year and you are just now getting around to telling me it was all a misunderstanding?"

"Yes, please forgive me and I— we really want you here. We want the whole family."

"I thought you said this was a surprise."

"Yes, I meant me and the kids. Can you come? It's very important."

"I don't know. I'll have to talk with Bill. He was very upset after that night. I don't think he's forgiven Tazeem yet."

"Please, we want your whole family here. You need to be here by five so we can get everything set up in time. I really need your help." Nina's eyes watered. She tried to blink the tears away. How could she convince her sister without saying too much?

"We'll see. I'll let you know."

"Please, you have to come."

"What's this all about?"

Too much. "You're my only sister and with mom and dad gone you're all the family I have left. This is an important day for Tazeem and I really would like to share it with you. I've missed you."

"I'll call you after I have a chance to talk with Bill." The line went dead.

What did she expect? Tazeem had said he would kill them if they ever came around his family again. She needed a better lie before she called Tazeem's parents. They hadn't spoken in years. A call now would raise too many questions.

I knew Sara could not have killed Todd. The pieces just did not add up. Tony had just gotten into the office. The thought that someone at Homeland had framed her infuriated him. He was determined to find enough evidence to put them away for a very long time. He plopped into his chair and tapped into Homeland's systems hoping to follow the money trail and find everyone involved. Their computers were unusually busy this morning.

Tony followed the route of highest activity. Files were being removed, not just files but whole top level directories were being wiped from the system. This was completely illegal without a Presidential order. Someone was obviously trying to hide their tracks and they weren't being very quiet about it.

He tried to kill the commands that erased the files, but because of the way he had punched through their firewall, he had too low a priority to override them.

If he couldn't stop the sabotage he could at least save some of the files. The repository of backups appeared to be the most intact. Copying the files over the web was too slow, he would lose most of them. Copying them onto another part of the same system was faster. But it was risky. He could get noticed. But it was a chance he had to take.

The disk usage command showed plenty of space on the system. He started duplicating the directories to an almost empty hard drive while changing their names, owners and permissions. As long as he went unnoticed, he believed he would be able to save most of the work and retrieve it later.

"You coming?"

Tony turned to see Chris at the doorway. "Booker just called a staff meeting. Everyone is required to attend right away."

"I'll be along in one minute." Tony verified that his program was still running before he left.

————

Tazeem sat in his car. He had arrived on time, but The Chemist was nowhere to be seen. That man showed him no respect. He should not have entered the building before Tazeem. He needed to learn who was in charge. Stepping out of the car, Tazeem made a promise to Allah. If this man could not honor the ways of Islam, he would die in the attack.

He walked briskly toward the door. They needed to get this test over with quickly so they could continue with the plan. He punched in the code and entered. It took a few seconds for his eyes to adjust to the dim light.

Noises came from the small room in the rear of the warehouse. It was an unused office that had been sealed off with sheets of plastic and was the only place this test could take place. The idiot was probably setting things up without him. Crossing the floor, Tazeem decided to show this man who was in charge. With each step his disgust for The Chemist grew, but he would have to control it for now. The Chemist was still needed for a few more days.

Tazeem entered without knocking and pushed the sheet of plastic aside.

"What are you doing? Do you want to die?" The Chemist's voice was muffled by the breather in his rubber suit.

An ionizer sat on the table. A fine mist was barely visible in the narrow shaft of light coming through a mostly covered side window. The table held several cages of lifeless animals. Tazeem took a quick breath, then realizing his error he covered his mouth as his eyes widened. That poor excuse of a follower had just killed him.

"Get out, now!"

The muffled voice made its way through the pain that was coursing throughout Tazeem's body. His muscles started vibrating as every fiber burned in pain. The Chemist's hands grabbed him, pushing him toward the door. Tazeem determined he would not die alone. He grabbed the man's hood and pulled it off his head.

Sam caught up with Lamar as they walked down the hall toward the conference room. "It's nice to know you are back at work. How's Kai doing?"

Lamar understood his concern. "She's a strong young lady. She's already up and around some. She helped Mary with dinner last night."

A slight smile formed on Sam's face. "I'm not surprised. Her dad was like that too."

"She asked me this morning if there was any way she could help."

Sam gave a barely perceptible nod. "We are short handed in the computer area. Ask her in the morning if she thinks she can handle a desk job."

"I'll do that."

The two men found seats near the front of the crowded room as Booker called the meeting to order.

"Ladies and gentlemen, there has been a major breakthrough in the murder cases of Agent Jenkins and Senator Henderson. New information has been brought to my attention by Agent Sam Freymen of the CIA." Sam stood and looked around the room. He received many astonished looks as he again took his seat.

Booker continued, "We will be working closely with the CIA and they will receive our full cooperation. Agent Freymen has evidence that the leak we have been tracking originated with these three agents from Homeland Security." The screen displayed pictures of Agents Landry and Hewitt as well as a woman that was unfamiliar to most of the people in the room. There was mumbling as people came to grips with the fact that they had all been working closely with terrorists.

"My contact at Homeland has informed me that all three of these people left the Homeland office earlier this morning. It is believed that they know their covers are blown and are now on the run. We will be using all of our resources to track them down."

Booker continued to explain all of what Sam had told her. She emphasized the importance of keeping the information about the attacks secret until they learned the details. The room was surprisingly quiet as the seriousness of the situation settled in. "So as you can see, we no longer need to be searching for Sara Beckwith. This new evidence clears her of any wrongdoing in this case. In fact, we are trying to reach her in the hope that she can help us find additional information in time to stop this terrible attack. But this may be difficult given the fact that she still believes she is being hunted. But if any of you come across anything that will help us locate her be sure to pass that information on to me.

"I have been in contact with all of the FBI offices across the country. Every resource is being used to track down the terrorists and find out the details of the attack before it occurs on Friday. Your group leaders will discuss the details of your individual assignments. Good luck. The fate of the nation rests in your hands." Without waiting for questions, Booker left the room.

———

"You're saying John Motova is involved with a Muslim terrorist group?" Derry paced the small library room and spoke in hushed tones.

"Yes—I think—maybe. That's what the evidence points to." Sara remained in her seat, looking up, following him with her piercing, light brown eyes.

"From what I know of him, which is only what you have told me, he's not the type. All other issues aside, Islam is a very strict religion. No drinking and no pork plus a whole bucket full of rules on prayer and nearly everything else. The way you described Motova, he is the complete opposite."

"Yeah, but he would fit right in with the way he treats women."

"Because of what he let his sons do?" His voice was tentative. He did not want to open the wound any wider.

"According to them, everything they did to me was somehow my fault. Isn't that what Islam believes? It's always the woman's fault?"

"A lot of Muslims interpret the Qur'an that way, but not all. Remember, lots of different groups all claim to follow the true path." But she had a good point. The radical groups looked for messed up people to recruit and turn into *suicide bombers*. "However, he might be the right type to buy into something like this."

"You need to call Sam and tell him."

Derry pulled the phone from his pocket and stared at it. "If I turn this on, we may be telling the FBI where we are. Are you ready for that? We're both still wanted."

Sara glanced at the laptop. "If Motova has hidden his tracks well enough and the Feds arrest us, he'll get away with it and we'll be in jail..."

"...waiting for the poison to fall from the sky." He finished her sentence.

Her expression took on a doomsday look. She focused on the computer. "We need more data to prove he's behind this, something Sam and the FBI can act on."

"How can we get that?"

"I'll hack back into Motova's computer. Something has to be there. I might even be able to run a trace on his phone, maybe even record his phone calls."

The sleepless night suddenly hit Derry like a brick. He pulled out his chair and plopped down next to her. "How long will that take?"

"A few hours." It was her shift.

Derry laid his head down. "That long? I don't think the library will let us spend the night." He smiled as he closed his eyes.

"We can come back tomorrow if necessary. We have until Friday to find them."

56

Jonas sat across the table from Dace while John Motova sat at the end. "We have come to help you prepare for the attack tomorrow. We understand that this sudden move has put you behind schedule."

"Nasir told me he was sending extra help. I did not expect two Homeland Security agents. You have no experience in what we are about to do. You are untrained. And now I find out we have to be ready two days earlier than planned. I fear we will not be able to make that deadline. We had begun to make the nerve agent before we had to move. It has taken most of a day to get the machine set back up and running. We still have much to do, and not much time. Right now we need help with the drones."

Dace scanned the area. "Where are the drones?"

Motova pointed toward the east. "They are at my warehouse in Aurora. The two of you and the pilots will go over there tomorrow to get them."

Dace showed uncharacteristic emotion. "You left them behind? Do you not understand their importance to this mission?"

"I had no choice. When the FBI took the money, I had to move quickly. Moving a drone is not like packing a suitcase for a vacation. I needed time to rent a large truck to move all four drones along with their controllers and fuel."

Dace stared hard and cold into John's face. "How do you expect to spread the nerve agent without the drones? Are you going to throw it into the air and hope the wind blows it across the city?" His accent grew as did his anger.

Before John had a comeback, his encrypted phone rang. All six eyes shifted to it. "It is Nasir." The composure of all three returned as

John placed the phone in between them and hit speaker. "We are here."

"Team three, have the new members shown up?" Nasir always spoke in some level of code, even on a fully encrypted phone.

John leaned in. "Yes, your friends have arrived."

"They may be somewhat incompetent on other matters but they can be trusted. They will help you complete your mission. But we have a problem. Team two is not answering my calls. I sensed problems in that group all along, but I had hoped they could make it to the end."

"Do you think they were discovered?" Jonas cut in.

"Not at this time. I have someone in the area monitoring the police radios. Nothing has shown up yet. But it may only be a matter of time."

"We have a problem at this location also." Dace declared.

"Something more than sending in two untrained members this late?"

John took over before Dace could put an unfavorable spin on his actions. "As you know, when we suspected that my company was under surveillance, I needed to move. Unfortunately, I had to leave the drones behind. If everything looks okay, I will pick them up tomorrow with a truck large enough to haul them without having to disassemble them."

Nasir was quick coming back. "We do not have time tomorrow. Send a team over today, now. You need them on location and fully loaded no later than three o'clock tomorrow afternoon."

"I do not have a way to move them today. I need a large truck. I have one reserved for tomorrow morning. We must delay things for another day. Also because of the move, we have only two liters made. If we wait until Thursday, I feel we will have time to make the remaining powder."

"That is not possible. It appears our enemy has learned of our plans. The FBI is looking for us as we speak. Any delay could cost us everything. We move tomorrow."

"But that is impossible." John bellowed.

"Do not disagree with me on this. I do not care if you have to steal a truck to move the rest of your equipment. Once you are done with it, leave it where no one will discover it for a day or two. If you are unable to do this simple task, I will transfer the leadership of your team to Dace and you can join your cousin."

John's face lost some of its color as his gaze shifted to Dace and back to the phone. "Yes, sir. I will get a truck. We will have the planes in position by three tomorrow." He ended the call and picked up the phone. Gripping it tightly he stood and paced as he talked. "I know of a truck we can 'borrow'."

———

"Mr. Jamshed, it's Nina, your daughter-in-law." The other end of the line was quiet. She heard nothing. Nina pulled the phone away from her head and looked at the display to make sure the call had not died. She put the phone back to her ear. "Dad, will you talk with me?"

It took another few seconds before Tazeem's father answered. "Is he okay?" The tone was flat.

"Yes, yes, Tazeem is fine." He wasn't physically hurt that she knew of, but he was far from okay. She was putting one lie on top of another, but she knew in her heart it was the right thing to do. "Well, I mean he's not hurt or anything like that."

"Does he know you are calling me?" This man was perceptive.

"—No."

"You are a brave young lady, but going against his wishes is wrong, you know that. Right?"

"I know, but—" *but what?*

The line remained silent.

"I know he will be very upset if he finds out that I called you, but I needed to call someone."

Mr. Jamshed mumbled something in Persian. She recognized the language from her husband using it whenever he got angry. The two men were so much alike. "If this is about problems between you two, I cannot help. You must work that out with my son."

How could she tell him that his son was planning to kill him and a million others? "That's not what this call is about."

"Has he done something stupid and gotten himself in trouble?" It didn't matter how Tazeem treated his father, the man still loved his son. His concern came through despite the words.

How could she answer and get the help she needed without breaking the promise she had made? She pondered the right words, but before they came, her father-in-law understood part of the problem.

"Is he in jail?"

"He is not in jail right now, he's at the warehouse, at work." That should send the right message.

"He is too extreme in his beliefs. That has always been his problem. He wants the whole world to think the way he does." Jamshed paused. "Tell me what this is about." His tone changed to one of understanding.

She respected her father-in-law and wished she'd had more opportunities to get to know him, but her husband would never allow it. "I can't, I'm sorry I called. I need to go."

"Nina, you called me for a reason."

"It doesn't matter anymore. You're a good father. I see that, even if your son doesn't."

"Has he joined one of those radical groups? Is he planning to do something to hurt others?"

She took a deep breath and in one rushed sentence she said, "You and Mom need to leave Atlanta before Friday and take your other children with you. But you can't tell anyone else." She hung up.

57

Mr. Jamshed sat in his office staring out the window, the warning echoing in his mind. What was his son going to do?

They hadn't spoken for years, not by his choice. And now what he feared was coming true. Someone had taken his son's hatred and turned it into a weapon.

Maybe Nina knows what is going on.

Is it possible? Could my own son be a terrorist?

After all the kindness this country had shown him, could his son truly turn his back on it and follow the misguided words of those that wanted to destroy the world?

Nina sure sounds like he has.

Or at least she believes he has.

If Tazeem was planning something, maybe he could talk him out of it. Jamshed checked the time. If he left right away he could make it to his son's work before it was time to change shifts.

Leaving his office, he informed his secretary that he had a client to see and would not be back today.

Tazeem lived south of Atlanta. The roads were crowded and the drive through Atlanta took almost an hour, then another hour to Tazeem's workplace. Waiting in traffic gave Jamshed time to think, perhaps too much time. As he pulled into the parking area, he hoped showing up at his son's workplace would not bring punishment on Nina.

He would make up a lie, tell Tazeem his mother was sick or something.

The shipping and receiving business Tazeem worked for dealt mostly in plumbing and electrical supplies for contractors. Jamshed headed for the small room stuck on the front of the large two story building. The warehouse struck him as a monster waiting to gobble up a meal. He stepped in and asked the whereabouts of his son.

"He no longer works here."

"What?"

"Why are you looking for him?" The small skinny man looked up from his keyboard.

"I'm his father. Do you know where he might be?"

The man's face took on a look of understanding. "He turned in his notice last Thursday." He gave Mr. Jamshed one last look before turning around and talking into his radio.

Jamshed decided to go see Nina. Maybe Tazeem would be at home and he could talk to him there.

———

Hearing the clicking of the keyboard stop, Derry lifted his head. "How long have I been out?"

Sara checked the time. "Long enough. I'm hungry."

Sitting up, he stretched his sore muscles. A table was not a good bed. He glanced out the window at the clock outside the room. "We've been here the whole day?"

"That's why I'm hungry." She picked up a paper that was lying on the table and put it to her mouth. She acted as if she were eating it before tossing it back on the table. "Did you know you talk in your sleep?"

"Did I say anything interesting?"

"Oh yes. I'll use it for blackmail later."

His neck and shoulders ached. Rotating his shoulders helped some. "Did you find anything we can use against Motova? Is he in on all this?"

"Very likely. A whole lot of stuff points that way. He has two phone numbers and four different email accounts, one personal, two for business and one that does not appear to be used at all. That is the strange part."

"Maybe it is an old account and he no longer uses it."

Sara moved her finger around on the mouse pad. "I thought of that first. But I went into the deleted messages which are cleaned out on a regular basis." She studied her screen.

"And what did you find?"

"The account has multiple users. They type up a message and save it as a draft. Then delete it. Then the only copy is in the trash bin. There, anyone with access to the account can read it, but since it was never sent, the FBI and NSA can't monitor it."

"That works?" It sounded so simple.

She shrugged. "Most of the time. As long as the account is not on a watch list."

"I assume you read through all of his emails."

"Of course. There was nothing interesting in his personal or company emails. The important information is in the deleted messages in the "unused" email account. The problem is, everything is coded, kind of like the files we found on Landry's computer only more so. I need more time to go through them. I think I can crack his code if I have enough time."

"Can you tell where the different users are located?"

"Not really. I might be able to get close by looking at the routing information but they seem to log in from different places each time." Sara leaned back and slid her hands into her pockets.

Derry leaned closer to her screen as he studied its contents. "But are they always in the same city?" He shifted away from the screen to look at her face.

Her eyes opened wider. "I'm so stupid. Why didn't I see that?" She pushed him out of the way and started going through the header data on each of the emails and pulling the login information over.

"I thought we were going to get some food."

"Shhh, you can wait."

Derry observed her speed on the computer for a few minutes before he stood and looked out the large glass window at the patrons on the fourth floor. Everyone moving around out there seemed to be content.

"L.A."

He turned at her voice. She was typing like a madwoman.

"Atlanta."

Minutes passed without any more comments from Sara.

"Okay, I think I've got them all."

"Just L.A. and Atlanta?"

"Also New York, Chicago and Detroit." She wrinkled her

forehead on the last city she named.

"What is it?"

"I'm not sure about Detroit. It popped up more recently than all the others. And it seems that there are a lot more messages coming from Detroit than from the other cities."

"It is pretty obvious that Motova is running a group out of Denver. So if you count Denver, that gives us six cities, but Sam's file indicated only five. You said Detroit popped up recently? Were there any locations that went away when Detroit came into the picture?"

Sara shifted back to her computer. "Maybe. There were several locations in the Middle East before that, but none since messages began in Detroit." She looked up at Derry. "That's it."

"What's it?"

"Whoever is behind this recently moved their base of operations to Detroit. That explains why Detroit only showed up in the last few days and why the messages from Detroit seem different." Sara stood and paced the room before stopping with her back to the window that Derry had been looking out. "Now we know more than enough to chance sending a message to Sam."

Derry inserted the battery in the phone, sent a text message telling about John Motova and the names of the cities, then removed it again. They immediately left before the FBI could arrive.

———

Mr. Jamshed pulled his BMW to a stop in front of his son's trailer. The hot box his son lived in disgusted and saddened him. One of the smaller windows had been replaced with scrap wood, just another sign of how bad things were for them.

Tazeem does not have to live like this. I would give him a well-paying job if he would only take it. If he would just put that godless hatred of his aside and think of his kids and his wife, things would be so much better for all of them. But no, he is so insanely stubborn.

Pushing his car door open he stepped out onto the crumbled asphalt. He slammed the door and started his march toward his son's rattrap. Reaching the base of the worn wooden steps leading to the front door, he stopped as his anger raged inside. His son's pride and stubborn adherence to a twisted version of his religion had started the years of silence. Looking off into the distance he thought of his son as a child, when they would play together and pray together. His son would ask him hard questions about what the Qur'an meant.

"Dad?"

He looked up to see Nina holding a toddler in her arms. "Please forgive me, but I had to come after that phone call."

Her eyes shifted to the street. "Are you alone? Did—Mom come?"

"No, she does not know about the call. I wanted to find out what this was all about before I involved her."

"It's nothing. I should never have called. If Tazeem finds you here, he'll never forgive me." Her eyes shifted toward the rutted road.

"Where is he?"

"At work. He said he might be late tonight."

He wanted to believe she didn't know that Tazeem had quit his job, but after the phone call he could not. "Nina," he looked deep into her eyes, "you know he's not there. Tell me where he is and what he is about to do." He moved up the steps past her, and invited himself in.

58

Faircloth sat in the black SUV watching the display. It showed video feed from each of the three teams. Several of the agents wore head cams. It was a practice that had taken him a while to find useful, but now he wondered why he ever resisted it.

With him was the backup team, to be sent in only if one of the other teams ran into problems. The three teams each had four components: the group leader, two shooters and one rear cover. Sam Freymen had passed on information that a John Motova had acquired the necessary supplies to produce a deadly nerve agent. These teams were about to enter Motova's warehouse.

One team moved in from the north, one from the east and the last from the south. The west side of the objective was pushed up against a dirt embankment. The lead team used a large rental truck as cover as it moved into position. The truck sat forty feet from the open bay doors.

Faircloth listened to the muffled voices talking through their gas masks. If they encountered the nerve agent, he prayed their protection would be enough. He took a quick glance at the beastly hazmat van sitting next to his SUV. Once the human threat was removed it would be their turn.

"IR scan shows two warm bodies near the north end of structure. I am unable to get a clear reading on the south end."

Faircloth pressed the talk switch. "Team three, remain where you are and guard the south entrance. Teams one and two proceed to the north entrance."

The two teams flanked the large doors. Once in position, the leader from team one used a hand cam to peek around the corner. It was clear as far as the camera could see. He signaled the others, and on the count of three, two men from each side rushed through the opening and headed for cover while the remaining men were prepared to provide cover fire if necessary.

The blast of small arms fire hit two of the agents as soon as they entered the building. Faircloth pounded his fist against the door. The men would live, their full body armor ensured that, unless the terrorists were shooting with a .50 cal. It did not sound like they were. But he hated to see any of his men go down.

The remaining agents poured automatic fire through the door toward the location of the terrorists. A member from team one lobbed a flash-bang into the mix. Two more members rushed into the darkness. Five seconds later the noise stopped. The whole shootout had lasted less than thirty seconds.

———

Sam sat in a small conference room with Booker and Lamar. They were watching a live feed of the attack by Faircloth's teams. Sam felt justified that the intel from Sara had been good.

Booker stared at the screen as the hazmat team began searching the warehouse. She felt a little relief seeing the four drones. Now the terrorists could not spread the chemicals in Denver. "Have you found the nerve agent?"

Faircloth talked with a member of the hazmat team before answering. "Negative. My guess is, it's been moved."

Sam heard Lamar mumble, "No duh."

Booker apparently did not hear him. "You know the drill. Have hazmat run the tests to see if they can tell us what type of biohazard we are dealing with."

Booker told Faircloth his team had done a good job before terminating the connection. "We have their delivery system. If they were planning to poison the city, they will have to find a different way to do it now. Lamar, have Tony send this information out to the other sites. It will tell them what to look for."

He nodded.

Booker rose. The meeting was over.

Sam spoke up. "Before you leave you need to know that I just received word that a man identified as a relative of John Motova has been found dead. His body was discovered in the trunk of a stolen car in

Detroit. His throat was slit. He was a chemical weapons expert in Soviet Russia."

Booker stopped halfway to the door. "If he was their chemical expert, why would they kill him?"

"These guys are playing a very dangerous game. They don't want any leaks." Sam closed his laptop and stood. "So far everything we have gotten from Sara has been good. I just wish we could find her and let her know she is back on the team."

Booker walked out of the room without a response.

———

Jonas gripped the wheel as he and Dace watched the FBI moving in on the warehouse. They had been late getting to the warehouse because of Motova's poor directions. It had saved their lives.

Once the shooting stopped and the rest of the FBI moved in, Dace reached for his phone.

"What are you doing?" Jonas asked.

Dace looked at him with his typical air of superiority. "We must inform Nasir. Our part in this mission is over." He punched in the number. "This city will survive a little longer." He sounded relieved.

Before Dace pushed the call button Jonas grabbed his hand. "Maybe not." He surprised himself. He actually wanted to see this mission go through to the end, and wanted to be part of the final act.

"We no longer have access to air transportation. How do you propose we deliver the neurotoxin?"

"It has to do with what you said earlier today, about tossing it into the air."

Dace gave a sardonic smile. "That comment was meant as an insult to show Motova's recklessness and lack of forethought. Tossing the powder into the air and expecting the results we need is a foolish delusion."

"Yes, it is. But what if I found a way to shoot it into the air, say up to around a thousand feet or more? Is that a foolish delusion?"

Dace put the phone down.

———

Gabriele observed the apartment building from across the street for several minutes. Finally, she was convinced that the FBI had not arrived yet. Quickly she walked across the street and up to her dwelling.

She grabbed her passports and cash along with a change of clothes. This mission was falling apart and it was time to leave. She hoped that by the time the FBI learned what she had done, she would be in some other country, under a new name, with a new look and working for a new employer. And after the attack, the government would be so busy keeping the country together, it would be years before they had time to even think about someone like her.

Her original escape plan had fallen apart when her cover was blown and she needed a new one. She decided to take I-25 south to Colorado Springs and catch a flight at the small airport there. She got into her car and pulled away. As she drove away from her apartment she continued working out her plan. She had only gone a few blocks when her mind snapped back to reality as she heard the cop's siren behind her. Glancing down, she saw she was doing just a few miles over the speed limit. Not much, but some of the Denver cops were notorious for handing out tickets. She pulled her car to the side of the road, but left the car in gear.

With one hand she lowered the car window as her other hand reached into the space between the car seat and the console. Gripping the butt of a pistol, she studied the man approaching the driver's side of her car. His left hand rested on his gun. A lefty, that would give him a slight edge.

He stopped a foot back from her window. "Turn off your engine and put your hands where I can see them, please."

"What seems to be the problem, officer?" she said very softly. She needed him to move in closer. Right now, his position put her at too much of a disadvantage.

He kept his hand on his semiautomatic. "Turn off your car, now. Then place both hands on the steering wheel."

She sighed, this was not going well. After putting the car in park, she reached up and turned off the motor. Resting her left elbow on the door, she placed her right hand on the wheel.

He relaxed his hand a little. "May I see your license and registration?"

She twisted her head toward him and gave the man an innocent smile. "I wasn't speeding, was I? I'm really sorry, sir, if I was going too fast."

He moved a half of step closer. "License and registration, ma'am."

This feels all wrong. He is way too guarded. "Sure, they're in the console." She turned so her body would obscure his view as she reached for the paperwork with her left hand and reached for her pistol with her right. "Here you go, sir." As she slipped the gun out of its hiding place, she turned back toward the officer using the papers as a visual shield, covering the pistol below.

He moved forward to take the papers and saw a glint of steel. Reaching into the car he used his right hand to push the weapon's barrel down and toward the front of the car.

Gabrielle pulled the trigger twice. Both rounds penetrated the door, coming through on the other side, missing their intended target. The officer's face was only a few inches away. She pushed up fast and hard with the heel of her left hand, smashing it into the officer's nose, trying to drive the cartilage into his brain.

He released his grip on her gun as he fell backward. She knew the hit wasn't hard enough to kill the man. Dropping the weapon to the floorboard, she started the car and dropped it into gear. Looking in the mirror as she sped away, she watched the officer quickly recover and draw his pistol. Her eyes stayed glued to the mirror to see if he would shoot.

He took aim and fired one shot as she ducked her head. It was a clear miss. As she rounded a corner, he was holstering his weapon and speaking into his shoulder mic as he rushed toward his car.

Maybe she was in the clear. Her hopes were dashed as she was first joined by one new police car, then by another. It did not take long before several of Denver's finest were following behind her. Her odds of finding a way out of this mess were growing ever thinner, but what choice did she really have? The attack would be happening tomorrow. Staying in Denver was a death sentence. She had to get away. No matter what it took, she would make it out of town.

As she approached the ramp leading onto I-25 southbound she saw police cars blocking the entrance. She refused to slow down. She aimed for the widest hole in front of her. She clipped both police cars as she forced her way between them and onto the ramp, cursing them for her loss of speed.

Punching her way into the traffic, she floored the accelerator as she weaved between and around the other cars, several times passing vehicles on the right shoulder. The information signs along the interstate were telling everyone to either pull over or exit the highway. At first, no one paid any attention, but as the area behind her filled with red and blue lights, more and more vehicles pulled off. Within three miles of entering this long stretch of cement slab, she found the view in front of her desolate except for her adversaries.

The last few non-police cars pulled to the side as a sea of bright lights appeared over a slight rise. Her only hope was to get past them before they were completely set up. She pushed harder on her accelerator only to find it was already touching the floor.

As she drew closer, she saw the lights formed a funnel. Police cars were parked on both sides of the road with each pair of cars closer together, forcing her toward the right side of the road. The cops knew what they were doing. They stood behind their cars, weapons drawn as she rushed toward sure destruction. As she sped down the track they had created for her, she saw something shiny lying across her path.

Strips of metal spikes were waiting to blow her tires. Gripping the wheel tightly she hit the brakes as she swerved to the right. Both tires on the left ripped apart, dropping that side of the car and pulling the wheel in that direction. She yanked it to the right to compensate, slamming into a police car. Bouncing off, she lost control. She traveled across the open lane, losing the other two tires on another spike strip and colliding with another police car.

As she spun around, the steel rims scraped across the surface of the road. Suddenly one rim caught on a crack causing the rear of the automobile to fly up, spinning the car sidewise before hitting a concrete barrier. The metal cage that contained Gabriele continued to bounce and twist before sliding to a stop upside-down.

Gabriele slowly opened her eyes as she heard several pairs of feet rushing toward her. She hoped her injuries were bad enough that they would have to airlift her to some specialist outside of Denver, but in her heart she knew she was a dead woman.

———

Derry stepped through the door with Sara behind him. The motel room was much better than he'd expected but still not what he would consider nice. At least this room's carpet wasn't covered with stains and the room lacked the odors of the previous place he had stayed. "We could have gotten a nicer room in some other part of town. East Colfax isn't the best area, you know."

"Yeah, but no one here cares what your real name is." Sara walked toward the bathroom. "It's better than Kai's old apartment."

"That's for sure."

She dropped the pack on the floor next to the inside bed. "This one's mine. You can sleep over there."

"That's fine, but I get first shower."

"Good. That way if there are any cockroaches you can kill them."

He studied her face as she grabbed the remote for the TV. "I think I'll take my shower now."

He was happy he did not find any cockroaches or other crawly things in the shower. Stepping back into the main room, he found Sara sound asleep. He removed the laptop from the bed and covered her with a blanket.

———

Jamshed did his best to comfort Nina as they waited. He had called a friend in the Atlanta Police Department and told him everything Nina had said about his son. The police had taken the threat very seriously and said they would locate Tazeem immediately. It had been almost two hours when the knock on the door finally came.

Mr. Jamshed answered it. The man and woman standing in the dim light both wore navy blue jackets with the letters FBI across the front. "Is Mrs. Jamshed home?" The female agent spoke.

He stepped aside and allowed them to enter. Nina's kids were in bed. She stood across the narrow room, wringing her hands. "I'm Mrs. Jamshed."

The female agent walked over as the man remained near the door. "Mrs. Jamshed, I'm with the FBI. I have some bad news for you."

Nina was speechless. It was like a scene out of the movies, shown so many times we all know its meaning.

"Using the GPS on your husband's cell phone we were able to track him to a warehouse outside Atlanta."

Nina silently waited.

"I'm sorry, but when we found your husband," she paused, "he was dead."

Jamshed watched Nina for a reaction. Her husband, his son, was a terrorist, that was certain, but he wondered how far she had been pulled into that world.

Nina first showed surprise, followed closely by loss. As her eyes teared up, they shifted toward him. He stepped closer and wrapped an arm around her shoulders. She did not lean or turn toward him, but stood like stone. What had his son done to this woman? "I am sorry, dear. We will make sure you and the children are cared for." *Was this partly my fault?* He looked at the FBI agent for more information.

The man by the door spoke up. "Sir, we want to thank you for coming forward with this information. It is very valuable and could save hundreds, if not thousands, of lives. We found a large amount of a very dangerous neurotoxin at the warehouse. That is what killed your son. But because of your call, we have secured the chemicals and the terrorists will not be able to use them to hurt anyone else. However, we know there were more people involved than the two we found at the warehouse. What can you tell us about your son's associates?"

"I made the call. But I only know what she told me."

All eyes turned back to Nina.

Nina moved to the kitchen table and took a seat. "I don't know anything. Tazeem never talked about his associates."

The female agent moved into the kitchen with Nina. "Do you know how many people he worked with? Who was in charge? Anything you remember could help."

Nina's hands rested under the table as she stared at its surface. "Tazeem led the group. He was very proud of that. I think there were four or five others. He never used names or told me much about them. He only went on and on about how America would suffer."

The agent sat down next to Nina. She placed her hands on the tabletop, folded together. "Do you know where the chemicals and equipment came from?"

Nina shook her head no. "All I know is he took several trips around the country. He put a lot of miles on our new van. Well, not our van. Someone gave him money for it. But when he wasn't driving all over the place I was allowed to use it to take the kids places. It was a lot better than trying to fit them all in our old car."

"Do you know how the money came to him? Cash or through a

Deadly Infiltration

bank account?"

Nina stared off into the distance. "I think it came in little by little to our bank. He said they were very smart to do it like that so no one would notice."

———

Sam looked up from the over-stuffed chair in his temporary office. Booker was at the door. "Yes?"

She stepped in but left the door open. "It looks like you were right."

"I know. – About what this time?" He sat up a little more and put his laptop aside.

She stayed close to the doorway, with her arms crossed, leaning against the wall. Her hair was a mess. Her eyes were red and puffy looking.

"You know we captured their drones."

He nodded.

"The hazmat team identified several chemicals at the warehouse. It looks like Motova has what he needs to make a very powerful nerve agent."

"Novichok?"

"Yes. Your informant was right."

"You mean Sara?"

"Yes. Sara. I guess I was wrong about her. I will remove the BOLO on her and on Derry Conway."

"Maybe we should still 'Be On the Look Out' for her. We need to find her."

"You're in contact with her. Can't you just tell her to come in?"

Sam gave a slight chuckle as he rubbed his hand across his face. "It seems to be a one-way communication right now. Their phone is off. But I'll try to send her a message."

Booker did not move, but looked out the dark window that showed the city lights to the north.

"What's bothering you?" Sam was concerned.

She walked over and took a seat next to him, folding her hands together and placing them between her knees. "We only found traces of the chemicals. The terrorists still have what they need to kill thousands of people. And we have no idea where they are."

Sam studied her for a minute. The strain was taking its toll. "I have some other news related to this case."

She spoke, but she did not make eye contact. "More bad news, I take it?"

"A contact of mine that works for Homeland in New York was found dead in her apartment today."

"How is she related to this case?" Booker glanced up.

"She contacted me about a week ago with suspicions about chemicals crossing the border from Mexico. I have been trying to track them down but have been unsuccessful. And until today I was not sure that her intel was even related to our case. I've requested her case files to see what else she might have learned. Maybe we will get lucky."

"It seems like every step we take just brings more questions than answers." She rubbed her forehead. "I'm just tired."

He raised his cup of coffee. "The magical bean."

Sitting up straight, Booker looked him in the eye. "I am not sure capturing the drones has really done much to stop the attack."

"As long as they have the nerve agent, we are all in danger. They may not be able to use the drones, but there are other ways to fly over the city. How hard would it be to rent a small plane?"

59

Wednesday

Derry opened his eyes to see Sara coming out of the bathroom, drying her hair with a towel.

"Good morning, lazy bones." She smiled. "You slept like a rock."

"I heard you get up. I was just checking my eyelids for holes." He closed his eyes to demonstrate.

She tossed the towel at him. "Right. If you were awake, then I suppose you heard my question?"

"Yeah, sure. What was it again?" He smiled at her. She looked better today. Some of the color had returned to her skin.

She plopped down on her bed, sitting across from the mirror on the dresser and combed her still reddish hair. Peeking at his reflection, she smiled. "You know, if you weren't so good looking, I'd trade you in for a more honest model."

"Thank goodness my girl is blind." He sat up. Swinging his legs around to the floor, he rubbed his face. "Three days' growth and you think I look good." Shirtless, he stood, went to the pack, and grabbed a clean shirt. "Give me a minute and I'll be ready to go. Are you hungry?"

"Not really. My stomach is not up for much right now." She stopped working on her hair and watched him. "I could get used to this."

He flexed his muscles and smiled. "Good." Slipping the shirt over his head, he added, "Well, I'm starved. What do you think about grabbing something at the fast food place across the street?"

She wrinkled her nose. "Yuck, now I'm really not hungry."

He grabbed the pack and shoved the laptop in. "Sorry. How about if I take you to that breakfast place down the road? They might have something that will sit well with your tender tummy. Then we can hit a different library and do more research."

"It's a deal. But I don't think we should go to another library. The FBI might have them staked out. There are lots of other places with free Wi-Fi."

He went over to the duffle bag and started going through it. "Okay, we can hit a coffee shop or something."

He tossed the bag on the bed. Standing, he looked around before going back to the pack.

"What are you looking for? Maybe I can help."

After ramming his hand down the insides of the pack, he searched around the room. "Did we leave the pistol behind?"

"Isn't it in there?"

"I put in in the pack yesterday, I'm sure of it.

He turned toward her.

She smiled. "You don't need a gun. Aren't you my big strong protector?"

"Where is it?"

"What makes you think I know where it is?" Her smile grew.

He walked over and held out his hand. She reached under the pillow and retrieved the pistol. "I've had it all night, just in case."

"I thought you were depending on me." He shoved the gun, along with everything else, back in the pack and placed it on one shoulder.

"You were asleep. You are not much of a protector when you're sound asleep."

"Are you about ready, brat?" Looking around once more, Derry made sure they had all of their belongings, few as they were, before picking up the duffle bag and tossing it onto the other shoulder.

Sara headed out the door as he brought up the rear. As they crossed the parking lot she looked up at him. "I'm glad you're here. When I was alone it was starting to feel like my old life." She dropped her head back down as she walked. "That's a world I never want to return to."

Jonas sat on one side of the table, with John and Dace on the other. They had been up all night working out the plan.

Dace was still a little skeptical. "If we can find the right building, with the right equipment, in the right location and gain access to it, then

I can see how this might work."

Jonas stared at him. "If not this, then what?"

Dace leaned back. "We have the option of leaving. Would it not be better to protect the remainder of the team and use them to inflict harm later, after the attacks in the other cities?"

This argument, phrased differently, had popped up about every two hours during their discussions, always from Dace. "What kind of damage could we inflict on this country after the attacks that would be more devastating than this? The whole nation will be on the highest alert and the FBI will be looking for us." Jonas looked at John as he worked to keep his voice in check.

John studied the map. "Any of the skyscrapers in the downtown area can work, some are better than others, but they will all work."

Dace again voiced his doubts. "Not all of them will work. The building must have the right equipment."

"Yes, yes, but most of these buildings have what we need. Without the drones our options are limited. If you have a better plan, we are listening."

Dace stared into his face for several seconds, before nodding in agreement. "If we are to go forward with this plan, we must notify Nasir. He must be told that the FBI has taken our drones and approve the new plan."

John made the call and again put the phone on speaker. After they explained what had happened at the warehouse, they fully expected Nasir to rip them apart. But before he could say anything, they told him of their new plan. Jonas took the lead. "We have devised a way to save this operation. We believe we can modify the canisters and strap them on top of the air conditioning units on the roof of one of the high-rise buildings downtown. The timers will open the canisters at the appointed time and when the fans kick on they will shoot the powder up into the air. The fans on these large air conditioning units are very powerful. They will push the chemicals at least a few hundred feet into the air. And the building will already be several hundred feet tall. The winds at that altitude will do the rest. The agent will be spread for miles around the city."

Nasir was silent while he processed this news. Finally, he spoke with a strained voice. "Things are falling apart. Our team in Atlanta has been discovered by the FBI. They now have our full plan." There was a short span of silence. "Fortunately, I believe they do not know what other cities will be hit and they believe the attack will come on Friday. We cannot afford to wait another day and we cannot afford to lose Denver as well. Your plan is risky, and it is unclear how well it will work. But I want you to continue with what you have outlined. You must have everything in place and ready to go at 4:00 P.M. Denver time. All the attacks must occur at the same moment." They worked out the details of the plan and Nasir felt they could make it work. They had seven hours. It wasn't much time, but the new plan was simple enough.

After ending the call, John called Segel, the man making the nerve agent, asking him to come to the office. When he arrived, John began, "How is the production going?"

"Right now I have a little more than four liters. I am making about one liter every ten hours."

"Not fast enough. What do you need to have six liters made by noon?"

Segel glanced around the room at the three men. "I would have needed to start a day earlier or have a second—"

"What if you had more help?"

Segel took another step into the room. "Adding an untrained person would only slow things down."

"What about your brother? You asked to bring him in on this before. Is he trained? Can he help you?"

The bewildered man looked at the floor as he shook his head. "He has the right skills but is at work today."

"Where does he work?"

"At the Republic Plaza, downtown. But even if he could get off, it would only make a small amount of difference in how much I can make in the next few hours."

John glanced at the others in the room before he stood and walked over to the man. Looking him in the face he asked his next question. "Does he know what you are doing here? How much have you told him?"

"Nothing. You said I would die if I let anyone know about the attack." Segel did not look at John as he answered.

"You know he's lying." Jonas cut in.

John put a hand on Segel's shoulder. "When is he planning on leaving town?" He squeezed tightly.

"Thursday evening."

"Do you want to save him? Do you want him to live past today?"

Segel looked up. "Yes, of course."

"Is he a believer?" John studied the man's face.

"As am I." Segel sounded offended at the question.

"Will he help us? Can he be trusted?"

"Yes."

"Are you sure?"

"We are very close. I am certain he would be willing to help if we ask."

Jonas smiled. "Perfect."

The man looked quizzically at Jonas as John went on. "Call him and find out if he is able to get us access to the roof of the building."

Segel nodded. "You don't want him to come here to help me?"

"No, whatever you make on your own will have to be enough. Make the call and let us know what he says."

Segel stepped out of the room.

Dace waited a second as the other two went back to the map. "You sure that building will work for us?"

Jonas typed the name into his map program and studied the images on the screen for a few seconds. "If I were to pick a building for this, the Republic Plaza would be the one I would choose. It is the tallest building in Denver and has everything we need. It is absolutely perfect." Jonas stood and walked over to refill his coffee cup with the rich black liquid. Dace held up his cup. Jonas filled both of the other men's cups as well.

Dace added a large amount of cream to his coffee. "What do we do next?"

John returned to his seat and started writing out a list on a notepad. "We will need a way to hook into the power on the roof so we can power the timers on each canister."

"We also need a way to secure the canisters in place. When the fans come on, anything not tied down will go flying off. I'll get started on that." Jonas also made some notes. "And how can we be sure all of the nerve agent will come out without a pump?"

"We can't, but we don't have time to do anything better. We will have to rely on the power of the fans."

Just then, Segel reappeared at the door. "My brother says he'll do it. But he wants a guarantee that his family will be taken from the city before we implement the plan."

"Assure him that we will take care of them," John said looking straight at Segel. "What does your brother do at his job?"

"He works in facilities. He helps maintain the building. He has access to the roof and will be able to escort you up there."

John looked at Jonas with a smile. "Excellent."

Jonas studied the man. "Can he control the airflow and temperature in the building?"

"Yes, I think so."

Jonas looked at the other two men. "Allah is smiling upon us. Allah be praised." Turning back to Segel he said, "Come back in about thirty minutes. I will have a list of instructions for your brother. He must follow them to the letter. Can he do that?"

Segel nodded.

"Good."

Jonas turned to Dace who now seemed unphased since the plan had been approved by Nasir. That was good. There was a lot of work to do and they did not have time to deal with bad attitudes. "Are you willing to get your hands a little dirty?"

"That all depends on the dirt you want me to stick my hands into." Dace almost had a friendly smile, but not quite.

"I need you to steal a van from a heating and air conditioning company."

Now Dace smiled. "That will not be a problem."

———

Booker, Sam and Faircloth stood near the front of a conference room filled with the team leaders of the Colorado contingent. On the wall was a display divided into several smaller screens. Each screen displayed the image of the leader from each of the other four cities involved. A full-fledged conference call was the quickest way to share information.

Booker directed her question to the leader from the Atlanta office. He was a large man, his figure filling most of the screen, his dark

Deadly Infiltration

skin glistening with sweat from the heat. "Can you please fill us in on what you know?"

The man's voice was deep and commanded respect. "Last night we received a call tipping us off to a possible terrorist attack. When we investigated, we found a manufacturing facility making neurotoxin. Evidently there was an accident and two of the terrorists were killed by the poison. The tip came from the wife of one of the men. She confirmed that the attack would take place simultaneously in five cities. The cities she named confirm the cities that you already suspected."

"Were you able to recover all of the toxin?"

He glanced at something off screen before he responded. "We believe that to be the case."

Booker continued, "Did you find any drones or other delivery systems?"

"Yes, we discovered four drones." Photos of the drones popped up in his place. "These are custom made vehicles."

"Yes, they look just like the ones we found here in Denver. I've had a team working on them all night."

"Then you will have more data on them than we will. The area around these drones was contaminated. We have not been able to really examine them." The drones disappeared as the man's face returned.

Booker introduced the next speaker as Denver's technical expert on drones. A young man stepped forward and brought up a slide show for all to see. "These drones are very high end and not something you can buy on Amazon. They are similar to the UASUSA Tempest drone. But they have been modified to increase payload and distance." He brought up a slide with yellow arrows. "As you can see here, the wings have been modified to add more lift. This would slow the plane down some, but it would increase the payload."

Faircloth interrupted. "Won't that also make it need more power?"

"Very good. They overcame that by changing out the motor and prop for a far more powerful and effective system. They also moved some structural supports."

Faircloth appeared satisfied.

"Next, they put in real high end navigation and flight control systems with encoded GPS. These babies can pretty much fly themselves once they are off the ground. The only thing missing that I would expect to find are cameras. There were none. My guess is they were left off for two reasons. One, to reduce weight, the other, to keep anyone from tracking the signal."

"Wow, these aren't like the RC planes I grew up with." Faircloth mumbled.

"They're not RC planes at all, they are drones."

"That's just a new name for the same thing."

The speaker looked over at Faircloth with an incredulous smile. "RC planes have been around for decades. Drones belong to a whole new class of UAV, unmanned aerial vehicles."

"Which means what?" Faircloth's tone was condescending.

"It's like comparing your handheld calculator to a computer. The computer does everything the calculator does but so much more."

"So it's a little fancier."

Sam took over before this part of the meeting got out of control. "It has to do with what keeps it flying and under control. Someone must control the speed and flaps remotely for an RC plane to stay aloft. An RC aircraft has no ability to fly or even stabilize on its own. If it loses contact with the controller it will almost certainly crash. On the other hand, drones have a certain amount of built in intelligence, depending on how much money the owner wants to invest. Like the man said, they can fly themselves. Some have a remote pilot to control them, but others are fully programmable.

Faircloth nodded a silent thank you to Sam.

The younger man went on. "The good news is that now that we know what they are using, we can stop them, by either jamming the range of frequencies they use or by hijacking their signals and controlling the planes ourselves." He smiled.

Sam stepped toward the young man. "You said their GPS was encoded and those drones could almost fly themselves. How do you plan on taking control if they get them in the air?"

He turned to Sam. "That is what we have been working on all night. We have broken their encryption code. We can take control by overriding their signal. I will send out the necessary information to all the other sites."

This was the first really good news they had had in a while. There was finally a glimmer of hope that they could stop these terrorists, at least in the cities using the drones. They still needed to find out what the terrorists in Denver planned to do.

60

Sitting at a corner table of a noisy local coffee shop, Derry typed while Sara got refills. The 60's music that played loudly in the background added to the energy of the place.

He took a break to study her outline. She was so frail. Going to jail could kill her. She returned with the two large refills. "Can't take your eyes off me, huh?"

She was right, but not for the reasons she thought. "Did you get me one of those pastries?" He diverted the conversation.

She skimmed the glassed in goodies at the counter before sitting down. "I can't believe you're still hungry after that breakfast."

"I'm not, but they look really good."

"You're going to get fat." She set her cup down and leaned over to see the screen. "You haven't done anything while I was gone."

He smiled and raised his shoulders. "Just waiting for you to get back. I was thinking about the information I sent to Sam." He surveyed those around him to see if anyone was listening or could hear over all the other noise. This wasn't something the public should know about. Lowering his voice, he inclined his head toward hers. "Is there any way we can see what the FBI is up to now?"

"Sure. There is always a way." Even though her mouth covered by the cup as she took a sip, he could see the smile in her eyes.

"How hard would it be?"

She set the cup down and reached for her computer. "I just need to set up a false node and a VPN within a VPN to hide my tracks." She typed as she talked. "Now I need to tell the system I am someone I am not." Here she slowed to a stop.

"What's wrong?" Derry was becoming alarmed.

It took a second before she answered in a whisper. "I'm using Todd's ID and login." All joy and joking was gone. She pulled her hands back and dropped them in her lap. Then, wiping away a tiny tear, she went back to work.

"Think this will work? Using Todd's login?"

"My guess is the Bureau has been too busy to delete him from the system."

Derry studied her eyes. The pain that was there would continue for a long time. The hard street kid that first caught his attention had evolved into a sensitive beautiful woman with a heart for God. A transformation that only God could accomplish.

"You know this isn't without risk." She turned and studied him.

"How much?"

"If we stay on the Bureau's system too long, there are a couple of people there that can punch their way through and find our physical location."

———

Booker, Faircloth and Sam sat in a small conference room. The large display on the wall had a four-way split screen showing Director Augustine, the head of terrorism for the FBI, his counterpart in the CIA, Director Rosenberg, Air Force General Schmitt, and his Army counterpart, General Franklin. Agent Sam Freymen was leading the meeting. He went over a summary of what they had learned and accomplished so far.

FBI Director Augustine spoke up, "Excuse me, Agent Freymen, let me be clear about your data. You believe we have stopped the attack that was planned in Atlanta, but have not stopped any of the attacks in the other four cities? Is that correct?"

"Yes. We do not have any idea where the terrorists are located within the other cities, and I think all we have accomplished in Denver is to irritate them by taking their drones."

"But we now know how they are going to attack, what cities they plan to attack, and what day it will happen."

"Yes, sir, that is all true."

CIA Director Rosenberg cleared his throat to get noticed. "This nerve agent is so deadly that one tablespoon could kill every man, woman and child in a small town, and they have," he reviewed something on his computer screen, "maybe six liters at each site. That's enough to kill most of the population in any major city in the U.S. We still have a very serious situation on our hands. Is it your belief that they will still use the drones in the other cities, considering we know all about them? Wouldn't it be more prudent for them to wait and develop a new method to spread the agent?"

Sam stood as he answered their questions. "If anyone else were in charge, that would probably be what they would do. But we have reason to believe that a very dangerous man named Nasir is behind these attacks. We have confirmed sightings of Nasir in the Detroit area and we have data that supports Detroit as the base of operations. He would only be in the U.S. if something big was about to happen. And he is not one to back down, even in the face of impossible odds."

Director Rosenberg responded. "Are you sure it's him?"

Sam nodded. "We have every reason to believe it is. He was seen in Canada close to the U.S. border several days ago. Then, a few days later, an analyst for Homeland Security started a trace on his whereabouts in the Detroit area. In the last week, four possible sightings have popped up. And yesterday that same analyst was found murdered. That cannot be a coincidence." He looked directly at the screen. "Also, I've been studying Nasir's tactics. This is just the type of bold move he would plan. So yes, I'm sure he's here and is behind these attacks." Agent Freymen returned to his seat.

Director Augustine cut in. "What else can you tell me about this guy?"

Sam brought up a file on his laptop. "He is relatively new on the scene as a leader, so we don't have a lot. But we know he is very aggressive and very intelligent. He doesn't mind being backed into a corner. In fact, that is when his true abilities come through."

"Over the last few years, the Middle East has been turning out a whole new level of leaders." This was CIA's contribution.

"One more thing," Agent Freymen continued, "He's not just after shock value. He likes high body count in his projects."

"So how do we plan to stop them?" Director Rosenberg cut straight to the heart of the matter.

Air Force General Schmitt spoke up. "With the information sent to us, we are confident we will be able to detect the drones as soon as they take off and then take control of the drones and put them down in a safe location. As long as they don't change the encoding on them, that is. And we believe they will not have time to make such a change before Friday."

General Franklin cut in. "And if they do?"

General Schmitt looked off screen and talked with someone before answering. "I have been assured that given the data recovered from the captured drones, we can run through the possible codes in a matter of minutes to reacquire a lock."

"We will have choppers in the air, just in case those minutes are longer than expected. We believe our choppers could get above the drones and force them down if necessary. It would be better for them to crash on the ground than to have time to disperse the agent in the air," General Franklin added.

Agent Booker took over. "That sounds very prudent, General, thank you." She directed her next question to General Schmitt. "How long before you'll have your men in place?"

The Commander thought for a moment. "Two hours, tops. I need to contact NORAD. They have the drone pilots and necessary equipment for this type of operation. But once we take control we will need eyes-on to safely maneuver and land them since the cameras have been removed." His eyes shifted. "General Franklin, we need to have cameras and men on your choppers to give a visual to our pilots in Cheyenne Mountain."

"We are always willing to help out the Air Force," he said with a smile.

Sam stepped closer to the monitors. "Even though our initial information indicated the attack will take place on Friday, I believe that date could be moved up. Nasir is one to think outside of the box and I believe it is very likely the attack could be on Thursday instead. Maybe even today, but that is more of a long shot."

It took a few seconds for both commanders to process this new information. "We will plan to be ready as soon as possible and be prepared to wait as long as necessary." They both agreed.

"Excellent," Booker breathed out.

"How will you know when to send up the helicopters? It will be hard to keep this quiet if we have Army choppers flying over the city for days on end," Faircloth interjected.

"NORAD will be monitoring the drone frequencies continuously in all target cities. As soon as they detect any sort of signal they will notify the Army to send up their choppers," General Schmitt responded.

Sam nodded. "I think that gives us a plan for L.A., Chicago, and New York. Now, what about Denver? Any ideas on how they will get the toxin into the air in Denver?"

"They could rent a plane," Booker suggested. "Or steal one if they have a pilot."

The FBI director responded, "We can ground all small aircraft. You can contact the FAA at any time you feel it is warranted."

Booker stood and moved to where the others could see her on their monitors. "We will get on that right away."

Director Rosenberg looked at Sam. "Do you have anything else that we need to know, Agent Freymen?"

"Yes, sir. We have captured one of the suspected terrorists. She was going by the name of Alex Taylor at Homeland Security. We have reason to believe she was the one who murdered FBI agent Todd Jenkins. She was pulled over and tried to shoot the officer. After that failed, she led police on quite a chase. Her car crashed into a cement barrier. She was pretty badly injured and is unconscious as we speak. I am not sure we will have a chance to question her before the attacks take place. But we will keep tabs on her progress."

"Let us know if you learn anything from her." The FBI director added.

"As always." Sam smiled. It was a known fact that the CIA did not always share information with the FBI right away.

Director Rosenberg cut in. "I am going to advise the President to take a short vacation, and the same for Congress."

Booker warned, "If even a hint of this gets out we will have mass evacuations and riots in every major city in the country."

"I understand. I will do everything I can to keep this away from the public, but I also have an obligation to the President." There was a short hesitation. "I'll hold off on informing all of Congress for now. I need you to keep working on this. We all know what is at stake. Agent Freymen, you have full authority to pull in all the personnel and do whatever you feel is necessary."

Director Augustine repeated the sentiment and the images disappeared.

Sam turned to see a man at the door. Booker asked him what he needed.

"Tony said he thinks he may have found Sara."

"Found her? Where?" Booker was instantly heading toward the door.

"She logged into our system remotely. Tony said he almost has her."

Booker stopped. "Where is she logged on from?"

"Tony's working on that. He said she had him going in circles for a while."

"Does he have her or not?"

Ernest took a breath. "She logged on as Todd. She was going through the reports on this case." He nodded toward the people in the room. "A flag popped up on Todd's system, the one I was using, and Tony took over. She's run through at least two, maybe more, VPNs."

Booker stepped closer. "Thank you for the summary, but I don't care how you find her. Do you know where she is?"

"Her physical location? No. But we have her IP address. From that Tony believes he can find her physical location."

"If he comes up with something, let us know." Booker turned away from Ernest. "We are very busy."

Sam stepped toward Ernest. "Do you think Tony can send her a message?" He joined Ernest at the door and the two walked out together.

———

"How is the production coming?" John asked Segel through the intercom into the production room.

Segel spoke through his breather. "Better than I hoped. I will be done by noon."

"Did you pass on the information to your brother?"

"Yes, everything is set. He will disable the air conditioning equipment for the building at 1:40. We should receive the call for repairs between 2:00 and 2:30. That will give us time to have everything in place by 4:00. Have you made arrangements for his family?"

"Your brother is taking your place in this attack. It is now your responsibility to take care of his family. You can leave here when we leave."

"That is fair." The man turned and went back to work, overseeing the filling of the canisters.

John walked back to the makeshift office where Jonas and Dace were breaking four rifles down. "Good news. Segel will have the full amount of toxin in time. We will have enough to destroy this city."

Jonas looked up. "Excellent. This will be the greatest disaster America has ever experienced."

"It will make 9-11 look like a walk in the park." John added.

"It will make Pearl Harbor look like a walk in the park. This country will never recover after this." Jonas slipped the two halves of the M4 into the long tool box. Grabbing fully loaded thirty-round magazines he placed several in with it. He and Dace repeated the process with the other three guns, putting them into different toolboxes.

"Is everything else ready?" Dace stepped toward John.

"As soon as the nerve agent is ready, Segel will finish filling the containers and wipe them down. At that point, they will be loaded inside these carts, along with the hazmat suits. Once that is completed, everything will be ready to go."

"Good." Dace leaned back in his chair.

John walked outside to the newly acquired van. He looked around at the other equipment inside. *Our stuff will blend right in. No one will give it a second thought.* He then headed back to the office. John was satisfied. The new plan should work. He rejoined the other two men.

Dace stood at the counter and looked over at him. "You are out of coffee."

"I did not expect two coffee camels to show up." John joined him and shook the empty can. "If you cannot live without it, there is a coffee shop a couple of blocks over." He waved his hand in the direction of the shop. "They call it Russian coffee but it is too weak for my taste."

Jonas looked up at Dace. "We have an hour before we are needed again. How about we get some fresh air and coffee?"

"You must be careful. Remember you are wanted men," John warned as they left.

61

Derry saw a new window pop up on the screen that Sara was working on. At first he thought she brought it up.

"Uh, oh. They found me," she piped up.

"What?" He looked around the busy room. Everything looked normal. People were coming and going and the line for coffee was longer than before. No one was looking at them.

"No, on here." Sara pointed to the screen. "But it was just a matter of time."

Derry looked to where she pointed and read the window's contents

```
This is Sam. You are no longer on the wanted list
but we need your help.
```

She leaned back in her seat. "Think it might be a trick? Them asking for my help?" Reaching forward, she started to close the lid.

He reached over and stopped her. "Hold on."

"They found the laptop. I don't want them to find us." She pushed down again, but he held it open.

"Just hear me out first."

With one hand on the lid, she looked defiantly into his eyes. "What?"

"If they were still hunting for us, why give us a warning?"

"Because they are stupid or they think we are." She kept pushing on the lid. "We still have a few minutes. I have this connection routed all over the world. Finding it at the end of an electronic trail is not the same as finding its physical location." She tried again to close the lid.

"Move your hand. I'm not going back to jail."

He reached over with his other hand and gently but with enough force, moved her hand off. "Before we run again, is there a way to find out if they are telling the truth?"

"Yeah, tell them where we are at and wait to be arrested." She twisted her hand out of his and placed it back on the lid, pushing down again. After a few intense seconds of staring into his eyes she relaxed a little. She couldn't out muscle him and they both knew it. "Look, the longer we wait, the more time they have to trace the physical links."

A new window popped up.

```
This is Sam again. I know you are in the downtown
area. We are not coming after you.
```

"It's a lucky guess." She let her elbow lower to the table but kept her hand on the lid. "They are hoping I will respond in that window so they can finish their trace."

He tilted his head. "I understand your paranoia. But we have sent them a lot of good intel. Sooner or later they will see the truth that you are innocent." He pulled his hand back, hoping she would not close the lid. She did not. "You read most of the Bureau's reports, several on the raid." He lowered his voice so only she could hear. "They have found drones and nerve agent just as we told them. It only makes sense."

A new message popped up on the screen:

```
Call me at 303-555-0134 ASAP
```

They both studied the latest message for a minute. Calling them would change everything and they both knew it. It was no longer a theoretical discussion.

"Well?" He would not make the call until she agreed.

"Do we have any burn phones left?"

"That we haven't used before?"

She nodded.

He held up one finger. She wordlessly held out her hand.

Reaching in the duffle bag, Derry grabbed the last unused throwaway phone and handed it to her. He wanted her to make the call. She had suffered so much. She should feel the reward of freedom first.

She held it with her hands folded around it. "Maybe you should make the call. You know him."

Derry smiled. "Not on your life. This is your time. Your freedom call." He reached over and placed his hand over hers. "Hey, he's Kai's good friend. He's not some scary spook."

She smiled back, and warily said, "Okay, I'll do it." Reading the number on the screen, she turned on the phone and punched it in.

She raised the phone to her ear as she looked around the coffee shop. Derry watched her face. It was filled with joy and relief, —for about five seconds. Suddenly the light left her face as she lowered the phone to her lap.

———

Lamar stood at the door, with Kai slightly behind him. "Did I hear correctly? Did you find Sara and Derry?"

Tony looked over his shoulder at his boss. "Maybe. She tapped into our system and I was able to run a back-trace on the node-tree she set up and send it through a set of filters that removed—"

Lamar held up a hand, telling Tony to stop talking. "Did you find her at the end of your bragging or not?"

Sam, standing across the room talked as he walked toward Kia. "We think we found her. I had Tony try to tap into her system and set up a link." He looked over at Kai. "How are you feeling? Did this oversized, over-zealous, beat-cop take good care of you?" He reached his hand out as she stepped in.

Taking it, she moved in and gave him a hug. "His wife did great." She smiled back at Lamar as she tucked in under Sam's arm. "Thank you for saving me," she added to Sam.

"I always take care of my people."

"If you two are through, tell me about Sara. Where is she? Did you get ahold of her? Is Derry with her?"

Kai took the only empty chair, clearly still a little wobbly, as Sam moved back against a desk across the room from Lamar. "Your man here traced her location to a coffee shop downtown. We are pretty sure she is either in or near it."

Tony injected his assurance. "I'm sure she's there."

"Well, send her a message or call her or something. If you have a link set up, turn on a camera, and let her see us. We need her here!"

Lamar was always the bear protecting his cubs.

"What's the latest on Sara?" It was Booker, coming through the doorway.

Lamar stepped back from Tony's chair giving him a chance to answer.

"I sent Sara some messages, but haven't heard anything back."

Lamar's face began to show concern. "Can you tap into the cameras at the coffee shop? Do they have any in that area that we can use?"

"I don't know but I will check." Tony turned back to his keyboard and started typing.

Booker stepped past Lamar and stared down at Kai. "Who are you and what are you doing here in the middle of my investigation?"

Sam answered in his relaxed, it's no big deal manner. "This is Kai Luana, my friend and co-worker of sorts. She's the one who identified Todd's killer and decoded the file that gave us much of our intel. And to set the record straight, it's my investigation and I want her here. We can use her."

When Sam said it was his investigation, Booker's expression softened as she looked back at Kai. "Sorry for coming across that way. With all that is happening, you understand I hope."

Kai nodded and gave a tiny smile. "It's fine. I'll do whatever I can to help."

"You've already done a lot for us, thank you. I heard you were poisoned and almost didn't make it."

"It was close, but Sam came to my rescue." Kai smiled up at Sam.

"I'm glad." Booker turned to Tony. "Don't waste too much time on Sara, we need your help finding Hewitt and Landry."

"I'm still running the search for them in the background, but Sara's the best on these tools and her being here would really help."

"What about looking for other buildings or property owned by Motova or listed under his alias?" Booker asked.

Tony turned to Ernest. "Can you take that?"

Ernest looked a little lost. "I guess. Should I start with the state records or city?"

Kai leaned forward in her chair. "Don't you have a tool to scan all the records under his aliases and cross check them against tax records and other transactions?"

Tony shifted his gaze to Kai. "Feel up to giving us a hand? Sara's system is just sitting there waiting for someone like you."

"What's with the yellow tape?"

Lamar grabbed it and yanked it off. "That was put there when they thought Sara was guilty. Tony get her set up." He nodded toward Kai.

Kai started to roll her chair over. Sam put his hand on the back of her seat and pushed her to Sara's desk. "I see your time in Homeland has paid off."

"I didn't spend all my time locked up in a tiny room with a psycho."

As Tony logged Kai into Sara's computer, Sam turned to Lamar and Booker, "I need to talk with you two in private."

Sam followed Lamar to Booker's office. "Agent Booker, would you call Agent Faircloth and ask him to join us? We need to figure out what the terrorists are going to do with their poison now that we have their drones."

The three of them talked about nothing in particular while they waited for Faircloth to arrive. Once he entered the office, Sam got right down to business.

"All the other major cities are looking for an attack from the air. We should be doing the same even though we have captured the drones. What other ways could we be attacked?"

Lamar walked over to one of the overstuffed chairs and placed one hand on its back. "Since we have their drones, that pretty much just leaves small aircraft."

Booker picked up a pen off her desk and tapped it against the palm of her hand as she talked. "We have that possibility taken care of. The FAA has received the order to issue a no-fly zone for small aircraft over and around Denver starting at 5:00 this evening. What about hot air balloons or some other method to get the stuff into the air?"

Faircloth moved away from the windows, toward the other three. "They would have to attack in the morning and even then it's iffy. The balloons can only stay up when you have a slight updraft. That's why you mostly see them early in the morning, when the ground is warming up. Plus, their direction is dependent on the wind. There really isn't a way to make them go where you want them to go."

Booker responded, "And how do you know that?"

Faircloth gave a shrug. "I was a ballooner a while back, before one came down too hard and I messed up my back."

Sam asked, "What about helium balloons?"

Booker had the answer for this one. "They would need a fair amount of helium. We can monitor the sale and transportation of the stuff for the next few days."

Faircloth interjected, "You still have the problem of control."

Sam was trying to think this through. "If you knew the general direction of the upper air currents, could they get the balloons over the city with a fair amount of confidence?"

"Yeah, I guess, if they got them high enough not to hit a powerline or the side of a building."

Lamar saw where Sam was going. "I will have someone from my team monitor the movement of helium within the state. We will look back thirty days and see if they had this as a contingency."

Booker nodded as she saw a puzzled expression on Sam's face. "You have something to say?"

"I know I was the one who suggested the possibility of balloons, but the more I think about it, the more it doesn't sound like Nasir." Sam went on. "From what I know of the man, he is somewhat of a control freak and this has too many variables."

"Not if he's been planning it as a backup all along and has studied the weather patterns around here."

Sam didn't look convinced. "Lamar, how much of your resources is this monitoring going to take up?"

"Hardly any, once it's set up."

"Ok, then go with it. Any other ideas on how they could deliver the poison?" Sam was really hoping they could out think Nasir.

"They could buy new drones, ones that are maybe not ideal, but could possibly work." Faircloth shrugged as he spoke.

"Not likely, but possible." Sam conceded.

Since no one had any other ideas Sam gave the new orders. "Faircloth, get all types of balloons added to the no fly list, and have the Army jam all frequencies commonly used by commercial drones, starting at 5:00 PM today. Lamar, have someone get word to the networks and other known users of drones to keep their equipment out of the air for the next few days. Make it sound like a military exercise or something that will not raise suspicions."

Lamar started to protest about letting the public know so much, when Sam's phone vibrated.

62

Derry watched as Sara leaned forward and dropped the phone into the pack, her eyes never wavering from a fixed point across the room. "We need to get out of here." She reached over and killed all links on her laptop, with barely a shift in her eyes. "Now." She shoved the laptop in on top of everything else and forced the zipper shut.

He looked to see where she was staring. Two men in their middle-thirties stood in line. He knew them instantly. They were the terrorists from Homeland. He grabbed the duffle bag. Sara picked up the pack and threw it over her shoulder. With heads down they headed for the door.

The line the men were standing in partially blocked the exit. Derry hoped they could get by without being noticed. Peeking out the corner of his eye, he watched the killers. They were at the head of the line.

With any luck, he and Sara could make it out. He saw Hewitt picking up two coffees and handing one to Landry. Reaching forward, Derry pushed the door open. Sara went through and Derry fell in behind her to protect her and shield her face from their view. They didn't know him, but they would know her. They had set her up for Todd's murder.

She stepped out onto the street with Derry on her heels. "That was close," she said without looking back. He started to express his relief when something sharp poked him in the back.

"Now don't you two make a nice couple."

His mind went into protection mode. "Sara, run!" Dropping the duffle bag, Derry spun around, bringing his elbow back to deflect and block the knife. Nothing, the knife wasn't where he expected it to be. Twisting farther, he brought his left hand up to smash into the large man's throat. The man pushed Derry's arm off course as his head moved slightly in the opposite direction. Derry countered by using his other hand to hit the man just below his sternum.

His punch was stopped, not just blocked, but completely stopped by the man's grip on Derry's wrist. Before he could break free, the knife penetrated between his ribs, and his wrist was twisted outward.

Sara started to run but was instantly stopped as Landry grabbed her elbow. "If you would like your boyfriend to live, you will keep your mouth closed."

The fight was over. Derry had not saved Sara. Hewitt held him in place with a strong clamp on Derry's arm and a knife in his side.

Sara's eyes flashed at Landry. Fear. Anger. Hatred. She yanked and twisted her arm, trying to break his grip, but she was too weak.

Hewitt leaned in so only they could hear. "Unless you want me to drive this knife all the way home, I suggest you not try that again."

Derry fought to control the pain and the rage. This man was a terrorist. And he had framed Sara and was about to kill them both. He had to stop him. The man rotated the knife a little as he smiled. "I still see defiance in your eyes." He was too strong and quick. Derry couldn't win, not right here. But there would come a moment when the man's guard was down. Derry dropped his gaze. He would bide his time.

"Much better." Hewitt pushed the point in a fraction more before pulling it out.

Hewitt smiled. "Next time you try something, she gets the blade. Now, pick up your bag and move."

People passed by, barely noticing them. No one cared. No one would help. The world was a place that did not want to get involved.

———

Sam said hello several times without getting an understandable response. Was it a wrong number? One of those irritating 'hitting the buttons while in someone's bag' calls? He started to end the call. They had work to do. But he thought about the message they had sent to Sara. Was she finally calling? He listened a little longer. A woman was saying they needed to get out of someplace. She sounded scared.

Booker looked over at him as she held up one finger toward Lamar to quiet him. She asked Sam if he had something.

He put the phone on speaker, hit mute, and turned up

the volume.

The others in the room moved in closer. All they could hear were background voices. Booker and Faircloth gave Sam inquisitive looks.

Sam softly answered their unspoken questions, "I think this is the call we've been waiting for."

Lamar mouthed "Sara?" as he tilted his head toward the phone.

The answer came from a man's voice over the phone.

"Sara, run."

Everyone in the room looked at Sam.

"I need to get this to Tony. See if he can trace it." Sam ran out of the room and down the hall.

Lamar, Booker, and Faircloth followed him.

———

Derry held his left hand over the wound to slow the bleeding as he watched for an opportunity to try something again. These men were very good, but he was not a sheep and he would not be led willingly to his slaughter.

While he watched for the opportunity, Sara talked, a lot. Asking them questions which they refused to answer.

After walking two blocks on East Colfax, they turned down an alley behind a few local businesses. Dace talked a little freer now that they were away from other people. "I see the police have not found you. You have served your purpose well." A French accent came through.

Sara knew these men were behind Todd's murder and most likely behind the texts that had made her run. But she was determined not to let them intimidate her. "What do you mean?"

"You have kept the FBI and police very busy. That has allowed us the time we needed to complete our plans."

"I told them all about your plans."

Dace stopped and spun her around. Derry almost plowed into him, and would have, if Jonas hadn't yanked him back.

"That is impossible." It took a moment for him to connect the dots. "Even if you found my emails you cannot know what they say. Without your FBI tools to decrypt them, it means nothing."

"Unless I have the encryption key. Then it means everything."

Derry wondered if she was always this talkative when about to die.

"Yes, if you had it. But that secret is impossible to find. So, what you may or may not have told the FBI would be nothing more than guesswork, and therefore wrong. So again, you have helped us. The FBI will be wasting the last few minutes they have by following your false information."

"Philippe Sauvageau." There was triumph in her eyes.

Dace grew pale as he glared at Sara

She continued, "How do you think the FBI knew where to find the drones? The FBI knows what type of attack you are planning and in what cities the attacks will take place." Her voice was strong.

"It will not matter. By the end of today—"

"Shut up." Jonas pushed Derry aside and grabbed Sara. He quickly ran his hands over her body. "She has been playing you for a fool and you like to talk too much."

"No one plays me for a fool. What are you doing?"

Jonas grabbed Sara's pack and dumped it on the ground. Two computers crashed to the concrete, followed by a phone and a gun. Jonas smashed the heel of his foot into the phone, twisting and digging it in deep. He retrieved the pistol and pressed it against Sara's forehead.

Dace stood with mouth agape.

"I should put a bullet—"

Derry jumped forward to protect Sara, only to be stopped by Jonas' fist in his throat. All his years of training were useless as he let his anger get control. He grabbed his neck and collapsed to the ground as he gasped for air.

63

Sam watched Tony as he tried to trace the phone call. Kai stood up and moved next to Sam.

"Did you get the location?" Booker stepped into the tiny office.

Tony did not even acknowledge her presence as he concentrated on his computer display. No one spoke as Tony continued to work. Three minutes later he answered, "The signal's gone now, but I was able to track it to a cell tower. It's on or near East Colfax. Around the eight to ten thousand block." He brought up a map of the area in one of the other windows on his screen. Looking at the data in that window he pointed to one of the buildings along Colfax. "That's the coffee shop she was tapped into."

Lamar looked over a Booker. "I'm taking a team down there." It was not a request.

"Take every available person. This is the best lead we have right now. It is imperative that we find these terrorists." Booker barked out orders, then remembering her place, she looked at Sam.

He nodded to Lamar.

Kai took a step toward Lamar. "Can I come?"

Lamar hesitated. "Sorry, no, too dangerous. And your skills are better used here." He stepped through the door.

Looking down at Tony, Sam took over the control of the search. "Bring up every city camera in that area. They should be on at least one of them. Let's see if we can track their movements." Then glancing at Booker, he said, "Did you catch the last thing he said?"

Booker nodded. "It's sounds like it's going down today." She stepped into the hall. "If Denver's attack is scheduled for today, the others will be also. I'll get word out and make sure the Air Force is up and running."

"And let the FAA know that we need the skies cleared immediately. All private aircraft need to land now."

Booker stepped into the hall to make some phone calls. Covering the mouth piece but keeping her ear to the phone she looked at Kai. "How good are you with tapping into city cams? Can you give Tony a hand?"

Kai moved back to her seat. "Tony, what was the address of that coffee shop again?" She glanced up at Sam. "Think anyone will mind if I also tap into a few private systems as well?"

"Whatever it takes."

As Tony, Kai, and Ernest worked, Sam stepped over to Booker and waited for her to finish her call. After she said goodbye and lowered her phone, he gave her his thoughts. "If the attack is going down today, I would feel a whole lot better if we had every police chopper in the air with a sharpshooter in each one."

"We're not even sure how the attack will come. Do you think we'll need them?"

"Call it a gut feeling."

She stared at him. "I hate it when people on my team say that, but too often they're right. I'll make the call to the Denver police department."

Sam checked the time as she hit another contact on her phone. It was just past noon.

———

Jonas kicked Derry's leg as he lay on the ground gasping for air and rubbing his aching throat.

"Get up. We need to move." Jonas glanced over his shoulder toward the road. "I can't have anyone calling the police about a person needing help."

Dace gave Sara's bad arm a squeeze making her wince. "If you try to escape or inform anyone, I will have Jonas twist this arm of yours off. Do you understand?"

She gave a rapid nod as tears rolled down her pale face.

Derry was lying in bits of asphalt and street trash. Something sharp poked him in the back. He slowly stood and took the pointy item with him, sliding it into his waistband. Once up, he reached for the duffle bag.

Jonas grabbed it and looked inside. "Well, well. What do we have here?" He held up a bundle of $20 bills for Dace to see. "I think I will take this off your hands." Jonas slung the bag over his own shoulder, while keeping the gun pointed at Derry. "Empty your pockets onto the ground." Jonas kept his body between the pistol and the road. No one driving by could see it.

Derry obeyed. There was not much in them.

Jonas told Sara to do the same. Before moving on, he patted them down to assure their pockets were empty.

Dace released Sara as a man stepped out the back door of one of the businesses. "We need to move."

Jonas slipped the gun out of sight as he whispered, "Say anything and you're both dead." As they walked off, Jonas waved at the man.

"Hey, is that stuff yours?" The man pointed at the backpack and other items left behind.

Dace slowly spoke over his right shoulder, with a hick accent. "Ain't mine. It was there when we got here." Almost as an afterthought he added, "It smells kind of funny. I ain't touchin' it."

The man peered at the stuff for a few seconds before turning around and going back inside the building.

The foursome headed back out onto Colfax. They crossed at the light, obeying all the laws. Dace held a small knife under Sara's armpit. If she made one false move, he could cut her artery and leave her behind. She'd be dead in three minutes.

A short walk on the north side of the street brought the group to an old one-story warehouse. Stepping inside, Dace led them past a company van and into a small office where two men were kneeling facing east and reciting Salat, a prayer that Muslims recite five times a day.

Dace and Jonas stood by quietly. Only one of the men looked like he was from the Middle East. The other appeared to be European.

Derry pulled his hand away from his side and looked at the wound. It was still bleeding but only a trickle now. Without his hand pressing on it, the pain increased. He put his hand back. He surveyed Sara's face. He wanted to see how she was holding up. Something was wrong. What little color had been in her face drained away, and her brown eyes dulled.

The men finished their prayers and stood. As the European turned around his face twisted and he whispered, "Sara?"

64

Sam sat absentmindedly staring into space when Booker stepped into his temporary office. She began to ask if any progress had been made, but seeing the look on his face instead asked, "What's wrong?"

"The more I think about how Nasir operates the more convinced I am that he has found a way to disperse the poison that we haven't thought of."

"There are only so many ways to drop a powder from the sky." Booker sat in a nearby chair.

"No, there is only one way to drop it, use gravity. The real question is how are they going to get it into the air to start with."

Booker shook her head while staring at the floor. "Is everyone at the CIA such a pain?"

"Most of them are worse." Sam's deadpan expression prevented her from knowing if he meant what he said.

Her phone buzzed. She answered and listened for a few seconds, thanked the caller, then hung up. "That was Detroit."

"News about Nasir?"

She nodded. "The data is a few hours old, but he was spotted by a traffic cam on the north end of town. They have three teams following up on it."

"Have you sent out a BOLO to Canada to watch for him crossing the border? If we stop this plan from succeeding, but Nasir gets away, he will be back in a year or three, with a new and improved scheme. We have to get him." Sam was very insistent.

"I'll make the call." Booker rose and left the room.

———

Derry studied the man across the room. He had heard many

terrible things about John Motova and what he and his family had done to Sara. But up until this point it was hard to believe he truly was part of a terrorist attack against America. Yet here was proof in the flesh. This evil man had caused Sara so much pain and now he was willing to take her life along with millions of others. He needed to be stopped for good.

Dace held Sara's arm and every time she tried to move, he applied pressure, making her wince in pain. But seeing the new look on her face he remarked, "I see you know this man."

Sara's voice was hard and low, "Yeah, an old enemy of mine."

Dace gave a sinister smile. "You appear to have many."

She did not acknowledge Dace's comment. Instead her hate was directed toward John. "Ever wonder what happened to your money?"

He took a step toward her. "I did until we got it back."

"What?"

John looked past Sara, at Dace. "Why did you bring them here?"

"We did not have a choice. They spotted us at the coffee shop. We could not chance the FBI learning our location." Jonas set the bag down against the counters.

"What is in there?"

Jonas smiled. "It looks like one of them robbed a bank while they were on the run."

"Money? That does not matter now. Tomorrow it will be worthless. After today's attack, the American economy will collapse. American dollars will not be worth the paper they are printed on." John studied Sara's face. "You are like a bad penny that keeps turning up. But today the bad luck is yours. I am sorry you will have to die for being in the wrong place at the wrong time." He looked up at Jonas. "Kill them both, but be quiet about it."

Dace started to pull Sara way. She cringed but held her spot on the floor. "Before we die, I want to know one thing."

"What you want is not important. You are to die." John nodded to Dace again.

And again, Sara fought to stay. "After what you allowed your sons to do to me, you owe me."

"You are a non-believer and what they did was their doing, not mine." He hesitated for a second. "But I will give you one question, that I may choose to answer or not." John nodded.

Sara pulled her arm free as the anger grew on her face. "How in the world did you get tangled up with such low life scum? I mean, you were pretty low to start with, but to go from poisoning one person to killing millions is quite a leap."

"We are not scum, but followers of Allah and his one true prophet, Mohamed."

Derry was surprised by this answer. This man did not behave the way that Sara had described. Even after her spiteful question, he kept his voice steady.

Sara commented to Derry. "You were right. Muslims are a bunch of godless, crazy maniacs."

John addressed Jonas again. "You know what needs to be done. Make it quick. We have work to do."

Sara twisted and raised her arm, keeping it away from Dace. Dace grabbed it and pulled it down. She cried out her request. "Being a Muslim has turned you into a wimp. The man who let his boys rape me would never be kind enough to kill someone quickly. Don't do me any favors you low life pig, rolling around in its own excrement."

Dace let out a small laugh. "I see she does not like you, John." He started to pull Sara toward the door.

John's hand gripped the back of his chair tightly. "You would rather I not be nice? You want to die by the poison? So be it. You can die in great agony like the rest of the city." She had gotten to him.

"If God doesn't strike you dead first." She spat at him. None of the spittle reached him, but his face began to grow red.

He continued to grip the chair as the veins in his hand popped up. It took a few seconds before he relaxed. Finally, he spoke to Jonas. "If they want a slow, painful death, we will give it to them. Tie them up and leave them in the bay. Oh, before you leave, you might like to know that while you were out I checked the afternoon's weather predictions. The winds are perfect. They are forecasted to be out of the west by southwest at ten to fifteen knots. It will spread the powder all the way to the airport." Looking at Sara he added, "And will cover this area with enough powder to give you that nice, slow, painful death you want." Glancing back at Dace he added. "Make sure the rope is tight."

Jonas pulled Derry's gun out of his waistband as he yanked on Derry's arm. Derry resisted. If he was going to die, fighting might not help, but it was better than doing nothing. Jonas struck him across the face with the pistol. The pain slammed through his head as he slumped against the wall, before being yanked back up. "Don't die on me, I want you two love birds to feel the agony of your coming deaths for the full twenty minutes." Leaning close to Derry's ear, he whispered. "Your skin will blister, as your lungs fill with your own blood. The pain will be unbearable when your whole body starts hemorrhaging, inside and out. Your little girlfriend over there will suffer beyond anything you can imagine and you will hate the world and everything in it as you see her scream in pain before she dies in front of you. But if you like, I can kill her now so only you have to suffer such pain."

What an offer, a terrible disgusting offer. Let her live and suffer far more or ask this murderer to kill her quickly. Derry knew there was no real choice. Their only hope was in stopping these men before they could carry out their insane plan.

God, this isn't right. Please help me know what to do.

65

Lamar sat next to Faircloth as they pulled into a parking lot at the east end of the seven thousand block of East Colfax. Two Denver police cars pulled in beside them. Four other teams quickly joined them.

Booker would have called in more help, but any more people would have raised suspicion. Lamar was the first out of the vehicle and called everyone together.

"We know the terrorists are somewhere in this area. They were at the coffee shop over there just a few minutes ago."

They all headed toward the coffee shop and then fanned out, checking every building, alley, and parking area for any signs of Sara and Derry or the terrorists. One team quickly came across a backpack with its contents lying scattered around it. In the center of the pile was a smashed cell phone.

Lamar looked around at the businesses that lined the alley. Most of them had doors opening onto the alley. He looked over at Faircloth who was also studying the buildings. "Think anyone around here happened to peek out and see our people?"

"I hope so." Lamar instructed the teams to talk to all of the shop owners on both sides of the alley. Working in pairs they hit each of the businesses, showing pictures of Derry and Sara as well as Landry and Hewitt, asking if anyone had seen them.

Lamar walked into a very neat, small copy and shipping store. "Excuse me, Miss." A young, dark haired woman who looked like she should be in high school was working at the counter. Lamar flashed his badge then held out his phone displaying Sara's picture. "I'm with the FBI and I have a few questions for you. Have you seen either of these two people?" He swiped the screen to show the second image. "They would have been with these two men." He swiped to Landry's and Hewitt's pictures.

She studied the images. "No, I don't remember seeing any of them."

"What about out back? Did you see or hear anything out of the ordinary today?"

She looked over her shoulder, toward the rear of the store. "Hey, Dad. The cops want to talk with you about what you saw."

Lamar saw a man step from the rear of the store. The girl's father examined Lamar and the police officer with him before speaking. "What can I help you with?"

His daughter spoke. "They want to know what you saw out back." She looked at Lamar. "Dad said there were some men back there a while ago, roughing up a young couple. He said he would have stopped it, but then the couple acted like everything was okay. Me, I would have called the cops and I told him we should. But he refused." She turned back to her dad. "Told you we should have called."

Lamar give a tiny smile as he showed the pictures to the father. "Are these the men that were *roughing* up these two?" He swiped through the four pictures.

"Yes, that's them. Are they okay? I started to stop them but, like my daughter said, before I could do anything, everything looked normal. They just walked off together, like friends."

"Did you happen to see which way they went?"

"Not after they crossed Colfax." He looked out the front glass of his store. "There was a van parked next door and I could only see them make it about half way across. Sorry I didn't call. I should have."

"Thank you. You've been a big help. If you think of anything else," Lamar pulled out a business card and wrote a number on it, "call this number. They will take a message and make sure I get it."

The two men left the store and contacted the other agents in the search through their ear pieces. They now knew Darry and Sara and at least two terrorists were on the north side of Colfax and most likely within walking distance. The teams shifted the focus of their search, as did Kia and Tony on the city cams.

———

Derry sat on the ground with his back to Sara as Jonas tied their hands together. "You don't have much of a boyfriend here. I offered to take your life quickly and painlessly so you would not have to suffer with the rest of the city. He said no. He must want to see you suffer along with him." Jonas yanked the twine tight as both of them yelped from the pain. "Maybe he believes that is some type of love."

Derry felt Sara's fingers squeeze his. A silent thank you. His wound was bleeding again. He could feel the blood trickling down his side.

Her voice was icy cold. "So you came over to gloat?"

Derry could not see who Sara was talking to but by her tone he knew it must be Motova. He wished he was the one facing the door. He hated not being able to see what was going on. He thought about the sharp item that was poking into his back. He was sure he could pull it out and use it to cut the twine. Now he just had to wait for the right moment. Rushing something like this could cost him his only opportunity to save Sara and escape.

The Russian's voice was condescending. "I know you think your life has been hard. Perhaps it has, and that may be what you deserved for not being a believer. Now you must die along with the rest of the infidels."

"You are the reason for my suffering, as always. You are the exact same pig you were when you held me captive." Sara's anger came through in every word she forced out. "If you feel so bad about it, why not let us go?"

"Death must come to all non-believers until the faithful are in power. True believers must and will rule someday. I am only a tool for Allah. He will receive the praise."

"You are killing us because we are Christians?"

"You follow false teachings and the Qur'an is very clear about what must happen to infidels and those who corrupt his teachings."

"If you are following this book of yours so closely, what does the Qur'an say about perverts?"

"I am a different person now. The person you knew no longer exists. What happened to you in the past does not change who you are today and what your punishment is."

"You are still a weak, little man. Before, you hid behind your wife, doing what she ordered you to do, letting your sons abuse me while you defended them and punishing me for complaining, then poisoning me with the chemicals in your basement. The only difference now is that you're hiding behind a false religion. You are still using me to fulfill some deep seated hatred toward mankind. Or maybe it's hatred of yourself."

With a calm voice he went on. "You are right about my life in the past. I was a sick, hopeless man. But as I said, that man is no longer alive."

Sara jerked her body toward him. "Then why not let me help you to your grave and you can join that man?"

As these two bickered, Derry got a peek of Jonas and Dace in the office on their knees. It was their turn to recite the prayers. He could not hear them over the other noises, but they were going through all the movements. His right arm was now out of view of his captors.

Motova continued, "Many will see their graves today. That is Allah's will. And with those deaths, Allah will show his power and hatred for the infidel and this nation."

Derry bent his hand up as high as he could without making it clear what he was doing. He could barely get his fingertips to the sharp tool. With only the ends of two fingers, he slid it up a fraction of an inch. The jagged edge cut into one finger.

Noises on his right caught his attention. Stopping, he turned his head to see the man who had been praying with John pushing a cart across the floor. The man carefully loaded the cart into a Heating and Air Conditioning repair van. On the cart, Derry could see metal canisters with some type of controls on the side and a few wires hanging out. What looked like an LCD clock was in the upper right corner of each control unit. After completing his task, the man signaled John.

John told him, "Very good. As soon as your brother completes his part and calls us, you may leave to get his family."

"It should be me up there and not him."

"Yes, that may be true, but he has the right job at the right time. Allah has other plans for your life."

He nodded but clearly did not agree.

Sara continued to challenge John. "You say you believe in the one true God. But God is not a God of hate, but of love and forgiveness."

The Russian moved to where Derry could see him. With the other man gone and John to his left, Derry stretched his fingers out again. The tips were sticky-slick from the blood. Each quarter inch cost more skin. He stopped several times when the pain got too intense.

"First, you are confusing the Christian God with the one true god. Christians are polytheists, worshiping three gods. Second, you say your God is a God of love and forgiveness. If that is true, why have the Christian nations gone to war every time Islam gets near them? You do not follow a God of love, but of fear."

Derry couldn't resist. "Can you tell us how Islam has been spread in most countries?" He folded his fingers into his palm and made a tight fist to stop the throbbing.

"Through the power of Allah."

"Through the power of war and millions of dead followers. Only in a very few places has Islam come in without an overthrow of the government and the destruction of all other religions."

"It is only right that we spread the one true religion by the means Allah has given us. Once Islam rules the world—"

"You sound like a broken record, saying the only reason you kill is to help the world. You kill because your kind of Islam is a religion of hate and bigotry."

"No, it is Allah's will we do what we do."

"And how do you feel about the Muslims in Iran?"

John's face tightened, "I am not here to debate with you how we are to treat blasphemers. If you want to ask me about the one true religion, I will answer your questions." John started to walk toward the van.

Derry didn't want anyone on that side. "Don't the Muslims consider Jesus a prophet?"

"Yes, he is. But much of what he said has been perverted by you Christians, turning him into one of your gods."

"It's not like that." Sara cut in.

"Really?" He checked the time. "I have a few more minutes. Tell me how it is."

Derry reached up again. Time was short. He would have to work through the pain.

"We believe there is only one God, in three personalities."

"Those are just words to confuse others."

Sara was quiet for a few seconds. John started to walk toward the van again. Derry pulled up hard on the piece of metal. It cut deeper.

"Let me ask you one more question?" Her voice was growing weak.

Good going, sweetheart. Keep him occupied.

John stopped and nodded.

"Do you act the same way around your family as you do at work or in public?"

"Are you trying to say I am like your God?"

"No—but the Bible tells us we are all made in the image of God. We are a poor reflection of Him. I can't fully explain it. But just as humans have different roles to play, so does God. It only makes sense He would have a spirit of protection, one of love and one of a counselor. We call these roles the Father, the Son and the Holy Spirit. They are three separate persons, but there is still just one God."

John started to speak but his phone buzzed. "Your time is up." He walked away.

After completing his phone call, they could hear him talking to the fourth man. "Segel, that was Magen. The air conditioners have been disabled in his building. We will head over there right away. You have until four o'clock to be out of Denver."

"Good, I just finished loading the hazmat suits on the carts." Segel stood near the rear of the van.

John, Jonas, and Dace slipped on coveralls. Jonas walked by Segel and whispered in his ear as he slipped him a pistol.

Segel glanced over at Derry and Sara before nodding.

Jonas patted his shoulder and joined the others in the van.

With no one observing him, Derry rubbed the jagged metal against his bindings.

Segel opened the garage door behind them. The van drove away and then Segel closed the door again. He then walked over to where Derry and Sara sat. When he was within a foot of them he pointed the gun at Sara's head.

"I was told to shoot you both once they cleared the building. We cannot take any chances of you surviving."

———

Kai called Sam. "I think I found them."

66

The terrorists removed the carts from the van and headed toward the building. It was a very hot August day and the temperature on the roof would be well over a hundred degrees. They entered the Republic Plaza and the manager met them twenty feet inside the door. "Thank you for getting here so quickly. The top fifteen floors had to be evacuated. The heat up there is stifling. We can't get this fixed fast enough."

Jonas stepped forward. "We will get right on it."

"How long will it take?" The manager looked hopeful.

"It is impossible to say without looking at the units to determine what the problem is."

The manager browsed the carts. "What in the world is all this?"

"The travel time from the roof to our truck is pretty long. We decided to take everything we might possibly need with us to begin with, but if you like we can leave the tools in the truck until we see what we actually need."

"No, taking everything with you to begin with is a great idea. The heat is killing us. The faster you get this fixed the better."

John smiled at the irony of his comment. "We need to know what floors are affected."

"All floors above the tenth floor."

"Alright. Do you have someone to show us the way?"

"Let me get the maintenance supervisor, he can help you."

The manager touched the tiny button on his ear piece. "Magen, I need you at the front desk, right away." He lifted his head and looked at John. "He should be here in just a minute."

Before Magen showed up, someone stopped by to complain.

"You better get the air back on soon. I am in the middle of a very important meeting with clients from Japan and they are only here for one more day. If I lose this contract, I will sue the owner of this building."

"Would it be possible to continue your meeting in one of our private conference rooms on the first floor?" The manager stayed calm despite the tenant's agitation.

The man looked around. "That could work, but I better not get charged for it."

"No, you won't. I'll have someone get you set up." The manager signaled to an assistant and instructed her to help the disgruntled tenant. At the same time, Magen stepped off the elevator and approached the group.

"These repairmen need to know the scope of the problem. You can explain the situation as you show them the way to the roof," the building manager clarified.

"The smaller bank of coolers is still running and is keeping the lower ten floors relatively cool. But the large set, which has three massive units, has stopped."

"All three? We better get up there and take a look. Mind showing us the way?"

Magen led them toward the elevators. John waited until they were inside to speak. "Quickly, put on your hazmat suits." All four men stepped into the bulky suits as quickly as they could in the cramped space.

"Your brother is headed over to pick up your family. You are a brave follower and will be rewarded for your help."

"Good. I told my wife that Segel was taking them up to the mountains for the day."

Dace stepped closer. "Your wife did not question that?"

He looked over and hesitated. The other men waited for the response. "Yes, she asked me why."

"And?" Jonas looked down on him.

Magen's eye's shifted rapidly from one person to the other. "I told her that I heard some men talking in the restaurant about a mass protest against Islam. And as we live so close to downtown it would be better if she and our son were out of town. Now she is worried about me."

"When this is all over, she will understand." Of course the FBI would learn that Magen was involved. And if he did not make it out of the country quickly, he would most likely be put to death. John wondered if Magen fully understood the cost of his actions.

As the altitude increased, so did the temperature. Beads of sweat collected on their foreheads and ran into their eyes.

"How did you disable the air conditioners?"

"I turned them off in the control room. Nothing but a simple command."

This was not what John expected to hear. "And what if someone else looks at the controls?"

Magen smiled. "I am the only one at work today that has the code to the controllers."

"And how do you expect to turn them back on when we need them? Will you have to return to the control room?"

"No, no. That system has a port in the maintenance shack on the roof. I can override the command from there."

Dace cut in. "We are not setting them off while we are up there are we?"

John thought little of the French man. He had done practically nothing to help today and now was acting like a coward. "Of course not. We have timers on our equipment. But I want everything else running when we step off this roof. I want to know that all three cooling towers are running at their top speeds." He checked his watch. "If we want to live, we have thirty minutes to get everything set up. That will give us forty-five minutes to clear the area."

Jonas, dripping with sweat nodded. "That will work."

Magen spoke up. "As hot as it is today and with the amount of heat built up in the building, the units will run for at least two hours straight. Most likely until sundown."

The elevator came to a stop on the top floor of the building. The doors opened and heat poured in. They thought it could not get any hotter than it had been in the elevator, but they were mistaken. John and Jonas grabbed the carts and pushed them out. They moved through a door and down a service hall. At the end of the hall they entered a freight elevator. Magen pulled a bundle of keys out and turned the lock to

Deadly Infiltration

activate it. The elevator took them to the roof.

The heat reflecting off the surface of the roof drove the temperature on the top of the building to a hundred and ten degrees. But that was cooler than inside the upper floors of the Republic Plaza.

Jonas, along with the other three, took a minute to tug at the collars of their airtight suits to try to get some air flow inside them. "I hope none of us passes out before we are done."

Dace headed toward the tall cooling units ahead of the others. He took nothing with him.

"Come back and help with the equipment. We do not have any time to waste." John pushed one cart as he wondered if he could leave the Frenchman behind.

————

Sam rushed over to Kai. "What have you got?"

"I hacked into several of the private security cameras in the area and found our people heading down this street here."

Sam checked the map and called in the information to the teams in the field. "Good job, little sister."

————

The teams had spread out on the north side of Colfax. Faircloth's and Chris' teams took the area one block north of Colfax, going from house to house as Lamar's and Kent's teams hit the businesses along the busy street. Several of the units were out of business and locked up tight, making them a perfect place to hide. Each one had to be investigated. It made the going slow, way too slow.

Lamar's headset pinged. It was from someone at the Bureau. He spoke into his mic. "Please tell me you've got something."

Sam was on the other end. "We found all four of them walking between some buildings." He gave them the address for the location. The message went out to all agents involved. They immediately headed toward that location.

"Lamar, it's Kai." Kai's voice cut in. "I brought up the satellite view of that block. There is a large warehouse on one side and a set of small business rental units on the other. I'll see if any of those businesses have a security system I can access."

"You can do that, but I'm not waiting. I'm going in." Lamar slowed as they approached the area. The warehouse had two large garage doors and a standard sized door on the west side. No windows.

The business units across the alley all had big glass fronts, making it hard to hide anything going on inside.

He signaled for Kent's team to hit the warehouse first. Kent and one officer went around back as Lamar and the other officer flanked the door on the front.

Faircloth said he was only sixty seconds out and told Lamar to wait.

The teams held their positions as they waited.

Creeping up to the cracked wooden door, Lamar placed his ear against it. He could make out voices but not what they were saying. Pulling back a little he reached for the door handle and slowly turned. It was locked.

He turned his head to see Faircloth and his team cutting through an opening between some houses, as two shots rang out inside the building.

Jumping back, he lowered his shoulder and plowed into the door. The obstruction splintered into several pieces.

67

Derry craned his neck to see Segel place the pistol against Sara's head.

"You two are the lucky ones. This way of dying will be much less painful than what so many others will suffer today." The terrorist sneered.

"I've made peace with my God. Have you made peace with your Satan?" Derry just needed one more second to free his hands. Just one more strand to cut through.

Segel gave a fake chuckle. "It is not the followers of Allah that will spend an eternity with Iblīs. But I do not have time or any desire to convince you of the truth. I must go and you must die."

Segel's smile faded and he pushed harder against Sara's head.

"OUCH!" She twisted her head and shoulders away from the hard barrel.

The assailant repositioned the pistol, this time an inch away from her skull. "Your pain in this world is almost over. What you suffer in the next life is of your own doing." Segel gently laughed.

"I love you, Derry." It was a whisper as one of her hands stretched its fingers out to touch him.

She had given up, that wasn't like her. "It's not over yet." Derry felt the straps connecting him to Sara fall away. He kept his arms tucked behind his back. With his head turned as far as he could, he concentrated on the man's hand.

The color of Segel's trigger finger changed shades. Derry waited the tiniest fraction of a second more before dropping his head down and pushing his back against his love, forcing Sara out of the way. Using one hand as support, Derry lunged for the gun with the other. The explosive blast next to his ear was followed by a sharp, intense pain as the bullet grazed the side of his head. His timing had almost worked.

Somewhere off in the distance Sara screamed above the loud ringing in his ears.

The searing pain in his head along with the sound of the blast, caused a slight delay in his actions. Derry twisted his head up to locate his objective and pushed up with his legs.

The recoil from the pistol had raised Segal's hands a couple of inches and he took a step back to reposition himself.

Derry rammed his shoulder into Segel's waist, just below the hands that were gripping the weapon. As his shoulder made contact with his would be killer, Derry arched his back up and drove hard, hoping to push the barrel above the level of Sara's head.

Segel took another step back and planted his right leg to stop his reverse movement. As Derry wrapped his arms around his adversary, the man's arms began to pound his back. Derry gripped hard and twisted the man's frame as he tried in vain to lift him. If he did not take control right now, this idiot would kill his girl. He drove his shoulder upward with more strength than he knew he had, lifting his heavier rival off the ground, if only for a second. It was long enough to achieve the desired results. Segel lost his balance, and Derry pushed him backwards onto the ground.

Landing with a thud on top, Derry released his hold around the man and rammed his forearm into the man's windpipe. His opponent dropped the gun he was holding.

Sara was somewhere out of his sight, screaming at their common enemy.

Segel twisted and pushed Derry off to his right. Both men scrambled for the gun. As they wrestled for control a loud explosion shattered the air.

68

Astonished, Derry realized he was still alive and Segel had suddenly stopped struggling. The pistol fell from Derry's hands. He first peered into the lifeless eyes of his dead nemesis, before he noticed the red appearing around a newly made hole in the man's chest. He tore his eyes from the man's body and turned toward the commotion.

Sara exclaimed their friend's name. "Lamar!"

Lamar stood near the door as several police officers rushed in behind him. Lamar kept his gun pointed at Segel as he quickly stepped up to the body and kicked the pistol away, before checking his pulse. "We won't get much out of him."

Derry suddenly turned toward Sara. The white skin that covered her face showed both relief and exhaustion. He rushed to her side.

She threw her arms around his neck and cried. After a couple of minutes, she pulled back and looked him in the face. "You saved me—again." She leaned back in and gave him another long hug. "I love you." The soft words came through her tears.

"I told you it wasn't over."

She pulled back again and looked at her blood soaked arm, then at the side of his head. In the struggle, blood had worked its way through most of his hair and onto his shoulder. "You're bleeding. He shot you."

Derry reached up and touched the sticky area. "Ouch." It was extremely tender.

A policemen approached and gingerly examined the side of Derry's head. "You are going to need stiches."

Lamar finished talking to Kent and stepped toward them.

"Where are the two men that brought you here, Hewitt and Landry?"

———

Sam stood behind Kai, listening to the live feed from the warehouse, while Tony and Ernest remained in their desk chairs. No one in the room had spoken since Lamar had reported that shots had been fired. Finally, Lamar gave a summary of Derry's and Sara's conditions and Sam relaxed. The two were hurt but nothing was life threatening. One terrorist was dead, but Landry, Hewitt and Motova were gone, along with the nerve agent. They had left less than fifteen minutes before the FBI had arrived.

The tension returned. They were so close, but had missed their targets again. The poison was on its way to be deployed.

Booker stepped into the room, stopping just inside the door. "Did we find them?"

Sam filled her in. Her face showed the disappointment.

"Mind stepping outside with me for a second?" She was looking at Sam.

"Sure." The two moved into the hall.

"I just got off the phone and want to bring you up to speed on the other cities. The Air Force and Army have everything in place. NORAD pointed out that since New York, L.A., and Chicago are all U.S. border cities, they are well covered with monitoring equipment. NORAD is confident the minute the drones are activated they will be able to take control of them."

"That's good news for the other cities."

"And NORAD feels they will be able to zero in on the drones' starting points. So we have a good chance of catching the people responsible. We've asked for police help in the involved cities. They have helicopters and SWAT teams positioned around town, ready to move in once the location is known."

Sam nodded. "Now if we could only find an answer for our situation."

———

Sweat poured off of the men as they worked on top of the massive air conditioners. The small cooling units built into each hazmat suit were not keeping up with the heat. To make matters worse, police helicopters were flying by every few minutes. Each time a helicopter passed near the building, Jonas ducked his hooded head, hoping they would appear to be nothing more than a repair crew working on a broken air conditioner.

After the latest chopper passed, Jonas returned to the job at hand, thinking about his plan. It was so perfect. No one would expect these large fans to be used to shoot the powder high into the sky. And starting on the top of the tallest building in Denver, with the help of these powerful fans, the powder would rise to a thousand, maybe twelve hundred, feet. At that point the winds coming off the mountains would carry it across the Denver-metro area, killing everyone in its path. Close to half of Denver would taste death today.

He pulled hard on the large zip-ties holding the cables down. He checked his watch to see how much time they had left. The heat and the cumbersome suits were slowing everything down. But none of them wanted to take a chance of being exposed if one of the containers was dropped or broke open when it was being installed. They needed another ten minutes or so. And that was all the time they had left.

He checked over his shoulder to see how Dace was progressing. Despite all his education the man was a slow worker. Clearly he was not suited for this type of work. His ineffectiveness would cost them escape time.

Movement off to his right caught his attention. Magen had walked out of the utility shed toward him. He signaled that he was ready to turn the power on as soon as everything was in place. Jonas held up his hand with all five fingers extended, five more minutes.

Magen nodded and went back into the shade.

Jonas waved at John, who was working with the timers. John was hooking them up to the building's power.

He looked up as Jonas approached and yelled as he handed him some wires. "Don't plug this timer into your unit until you have everything ready. Any static buildup could trigger the boxes."

Jonas nodded and carried one of the timer wires over to Dace and repeated the instructions.

Dace shrugged and plugged his in. "These units are ready. It is time to leave."

Jonas first looked at the man then at his work. Dace was both irresponsible and unskilled. Jonas reached down and tugged on the housing. It was loose but it didn't come free. He turned away and finished his own unit as he hoped for the death of the man he had put up with for the past three years.

Everything was a go. Now they just needed to get out of the city.

69

An ambulance had been called for Sara and Derry. While they waited, one of the Denver police officers dabbed Derry's head with some white cotton. Derry could hear the sirens as the ambulance approached.

While Faircloth and Lamar questioned Sara and Derry, other FBI agents combed the building for evidence that might indicate where the terrorists had gone.

"It has to do with where that man's brother works." Derry nodded toward the body, as the officer asked him to hold still.

"Do you know this man's name?" Faircloth was doing most of the questioning.

"I heard him called Segel, but no last name," Sara responded.

Lamar put a call into the Bureau. "Tony, that picture and prints I sent in, we need to know where his brother works. The deceased's first name is Segel."

While Lamar waited, Faircloth asked the next question. "You said they left in an air conditioning and heating company van. Did you get the name of the company or a plate?"

Derry shook his head. "I know it was a white Chevy, about four or five years old."

Sara looked down at the floor, "It started with an A, but I couldn't really see it from where I sat."

"That's a start." Lamar's earwig pinged. "Wha'cha got?"

Derry and Sara watched in silence as both Lamar and Faircloth listened to the voices in their ears. After a few seconds Lamar looked at Faircloth. "Did you get that?"

"Yeah, the Republic Plaza, downtown."

"It's an office building. They will want to hit it before people start leaving for the day." Lamar checked his watch. "That doesn't give us much time."

Sara reached out and tapped Lamar's arm. "I don't think they are planning to kill just the people in that building, at least it didn't sound that way."

Faircloth cut in. "With the amount of toxin they have they could be setting up to hit several buildings at once. But that would take more manpower than we believe they have."

Derry stood up despite the repeated requests of the man trying to tape his wound. "I think she's right. They were talking about how we would also die here in this building in the attack."

Faircloth looked over at Lamar. "Do you think they have other drones in their van?"

Lamar responded, "The Republic Plaza has a flat roof. They could be planning to use it as a launch point. But getting even one drone to the roof without questions would be hard. I don't see how they could do that." Lamar turned to Sara and Derry. "Did you see them put anything in the van? Or see inside the van?"

Derry answered, "Nothing big enough to be a drone or anything else that could fly."

Faircloth began to pace. "Then how in the world are they planning to get the poison into the air? Throw it off the side of the building?" Frustration came through loud and clear.

"However they are going to do it, I need to get over there and stop them." Lamar put a call in for a police chopper to come pick him up.

"Why an air conditioning van?" Sara looked at Lamar, then Derry.

Derry answered, "I believe their plan has something to do with the air conditioning units themselves. They seemed very important. And I watched him load up the van." Derry nodded toward the body again. "He didn't put much in it other than a few metal boxes and rolling carts. No drones or blowers or anything else that could be used to shoot the stuff into the sky."

"If they aren't taking the delivery system with them, it must already be there." Sara reasoned.

Lamar looked down at her. "What are you talking about?"

Sara took a breath as she rose with Derry's help. "They sounded like they planned to be out of town when the nerve agent was released. We didn't see any drones so let's assume they don't have any. If that is true, they must be planning to use something else that is already on the roof."

Everyone nodded in agreement as Derry said. "And it sounded like they just picked this building today, so it has to be something that is always there."

Sara shifted her focus from Lamar to Faircloth and back before looking at Derry. "Where do buildings like the Republic Plaza have their air conditioning units?"

Lamar answered for him. "Normally, on top of the building." Then he suddenly realized what she was saying. "Of course. They don't need to bring their own fans. Those large air conditioners have massive blowers, large enough to throw the powder high into the air. It could travel miles before all of it comes back down." He looked at Faircloth. "Get this information to Booker. I'm catching a ride downtown." Lamar hurried out the door as he heard the chopper approaching the parking lot behind the building.

———

Lamar asked the chopper pilot to stay as low as she could as they approached the Republic Plaza from the east. Two other helicopters were hovering within a quarter-mile and staying low. One of them was also a police helicopter while the other was Army.

Halfway there he got a call from Faircloth. The building management said that the van was still out front, but the cooling units had just come on.

"They need to be shut off immediately," Lamar yelled over the thumping of the blades.

"He's working on it, but said everything in the building is password protected. They were afraid of someone hacking in. The head of maintenance appears to be in on it. He went up to the roof with the terrorists. They will have to track down someone else who has the password."

Lamar pressed the intercom button. "What's our ETA?"

"Three minutes. I could cut that down if I fly a little higher."

"Do it." Lamar sat behind the two police officers. "Also, can you patch me through to the other two choppers?"

The co-pilot flipped a switch. "You're on."

"This is Special Agent Stover of the FBI. The men we are after are suspected of setting up a nerve agent device on the roof of the Republic Plaza. We cannot let this unit be detonated."

One of the police choppers cut in. "Agent Stover, I did two flybys on that building in the last forty minutes. I spotted two, maybe three, men working on the air conditioning units on the roof."

"When was your last flyby?"

"Twelve minutes ago. They looked like they were finishing up. The cooling units appeared to be on and they were leaving.

The pilot signaled to Lamar that they were a half mile out.

"I need the other choppers to move in now. I repeat. Move in now."

———

Nasir wanted out of America before the borders were shut down. The attack would be underway in less than an hour. The minute it happened, the U.S. would shut down all incoming and exiting traffic at every border. He rubbed his face where his beard had been. With the change in hair color and the clean face, he would be able to drive across the checkpoint without anyone suspecting his dedication to Islam.

Before leaving the International Bridge at Sault Ste. Marie, he peered over the side to his right at the very green St. Mary's Island. The landscape was breathtaking. Coming down the ramp, he pulled his car to a stop at the Canadian checkpoint and held out his fake Canadian passport, filled with forged crossing stamps. The officer took it and stepped away from the car and into his little room to scan it.

Nasir watched in his mirrors as other border guards checked other cars and went about their busy, boring day. He smiled to himself, as he knew that soon that would all change.

The guard stepped out of the door and approached. "Excuse me, sir. Would you mind opening your trunk?"

"Is there a problem?"

"Please open your trunk, sir."

Nasir reached down and pulled the handle to release the trunk lid. It popped up.

The guard's hand rested on the butt of his pistol. "Now, would you mind stepping out and around to the rear of the car while I go through your trunk?"

This was humiliating. Their words sounded fine, but their tone was anything but respectful. He should have gone by boat as he had done before.

The guard stepped back as Nasir opened the car door. "There is nothing in the trunk. I don't understand why I need to get out." He looked in the guard's face as he moved toward the rear of his car. The guard's eyes were never actually focused on him. The guard gave a quick, lifeless smile. "We've had a lot of problems ever since some of the states legalized pot."

Another sign of how far America had fallen. Maybe this guard also felt America needed to be punished.

Coming around the trunk lid, Nasir saw two other guards with guns pulled. He started to turn, only to be pushed against the back of the car by the guard behind him. Before he could react, four guards surrounded him with semiautomatic pistols pointed at his head.

How could I have not seen this trap?

70

Everything was in place. The timers were set to go off in forty minutes. Jonas walked over to the others in the team. They were all standing behind the large structure that sat in the middle of the Republic Plaza roof. John and Magen used a large hand-pumped jug to spray down Dace. Each member would be sprayed down, in case some of the poison had made its way out. "We need to hurry," Jonas declared.

John, holding the spray wand, nodded to Jonas. "You're the last one. Stand over there and rotate around slowly."

Already coated with the neutralizing solution, Dace, now mostly out of his hazmat suit asked about the carts.

John answered without looking at him. "Leave them. Leave everything, we no longer need any of it." John released the grip on the wand. "You are done. Magen, help me get Jonas out of his suit."

They worked quickly. Their clothes were drenched in sweat. But that would just make them blend in with the other occupants of the overheated building. They would be able to walk out without being noticed. They headed around toward the door leading to their escape route. Magen pulled his phone out and placed a call.

Dace reached for the man's hand. "Who are you calling?"

"My brother. I must make sure my family is safe."

"And if they are not?"

"I will take my car to get them. Do not worry. I will tell no one."

Dace looked over at Jonas. His eyes shifted between Jonas and Magen three times. He wanted Jonas to kill the man.

Jonas wondered if that was necessary. The man had held up his end, but what if he let something slip? The police could find out and stop the timers. Jonas gave a nod.

Deadly Infiltration

Dace pulled the phone out of Magen's hand. "You may not contact them or anyone else. Is that clear?"

"But, our deal was my help in exchange for their lives. If they die because of you, I—"

Jonas pulled his pistol and placed it against the back of Magen's head. "We cannot have someone on the team whom we cannot tr—" Before he could finish his task, a loud noise drowned out his voice. He hesitated then lowered the semiautomatic. He turning to see a police helicopter rise into view at the far edge of the rooftop.

Jonas yelled to the others, "Wave at them and keep moving." He did as he had told the others to do. Dace moved in behind Magen.

A second helicopter came into view on the north side, followed by the deeper sound of a larger chopper behind them. Jonas gripped his pistol as he spun toward the newest intrusion. The latest helicopter to join the party was military. As the two police units stayed fifteen to twenty feet off the roof, the military chopper moved into a covering position. Rising higher than the others, it turned sidewise. Jonas saw an open door and two riflemen facing them.

Regret at his over confidence and lack of planning washed over him as he realized they could not reach the rifles in the carts. He tried to formulate a plan. No matter the cost, they had to protect their position, as weak as it was. "John, get back there and detonate it now. We'll cover you." Jonas dropped to one knee and fired two rounds at the closest police chopper pilot with his pistol. The slugs hit the transparent shield but did not penetrate. The pilot veered off to the left. The rounds Jonas had in his gun were not adequate. He needed his rifle.

Death would come early for Denver. He glimpsed over his shoulder to see John running toward the air conditioning units. Today, no matter the outcome of this battle, all four of them would find their way into paradise. This type of death would guarantee their place.

The nose of the military unit dropped slightly as the back end swung around. Jonas knew this move. He jumped behind a short wall as the area was sprayed with bullets.

Dace's slowness cost him his life. The shooters took him out of the fight, just as his gun cleared its holster. The only round he got off just put another hole in the roof. Dace's body jerked from the multiple hits. His carcass dropped to the roof as the shooting stopped.

Magen raised his hands and went to his knees, still alive and completely unhurt. It was infuriating to Jonas. Someone on a loudspeaker told him to lie face down. The little traitor fell forward, arms outstretched.

The pig deserved to die and Jonas would have dispensed the worm's punishment if it would not have cost him his much needed ammunition.

"Stop where you are." The booming voice came from the first chopper which had recovered and positioned itself close to the cooling units. John was less than forty feet away from the timer, but that forty feet might as well have been forty miles. He wouldn't make it without help.

Jonas rolled out, and lying prone, took aim at the pilot of the chopper that was stopping John. He squeezed the trigger. As he felt his pistol jump, the area around him became a sea of flying material as dozens of .556 rounds turned the roof, and his body, into a bed of holes.

John realized that his commitment to Islam was not as strong as he had thought. Upon seeing Jonas' fate he immediately sank to his knees with his hands in the air.

In New York, several choppers, both military and police, blanketed the city and surrounding area, waiting for word from NORAD. As much as possible, they kept the choppers low and out of the downtown areas. They didn't want to alert the terrorists that they were aware of the date change.

The Army had set up decontamination stations in each city, giving NORAD safe locations at which to land the drones. The FBI in Atlanta had discovered the canisters carried timers. It appeared that the terrorists would launch the drones and leave town. The drones would then fly a preprogrammed route and the toxin would be released at a set time. As nearly as the FBI could tell, they would only have a few minutes to take control, land, and spray down the drones before the canisters released their deadly cargo. Each site had the equipment to spray the drones with a neutralizing foam and a team of weapons specialists who could disable the canisters once the drones were secured.

NORAD detected the first drone activity at 5:50 New York time. Within three minutes they detected launches in the other two cities as well. NORAD took control of all 12 drones quickly. In New York, two military choppers flanked the drones as two more moved in behind, ready to force them down if need be.

NORAD flew the drones to the decontamination location on Riker's Island, a place in the middle of the city but easily closed off and isolated. The NORAD pilots set the drones down on the long straight road running down the center of the island. Within seconds, military trucks converged on the drones, covering them in the neutralizing foam. Underneath the heavy foam shell, weapons disposal experts disconnected the timers and secured the canisters.

At the same time, the FBI went after the point of origin, an industrial park in Newark, New Jersey. The location was also radioed to the Newark Police, which had teams standing by. The New York police choppers didn't wait for a go ahead to assist, but flew across the Upper New York Bay and Newark Bay to the park at the interchange of I-95 and I-78. This location gave the terrorists multiple escape routes.

The New York choppers arrived at the industrial park to find four Newark police helicopters chasing a rental truck across the open area of the industrial complex. The terrorists were headed for an on ramp to I-95. At this time of the day the traffic on the interstate was moving slowly, but if the truck mixed into the flow, it would limit the options the police had for stopping them. Two of the Newark police choppers opened fire on the cab of the truck. The truck veered off course and into the cement wall of the on-ramp. Men on the ground quickly moved in to secure the terrorists.

71

Three months later

Derry looked over at his future wife. She sat silently as she stared at the table that separated them from the open floor and the judge's bench. Winds blew heavy wet snow against the courtroom windows. The forecast predicted four to six inches by morning.

In the weeks that followed the terrorist attacks the federal and state governments had worked hard to quiet the fears of the public. Some details of the events were sealed, those items that showed just how close the terrorists had come to succeeding and how deadly the nerve agent had been. But enough details had been released to satisfy the public's curiosity. And most of the terrorists had been either captured or killed.

The terrorists who survived had been given a choice. Either give up every name, place and detail of the operation, or be shipped off to Gitmo where everyone but the CIA would forget about them. Most chose the CIA captivity. Two chose to tell what they knew. One of them knew almost nothing and was killed by a fellow Muslim one month after being incarcerated in a U.S. prison. The other terrorist, John Motova, after telling all he knew about Nasir and his finances, was moved out of the general prison population. He was kept in isolation and received few visitors.

Gabriele Dieter, who had murdered Todd Jenkins, spent a month in the hospital recovering from her injuries. She was currently awaiting trial and was expected to get the death penalty.

Nasir, who had masterminded the whole attack, met with an unfortunate accident while being transported from the Canadian border to a federal prison. The transport vehicle he was in exploded just as the Federal Marshalls got out of it. The CIA claimed it was not their doing and they were investigating possible terrorist connections, but no one was ever sure. Regardless, many people felt that Nassir had received his just reward.

Although Kai had worked with the terrorists to decode the stolen files, she had no knowledge of their terrorist activities and had worked with the CIA to help bring them to justice, so no charges were filed against her.

Today's hearing was to decide what charges would be brought against Derry and Sara. Sara had broken her probation. She and Derry had both disobeyed an order given by a federal agent, and could possibly be charged with impeding a federal investigation. There were also several possible charges related to illegally accessing computer systems. On the other hand, they had both been instrumental in stopping what potentially would have been an unprecedented terrorist attack. Today they would find out which was more important to the courts.

Derry again studied the door that led to the judge's chambers. It had been over an hour since Lamar, Booker, Sam, the U.S. Attorney, and their defense attorney had disappeared through it. Derry thought the discussion should have included them as well, but they had been excluded.

Sara reached over and lightly rubbed the bald spot on the side of his head. The doctor said the hair would most likely never grow there again. It didn't matter, Sara said he was just as handsome as ever. More importantly, Sara was safe and getting better each day. The treatments she was receiving to remove the toxins from her body were really helping her. She had even gained a few pounds, and was now complaining about getting fat.

"We are praying for you two." Mary's reached out and squeezed Sara's shoulder. Mary sat behind them with Kai beside her.

Derry turned in his chair to thank Mary. The courtroom they were in was small and only a few close friends had been allowed in.

Faircloth had also gone into the judge's chambers, but had returned to the courtroom about twenty minutes earlier. He now occupied a chair in the back.

Derry's head snapped to the front upon hearing a click. The door opened and everyone but the judge walked in and took their seats. As they passed, each one smiled at Sara and Derry. Their lawyer was the last to come through. He sat next to Derry and whispered, "It was a good meeting."

"All rise." After the formalities, the judge took her seat behind the bench. After everyone was seated she asked Sara and Derry to rise again.

Before speaking, she scrutinized both of them for a couple of seconds. "This is a very interesting case. One I am pleased to be involved with. You two were very busy, breaking into Homeland Security's computer network as well as private computers, stealing money and moving it to unsanctioned locations, disobeying federal law enforcement officers and," she examined a paper on her bench, "a whole list of other crimes."

"Your Honor, I can explain. We had reasons for—"

She held up her hand. "Please young man, do not interrupt a judge— ever."

"Sorry." Derry bowed his head a little.

She smiled before continuing. "Before I announce my decision, I would like to ask Ms. Beckwith a few questions." She was looking at Sara.

"Yes, your Honor." Sara's voice was soft.

"I understand you have made several visits to our prison, as many as three times a week."

Derry wanted to answer for her, but one rebuke was sufficient.

Sara held her hands folded together as she stared at the floor. "Yes, Ma'am. To see John Motova."

"From what I understand Mr. Motova has caused you a great deal of pain. Why would you want to visit him so many times?"

"It is true that Mr. Motova is an old enemy. But I have learned to forgive him for the things he has done to me."

"Mr. Motova is a terrorist. He has confessed to being one of the architects behind these attempted attacks. He tried to kill millions of our citizens, including you. And you tell me that he is forgiven? What gives you that right?" The judge obviously disapproved.

Sara's head dropped a little lower.

How could this woman ever understand?

"I cannot speak for the others he hurt. I can only speak for myself. He abused me and allowed his boys to do many unspeakable things to me. And for years I hated him for what he had done to me."

"As is completely understandable. Yet now you say you have forgiven him completely?"

"Yes, your Honor."

The judge leaned back in her seat and was quiet for several seconds as she studied Sara. "How can you forgive him? I don't normally interject my opinion in cases outside of my courtroom, but he is one of the worst individuals I've ever heard of."

Sara glanced up at Derry. In that short glimpse he saw all the pain and struggle she had gone through. He replayed in his mind the events leading up to this moment. Until a few weeks ago, Sara had hated John Motova. She had wanted to see him not just die, but suffer greatly in the process. She had wanted to see him destroyed. Every day after his capture she had talked about how his deal with the government let him off too easy. Every day the hatred took more from her. The treatments to remove the toxins from her body did not seem to be making her any better. Finally, her disgust for John Motova drove her to go see him.

Sara gloated over his capture and told him how much she despised him. She blamed him for ruining her life. She told him how she had been poisoned at his home. How the toxins were robbing her of the chance to be a mother. Sara thought that getting everything out in the open would help her feel better, but it didn't. It only made her sicker, until finally she ended up in the hospital.

Derry had been trying to reason with her for weeks, but to no avail. However, once she entered the hospital her attitude changed. Sara realized that everything Derry had said was true. Her hatred was killing her. She knew she had to let it go. But this was more difficult than she had imagined. She had hated the man for so long the hatred had become an old friend. Finally, she prayed and asked God to help her let go of her anger and her desire for revenge.

After two days she was released from the hospital. The first thing she did when she returned home was to ask Derry to go with her to visit John again, but this time to tell him she was done hating him. Derry agreed.

Motova was surprised to see Sara again. "Come to scream at me some more?"

"No, I have come to tell you that I am done hating you. You no longer have any power over me."

Motova stared at her. It was obvious that something had changed. She looked like a different person. As she was walking away, he asked her one question, "Are you saying you have actually forgiven me?"

The question pierced her heart. Had she really forgiven him? She whispered a quick prayer, asking God to help her really forgive this man. Derry prayed for her as he saw the struggle on her face.

Sara turned back to Motova and suddenly, for the first time, she no longer saw the monster she had known for so many years. Instead, she saw a hurting man whose choices had ruined him. She saw a soul that needed to be saved. She truly saw John Motova through Christ's eyes. She was able to forgive him for all that had happened at his hands. Peace washed over her. She realized that God was working in her, changing her. She could now truly trust God with her future.

Sara's words to the magistrate brought Derry's mind back to the courtroom.

"I can forgive him because I am forgiven. If I keep the hate in my heart, it will not only destroy me, but it will also mean that the enemy has won."

The judge leaned forward and asked, "So, he is still your enemy?"

"No, not Motova. He was nothing more than a tool used by our enemy, the one that wants to destroy all of us."

The judge leaned back a few inches. "The jihadists?"

"They also are just tools used by Satan." Sara kept her gaze on the judge. "In the eyes of this court and this world, what Motova did is only forgivable by serving time or trading secrets. But in the eyes of God we all deserve the same punishment, for we are all sinners."

"I did not call you up here for a sermon." The judge skimmed the courtroom before looking back at Sara and Derry. "I see no problem with you visiting this man as long as he is willing to see you. But it's beyond me why you would want to do that."

The woman behind the bench sat up straighter and folded her hands together. "I have to say it appears that you two have some powerful friends. And after studying the records and listening to the testimonies concerning what went down, I can understand why." She raised her voice so all could hear. "After thoroughly reviewing this case, and on the testimony of all parties involved, and on the recommendation of the U.S. Department of Justice, I am dismissing all charges against Sara Beckwith and Derry Conway."

She pounded her gavel before going on. "The State, along with millions of people, are in your debt. Your actions, though illegal in some instances, saved countless lives. We thank you."

Derry reached over and grabbed Sara's hand and gave it a squeeze.

The judge looked intently at Sara. "Now I have a special ruling for you. At Special Agent Booker's request, for your outstanding contributions to the FBI and help in this matter, your record will be sealed. All past charges and verdicts against you are to be expunged as of this date."

Sara leaned forward a little. "What does that mean exactly?"

"It means you have been released from your probation. You now have a clean record, as if you never broke the law. You are free to live your life as you choose. Just try to stay out of trouble from here on out."

———

After the hugs and congratulations, Booker approached Sara and pulled her aside. "You know, you truly were a big help in solving this case."

"Thank you."

"People like you are a great asset to the Bureau. We would hate to lose you."

The thought had never entered Sara's mind. "Are you letting me go?"

Booker smiled broadly. "Never, but we can't make you stay now. You can go anywhere you want."

Sara thought about this for a second. Anywhere? She was free?

"What if I don't want to leave?"

Booker smiled. "I am sure I can push through the paperwork to keep you if you are willing to stay. Tony and Kent have been going through the files Tony was able to save off of Homeland's computer system. They have given us some insight into how three terrorists made it past all the security checks. I can't say much more until we get you sworn in, but I can tell you it will take someone like you to plug the holes they exploited."

"Excuse me, but I won't let her start a new job until after our honeymoon," Derry butted in as he slipped his arm around Sara's waist.

"Of course. That will give me time to get everything arranged. If you are sure that is what you want?" She waited for Sara's nod. "Very well. Enjoy your honeymoon." She turned and walked toward the door.

Sara smiled up at Derry. "Can you believe that?"

Before he could answer, Kai stepped in. "So you're sticking around here?"

"It looks that way. You want to come work with me? It could be like old times, only better."

Kai's eyes met Sam's across the room. "Sorry, I have taken a job with a competing agency. I am going into my father's business. The CIA has offered me a job."

Sara reached out and took Kai's hand. "You're really going to be a spy?" There was a giggle in her voice.

Kai gave her an indignant look. "We don't use that term anymore. I'm going to be an agent."

"A spook. Are you going to have to go to spy school or do you come by it naturally?"

"Can't tell you because—"

A noise in the rear of the room changed everyone's focus. "I told you before, no reporters allowed. Stay out." Faircloth raised his voice as he blocked someone from passing.

The young man with almost black hair and light brown eyes, stuck his head around Faircloth. "Sara. Tell this goon who I am."

Sara looked at him. It took her a moment to place where she knew his face. Suddenly memories from her childhood flooded her mind as she recognized the man. "*Colby?*"

Faircloth glanced over his shoulder. "You really know this low life reporter?"

Sara weaved her way to the back of the room. "Is it really you?"

"Sara, I've been trying to see you for months."

The only person now between her and the intruder was Faircloth. She reached out and pulled down on his arm. "He's my brother. Please let him in."

Faircloth looked hard at Sara before stepping back and allowing the man to enter.

"Your friends are very protective." Colby looked around at the others, all of whom were staring at him.

"Where have you been? What have you been up to? How did you—"

"Hold on. One question at a time."

Derry stepped up next to them. "This is your brother?"

She didn't answer, but smiled and hugged her brother tightly. Holding his hand, she took a step back. "How in the world did you find me?"

"Mom told me you worked for the FBI. I tried getting ahold of you, but some joker named Lamar Stover blocked my calls. Then the paper sent me on assignment overseas. I have been out of the country for the last two months. I just got back yesterday. Last night I saw on the news that you were being arraigned today and headed over here as soon as I could."

Sara appeared not to hear anything her brother had said except one thing. "What? Mom? You found her?"

"Yes, in a dump. The place she was living was killing her. I got her out and into a rehab program. Once she was sober she started going on and on about seeing you. She sounds proud of you."

The End

About the author

W. Richard Lawrence comes to the writing table with a different background than many authors. He grew up in a military family, which meant he moved a lot. He spent nine years in Germany and three in Hawaii, plus lived in nine different states on the mainland, most of them along the east coast. By the time he was seventeen, he'd lived in seventeen different places. As an adult he joined the Army where he worked as a technician. After his enlistment was up he went to the University of Colorado where he studied Electrical Engineering and also met the woman of his dreams. It was during this time that he gave his life to Christ. After twenty years working in the high-tech world of integrated circuits, he left the engineering field for new opportunities.

He now lives in northern Colorado with his wife, Debbie, who works as his sounding board and editor. Debbie and Richard both have backgrounds in electrical engineering and together have written 12 award winning science books. They also ran a science supply company for several years. After "Answers in Genesis" started publishing their science books, they shut down their business. That's when Richard began writing high-tech novels filled with distrust, deceit, murder, treachery, faith, love and at times, the ultimate sacrifice.

Richard's background has given him a unique perspective on life, which comes across in his writings.

www.ingramcontent.com/pod-product-compliance
Lightning Source LLC
Chambersburg PA
CBHW030539260626
47157CB00006B/2101

*9 7 8 0 9 7 7 4 4 3 2 1 5 *